summer
of the
soldiers
sandra chastain

PINNACLE BOOKS
WINDSOR PUBLISHING CORP.

For Pepper, who stored up memories of the "fifties," and helped me capture the flavor of our time on paper.

And for everyone who knows you really can't turn back the clock, but would, just once, like to try.

PINNACLE BOOKS

are published by

Windsor Publishing Corp.
475 Park Avenue South
New York, NY 10016

First Printing: January, 1993

Printed in the United States of America

PART ONE

The Summer

"And awa-a-ay we go."
—Jackie Gleason, 1954

One

The Fourth of July, 1954

The summer was setting a heat record. The temperature was already over a hundred degrees and July had only just begun. Farmers said that watermelons in the fields were popping as loud as cherry bombs. There was no promise of rain and the sky, high and blue, seemed to move in endless tandem with the earth.

The townspeople of Galilee, Georgia, drank iced tea for breakfast as they thumbed through their Sunday *Augusta Chronicles*. They skimmed the stories about ending the war in Korea, the rising crime rate, and the threat of polio, and went straight for the comics and the latest escapades of *The Phantom* and *Joe Palooka*.

At Mrs. Lacey's Boarding House, Frank Eden, the high school history teacher, gave sympathetic lip service to Perry Sims, whose contract to teach English had been terminated because he'd dared to write and produce a one-act play about the impotent war veteran who could no longer satisfy his wife.

Down Main Street, Mayor Jordan read about the Supreme Court's decision to ban school segregation and practiced sounding wise by announcing that his black folk didn't want to go to school with the whites anyhow.

Sweeping changes were about to begin, changes that for the most part went unremarked upon by the residents of Galilee, Georgia. Sooner or later, the ones who might have cared left town; those who stayed were too involved in their own lives to take a stand. Life in Galilee, Georgia, went on as it always had.

Margie Raines got up from her grandmother's breakfast table and went back to her room to dress for church. She looked forward to the Fourth of July celebration and dinner on the church grounds after Sunday services. The event was the highlight of the summer.

For three years Margie had marked the stages of her life by events. This Fourth of July signaled the last major milestone of the countdown. By Labor Day, she'd be in Atlanta where nobody would know what she'd been. She could create any kind of past she wanted, and make her personality whatever she chose. She could be smart and dedicated like JoEllen, who'd graduated a whole year early and was already in nursing school. She could be sweet and kind like Susan, who would take a business course and marry Sam. Or she could be exciting and unpredictable like Glory, who changed her future from one day to the next.

Margie looked impatiently past this day. This time it didn't matter if a boy looked at her, or sat beside her, or even talked to her, because this day marked the ending of the "getting ready" part of her life. She didn't know yet who she was, but she was about to find out.

Perspiration beaded Margie's forehead. She cupped her lower lip and blew a puff of air upward, fluttering the curls already hanging damply on her face. The day was going to be a scorcher. Even with the new overhead fans, the church would be stifling. A hundred hand-held paper fans with a picture of Jesus on the front and one of the Wilhoit Funeral Home on the back would flutter like butterflies as big-bosomed women tried to snatch a breath of air to dry the staining circles of perspiration spreading outward from beneath their arms.

Dinner on the church grounds would be shaded by the tall cool trees, but nothing could force a breeze where even the air was blistering. To Margie, the only hope for salvation this day was not in the church, but in going to the lake and swimming in it afterward.

And the soldiers.

Three busloads of soldiers from the Camp Gordon Army Base, outside Augusta, were to be guests of the Galilee Methodist and Baptist churches for the day.

Margie and her friends, caught up in their graduation and the senior trip, weren't exactly sure why the soldiers were invited. The best explanation they could find was that it was something patriotic, something to do with taking care of the boys who served in the Korean War, as the citizens of Galilee had done during World War II. It seemed fitting that the Fourth actually fell on Sunday this year.

The young ladies in the community had been asked to serve as hostesses and told that the injured soldiers, who'd been released by the base hospital for the day, should be kept comfortable. The girls should be friendly, they were told,— but not *too* friendly, toward their guests.

To the residents of Galilee, there was sin aplenty waiting out there in the big world, and offering these innocent boys a holiday with good people was the Christian thing to do. If there was one thing the small central Georgia town of Galilee had plenty of, it was Christian charity.

That the Korean War was nearly over before it occurred to anybody to acknowledge their patriotic duty seemed incidental. Where almost every family had lost someone during the big war, this one made barely a ripple in the town. Perhaps the town's shrinking population accounted for the present apathy.

One vocal exception to the malaise was their English teacher, Mr. Sims, a Korean veteran who'd come to Galilee, in 1952. He was a dark, moody man who had some kind of war wound that nobody was quite sure about. It was his wound that accounted for the town's interest in him during his first year. The second year, attention switched to his classroom reading of Arthur Miller and Aldous Huxley, and his writing dramatic plays that were much too modern and wicked for innocent high school students to perform. To Margie, he was the best teacher Galilee had ever had.

The citizens' Christian charity in hiring an "outsider" was a short-lived lie. The truth was, Perry Sims was the only teacher they could find. But he didn't belong. He was too different. Two years was long enough. The day after graduation he'd been fired.

9

Margie wiped the perspiration from her forehead and fastened her white clip-on ear bobs. She wished she had a smart new sleeveless sack dress to wear, but her grandfather wouldn't consider that proper for church. And Margie operated on her own kind of honor system. She wouldn't do anything to disappoint her grandfather. Her wayward mother had done enough of that for a lifetime.

She would wear the dress her mother had sewed and sent her to wear under her white graduation robe. That was playing the game properly. The dress was made of white dotted Swiss. It had a gathered skirt covering the starched crinoline petticoat, and a scooped neck that displayed a bit too much of her full breasts and gave her a lush, earthy look. With her blond hair and fair skin she thought the dress made her look virginal. But she was wrong.

Dabbing a few drops of Bond Street cologne between her breasts, Margie decided that even if the neck was a bit low, her mother had made it, and it was the coolest thing she owned. She wished she dared sneak one of the Herbert Tareyton cigarettes she'd hidden in the back of her bureau drawer. Smoking was part of her new, sophisticated image.

Margie didn't fool herself that she was beautiful. She understood why the boys at school had nicknamed her TNT. She'd told herself it stood for Dynamite, not, as they whispered behind cupped hands, Tits 'n Tail. Today's whispers would be different. The soldiers were men, not boys.

Men liked her, older men, the married kind who were usually half drunk when they drove her home after a Saturday night babysitting job. "You're a pretty girl," they'd say. "I like your hair." But it wasn't her hair they looked at, or tried to touch when they got her in their cars and pretended to be even drunker than they actually were.

"Margie?" her grandfather called from the end of the hall. "Are you ready? Don't want to be late this morning. We won't get a seat in church."

He'd have a seat, Margie thought with affection. Jim Burge had claimed the outside seat on the center aisle of the seventh pew for as many years as Margie could remember. Nobody would sit in Mr. Jim's place. In the Baptist church, across the square, the families donated and sat in their own pews, but the Methodists—the newcomers, having been here

10

less than a hundred years—brought thier pews one at a time with funds raised by all the members.

Sometimes Margie wondered if her mother had felt as disconnected from the world as she did. Was that why she'd left with the man she married during the Depression, left and never come home except to leave Margie with her parents?

Walking home from school Margie would come down the tracks beside the big ditch, dreaming of climbing on a train and leaving Galilee behind. She'd even lie down, pressing her ear against the rails, to listen for the thrumming sound that meant the four o'clock from Centerville was on its way.

Margie's grandmother, Alice, seemed content with her life. Alice was the hub around which all their lives revolved, but she never intruded between Margie and her grandfather. In later years Margie would remember her grandmother cooking, washing clothes, and ironing her grandfather's stiff overalls on a shaped board that was laid across the open doorway, one end resting on the kitchen counter and the other on the electric stove. But she didn't remember Alice ever sitting on that pew in church.

The lines in her grandparent's lives were carefully drawn. Alice ran the house and Mr. Jim earned the living and made the decisions. Other men didn't go downtown every morning and select the food to be cooked for the noon meal, but Mr. Jim did. He decided when it was time for Alice to visit her sister and when they'd have company for Sunday dinner.

Most of the time, Margie—and her grandparents, too, she thought—avoided thinking of her mother and father. They were always gone, until something bad happened and then they'd return, amid whispers and frantic looks. Dutifully Margie played the game of planning how she'd go with them when her father found another job, but it never happened.

This morning, as they did every Sunday morning, the Burges and Margie climbed into the maroon '47 Chevrolet and drove six blocks down the Winslow Road to Church Square. On one corner facing Main Street was the neat gray rock Baptist Church. On the other, the pristine white Galilee Methodist Church faced Winslow Road. The cars were parked between the two churches on the black dirt beneath the trees.

Funny, Margie thought, it was as if the two churches

11

turned their backs on each other. Both churches had Sunday morning services, but they alternated evening services because each pastor had circuit churches where he also preached. The youth groups drew a big crowd in the late afternoon; the kids didn't have anything better to do.

Bible study first. Then, for those who skipped church, there might be a secret trip to the lake where the girls practiced smoking and boys filled with bravado told dirty jokes and pretended they understood what they meant.

On the surface the churches were joined in Christ's work, but each was convinced that the Lord had a scorecard by which they were individually measured. The race for souls was deadly serious, beginning with Mrs. Loretta—pronounced Low-retta—Green, who privately told her little troop of G.A.'s that only the Baptist children would go to heaven. None of the Methodists professed to take this seriously, but enrolling their daughters in the Girl's Auxiliary wouldn't hurt.

Mr. Green never attended church and nobody seemed to think there was anything odd about Mrs. Green's call to save the children. Mr. Green worked for the railroad, keeping the steam engine loaded with wood to fire the boiler and with sand to be released on the tracks to stop it. The railhouse was located in a section of town that most white people avoided, unless they were picking up the maid or the yard man. But Mr. Green spent most of his days there, and an occasional night as well.

On this Fourth of July morning both churches were teeming with activity. The men had completed the arrangement of saw horses on which they laid sheets of plywood covered with crisp white cloths. There were tin washtubs filled with blocks of ice being chipped by hand to fill the cups of lemonade and sweet tea. Other tubs held churns of ice cream already cranked firm, draped with gaily colored feed sacks and left to harden.

First the services, then the food. Afterward the older people would stay around to sing patriotic songs and hymns, the Methodist church had even invited the Harmony Gospel Quartet from Augusta to lead the event. The younger people would head for the lake. The soldiers, who'd been told to bring swimming trunks, would be given their choice of the

12

two activities. A late afternoon wiener roast, where the girls would have sparklers and the men midget firecrackers, would finish off the day before the soldiers would be driven back to the base. Nobody considered it silly to offer firecrackers to combat veterans to celebrate a war for independence. In the past they'd had Roman candles, but today wouldn't be dark enough for them. Besides, firecrackers and sparklers were cheaper.

Margie helped her grandmother carry their dishes into the Methodist church kitchen where fans had been set up to keep the food cool during the service. Margie carried the fried chicken and Miss Alice held a large dishpan filled with hot chicken pie complete with a crust to cover the dumplings. Mr. Jim leaned against the car and waited patiently until the women had finished unloading all the food.

Margie made a place on the counter for her platter, but her mind was on the time. Where were the buses?

Catching sight of Susan through the window, Margie said a silent thank-you, and escaped. "Hi, Suse, I'm glad you got here. Is Glory still coming?"

"Who knows what Glory will do. I wouldn't be surprised if she personally drove up to Augusta and picked up a soldier or two herself. You know Glory, she's always doing something wild."

"Don't be catty. Like Mr. Sims says, Glory just marches to a different drummer. Do you suppose the soldiers will really come?"

Susan pushed her dark hair behind her ear and looked around, a worried expression on her face. "I guess what Mr. Sims says doesn't mean much anymore, does it? I mean he's about to find himself a different drummer. You know he's been fired, don't you?"

Margie knew. She just didn't want to think about it. She liked writing and literature. She'd already read every book in the tiny school library. Secretly, she wanted to be a writer, like Mr. Sims. She'd sit in the back of the classroom and pretend that she wrote great plays, picturing herself coming out on stage after the performance and receiving a standing ovation. But something about Mr. Sims was too intense, as if he could look at her and know just what she was thinking. He'd smile an exasperated smile that said she was ignorant,

13

that she'd never get out of Galilee.

He was wrong. She'd show him, and she'd show Glory and all the others, too. Sometime during the last year she'd made up her mind that she and Mr. Sims were changing places. He had come to her small, ignorant country town, where he was the one who was different. And she was leaving.

"The school board is blind, Susan. Mr. Sims is the best teacher we ever had. I don't guess he'll be here today, will he?"

Susan gave her an odd look. "He never comes to church, Margie. *I* almost didn't come. Sam doesn't want me here, even if it is a church picnic. He certainly isn't excited about me acting as hostess for a bunch of men."

"Oh, fudge. Sam may be the richest, best-looking boy in town, but I don't believe he ever gets excited about anything. Besides, if he's so worried, why didn't he come?"

"Granddaddy Winslow thought he ought to go back to school. He's on duty at the agriculture barn today. Sometimes I think he's more interested in pleasing his grand-daddy than in me."

"I don't doubt it. You know how powerful that old man is."

"Yes, and Sam's getting to be just like him."

"Susan! Did you and Sam have a fight?"

"Of course not. A Winslow doesn't fight, he *commands*. But sometimes Sam just isn't fair. I mean he's off at school, doing who knows what, but I'm supposed to stay at home and behave myself."

Who knows what? "What does he think you'll *do?*"

"I don't know. All I know is that he doesn't try anything with me. It wouldn't be proper. I figure that's because he finds other women to . . . you know."

"He doesn't try to—to . . . ?" Margie couldn't keep disbelief out of her voice. She glanced around and lowered her voice. "But doesn't he get—you know—*excited?*"

"Yes," Susan whispered. "Sam gets excited. He just doesn't show it."

"Then how can you tell?" Margie asked.

"Because when he kisses me, he gets all stiff and distant, like when you were little and tried not to fall playing Stitch Starch."

14

Margie identified with the *stiff* part of Susan's answer, but it didn't have anything to do with the game Susan talked about where two people joined hands, planted their feet together, and leaned back as they whirled around in a circle pulling against each other. "You aren't close when you kiss?"

"Yes, for a while, then he gets fidgety and starts acting real solemn. That's when he holds himself away."

"From what I can tell, Sam's always solemn."

"Well . . . not always. There are times when he forgets for a few minutes and—" Susan broke off.

"Tell me! Susan, tell me!" Margie couldn't believe that Susan was speaking so freely. She'd never done that before. Something pretty awful must have happened to cause her to say anything. "We've been best friends since second grade," Margie said, sliding her arm around Susan's waist. "What does Sam do?"

Susan looked miserable for a moment, then, as if gathering up her courage, she answered quickly, all in one breath. "Nothing. And that's the problem. Sometimes I wish he'd just let go and be excited. I'm tired of him saying we have to wait until we're married." She paused and took a quick breath. "How am I supposed to know if I really want to get married if he never lets me find out what it's like?"

Susan's honesty startled Margie. Everybody wondered what Susan and Sam did in her living room night after night when he came to her house. But Susan had never said.

Boys were sure that girls talked about kissing and sex, but they really didn't, Margie thought. Probably because those girls who let boys do things to them weren't certain that the others did it, too. And those who didn't, didn't want anybody to know the truth. Silence protected everybody. The only discussions about sex were about the "bad girls" who everybody suspected of going all the way.

Everybody knew that Susan wasn't one of those girls, though she and Sam had been going steady for so long she'd certainly had plenty of opportunity. She and Sam had become a couple from Susan's first day in eighth grade. Margie didn't know what the Winslows thought, but Mrs. Miller certainly approved of Sam for her daughter.

Sam was a Winslow and the Winslows were the oldest,

15

most prominent family in the county. Sam's grandfather's ancestors had founded the community of Winslow before the War Between the States, when cotton was king. They owned a plantation, the cotton gin, and had built their own railroad to take the cotton over to Augusta to market. Back then, Galilee, only five miles away, was only a crossroads.

Grandfather Winslow had three sons, each of whom had one living child. The present-day Winslow cousins were Steven, the oldest, who was graduating from Harvard; Sam, four years younger; and Glory, the first girl in three generations. The Winslow fortune, though still large, had diminished, but the name still commanded respect.

Everybody acknowledged that Susan would make Sam a perfect wife. She could cook and sew, and she played the piano privately for him as he sat on the couch in the front room of the house.

Some of the boys used to sneak up and hide beneath the open window, trying to spy on the couple, but all they could hear was the sound of Sam and Susan's voices. They talked a lot. But about what? Margie couldn't imagine. Neither Susan nor Sam ever seemed to have much to say about world problems, or literature, or the theater, or even sex. Susan didn't care that Mr. Sims had been fired. The most anybody could get out of Susan was what was in the latest *Seventeen* magazine and what was playing at the Dixie Theater downtown.

Sam was the intense, silent type, never late or disrespectful. He was interested only in his family's farm and his buddies. He participated in the high school activities— playing basketball, building mailboxes in shop class, joining the Future Farmers of America— but with no emotional involvement in any of it. Then, last September, he went away to agriculture school as his grandfather had directed.

Susan's confession brought a telltale flush of embarrassment to her pert round face. Margie tried to put herself in Susan's place and imagine being kissed by Sam. She couldn't.

There were more girls than boys in Galilee attending high school. If you didn't stake your claim early, you'd be left out.

Margie had spent a few awkward minutes with most of the local boys, walking around the block in what was euphemistically called a "prom." But she'd never prommed with Sam. By the time Sam entered Galilee High School the promenade was gone and dates were in, dates where first kisses and experimental groping took place more privately and less hurriedly.

The only time Margie had ever been close to Sam was when they danced. He remained the only boy in town who Margie couldn't follow on a dance floor, probably because he was the only boy in town who she hadn't taught how to dance. She was too much in awe of his mysterious silence to relax.

As the organ began to play, calling the worshipers inside, the army buses drove down Main Street and pulled into the church parking area.

"Well, they're here," Susan said.

Margie looked through the open bus windows at the sea of faces. "Look at all those men, Susan. Aren't you glad you came? I mean, it *is* our patriotic duty."

"That's why I came. Being a hostess for the church isn't really 'going out with other boys.' Besides, Margie, most of them are probably married."

"So? Being married doesn't stop any of the men around here from being friendly. And this is for a worthy cause. Relax, Sam's not here anyway."

Sam *wasn't* there. And Margie knew that Susan would be nice to the soldiers. But Margie didn't doubt that what Susan wanted to do was turn around and run.

Then, as if remembering her instructions, a stiff smile formed on Susan's face. "You're right. If Sam can have friends at school, I can certainly spend an afternoon being friendly to . . . to whomever I wish."

The buses began to unload. The soldiers, in their sharply pressed khaki uniforms, filed out, the injured ones first, some with casts, some on crutches. They glanced around the church square suspiciously.

From the back of the first bus, Nick Zambino gave a whistle and stuck his head out the window. "Well, well, will you just look at all those girls, just waiting to make us happy. We've been dropped into heaven. The big girl in the white

17

dress is mine, boys. Let's get off this bus so we can sample the sweets."

He stood up, slid the gold band from his finger, and put it into his wallet. His wedding ring was protection from any messy entanglements in the hospital where he served as an orderly and self-appointed ladies' man, but here it would put up a barrier that could spoil the day. Inside his wallet it made a neat little circle right next to the foil-wrapped packet that he always carried. Nick always kept a supply of "skins." He always needed them.

Humming "Bringing in the Sheaves," Nick left the bus and walked lazily across the grass toward the church. He stopped and allowed his gaze to slide up and down the two girls standing together. The shorter girl had dark curly hair and a slim figure. Her long fingernails were painted a bright shade of red that matched the red-print skirt she was wearing with the neat white blouse with a Peter Pan collar. But it was the other girl, the taller girl with the full figure wearing the white dress that he was really interested in. He noted, with a certain amount of pleasure, that she was aware of him, too.

Nick removed his cap, folded it neatly, and slid it beneath the loop on the shoulder of his shirt. He didn't move any closer. He had all morning to make his move. For now it was enough she noticed him. As two of Nick's buddies joined him, they made a right turn and assembled at the door to the church. Meanwhile, the other two buses unloaded and the men divided themselves between the two churches and started inside.

There's definitely something about a uniform, Margie thought, feeling the distinct thump of her heart. As Glory had predicted, today was going to be a grand adventure, though if Glory didn't hurry up, she was going to miss the church service. Not that missing church would be unusual for her. She was an irreverent and outrageous girl, and though Margie and the others professed concern over her lack of respect for tradition, her dominance of the group was unchallenged. Like metal shavings drawn to a magnet, Margie, Susan, and JoEllen, had always been drawn to Glory. Glory was a Winslow.

Sitting on the front steps of Margie's grandmother's house in the darkness the night before, while Susan and Sam had been doing whatever they'd been doing, Margie and Glory had fantasized about the soldiers. Margie imagined a man like Farley Granger, who would take one look at her and fall passionately in love. She had never expected to meet a man who would announce so blatantly with his eyes that he was interested in her.

In the dark, on her own porch, it was easy for Glory to visualize playing in the lake with the unknown *him,* finding a private spot in the woods, and lying in *his* arms. Kissing, touching, feeling *his* hand on her breasts; that far she could go. Further was deliciously uncharted ground.

Margie was no stranger to necking. The feel of an erection pressed against her abdomen was familiar but always ignored and unmentioned. Warding off hands that inched closer and closer to her breasts during heavy petting sessions was routine, part of the game. Like Glory, Margie wore her cardigan sweaters buttoned down the back and, for dress up, donned black-seamed stockings and ballerinas. But it was the game, not the touch, that excited her. And though she daydreamed, she never considered giving in to the fevered pleas of her dates.

Margie had even understood what her date was doing when he'd finally leave the car in frustration and disappear into the darkness to, as he'd explain, "take care of the pain she'd caused, since she wouldn't."

For a long time she'd thought they were peeing, until one night her date hadn't gone far enough and she'd heard his frantic hand motions and the forthcoming groan of agony. Though she lacked real knowledge, she'd been able to guess what he'd done to himself. But a girl actually "doing it" for a guy was beyond her imagination. Whatever secret sexual excitement was supposed to sweep her into complying was more vivid in her daydreams than in reality.

What was harder for her to understand was why boys took her out for a while, then didn't call again. She was certain that she didn't do anything that other girls didn't do. All girls were teases, they had to be, and Margie was certain that the others stopped, just as she did.

Now, as the intense expression in the eyes of the Marlon Brando lookalike with the jet-black hair, captured her, she allowed herself to acknowledge a shiver of desire. Her

19

excitement was tempered with fear. She knew immediately that he was the one. This man would be a test, an omen for her future. This time she didn't intend to lose. This man was hers.

Margie looked at Susan to see if she had observed the exchange, but Susan was staring equally hard at a slim, dark-skinned boy leaning on a crutch.

There was a gasp. "Margie, look. A Nigra."

Susan was right. There was actually a colored boy standing by the bus, in uniform, just like the others. "I don't believe it," Margie whispered. "What will we do?"

They watched him move awkwardly toward the church, past the spot where the two girls were standing. He wasn't coal-black like the black people they were accustomed to seeing. His features were softer, more like their own. His skin was a warm brown color, like coffee mixed with cream. Still, he was unmistakably black, and his hair was a mass of tight, glistening curls.

The church members standing outside the entrance made a wide path. They were so startled that they didn't even comment to each other about what they were seeing. Just as the black boy reached the door, his crutch hit an uneven spot in the grass and he stumbled.

Without thinking, Susan went instantly to his side. "Look out," she said, and leaned against him so that he was steady again. The soldier managed a squeaky "Thank you, ma'am" and accepted her help as they walked the few feet to the steps where he caught the wrought-iron rail and pulled himself up to the vestibule.

Margie hung back until she saw the boy look into the church. She watched his face contort in fear at entering, while the church members stared at Susan in silent disbelief. Oh, Lordy, Susan had really done it. *This* is *a church,* Margie admonished silently. *Jesus would never turn anyone away.* But Jesus didn't live in Galilee, Georgia.

Susan took a deep breath and stepped in front of the boy, preceding him into the church, then making a place for them both in the last row.

Margie shook her head in disbelief. Glory might be expected to do something like that, but not Susan. Still, it was Susan, who, already worried about what Sam would think, had befriended a black soldier with the entire town looking on. Of course, everybody knew it was only an act of Christian kindness. Didn't they?

Everybody knew that Susan wasn't the type to take chances. She'd never do anything that wasn't considered absolutely proper. But a young girl publicly coming to the aid of a black soldier would never be acceptable. Margie glanced around, caught sight of her grandfather's frown, and was glad that it had been Susan instead of her. She wondered what Sam would say if he were here.

Nothing, Margie decided. Susan was protected by her reputation. As a senior she had won the district typing award and that got her an offer of a job in the local bank as soon as she was finished with her business course. She'd save her money and she and Sam would marry when Sam finished college. Nobody would say a word, because Susan was a good girl and she was to be a Winslow.

Margie, who'd always considered herself brave, suddenly wasn't so brave anymore. She wasn't even *good*. She felt guilty over her lack of courage. Her determination to become smart like JoEllen, good like Susan, sophisticated like Glory, had yet to be realized.

She wondered briefly where Glory was, then answered her own question. Glory would make an entrance at the very time she was sure to make the greatest impact. She'd be surprised by Susan's brash move. But, Margie consoled herself, Glory would be even more surprised by Margie's black-eyed soldier. For once in her life, Margie Raines would be as popular as Glory Winslow.

Margie wedged herself in beside her grandfather and, under the guise of locating the first hymn in the book, searched the church for her soldier. As her gaze slid across the pews, she found him, watching her from the end of the pew in front at the other side of the church. The curve of the pew turned him slightly toward her and she felt his eyes on her. Throughout the service she tried not to look, but every time she glanced across the church he was watching her. The last time, he gave her a straight-faced, solemn wink.

At the back of the church, Susan's attention was planted firmly on the choir. When the singing began, she gave a timid smile to the officer who offered to share his hymnal. On her other side, the black boy didn't even open a book. He didn't need it: he joined in, singing from memory. His voice was too loud, but he didn't know it. This was God's house and everybody belonged.

The heat increased.

The paper fans waved in unison, but their frenzied movement only fed the underlying currents of tension rippling through the sanctuary on that morning of July 4, 1954.

Two

Glory Winslow had told her mother that she was on her way to Galilee to the Fourth of July celebration. Instead, she drove her graduation present, a coral-colored Ford convertible, down her driveway, past the First Baptist Church and took the highway out of Winslow.

She didn't mind the temperature. Already the heat rising from the highway made it look like rippled waves of water in the distance. Glory liked the way the sun felt beating down on her, the way the wind caught her short auburn hair and tousled it. Her heart was racing. She felt as if any second she might burst into a million pieces and fly away.

Glancing in the mirror, she checked her Fire Engine Red Revlon lipstick and smoothed her thick eyebrows with her index finger. Glory wasn't pretty. Her fiery red hair and great green eyes were dramatically set in a face that might have graced the front of a Terry and the Pirates comic book. Depending on whether she set out to vamp, or to outrage, her manner of dress alternated between solid, vibrant colors that exaggerated her exotic features and the avant-garde look that set her grandfather on edge. This morning her goal was entirely different: ease of *un*dress.

Glory pushed in the lighter, reached into her purse, and fished out a half-empty pack of Pall Malls. She rapped the pack on the steering wheel, fanning the cigarettes out so that she could take one between her lips and light it. Up to now, Glory's smoking had been more for effect than enjoyment, but today she took a long drag and let it out slowly.

She recognized her problem—desperation. From the moment she was cast in Mr. Sims's play as the unsatisfied wife of a wounded man, Glory had known that this day would come. In the play the conflict focused on the physical problem that prevented him from satisfying her, which in turn, hid the emotional dissatisfaction in the marriage. Glory's focus was more elemental.

Perry, as Mr. Sims allowed them to call him privately, had even encouraged her to say a curse word, on stage, before everybody in town. Glory had been indignant when most of the audience gasped and left before the climactic moment. She'd been sorry, but not surprised, when she'd learned that Perry's teaching contract wouldn't be renewed. Too bad. He might have made a difference. But being different wouldn't be tolerated. Glory could attest to that.

Very soon, thank God, she would be leaving all this small-mindedness behind. Sometimes Glory thought that only she and Perry understood that there was more to life than *Millie and Archie Go to the Prom,* or the spring beauty contest. That's why she'd made her plan so carefully.

Glory crossed the railroad tracks and glanced over at the ruins of the old train station, rebuilt after the War Between the States, only to collapse again thirty years later. As a child, she'd seen *Gone With the Wind,* and for weeks afterward, she and her cousins had played at the station, pretending that she was Scarlett and that Atlanta was burning. Sam was a reluctant Ashley and Steven was Rhett Butler, but in Glory's version, Scarlett desperately wanted Rhett, not the silent, ever-suffering Ashley.

At the edge of the city limits of what was still euphemistically called the Beautiful City of Winslow, she flipped her cigarette out the window and turned off the main highway, circling the town from the back side. She drove past the cemetery and cut down a little-used road leading into the woods joining Steven's house. Glory was supposed to be meeting Margie and Susan in Galilee for the big Fourth of July celebration, but Glory intended to be very late.

Her mother and Aunt Evelyn would be in Sunday school now. Immediately afterward, they'd don their red robes for their duties in the choir of the Winslow First Baptist Church. If the morning went as usual, they'd be the last ones to leave the church. Since today was special, with any luck the services would run long. And today Glory felt lucky. The rush of adrenaline that swept through her promised success.

This morning was Glory's last chance.

Glory parked the convertible, turned off the engine, and sat there, holding the steering wheel tightly in her hands as she contemplated what she was about to do. It had to work. She had to do it. Steven was home from college, for the last time before leaving for New York and his new job on Wall Street. Steven was always leaving, going away to camp, away to school. But always before, he had come back.

Glory hated being younger than Steven. If they'd been the same age they could have been at the university together. They could have had four glorious years side by side, away from Winslow and the small-minded people determined to keep them apart.

First, Steven was sent to Harvard, too far away for her to even visit on weekends. Now, four years later, she'd be attending the University of Georgia, just as her mother had before her. She'd be expected to join her mother's sorority and find a husband proper for a Winslow woman. Frustration and a deep-seated anger swept over her. This morning she'd do what she wanted to do. This was her last chance before Steven was gone forever.

At first Glory didn't understand Aunt Evelyn's sudden coldness, or why her own mother didn't want Glory and Steven to spend time together anymore. The Winslow cousins, Glory, Sam, and Steven had been a threesome all their lives, inseparable as children, best friends, and later, for Glory, and Steven—more.

Once Glory had tried to explain that she'd loved Steven, *really* loved Steven, ever since that summer she was five years old. Her mother had laughed at her. Of course she loved her cousin, she'd said. That was to be expected. But to Glory, loving Steven was more than that, much more.

That was the summer her black-eyed, laughing father had been killed in the war and the thin, intense boy had comforted her and told her that she had Mona Lisa eyes. She hadn't known who Mona Lisa was. She'd just known that Steven made her feel good when nobody else seemed to notice a five-year-old's grief and loneliness. That feeling intensified through the years without Glory's understanding what it meant.

Two summers ago, just before Steven went back to begin his third year of college, Sam, who was going steady with

25

Susan, had deserted their trio. That left her . . . and Steven. Without intending to, they found out what being alone could mean.

Glory was fifteen then and Steven was nineteen. For that glorious summer there was just the two of them, best friends, swimming together in the lake, having long philosophical discussions on the porch while they listened to records and tried to unravel the mysteries of men and women. It started with kissing and simple touching, touching that had intensified, as had the frustration, and Glory knew that there was more. But it was Steven who wouldn't let it go any further.

Last fall, Steven went back to school, leaving her with a wild anxiety that never went away. She was impatient to discover the final wonder, but Steven was gone and he was the only person with whom she wanted to share that wonder. At Christmas when Steven returned, she'd been determined to change that.

The first night of Christmas vacation they'd slipped away and talked until dawn, when Aunt Evelyn had discovered them together in Steven's room, in Steven's bed, in each other's arms. Evelyn called Glory's mother, who came over immediately. The sisters faced their children in shock.

"Steven, this can't be," Evelyn finally said.

"You're older," Adele added. "You should never have let this happen."

Glory had pulled herself unself-consciously against the headboard and lit a cigarette. "Goodness, Mother, you'd think you were living in the forties. This is 1953. Besides, we weren't doing anything."

"That isn't the point, Glory. You and Steven are first cousins and you can't—you just can't—"

"Be serious about each other," Evelyn concluded. "It isn't natural."

Steven, who had remained silent, sat up, threading his fingers through his hair. "Don't worry, Mother. Glory's right, nothing happened."

"But suppose it had. You know what can happen— genetically. Your grandparents were first cousins. Adele and I are sisters. And your fathers are brothers. The consequences could be disastrous."

Glory let out a sigh along with a stream of smoke. "Sure,

26

Aunt Evelyn, we could have one-eyed children—if we were to become lovers and I got pregnant."

There was a long, shocked pause.

"Glory, hush!" Adele finally said. "You don't know what you're saying. I never told you, but before Steven, there were two other children who weren't 'right.' That's why you're our only children."

Glory and Steven were told coldly, and without question, that they could never be sweethearts. Not only was it illegal, it was genetically disastrous and morally unthinkable.

Steven never came for her again. This summer, he'd only be home for a week. Then he'd start his new job. But he'd avoided Glory. His denial made her wanting even more desperate. Glory had to be with Steven. She was ready to give herself to him, fully, completely. And she only had a few days to find a way to force him to make love to her.

That was the way Glory thought about it—make love, not "do it," as if sex were a thing apart from love. It wasn't even discussed in the marriage part of home economics class. They learned to plan a menu, but not a honeymoon. Satisfying the body's dietary needs took nine weeks to learn. Satisfying the body's physical needs was classified as sex and was covered in one brief movie shown at the local theater, the home economics teacher took the girls to see it in the morning and the shop teacher took the boys in the afternoon.

The movie used technical terms: penis, vagina, intercourse. Afterward, the boys giggled and made crude comments. The girls blushed and ignored their comments. There was no connection between that movie and the way Glory felt when Steven touched her. The movie made everything seem secret and anxious. Sex was to be avoided at all costs until marriage, when sex suddenly became making love. But Glory knew better.

It was on New Year's Eve that she'd actually watched her mother with a man, in bed. She'd learned how arousing and exciting sex could be. Her mother's actions had made Glory sick to her stomach, but she'd learned something very important. She'd learned about rubbers and what they were used for. The next day she'd found the box in the night table beside her mother's bed and pilfered one. It now rested securely in Glory's pocket.

Glory intended to breach Steven's wall. She didn't know about genes and chromosomes. She didn't care about morals. She'd leave the moral issues to her mother, who kept a lover in her bed and a choir robe in the closet. Glory loved Steven and that was all she needed to understand.

Loving Steven was the one constant in her life, the light to which she moved through the darkness. After this morning he wouldn't be able to leave her. He'd never again tell her about the queens and kings of England and what happened when cousins married, for now she had an answer: she and Steven simply wouldn't have children. And she had the means in her pocket. Now nobody could keep them apart ever again.

Silently she crept around the side of the house and slipped in the back door. The house was already hot. All the doors and windows were open. She knew her way to Steven's room; she'd played there all her life and found a way to get inside every time she came to her aunt's house. She would lie down in Steven's bed and touch herself and imagine it was Steven doing that. She opened the door quickly and stepped inside, closing it behind her.

He was there, lying across the bed with his arm twisted beneath his head in sleep. In contrast to his light coloring, his face was stubbled with dark hair. His body was no longer thin and lanky, he had muscles that she'd never noticed before. Her gaze lowered. Wearing only a pair of white briefs, his body—his—*it*—had found the opening and stood erect and exposed.

This wasn't the first time she'd seen Steven naked, but it was the first time he'd been so—big. Seeing him, and Sam, too, as children, then later as they'd grown up, had seemed natural at the time. There was nothing sexual in their childish examination of each other, until that summer when she was fifteen. That was the first time she'd seen both of them hard, and understood why, Steven and Sam had been embarrassed around her.

To Glory it had simply been a part of their relationship, and nothing about their exploration of each other had been frightening. She'd forced them to let her touch them, allowed them to examine her body as well. As she felt their response to her touch, she'd realized her power. But Steven always pulled back. Then later, after Sam defected, Steven refused to let it happen anymore. And being together became strained. They'd been miserable together, but more miserable apart. And for Glory, pulling back was too late. They'd opened the forbidden door that could never be closed again.

It was the next summer, when he was twenty, that he'd finally lost control and taken the touching further, when they'd learned about intense desire and unfulfilled passion. They'd never completed the sex act, but they'd explored every part of themselves and she'd learned new ways to satisfy and be satisfied by a man. This summer she didn't intend to let him push her away again.

Glory took a quick look around Steven's room. Neat, carefully organized, like Steven himself. Heavy oak furniture with uncluttered surfaces; a beige rug on the floor. Above the bed was a painting that Steven had brought back from Boston, a painting of a bullfighter extending his hat to a fiery-haired señorita in a red dress. Glory always thought the woman was herself and she liked the thought of looking down on him when he slept. Steven said he'd bought it because her dress matched his bedspread. He was probably the only man in the county with a scarlet bedspread.

Taking a deep breath, Glory removed her clothes, folding them into little piles and placing them in the chair by the closet. She looked down at her breasts. They were knotted in tight, dark beads. She had never seen another girl with such large circles of a tan color around her nipples. She always wondered if she were some strange throwback to another race. Perhaps her great-great-great-grandmother had made love to a slave and had a child!

Glancing at her watch, she knew she had to hurry. With her heart thudding so loudly that she expected it to wake Steven, she crept toward the bed and sat, leaning back with slow, easy movements until she lay beside him. She turned toward him, feeling the heat of his body against her bare breasts where they touched.

Steven came slowly awake as Glory kissed him. For a moment he held back, then with a groan pulled her over him and held her so tight that she could hardly breathe.

Finally he tore his mouth away from hers. "What are you doing, Glory?"

"You were going to leave without saying anything. I couldn't bear that."

"Glory, This is . . . this is—wrong. You have to stop. We can't."

But his body was probing, undulating, pressing against her.

She could hardly breathe. Her breasts were on fire. Already she felt the warm moisture collecting between her legs.

"No, I won't stop, Steven. You love me. I know you do. And I need you, Steven. I'm dying without you." She slid up and down, trying desperately to position herself so that he'd slip inside. "I've always loved you and I am going to be with you once, before you're lost to me forever."

Sarah Bernhardt couldn't have played the scene better. Just enough pathos to be convincing, and just enough desire to push Steven beyond the breaking point. Glory knew what she was doing. She'd practiced it with every boy she'd gone out with since Steven left her.

Glory had driven them all mad with wanting her, taken them to the edge of desire, and devastated them by refusing them the final entry. After frustration turned into anger, she found other ways to give them their release, a subject whispered about but never verified by those to whom she offered the privilege. Glory found that she could enslave them. Out of sheer gratitude, and the promise of more of the forbidden, the boys pledged their love forever and even swore to keep the secret of what they'd done.

She was the mysterious, unchallenged leader of her group of Glory worshipers. Her word was law. And the boys were willing to keep their bragging to themselves to keep their place in her circle of admirers. And for once nobody told the truth, and nobody lied. Because nobody really knew what was happening.

But this morning Glory intended to find her truth. Steven would make love to her, once, just once, before he left again. And she knew, in that secret part of her, that he'd be tied to her—forever.

She felt him shudder and try to push her away.

"No, Glory. We mustn't. Suppose . . . suppose—"

"It will be all right. I have a rubber."

"A rubber?" He groaned, closing his eyes. "Where'd you get a rubber?"

"I always use one," she lied. "Steven, make love to me,

30

once. I'll never ask it again. Nobody will know. Oh, Steven, I want you. I want this. Steven," she whispered dramatically, and touched him, setting off a trembling reaction that he couldn't hide.

Steven opened his eyes, seeing her naked body openly and completely for the first time in a year. "Glory! Tell me you haven't been doing it with somebody else."

"I wouldn't have, if you'd loved me. But you didn't. You turned me away. I had to do it, Steven. Other boys don't refuse me."

She reached down and began to touch herself. She heard him gasp. "They've touched me here, too, just like you want to. I see it in your eyes and you're already so hard." She ran her wet fingers up and down him, smiling as he jerked beneath her touch.

Steven glanced down at his body and winced. There was no hiding what was exposed. "Glory, you don't understand, men . . . I mean, this isn't what you think," he protested. "I wake up like this every morning."

"But you don't have me in your arms every morning to take care of it, do you? You dream about me, don't you? You dream about being inside me, about touching my breasts and feeling so good." She closed her eyes and sighed heavily. "Such a waste."

When she leaned down to kiss him this time, he didn't protest. He shuddered as she rubbed her nipples against his chest.

"Don't worry, darling Steven. I belong to you. I always have. We never had any secrets between us. You were the first to touch me, the first to kiss me, the first to undress me. I watched you play with yourself when you could no longer stand it. But you don't have to do that anymore."

With a roar he tightened his arms around her. She knew that this time he couldn't stop himself. Kissing her, touching her. She was wet and ready. He was ready. When she slid forward and took him between her hands, he trembled.

"Don't Glory, I won't be able to stop."

"I don't want you to," she whispered, rolling over and pulling him on top of her. There was no more restraining him then.

He plunged into her.

She was a virgin. She'd lied to him.

31

Steven drew back in surprise when he realized what had happened. But he was already inside her and he couldn't have stopped if he'd wanted to. And then he didn't want to.

Glory was noisy. She'd waited all her life for this and she gave in to the feelings freely and with all the pent-up desire inside her. Others might have to learn about sexual fulfillment but she'd been so ready for so long that her orgasm exploded through her with more intensity than she'd ever expected. It rippled through her body like great waves of heat that bucked and rolled down her nerves and muscles like an earthquake, subsiding temporarily, only to begin to build again.

They only had an hour, but in that hour they stored up a lifetime of forbidden loving. When she finally stood up to leave, she realized that the rubber she'd stolen from her mother was still in her pocket.

"You know," Steven said sadly as he watched her dress, "this only makes things worse. It doesn't change anything. We still can't be together."

"Oh, but I've figured that out," Glory said confidently. "We just won't have children, then everything will be fine."

"No," Steven repeated, his voice cracking in anguish. "Oh, Glory. I should never have let you stay."

He stood ubruptly and walked to the window, staring out at nothing. Guilt, worry, pain warred within him. "It was wrong. I always knew it was wrong to feel the way I do. I tried to stay away. I didn't say anything because I didn't want to hurt you, but I've decided to get married. I'm engaged."

"You're what?" Glory felt her knees sway like tall blades of grass in the wind.

She stared at him in shock, feeling as if a cold white light had fallen over them, taking all color from their skin, chilling their blood, freezing their speech. Her heart seemed to stop beating and she thought in that moment that she knew how it felt to die.

He loved her. She couldn't be wrong about that. They'd just made love for the first time, it was beyond anything she'd ever hoped for. But he was going to marry somebody else. She'd given herself to him, risked everything, and he was rejecting her.

"It's best, Glory. I'm going to marry the daughter of the owner of the investment firm I interned with. It's all arranged. It will mean a career opportunity for me that I can't turn my back on."

"But you love *me*. Say it, Steven. Say you love me, damn you!"

"No, I can't. I won't. Forgive me, Glory."

"But . . . but what if—" She cast her mind desperately for something to stop him. "What if I'm pregnant?"

He thrust his fingers through his hair. "God, I—I don't know, Glory. If you are, write to me. We'll figure out something."

"Figure out something?" Glory began to laugh. The only thing Steven had figured out was how to get himself engaged to someone who could further his career. It was too late. She'd waited too long. She wanted to die.

"I'm sorry. I should have told you." His voice was anguished, but he wouldn't look at her. "Glory, it isn't what I want, but this is all there can ever be."

Glory stopped laughing and stared at him in cold fury. Silently, she finished dressing and walked slowly to her car. As she drove blindly toward the church picnic in Galilee, she swore that even if she was pregnant, she'd never tell him. Steven belonged to her and she belonged to him. It had always been that way. She couldn't change that, and neither could he. But she'd never offer herself to him again.

With the top down on her convertible she felt the wind tug at her hair. It seemed to pull her along. She pressed even harder on the gas pedal. Still, she couldn't get away from the taste and smell of him. She carried it, and him, with her as she drove.

The church service was over when she arrived. That was just as well. She'd never have been able to sit still. After a casual survey of the soldiers, she settled on the young doctor who had come with a group of his patients. She was through with boys. Steven was right. She was a Winslow. A Winslow woman married a man who had something to offer, not necessarily the man she loved.

God, it hurt. She felt like Mr. Sims. Mr. Sims had revealed his soul and he'd been stabbed in the heart for his honesty. Glory understood pain, but she'd survive. Like Scarlett she'd do whatever it took, she'd make Steven sorry for what he was doing.

The doctor wasn't wearing a wedding band. He wasn't a

33

boy. He'd probably been in the war. He knew about women. Perhaps he would find a high school girl intriguing. She wondered if he'd ever been with an almost-virgin?

Camp Gordon was less than sixty miles away. The summer loomed empty before her. Somehow last summer's spend-the-night parties and swimming at the lake seemed a million years ago. Shopping trips to Atlanta? What did any of that mean now? What did anything matter? Everything had changed. Steven was leaving forever. She'd been rejected by the man she'd loved all her life.

The rubber was still in her pocket.

Three

JoEllen Dixon sat in the middle of her bed and wished she'd never volunteered to come home for the Fourth of July activities.

Back at the dorm it had seemed like such a good idea. Not only would her friends be there, but Teddy would see her in action in her student nurse's uniform. That made her feel proud. Teddy would see why she'd been working so hard that she hadn't come home on weekends like she'd promised. But now the excitement over seeing Glory, Susan, and Margie was gone.

It was all Teddy's fault for surprising her. He'd borrowed his brother's car and appeared unexpectedly at her dormitory to drive her back to Galilee for the weekend. Except they hadn't gone home, they'd gone to a motel.

JoEllen glanced across the room at her dressing table with the chintz skirt tacked around the kidney-shaped top. The oval wicker mirror reflected her serious wide-eyed expression, her neat brown hair that could be tucked trimly in a bun beneath her starched nursing cap. She looked like her father. At least she had his build, slim and lean. She had her father's name, too—Joe. She thought about a song she'd heard recently. *Goodbye Joe, me got to go. Me-oh-my-oh."* The song could have been about her father. Joe had left a long time ago.

She glanced around her room and saw it as the sum of her childhood, shabby odd pieces of furniture covered by innocent little-girl prints. She was like that furniture, she decided, except she wasn't innocent anymore.

JoEllen looked at her calendar and counted again. She ought to be safe. She'd studied biology and she'd learned about reproduction and pregnancy.

In two more years she would graduate from Lawson General and be a registered nurse. Her future was planned. She intended her life to make a difference. When she had children, they'd be proud of her and what she did. To begin with she hadn't been able to see beyond the prestige, but now that she was working with sickness and healing she was beginning to understand that there could be so much more.

The Dixon family needed to feel pride. JoEllen knew she had something to give. Her success would wipe the beaten look from her mother's tired face and make her brother Skip stop thinking he had to be such a show-off to be important.

Teddy didn't understand her determination, but he would. By working weekends in the lab at Camp Gordon she could earn enough to finish school without asking her mother for money. Teddy would take an accounting course and get a job according to the plan she'd laid out. Then she could help out at home. Years of watching her mother work two jobs to support her children made JoEllen determined to have more.

Why couldn't Teddy have been in her class? They were almost the same age. Her birthday was in June. His was in December, and he hadn't been permitted to begin first grade until the next year. Then he'd been kept back in the first grade—too immature, his report card said. Throughout high school it hadn't mattered. Teddy was big and blond and golden with a smile that stunned. As the captain of the basketball team and the football team, he was every girl's fantasy. Being Teddy's girl took away the stigma of living on the wrong side of town.

But her life was different now. She was already enrolled in nursing school and Teddy still had another year of high school. She had to wait for him.

JoEllen should have made *him* wait last night, but he'd been so sweet, and so determined. She didn't have the heart to refuse. For two years she'd restrained him. But he'd waited so long, and all their plans were made. There'd been no doubt in her mind that they'd get married—someday.

Teddy was the kind of man she could depend on, not like

her father. Teddy would never disappear. And if he didn't share her drive and ambition, she'd teach him how. Teddy could be controlled. Until last night.

JoEllen gave a sigh and began to dress. She pulled on her white nursing stockings, secured them with wide white garters, and stepped into her starched uniform. It was so different an outfit from the clothes she'd donned the night before—after . . .

Fron the minute Teddy picked her up, she'd known something was different. At the motel JoEllen had been uncomfortable, afraid that someone would see and recognize them, or the car. But she hadn't said no. Even now she wasn't sure why she hadn't. Once inside the room Teddy locked the door and grabbed her, holding her in the air as if she were a football and he'd just crossed the goal line.

The room was awful. There was a bed covered by a green-plaid spread patterned differently from the drapes over the window. The carpet was stained and the light in the lamp was so dim that without the overhead light a person couldn't have read a newspaper.

"The guy at the desk didn't even ask questions, Jo. He didn't care whether I was twenty-one or not, just if I had the money for the room. Oh, Jo baby, isn't this great. We can finally be together."

"But, Teddy," she said stiffly, "we can't. You know we have plans. We can't take a chance on anything happening now. We're too close."

"Oh, baby, you don't know how close I am. Just feel this."

He took her hand and held it to him. But this time he unzipped his pants and, holding her fingers, pulled himself out so that she could see.

"And you don't have to worry. Otis got me a pack of rubbers. I'll take care of you. I promise."

He was so aroused that he'd ruined the first rubber in his haste. JoEllen had turned off the lights, embarrassed at his eagerness. She felt awkward as she took off her clothes and put them on a chair. Teddy shed his shorts and shirt and left them puddled on his trousers where they lay. Then, finally ready, without even pulling back the spread, they'd made love for the first time.

Afterward JoEllen had cried. Not because it had hurt, as

37

Teddy thought, but because it had been such a disappointment. She hadn't known what to expect, but this wasn't it. Teddy apologized that it hadn't lasted very long. The box only contained three rubbers and he'd torn the first one. The next time would be better.

It wasn't. JoEllen lay stiff and angry in his arms, refusing to spend the night. He'd rented the room for sex. They'd had sex. The room smelled like sex, and she wanted nothing more than to get out of that awful place and go home.

But Teddy continued to kiss her, repeatedly. Now that it was too late he began to explore her body, admire the breasts he'd felt but never seen. Finally beginning to warm to his caresses, JoEllen agreed that she'd let him put it in again, just for a moment, if he'd take her home. By that time, Teddy would have agreed to anything.

As he lowered himself over her, he lifted her legs, forcing her to cup them about his body. JoEllen felt a stirring that was new, and for a moment she allowed herself to move with Teddy. Then he began to groan.

"No! Teddy, you promised." At the last minute he had pulled it out, spraying the warm, sticky substance all over her stomach.

She'd sent Teddy out to the machine for a soft drink that she uncapped and shook until it exploded inside her body, hoping that it had washed away any of his ejaculation that might have escaped before he pulled out. That had been a mistake. If that worked, Teddy reasoned, there was no reason why he couldn't do it again. Once more, he'd promised, and then they'd leave. And she couldn't stop him.

For Teddy it was all wonderful. For JoEllen, that second time erased any promise of fulfillment. Now, besides her anger over what Teddy had done, she'd felt as if hundreds of spiders were crawling beneath her skin. She wanted to scream or cry, but there was no way she could let go. It hadn't helped matters that Teddy brought a washcloth and cleaned himself from her body. His washing left her twitching beneath his touch.

True to his promise, they checked out of the motel and drove back to Galilee. JoEllen hadn't known until then that he was going to spend the summer with his father in Texas.

38

She wouldn't see him again until September.

"September?" What had loomed as a problem for her had suddenly taken care of itself. He wouldn't even be here to argue with her about taking a part-time Sunday job at the base hospital at Camp Gordon instead of saving Sundays for him.

Teddy had said that if it was up to him, he would never go to Texas, not now, not after last night. But his mom had laid down the law. For years Teddy's father had drifted from one job to another, staying just long enough to earn a position of responsibility before going on a drinking binge and being fired. Everybody knew he couldn't handle responsibility. But this time he'd been on his job for nearly a year, and he wanted to see Teddy.

"Of course," JoEllen had agreed, secretly glad that he would be away. She still couldn't figure out what had gone wrong in the motel, but she knew it had meant more to Teddy than it had to her. She'd come so close, so often, to allowing Teddy to make love to her, wanting him to make love to her. Then when he had, it hadn't been what she expected.

They'd been alone in the room, in a bed instead of the backseat of a car, so no one would catch them. Teddy had protected her, at least he'd tried. They were going to be married. Teddy loved her. It should have been wonderful. But every moment she'd felt as if she wanted to scream.

All the way back to Galilee Teddy was on top of the world. She still hadn't gotten past the embarrassment, the physical frustration that seemed to intensify by the moment. She'd barely been able to tolerate Teddy's goodnight kiss. Nor did she want to acknowledge that he was already aroused and ready to take her again, right there in her driveway, with her mother and brother inside the house. It was good that Teddy was leaving.

JoEllen sighed. It was good that she didn't have to face Teddy today. She'd slept badly and she knew she was barely holding on to her control. She took one last look in the mirror and started out of the bedroom. Her brother Skip, two years younger, was standing quietly inside the bathroom between their rooms, watching through the cracked doorway.

"How long have you been standing there?" she asked.

"Long enough. You're finally getting some tits, Jo. Nice. Does Teddy like them?"

"Shut up, you dirty-minded little twerp! Teddy doesn't—" She flushed. Teddy *did,* and he liked them very much. She felt a blush steal across her face and ducked her head under the guise of checking her shoelaces.

"Oh, ho. I thought so. Better not let Mama know."

"Skip, I know that you're at the age where hormones control the vocal cords, so I'll forgive you, but," she turned to him seriously, "I'm older now and there are things you don't understand."

"Oh, I understand, JoEllen. I just haven't had any personal experience yet. Don't suppose you'd like to give me a little demonstration, would you?"

JoEllen glared at her sixteen-year-old brother. They'd always been close, the poor little Dixon children, wearing hand-me-down clothes and pretending their daddy was just away, not gone. She'd defended her little brother, protected him, and watched him grow up while her mother worked. But he wasn't her "little" brother anymore. In the last year he'd become a man and she hadn't noticed.

"Forget it, Skip. I've got to go." JoEllen picked up her purse and her name badge and ran out of the house. She wished she were back in the dorm. She wished she'd never come home. Nothing was the same. Even the town had changed. As she drove up Main Street she noted the deterioration. The houses on her end of the street were the oldest in town, the first to be turned into apartments, like the one she lived in.

Her mother was already at church. She'd gone to Sunday school with the neighbor who lived in the other half of the house, leaving the car for JoEllen and Skip. Skip! JoEllen had driven off and left him. Well, he could find his own way.

All the way to church she was quiet. She felt tears well up in her eyes. She needed to talk to somebody, but she couldn't, not about Teddy, or her brother. Even with her best friends she'd never discussed anything like that.

JoEllen doubted that any of them had actually done it.

40

Glory had so many boyfriends that somebody would have said something if she'd ever let them go all the way, and nobody did. Teddy said the boys could look at a girl and tell, but that seemed unlikely. Susan and Sam were probably making love, but Susan hadn't looked any different. She never said a word, and JoEllen didn't dare ask.

She had a horrible thought, What if she asked? What if she admitted that she'd done it and then found out that she was the only one who had. Her face burned as she considered the consequences.

She'd counted her days again. She ought to be safe. JoEllen wouldn't say anything to her friends. Already she felt a little out of place with them. They were still involved in high school things, and all that seemed like a lifetime ago to JoEllen. Teddy was gone for the summer and she wouldn't be coming back home for a while. Nobody would know what happened. Her secret was safe.

Dinner on the church grounds was in progress when JoEllen pulled up. Glory Winslow had already staked her claim on Dr. Sasser. JoEllen recognized him from the base hospital. The times she'd seen him when she'd made her rounds to pick up blood for the lab he'd always seemed friendly but harried. Gossip was that he was a nice person, ambitious and in demand. His time in the Army was almost up.

Margie was sitting with a stunningly handsome man. JoEllen recognized him too; every nurse in the hospital knew the "Greek God of Love." He was a medic, assigned to the therapy ward, and she'd heard that he was turning into a good technician. But the soldier leaning on one crutch and talking to her friends was the big surprise. He was black.

There were many black soldiers in the hospital, but she knew that this soldier wasn't supposed to be here. Somebody had fouled up. She touched her badge as if to assure herself that this was an official function and strolled over to speak to her friends.

"Here's JoEllen," Susan said eagerly. "Don't you look smart in that uniform."

"Thanks. Hello, Dr. Sasser." She gave a hug to Margie

41

and Glory, ignoring the black soldier, then feeling ashamed of her snub and turned back to greet him.

"Hello, Private, are you okay?"

"Yes, ma'am. I'm fine. These folks are making me real welcome."

"Aren't you the patient who plays the piano?"

"Yes, ma'am. I play some."

"You do? Wonderful," Glory spoke up. "Let's go back into the church and sing. Can you play boogie?"

"Glory!" Susan said in horror. "Not in the church. It's Sunday."

"What's the matter?" Glory asked. "Don't you think that God boogies? I'll bet he'd like some music with a little get up and go. What do you think . . . ?" She stopped. "What is your name anyway, soldier?"

"Private Joseph Cheatham, Jr. And I think that the Lord likes for us to be happy. Back home in Muscle Shoals, Alabama, we clap our hands and dance in the aisles. At least . . ." He looked down at his bad leg. "At least I used to. They tell me that I'm lucky to still have my leg. But they won't promise me I can still boogie when I get out of here."

Looking at the cast on the soldier's leg, JoEllen sighed. Boogie? She didn't think so. She was familiar with that kind of cast. Some of the joy seemed to drain out of the private's face as she watched.

JoEllen felt out of place. She and Glory and Margie were all the same age. They'd been inseparable, best friends. She would be where the two of them were right now if she hadn't gone to summer school and skipped her senior year. It had seemed like a smart move at the time. She'd pick up a year so that she'd have two years of nursing school behind her when Teddy graduated. But she'd missed that final year in school with her class, missed the basketball games, the spend-the-night parties.

Now Teddy was gone and JoEllen felt as if she'd been cheated. She felt the spiders under her skin begin to quiver again and she forced herself to circulate. She was both nurse and hostess and there were patients here who might need her help.

She managed to fill a plate and pick at the food until everybody finished. Then she assisted the soldiers into buses

42

and cars to be driven to the lake. Dr. Sasser and four other soldiers rode with Glory in her new convertible. JoEllen, Susan, and Margie piled into the bus with the men so that they could direct the lead driver to the lake.

This time they left behind the older church members and a few of the soldiers. There would be hamburgers and hot dogs at dusk to close out the day for the young people. For now, there were two young married couples to serve as chaperones for the high school girls who were the hostesses.

JoEllen looked down the row of soldiers on the bus. There had been a time when she would have been as excited about the day as the other girls. But her life had changed, even before last night. The patients in the hospital blamed the modern world for their problems. The soldiers in the base hospital blamed the war. She had nobody to blame.

JoEllen looked at the short military haircuts of the soldiers and compared them to Teddy's crew cut, to the kinky curls of the blacks with whom she'd grown up. At least in uniform they all looked pretty much the same. She watched them with their filter-tip Viceroy cigarettes in their pockets as they bragged about their conquests. JoEllen wondered if they were really as experienced as they claimed.

Styles were changing. JoEllen remembered when her mother went to the beauty parlor and had her first permanent wave with electricity that fried her hair into a frizz and made her smell like a singed chicken. Now the machine that cooked curl into hair had given way to a cold wave.

Margie had one of the new Toni home permanents. JoEllen simply swept her hair straight back to keep it neat under her pert little three-cornered nursing cap. Susan's hair was naturally curly; Glory's was so thick that she could simply have it cut in layers if she wanted the illusion of curl, or leave it straight in a Rita Hayworth look.

The residents of Galilee considered their town to be as modern as any other small town. But JoEllen knew that other towns didn't have theaters that still gave away dishes on Wednesday night, or had only two policemen who rarely left the one-room police station on Main Street in the middle of the one-block-long town except on missions of mercy.

Margie's Bond Street cologne and Susan's Evening in

Paris perfume came from Benny's Drug Store. Benny, the pharmacist, knew everybody in town, so that any of the high school boys who wanted to buy rubbers had to wait until Otis Jones came to work part-time after school or else go over to Lynville. Otherwise they faced the fear of Benny calling their folks.

JoEllen thought about the changes she'd seen in just one year and she recognized how truly ignorant her generation had been kept by their parents. Even their teachers taught them only what they needed to know, except for Mr. Sims. Using the senior class of 1954 as his instrument of truth, he'd dared to tell the students something about real life. Even he hadn't expected the town fathers to walk out on a play starring their own children and fire their teacher. That one play was probably the end of the serious drama in Galilee High School.

Now high school was over. And unlike their parents, who never dared to dream so big, or take such chances, these girls had plans for their futures; plans that, except for Susan, would take them away from Galilee. JoEllen suddenly felt very wise.

She'd listened as they'd bravely sung "You'll Never Walk Alone" at the graduation she'd missed, and she'd understood. She and the others would have a very different future. The class of '54, more than any before, was ready.

JoEllen looked about her. She was more nurse than hostess now. And as she listened to Margie chattering with the soldiers, JoEllen knew that she'd already left behind her past. She felt as if she were swimming and the undertow was tugging her back. She didn't belong here, but she didn't know where she did belong.

Susan would marry Sam and live the kind of life they'd been brought up to expect here in Galilee. Glory would go away to school and entice newfound friends into scandalous adventures until she found whatever it was that she seemed to be looking for.

About Margie, JoEllen was less certain. Margie never mentioned her parents, but JoEllen knew that there was some problem there and, because of it, Margie kept a shield around her emotions. She was bright, creative, always seeming to bubble with self-confidence, too much self-confidence. Margie would grin and say that there was a comet out there with her name on it and when it finally came, she would catch it by the tail. "Someday," Margie would say with a faroff look in her eyes, "someday, Margie Raines will be somebody."

For now, for all four of the old friends, there was the day to get through, then the summer.

The summer of the soldiers.

Four

At the lake Joseph pulled a harmonica from his pocket and began to play. He played "Side by Side," "Little Church in the Wildwood," and "Seven Lonely Days"—all tunes they could hum along. "Joseph" soon became "Jody."

And suddenly, sitting beside a black boy, clapping her hands didn't seem so strange to Susan anymore. One by one those who brought swimsuits went inside the bath house to change and started toward the lake.

Maybe if Susan hadn't felt abandoned by Sam, or maybe if she hadn't had her period, nothing would have happened. Years later she'd wonder about that. But wondering hadn't absolved her guilt. When the other girls excused themselves to change, it put the spotlight on her. She couldn't very well say, "I'm sorry, but it's my time of the month. I can't go in the water, so I didn't bring my suit." Instead, she covered the awkwardness by saying, "All the soldiers can't go swimming. I'll just sit here and talk to them."

But most of the soldiers, wandered away with other girls, until only she was left—with Jody. And she knew how he would feel if she disappeared, so she decided to stay and talk.

"What did you do before you went into the service, Jody?" she asked.

"Nothing you'd be interested in. My daddy was a sharecropper. I tried, but I wasn't much good in the fields and he didn't want me to pick cotton all my life."

"At least you have a father," Susan said without thinking.

"My father lives in Chicago. I haven't seen him since I was seven. He doesn't care what I do with my life. He's married again."

46

Susan was the youngest, but she'd realized, even back then, that her father, in his pinstripe suits and polished shoes, didn't come home at night like the other fathers on her block. He never attended events at her school. In fact, the only time she remembered seeing him was at Sunday dinner, when her older brother and sisters were required to report on their week's activities. She lived in fear that he'd call on her, but he didn't. In fact, he never seemed to look at her at all, and when he did, it was with annoyance.

After the heavy Sunday dinner, they would be dismissed, and her father would disappear shortly after. Susan decided that lawyers must be in great demand, for her father always had some legal matter to atttend to, or some meeting of the war ration board on which he served.

The older children often whispered about him, but they never shared their gossip with Susan. She was the baby and too young to understand. Soon, her older sisters and brother were gone, taking war jobs and joining the service. One day in December, when Susan was in the second grade, she'd come home from school to find her mother standing in the hallway with packed suitcases and a strained expression on her face.

"We're going to Galilee," she'd explained. "Going back to Georgia, where I belong."

Home for her mother might have been Galilee, but to Susan the move was a frightening trip on a slow, jerky train that stopped at every crossroads. "Delivering the mail," her mother explained. The smoke-filled passenger cars were so crowded with soldiers trying to get home for Christmas that Susan had to sit in her mother's lap. The ride was long and loud and confusing. Only the soldiers' gifts of chocolate and gum drew Susan's face away from its hiding place between her mother's ample breasts.

They were finally let off at a depot in a small town where there was neither bus nor taxi. Her mother arranged to leave their cases at the station until they could be fetched the next day, and, tired and sleepy, they walked up the dark street to a house with a big front porch.

"Your great-aunt Susan lives here, darling, the one you were named for. Be nice now, and don't cry. We want her to like you."

Susan sensed the tension in her mother's voice. She

promised she wouldn't cry, but she knew she was going to embarrass herself if she didn't find a bathroom soon. She tightened her legs and whimpered as she looked up at her mother in the darkness.

"Do you have to go to the bathroom?"

Susan nodded her head.

"Well, I don't know." Her mother looked around desperately. "You should have said something at the station."

Susan took in the dark shadows and the strange silence that seemed to envelop her. Her mother's anxiety was growing and Susan swallowed hard. "Mama—" She felt her control give way and the gush of warm liquid run down her legs. Then she did cry as the warm odor of urine permeated the night air.

"Oh, Susan." Her mother peeled the wet panties from Susan's legs and repaired the damage as best she could with her handkerchief before she squared her shoulders and knocked on the door.

For the rest of her life Susan remembered arriving in Galilee with wet socks and no underpants. She lived with the disapproval of the great-aunt for whom she was named— a woman suddenly forced to share her small living quarters with the niece she hadn't seen in twenty years. Susan never saw her father again. She always associated him with the acute embarrassment she'd felt over wetting her pants. Soon she locked both memories away in a place where she was safe from the pain.

In fact, Susan wasn't the only one without a father. None of the four best friends had fathers. JoEllen's had deserted his family. Glory's was killed in the war. Margie's father wasn't dead, but he and her mother were vagabonds who were never at home. Margie had her grandparents, but Susan didn't think that was quite the same. Maybe that was why they'd formed a foursome. They shared a common bond: no father.

"I joined the Army as soon as I was old enough to go." Jody was saying. "I like it. I wanted to make a career of the military."

"Why don't you?"

"Because my leg won't ever be right. They done—the doctors said that when they take the cast off, it will be shorter

48

than the other one. They want me to wear one of them shoes with a big sole on it."

"Oh," Susan didn't know what to say. She'd never spent any time talking to a black person. She couldn't say, "What did you think of Elizabeth Taylor's dress in *Father of the Bride?*" She didn't even know if black people got married. She was fairly sure they didn't have weddings like Elizabeth Taylor had. He saved her the embarrassment of coming up with another comment.

"Tell me about you, Miss Susan, what will you do now that you have your diploma?"

"I'm going to take a bookkeeping course over in Augusta and then I'm going to work in the bank."

"Don't you ever want to get out of this town, go somewhere else, see something of the world?"

"No, I don't think so. I lived in a big city when I was little. Then one day, we packed and left. I like Galilee. It's like a big family where everybody cares about everybody else. I never want to go anywhere else."

"I guess for you it will be good. Working in a bank will be nice, all clean and pretty."

"Yes, and we have good hours, including being off on Wednesday afternoon."

"Don't people in Galilee, Georgia, do any banking on Wednesday?"

"No, and not much of anything else either. Every business in town, except the drug store and the cotton gin during the summer closes Wednesday afternoon. Of course, the stores are open Saturday morning instead. Eight to five and an hour for lunch, forty hours a week."

"Imagine that. Working forty hours a week. My mama works for a family in Muscles Shoals, seven to six, six days a week. What does your father do?"

"My father is an attorney. He left us—married his secretary. We never hear from him. He has another family now."

"No kidding? I'm sorry. It must have been hard on your mama."

Susan thought about that for a moment. She didn't know the answer. Her mother's life had changed drastically, but she'd always seemed tired, resigned to whatever happened. And she'd had to go to work, which she'd never done before.

49

"Yes. We came to Galilee so that she could be near her family. But by the time we got here they were mostly all gone, except for Aunt Susan, who let us live with her. My older brother lives in Lynville, but my sisters live far away," Susan said quietly. "My mother works in a drapery factory, sewing, on production. I think her job is hard, too."

"There were twelve of us," Jody said, "living in a four-room house. No indoor plumbing. No electricity. My oldest brother Buck got killed in the war before I ever joined. They sent my mother a flag to drape over his coffin and she was so proud."

"Oh" was all Susan could say. Except for Aunt Susan, she'd never been around death. She couldn't imagine not having electricity, not having a bathroom.

"Do you have a girlfriend, Jody?"

"No, at least not anymore. There was one girl back home, but she got a baby by the man her mama worked for and she quit school when she was fifteen."

"Oh, I'm sorry."

"She wasn't. She's had two more since then. Same man. He gives her a house and money. She thinks she's better off than any of her friends. Maybe she is."

Jody began to play his harmonica again, a sad, keening song that Susan didn't know.

She listened and thought about Sam not wanting her to come to the picnic. She never talked to Sam about her feelings for her father, not like she had to Jody. Sam wouldn't have understood. His grandfather set the standards, and Sam never considered not living up to them. It seemed odd to Susan that Sam's own father seemed to be excluded from those standards. Since the night he'd caught her in the hallway at Grandfather Winslow's house, she'd avoided Sam's father, which wasn't hard to do since he was rarely there anyway.

She thought about what might have happened if she'd been black and encountered Sam's father in the dark. She shivered. Having an illegitimate child and being kept by a man was beyond Susan's comprehension. She was sure that Sam would never do such a thing. His grandfather wouldn't approve.

Sam wouldn't approve of her spending time with Jody Cheatham, either. But looking around, she decided that being with Jody was probably safer than being with any of the other boys. Jody wasn't interested in her that way. He was quiet and nice. And, suprisingly enough, in trying to talk to him, she had opened up and told him things that nobody else knew about her.

For most of the afternoon they talked. She learned that Jody was the youngest child, that his mother played the organ for the church, and that he sang in the choir. He'd thought he wanted to be in the infantry until he'd been sent to Korea. He liked Army life, but he'd hated the fighting. Now he would go back home. His father wouldn't say anything. He'd accept Jody's injury just like he'd accepted his own life. But he'd be disappointed. He wanted more for Jody.

Susan thought that Jody wasn't so different from the boys in Galilee.

At least Jody had tried to better himself. He'd been assigned to the medical corps rather than the infantry. He'd thought that working with those who did the fighting instead of having to do the killing himself would be better. But dying was dying, and he had watched too much of it.

"Miss Susan," he said finally, "I've never told another soul this, but I don't want to go back home. I don't fit in there anymore. I'm not a farmer and nobody else in Muscle Shoals, Alabama, is going to give me a job."

"Can't you do hospital work?"

"Sure thing. I can be a janitor, maybe. They won't let me be an orderly. I can't pick up a patient and handle him like they'd expect. And there ain't no other colored boys allowed in the ward."

"Maybe you could change that, Jody," she said, knowing all the time that he was right.

"Yess'um maybe. Maybe I'll try. But you know what I really want?"

"What?"

"I want to go to college. I think I might like to write stories. But I don't know if I can."

"Sure you can, Jody. Isn't there a G.I. bill that could help you? Our English teacher, Mr. Sims, told us about it. That's how he finished his college education."

"Help a black boy? I don't know."

She wanted to say that he could do it, but the truth was,

51

she didn't know. She was discovering that there was a lot that she didn't know. So she said nothing.

Susan finally found an excuse to check on another shore-bound guest and managed to avoid sitting with Jody for the rest of the afternoon. But avoiding him made her feel as guilty as sitting with him had.

Susan wasn't accustomed to being uncertain. Everything in her life had been simple. Even Sam. She didn't remember when they decided to get married. It had just been assumed. During her four years' home economics, they'd planned a wedding and she'd asked Sam's opinion on every step of the event. He'd approved of the china pattern, the silverware, and the music for the ceremony. The budget that followed was based on what Sam expected to earn.

Now she looked at Jody and realized how different their lives were. He had dreams, just like she did, but he had dreams of doing something better. He was looking for change. She just wanted everything to stay the same. She'd never realized how easy her life was.

Five

Glory welcomed that quick rush of adrenalin that always came at the start of something new. This time the rush was more powerful. As she pulled on her red two-piece swimsuit she turned off the picture in her mind of Steven lying back against the pillows, Steven confessing that no matter what they were to each other he couldn't marry her. So be it. Glory knew that Steven would always love her. But he was going to marry someone else.

Packing her skirt and blouse in her canvas bag, Glory left the dressing room, threw her towel and her beach bag over her shoulder, and glanced around for the doctor. She knew that she was being stared at. She expected that, and she relished the acceleration of her pulse at the same time a cold calm settled over her, banking the fire still raging inside.

Steven had rejected her. Fine. She didn't need him. Never again would she waste her energy on a man she couldn't control. She was sure the doctor was interested in her. Men always were. She scanned the crowd until she located him.

He was sitting apart from the others, perched on a picnic table with his feet on the bench and his elbows planted on his knees. He was pretending not to notice her swimsuit, just as he'd pretended not to notice her in the car on the drive to the lake.

"Hi, are you enjoying yourself, Dr. Sasser?"

"Yes, I am, Miss Winslow."

He had a stocky build. His light brown hair was cut in a standard G.I. crew cut. A scattering of pale freckles were clustered across the bridge of his nose. Nice, clean-cut. Under other conditions Glory might not have noticed him, for she

53

preferred the tall, dark, mysterious type, but today he was her target. He was a doctor and he was older.

Her grandfather would be pleased, she thought with amusement. A doctor or a judge was the programmed husband in Glory's future. Dr. Sasser would be more than acceptable, providing his family background measured up. All her life she'd fought against following her grandfather's wishes. Now she was going to do just what he would have wanted. Up to a point.

Glory never understood why her mother had married her father. Blackie was the ne'er-do-well Winslow, a soldier who wasn't even good enough to survive the war. But sometimes in the dark, at night, Glory could still remember him, the handsome, black-haired man with the big smile and laughing eyes. And he was a Winslow.

Glory still remembered the way her grandmother had winced and narrowed her lips in disdain when Blackie Winslow's name was mentioned. It was as if her mother Adele were the true Winslow and Blackie the outsider. And until she died Grandmother Winslow had filled Glory's head with stories of the Winslow women and the kind of men they were expected to marry. Her grandfather decreed, somewhat sanctimoniously, that the women were expected to be pious, subdued, and respectful.

Both Adele and Evelyn were widows after the war. Neither had married again. Aunt Evelyn always said that all the suitable men were either already married or they'd been killed in the war. Sam's father was the only Winslow brother left and people whispered that he was a little "odd."

"Do you have a first name, Dr. Sasser?"

"Yes, I'm sorry. It's Roger."

"And I'm Glory."

"What an unusual name."

"Yes," Glory laughed lightly. "I'm told that my mother said, 'Glory Hallelujah!' when I was finally born. I took a long time coming. My father called me his crowning glory. What do you think?"

"I think if I had to choose, I'd call you Morning Glory. They're so bright and colorful when they open in the morning."

"Ah, yes, and Morning Glorys close when the sun goes

down. I like the darkness. I like a person not being able to see what I think and how I feel. It gives me the advantage."

"And you like having the advantage, Miss—Glory?"

A car radio was playing. She could hear Nat King Cole's voice wafting across the lake.

"I intend to always have the advantage, Dr. Sasser. Do you like Nat King Cole?"

"Yes. He has a nice voice."

This wasn't going to be easy. Glory considered how best to reach him. He wasn't automatically entranced like the boys she usually met. Rather, he seemed to be acting deliberately cautious. One thing Glory wanted to be sure of was that she didn't sound too juvenile. "I just got back from New York," she said. "All the record shops up there are playing his songs."

"That's what your friend Margie said at lunch. Your class raised enough money to pay for the entire group to go on the senior trip? That's amazing."

"Not when you consider that there were only thirty-five in my class. And one of them joined the Army and didn't go on the trip."

"Welcome to the club," he said.

"You joined the Army?"

He laughed and swung around to meet her. "No, not then. I just meant that my class was small, too. Would you like to sit down?"

That was a mistake, he decided. This girl was seventeen going on twenty-five. She was pure trouble, and he was the fish she was angling for. Auburn hair, sea-green eyes that seemed to burn with intensity, a lush figure, precisely proportioned, and the breeding was there in every nuance of her stance.

"I came from a high school with a class that was only a bit larger. We had forty-nine. And the most we did was have a class picnic. They wanted to go to Florida but most of us couldn't afford it."

"One girl in my class bought Nat King Cole records in New York. Brought them all the way back from New York on the bus, holding them in her lap. Then while we were unloading the bus, one of the boys was horsing around and crashed into her. I guess you know what happened."

55

Out of sight of the church chaperones Glory pulled her cigarettes from her beach bag and shook one out. Catching it between pouting lips, she widened her eyes and tilted her head to glance up at Roger.

"Do you have a light, Doctor?"

"No. I don't smoke."

"Oh." Glory seemed nonplussed for a moment, then looked back at him with more interest. She replaced the cigarette in the pack. Only she and Margie were brave enough to smoke openly. Still, she was surprised. In her mind all soldiers smoked.

She dropped the pack into her bag and glanced down at her breasts swelling out of the top of the Rose Marie Reid swimsuit as she considered another approach.

"Aren't you going in the water, Dr. Sasser?"

"No, I'm afraid I didn't bring a suit."

"No problem," Glory said with sudden inspiration. "Come with me. There's a place around those trees where you can swim privately. I'll show you."

Roger groaned. He'd thought that she was trouble. Now he was sure of it. Saucy little rich girl, leader of the pack, driving her own convertible, probably a present from her daddy, practically dragging him into the car when they left the church. There was a time when he'd have been flattered, but age had brought a certain amount of wisdom. Once you added the word doctor to your name, doors opened. And open doors were what a bright young surgeon was looking for. Not this kind of trouble. She was seventeen and he was twenty-seven. She was the last thing he needed.

Trouble was, he'd been just as lonesome as the other soldiers, more maybe. And she was beautiful.

"Thanks, but I don't think so. I'd better stay where I can keep an eye on the men. Some of them haven't been out of the hospital before."

"Oh." He was turning her down. An experience which only made him more intriguing. "Come now, Roger, look around. Do you see any of your men who aren't being very well-cared for?"

She moved from the bench up to sit beside him on the tabletop, crossing her legs so that suddenly their hips were touching.

Roger looked around. She was right. Women gravitated to men wearing a uniform. If the uniform didn't get them, the bandages did. Every man under his immediate care had found someone to see to his needs. Even Jody, shy, inexperienced Jody, the lone black soldier, was sitting quietly with a small dark-haired girl who was sporting a class ring wrapped with tape to keep it on her finger.

"Tell me about yourself," he said.

She leaned her head closer, tilting it so that her large green eyes would seem to devour him. She'd been told that was her most seductive look. "I'll be at the University of Georgia in September. I'm going to be an actress."

"Oh? I graduated from Georgia, too," he said. "It's a pretty big school for a small-town girl, you know."

"I'm not a small-town girl, Roger. I've had enough of small to last all my life. There's a whole world out there and I intend to enjoy all of it. Where are you from that you had a class of only forty-nine seniors?"

"One of those small towns you're trying to escape from, a little place outside Athens called Maysville. That's why I went to Georgia. I could stay at home and go to school. And of course that made it easier to go on to the medical college in Augusta."

There was a vitality about the girl. Something about the way she focused all her attention on him reached down and jerked at his insides. In some strange way she seemed to transfer that vitality to him. He didn't like the way he responded and yet he couldn't seem to stop himself.

Roger had known a few women, not when he was her age, but as he'd made his way through medical school, and later with a few staff nurses where he served his internship. Then he'd graduated, been drafted, and sent to Korea. He only had a year in the war zone, but that was long enough to know that war accelerated everything: growing up, women, sex. Now, back at the military hospital, he was having trouble reprogramming himself. Tent hospitals on the battlefield had taught him to move at a frantic pace, but peacetime, where he had to deal with rules and regulations and mountains of paperwork, was driving him crazy.

"If you don't want to swim, would you like to go for a walk around the lake?"

57

"Fine." A walk seemed a good way to work off the tension that was building inside his mind, to say nothing of the pressure of Glory's leg against his. In truth, Roger *was* a small-town boy. He was the youngest of a family of four boys, three of whom were athletes. Roger was always the brain, the one who was chosen last for games. Until he became a medical student he was passed over by the popular girls, leaving him with what he knew was an inferiority complex. Glory took him back to that part of his past. Being singled out by a girl like her was new, and he wasn't certain what she expected.

He turned and offered her his hand as she stepped down. She didn't release her grip and they were walking toward the lake hand in hand. Damn! He couldn't seem to find a way to unclasp himself. Her thumb slid between their palms and began making a half-moon circle back and forth. The little witch—with those big, innocent eyes. She knew what she was doing. He was worried. He was older than she, and he was a senior officer. It was his responsibility to set an example. And leaving the group with a seventeen-year-old girl was asking for trouble.

"I love the sky in summer," she said softly. "But I like it best in winter, just before a storm when it's all purple and black. That's when it's exciting. But this is nice, too."

"Yes. This is nice."

They were moving away from the area where the others were playing in the water. The sounds of Nat King Cole faded into Eddie Fisher's "I'm Walking Behind You on Your Wedding Day." They had to circle a stand of trees and a blackberry thicket that extended to the water's edge. Once inside the shadowy woods, Glory stopped and turned to face him.

"Don't you like me, Roger Sasser?"

Oh, hell, he should have known. She wasn't going to let him escape.

She slid her hand behind her back. "Don't you want to kiss me?" She parted her lips and moistened them with her tongue. "I want to kiss you. I want very much to kiss you."

He might as well kiss her. She wasn't going to let him get away without it.

"What are you doing. Glory? Does every man have to want you?"

His words stung. "Every man always has," she whispered, as she pulled his face down to meet hers.

Glory, who had grown up thinking that making love meant marriage and commitment forever, understood that summer day that she'd been wrong. To a man, marriage was simply the price he paid for the privilege. Steven hadn't paid the price, so this man would have to do it for him. Glory's forever was wrapped up in one day. This day. Forever was now.

Roger Sasser was trying to back away from her. She'd been spurned once. She wouldn't allow Roger Sasser to turn away. She'd make him want her. He'd writhe in agony with wanting her from now on. And she'd enjoy his desire until *she* made the decision that she was through with *him*. She might not marry him, but she'd make him ask her. Drawing on some instinctive, primal knowledge, she parted her lips beneath his and began her deadly assault.

Always before, with other men, it had been the game that had been important. Life had been a constant proving ground. She wanted a boy, she got him, even if he already belonged to another girl. Then, once he'd proclaimed his undying love for her, she was through with him.

Acting was her outlet for her emotions. And always the lead role. On stage, she always played some part of herself. She simply reached down and found the character she was to portray. She'd even been offered an acting scholarship—to the University of Georgia—something that was unheard of in a town with only thirty-five seniors.

"Of course you won't take it," her mother had said in horror. "You'll major in fine arts, certainly, but not for the stage."

"Of course not," Glory had agreed, knowing all the time that once she got to the campus she'd do exactly what she wanted to do. She always had.

And what she wanted to do now was make love to this soldier. She'd used him to erase Steven from her body, the smell of him, the feel of him, the memory. This man would give her the adoration that Steven had denied her. She'd let him—no she'd *force* him—to make love to her. She was no longer a virgin. She'd given that to Steven who hadn't valued her gift.

What was done was already done and couldn't be changed. Suddenly she was glad. She didn't have to say no anymore because she was no longer a virgin. And she'd liked it. Sex had been the ultimate power. And she held that power.

She wondered briefly if the doctor would be able to tell, but from the way he was breathing as he looked down at her, she didn't think it mattered.

Let him think he was in control.

She knew that he wanted her.

She pressed her body against him, felt his erection, and gave a wicked wiggle as she smiled. "You understand that I'm very particular about who I choose to give my kisses to. And today, I choose you."

She stepped away, far enough so that he could see her. She smiled. Slowly she untied the straps behind her neck and let the halter of her suit fall forward, exposing her breasts. She slid her hands around to her back, unhooked it, and dropped it to the ground. She stood, looking at him for a long time before she held out her hand.

Roger knew what he was doing. He could never say that he didn't. When he kissed her and she pulled him down to the carpet of pine needles, he went willingly. Her body was impatient and demanding, her breasts throbbing beneath his lips. Without knowing how or when, the bottom of her bathing suit was gone.

He never got undressed. Only his shirt was unbuttoned and his pants unzipped and bunched around his thighs. The girl was a whirlwind of heat than enveloped him. Never before had he encountered such intensity, such raw desire. Only when he collapsed against her did he realize what he'd done.

"Oh, God, Glory. Do you realize that I didn't use anything?"

She only smiled. "Are you worried that you'd have to marry me?" she asked. "Or are you already married?"

"Yes. I mean, no, I'm not married. I mean, it shouldn't have happened. I'm older than you, and I'm a doctor. I should know better."

"But it did happen and you enjoyed it. And so did I. Now that I have you half undressed," she said brightly, "let's go for a swim. I'd say that there's no point in closing the barn door after the horse has escaped."

She stood up. Her small, lush body was beautiful. He couldn't understand her casual acceptance of what had happened. She was little more than a child. He was an adult. Yet he was still reeling from the impact.

"Take off your tie, Dr. Sasser. I'll do the rest. She knelt down and unlaced his shoes, lifting one foot, then the other as she removed his socks. Peeling his wrinkled trousers down his stocky legs, she openly examined him.

"Men are interesting," she observed. "You're the first *man* I've had the opportunity to look at up close." Steven had always been hard when she watched him, as he was this morning. This morning. She sighed.

The moment Steven's arms had tightened around her, everything had been too intense, too new, too powerful. Her eyes had been planted everywhere but on that part of him. Yet now, even in her passion, she'd realized that Steven was different from this man. The doctor was shorter and stockier and so was his—penis. She made herself think the word. No more oblique references. No more secretive half-thoughts.

Today was different. Today she'd been with two men and she'd intimately examined two penises, in the light, without pretense.

Roger removed his shirt. He found it unbelievably stimulating being naked beneath her open examination. Unlike other girls he'd known, she wasn't embarrassed or nervous. She was curious and she looked. She didn't simper and try to cover herself. And she was beautiful. When he felt himself begin to harden again, he grabbed her hand and searched for the direction to the lake.

"Which way?" he asked in desperation.

"Why the big hurry?"

"I'm hot."

"So am I," she admitted with amusement. "It's just not as obvious on me as it is on you. Follow me."

The finger of water was secluded. The lake was cool, but not cool enough. Glory was willing and Roger couldn't turn her down. Once he'd touched her, he was lost. He suspected

61

that she hadn't reached a climax when he had, but he didn't know how to ask her and nothing he did slowed the intensity of her passion.

They waded out into the water, Glory squealing with every step.

"I hate mud," she said as the water reached her breasts. She caught Roger around the neck, her legs circling his waist. He was instantly inside her.

Roger didn't dare look around to see if anybody was watching. He only hoped that the spit of land was still hiding them. As Glory began to ride him he felt the power she'd induced. Roger groaned and headed deeper into the lake.

Six

Across the lake, Nick Zambino watched the doctor and the saucy redhead disappear into the trees. The doc was a sly one. Nick might have gone off with a girl in an instant, but the doc was more reticent. Gossip was that none of the nurses could get him to the supply building, which was good, for Nick had fashioned a section of one of the linen closets for his own amusements.

Nick glanced at the blond girl in the water beside him. She was kicking her feet, holding on to the pier where he was sitting, looking up at him with open adoration. He'd already seen enough of her breasts to know that she was well filled out and he'd managed to gaze at her intently enough to feel her shiver of response when he touched her shoulder with his leg.

Time for Nick-the-Magnificent to swing into action.

He slid into the water, turning his body just enough so that he could catch the back of her suit and pull her down with him. Beneath the cover of the dark lake water he slid his knee between her legs and pressed her against him.

When they surfaced he gave her a smile.

"Wow, you've got some body, babe. I really like you."

"You do? I'll bet you tell all the girls that."

"Not unless they look like you. Can't we get out of here and lose these people?"

They were treading water, his knee still pressing against her with every kick. His hands were constantly in motion, touching, nudging, squeezing.

Margie gasped. True, she'd flirted with the guy. She'd wanted the other girls to see what she'd caught, but now that

63

he demanded she follow through, as always, she began to pull back.

"No. What would everybody say?"

"Who's *everybody*, Margie? From where I stand nobody is interested in what we're doing, except a couple of the guys who'd take my place in a heartbeat."

"Why, the chaperones, of course. And your superior officer. We're supposed to behave properly. You don't know what a bad reputation can do to a girl in a small town."

"And you have a good one?"

"Certainly I do." Margie pulled away and lifted herself back onto the float.

"What does a girl with a bad reputation do?"

"Well, she—she . . ." Margie's voice trailed off. There was something about the man's gaze that held on and wouldn't let go. He was big and muscular and movie-star handsome, and he'd picked her. For the first time in her life she'd been the lucky one. Nick was far and away the best-looking guy in the group. She knew that she was playing with fire, but all too often she'd backed away and later, when she'd shored up enough courage to go after what she wanted, she'd been too late. The world might think that she had no fears, but Margie knew what a coward she really was.

Not this time. Nick Zambino was her test case, her yardstick for the future. He was the embodiment of her wildest fantasies and she wasn't going to be sorry tomorrow that she'd been a shrinking violet. She could do whatever she wanted to. Nobody would have to know. And he wouldn't be around after today to gossip about what she did.

"A girl can get a bad reputation if she lets a boy go too far."

"You mean," Nick said in a low voice, "like your friend across the lake with the captain?"

Margie turned her head, searching for Glory. She could just barely see the heads of two swimmers treading water.

"What do you mean?"

"Well, if you watch until they come out of the water, I think that you'll see they're naked. And their heads are awfully close together to be taking swimming lessons. Why don't we join them?"

"I don't think that's a good idea."

"Well, okay. I guess I'll see if I can find some other girl

who isn't quite so innocent." He made a motion to move away.

"No! I mean, I suppose we could take a walk around the lake if you'd like. But, that's all, Nick. I'm a nice girl."

"I never doubted it for a moment, sweet thing."

"You promise that you'll be nice, too?"

"You can trust me. I'll be very nice. I promise."

And he was. When he kissed her, it was nice. His kiss set off an emotion that slid down her spine and rippled the tendons in the back of her knees until she could hardly stand. He didn't ask or cajole. He simply took charge. When he peeled the top of her bathing suit down to her waist and kissed her breasts, she watched in amazement as her nipples darkened and formed hard little knots.

But when he began to pull the suit lower she shook her head. "No, I can't. I trusted you. You promised."

"That's all right, darling," he whispered, and kissed her again. This time his hand left the suit and slid down the seam to the bottom of the leg, where he ran his finger back and forth until he reached the part of her he was seeking.

"What are you doing, Nick?" she said, trying to move away. But this time he had her captured in his arms, pushed against a tree. This time, when his finger moved beneath the crotch of her suit and slid into her, she gasped out loud. She hadn't expected it to feel so good. In spite of herself, she shivered.

"I'm just showing you that your body wants to know mine. I won't force you to do anything that would frighten you. But if you're going to be the one I spend my afternoon with, I ought to get something in return. That's only fair."

He placed her hand on him, the hard part of him pressing against her. "Feel this. You're responsible."

"No, Nick. I don't do this. Please. Stop! Stop!"

"You can do it, baby. You got me like this, now you've got to help me out."

"I can't. No!" Now she was scared. She could cry out, but what would happen then? She'd be found out. She'd be embarrassed before everybody. That would be the end of any reputation she'd ever had.

"Okay, Margie," he said, beginning to breathe heavily. "I won't force you. There are other ways." He rubbed her one last time and reluctantly removed his fingers from beneath

65

her suit and let it slide back into place.

"What?"

"I'll show you," he said, taking her hand and slipping it inside his suit. "Hold me tight, like this." He clasped her hand and pressed it around the length of him, moving it up and down briskly. Then, just as she felt a shudder begin, he pulled from her clasp and thrust himself between her legs. He didn't try to stick it inside her. Instead, he held her legs tightly closed as he slid it in and out, until he moaned.

Margie shuddered. In spite of her fear, the pressure of him between her legs was stimulating. Of course he hadn't done anything to her, but the feel of him against her left her aching for what she'd refused.

She stared at the handsome man in dismay. Then he stepped back, turned aside, and started to urinate. Right there before her, he was peeing. She'd never seen a man do that before, but she couldn't turn away.

"If I were you, babe," he said, stepping back and shaking the last drop of liquid from himself, "I'd jump in that water and wash myself off. I didn't come inside you, but those little fellows could run up there by themselves. You're pretty juicy and inviting."

Juicy? God, she was swimming in moisture.

Giving a cry of dismay, she turned around and, without worrying about who might be watching, she headed back toward the lake and jumped in. She wouldn't cry. She wouldn't. She'd decided before she came to the picnic that she wouldn't back away, and she hadn't, at least not completely. Why then, did she feel so *awful*?

Because she was a coward. Sometimes she felt as if she were transparent. JoEllen, Glory, even Susan, all seemed to know exactly who they were. But not Margie. Deep down inside, she knew she was a failure. She was only fooling herself about her great dreams. She didn't really have the courage to do what she wanted when she had the chance.

She walked back toward the dock and stayed with the crowd until the chaperones began building the fire for the hot dogs. She avoided Nick, who was sitting by the black soldier, and wondered if anybody had noticed that she and Nick were no longer a pair.

Nick watched her with something like regret. He never had much occasion to get acquainted with that feeling. All the women he went after came willingly. But this time, he hadn't even been able to get her to let him take off her suit. He'd tricked her. And he felt a tinge of conscience at shocking her, which also was new to Nick.

"Hell, Joseph," he told the black boy sitting beside him, "what we need is a drink of real whiskey, not this soda pop and chocolate milk."

Joseph agreed. *Where would we get it?* he wanted to ask the big guy. *Any places in this town that would serve you wouldn't serve me.*

Roger Sasser was physically and emotionally exhausted. The sun had slid behind the trees. He and Glory had been in the lake for a long time. When they got out of the water, he dried himself with his underwear, then pitched it into the bushes and pulled on his uniform.

His body felt strange wearing pants with nothing beneath. The starchy seam rubbed against him and he knew he was going to be constantly stimulated until he got back to the hospital. Looking at Glory told him that he'd be in that state even if it weren't for the seam.

Pulling her skirt and blouse on over her swimsuit, Glory was strangely silent. Gone was her exuberance. Gone was her laughter. There was a stillness about her that was almost deadly.

He caught her chin with his finger and lifted her face. "This—it never should have happened. But you—you've been wonderful. I don't know what to say."

"Say you love me," she said.

"But—"

"Say it, Roger. I need to hear you say it. You do, don't you?" Her voice was almost desperate. "Say you love me."

"I love you," he answered. And for that moment, he did.

JoEllen circulated among the hospital patients, making certain that they weren't getting overtired. She watched as Margie avoided the tall Greek man who had taken her for a walk. Susan had found a spot away from the black soldier now that everybody had returned from the lake. Glory and the doctor rejoined the group, strangely awkward with each

67

other. Something about the way they didn't look at each other made JoEllen wonder if Teddy could be right. Maybe you could look at a person and know if she'd made love. She wondered if her friends sensed anything different about *her*.

That awful memory came crashing back. In her mind JoEllen could still feel Teddy's body plunging inside hers. She could still feel his desire and she cringed at the sensation that was nothing short of revulsion when he'd collapsed on top of her.

But the thing that kept replaying in her mind was when he'd removed the prophylactic. He'd given a nervous laugh, tied a knot in it, and joked, "If he gets out of there, we'll call him Dick Tracy."

Maybe it would have been different if she'd enjoyed it, but she hadn't. It had been awful. Maybe there was something wrong with her.

JoEllen wished the night was over, the soldiers gone. They were all too male, and she was too vulnerable.

On the other side of the fire, Nick considered his behavior as he ate. Perhaps he'd been too crude. After all, he could be at Camp Gordon for another month before he'd be assigned. Then his wife would probably join him. Instead of bird-dogging women, he'd have to be a husband to a woman he could hardly remember marrying.

She'd been a waitress at the tavern in town. They hadn't known each other very long. Marrying her just before he'd shipped out to boot camp had seemed a proper gesture when he was on the way to war, even if it was only called a peacekeeping venture. But now he wondered. Since he'd been away from New Jersey, he'd learned that there were too many girls out there for any man to be tied to just one.

Nick watched Margie leave the dressing room and find a seat by the fire. She was a nice girl, and innocent, in spite of her looks. She was a real looker, even if she didn't know it yet. And he'd shocked her. Maybe he'd come back and see her again, just to apologize, spend some time with her. For a month Margie could be an interesting amusement. He knew that she'd give in to him eventually. They always did.

He stood up, walked around the campfire, and forced himself into the space next to Margie. He leaned over and whispered in her ear. "I'm truly sorry if I offended you, baby. You just don't know what looking at you in that suit does to a guy. I really like you. Will you forgive me?"

Margie tugged at the neck of her dress and thought about her answer for a moment. Forgiving him was safe now. They were in a group and the day was over. Nobody would ever know what happened in the woods and the other girls were looking at Nick with envy. She could afford to be generous now when it didn't matter. And for a moment she was as confident as her friends.

"Sure, Nick. I forgive you."

"Then let me put my arm around you," he whispered, "and let me pretend I'm back home with my girl."

He put his arm around her and pulled her close while they watched the girls twirl their sparklers in the late-afternoon sunlight. Packages of midget firecrackers were dutifully set off. After all, it was the Fourth of July and they were here for a celebration.

Margie let herself repeat Nick's words. With his *girl*, he'd said. He had a girl back home. Of course he did. They probably all did. This day had offered them substitutes for the women who'd already claimed them. But that didn't matter. The others didn't know. Margie leaned back and smiled up at him provocatively.

Being with Nick ought to make her feel good, but it didn't. As always, the uncertainty lingered. She was fooling herself. Today had turned out to be a tease, a promise unfulfilled, and she was the one left wanting. She glanced around the fire at Susan and JoEllen. What would they say if she told them what she'd almost done? They'd be horrified. They'd never allow a boy to touch them as she had. They simply wouldn't. About Glory, she wasn't sure. They didn't know how much she'd wanted to give in to Nick. And she wasn't sure her morals were worth the regret.

Later, as they took their soldiers to the bus, Margie allowed Nick to kiss her goodbye. The others were doing it, so it was safe. Even Susan shook hands with Joseph and wished him well. Glory and Roger didn't kiss, but the tension between them was evident to everyone.

"I'll write to you, Margie," Nick said, and kissed her again, sticking his tongue in her mouth suggestively. "Will you dream about me tonight?"

She didn't answer, for she didn't know. Closing her eyes, she said a silent prayer. She couldn't control dreams. Dreams were visions in a way, and a vision could be very real. For now, she didn't need sleep. She could create her own dream even if she was wide awake. Someday she would be somebody—somebody everyone would envy. And all this would be remembered as just what it was—nothing.

On the way back even Glory was quiet. Susan, sitting in the middle, felt as if she were being assaulted by waves of unspoken words. Glory and Margie were both smoking, both changing positions, moving restlessly as if they had to go to the bathroom and were trying to conceal their need.

Susan didn't want silence. She didn't want to think. She wanted to talk, to say something about the day. About Private Cheatham. She needed Glory's outrageous need to shock to praise her boldness. She needed Margie's philosophical outlook to find an acceptable reason for her actions.

But nobody spoke. And Susan wished she'd taken Sam's advice and stayed at home.

JoEllen rode back to the church in the bus with the soldiers. There was joking and good-natured teasing among the guys. And there was quiet, too. Some of them seemed depressed. They probably missed home and family.

As she drove home she could identify with that, at least with the idea of home as it should be. Nobody knew how much JoEllen wished for a mother who wore ruffled aprons and baked cookies. Her own mother managed to provide the necessities, but little else. It wasn't the cookies that JoEllen missed, but the apron with the ruffles and the mother who understood their importance.

JoEllen passed the telephone company where her mother worked the night shift and wondered if her mother was ever lonely and uncertain. Did she regret her life? Somehow she couldn't see her mother feeling anything at all. She refused to talk about their father and, as far as JoEllen knew, she'd never been with another man. She and Skip were the result of a marriage that had ended before her brother was born.

There'd been no divorce. Her father had just disappeared one day and never returned.

JoEllen took off her uniform and repacked it in her suitcase. She'd catch the bus back to Augusta tomorrow and put this weekend out of her mind. She wished she were already back in the dorm. She wished this weekend had never been.

Seven

The next week JoEllen was back on the hospital floor and in class. Glory, Margie, and Susan spent most of the week poring over pattern books and back-to-school fashion magazines, planning their wardrobes for the fall.

They discussed an incident that had the town in an uproar. On the streets of downtown Galilee, a car full of black people driving down Number One Highway from New York to Florida had stopped at the Galilee Hotel and asked to use the restroom. When they were denied access, one of the women pulled down her pants and urinated on the sidewalk.

"Can you believe it?" Susan said, her eyes wide in wonder.

"What else can you expect? You know the Supreme Court just passed that law," Glory said. "Now they'll all think they are as good as we are."

"People in Galilee won't go along with it. Our blacks don't want to go to school with us. They'd be just as uncomfortable as we would." Susan repeated the statements she'd heard all her life, then thought of Jody. Jody was prepared to go to school with white people, if it meant getting an education. Susan thought about what he'd said, but she didn't tell the others.

"I'm just surprised that we didn't get more of them at the picnic," Margie said. "You know the Army is integrated. They all live together."

All three girls digested that thought with a certain amount of shock. "What would we have done?" Margie asked.

She wasn't quite sure what she thought about that. She'd like to think that she'd have been polite and reasonable, as Susan had been, but thinking and doing were two different things, and the manners she'd learned didn't cover that kind of being polite. If Mr. Jim had known that she had anything to do with the Nigra, he'd have come and taken her home. He wouldn't have said anything, but she would have recognized that look; the look that said "don't be like your mother."

Come September, Margie thought, she would be in Atlanta, where scandalous incidents happened regularly. She'd stay temporarily with her mother's old friend, but once she found her own place she could do whatever she wanted.

The thought of being able to form her own conclusions was deliciously frightening. She would make her own decisions, honestly and without worrying about what someone else might think. She wouldn't be her mother's daughter, or Mr. Jim's grandchild. She'd just be Margie Raines.

Attending the downtown Atlanta Division of the University of Georgia wasn't the same as going to the actual university, but it was all her grandfather could afford. And she'd learned long ago that her father's promises to find the money to pay her way led to disaster.

It did seem unfair that there were no facilities in Galilee for blacks. What were they expected to do when they came into town to spend their money in establishments that were owned by whites? "If they stayed at home," her father would have said, "then they'd know where they could go." Her father had a great deal to say about morals when he was around, but they seemed always to apply to somebody else. And the only time he was around was when he needed money.

Though Margie worried about her mother, she was secretly glad to be getting away from all the problems that seemed to follow her parents. She felt bad that the relief was so great, then she felt guilty for feeling bad. It ought not to be that way.

A rare letter from her mother had promised that her father's new construction job in Florida would offer a guaranteed salary and she'd send money for the material to make Margie new clothes. Margie had heard that before. Her mother meant well. She always tried to make Margie's father look good, but something always went wrong. He'd never been successful. But *she* would.

*   *   *

For most of the next week the three girls talked on the phone and planned the upcoming week of vacation bible school where they'd be teaching. One afternoon they drove back out to the lake and, convinced that they were the only ones around, followed Glory's suggestion that they go skinny-dipping. They came out after a quick jump in the water and, uncomfortable with their nudity, donned their suits and lay on the float in the sun.

They didn't go to the lake again. In some kind of unspoken agreement they transferred their swimming excursions to the local pool.

"You know," Glory observed, perched on the pool's edge "this summer isn't turning out to be much fun."

"I know," Margie agreed. "We haven't had one spend-the-night party."

"After what happened last summer I'm not sure I want to," Susan said. "I still can't believe they thought we were out here at the pool swimming in the nude with *boys.*"

"There weren't any boys!" Glory said. "The one time we *don't* do something wrong, we get accused of it."

Susan opened the bottle of suntan lotion and began to spread it on her arms. "My mother never believed it."

Glory sighed. "That's because nobody would ever accuse Susan Miller of doing anything wicked. Susan is a good girl. She looks after her mother and goes to church every Sunday."

"So do I," Margie said sharply. "Go to church every Sunday, I mean."

"Yeah," Glory agreed, "but let's face it, Margie, with a body like yours, you just *look* guilty. You saw what happened with the Greek god. He took one look and zeroed in on you. You've got it, Margie, what men go for, and you don't even know it. You didn't let him do it, did you?"

Not once had they mentioned the soldiers until then.

"No, of course not! I mean—not really. But how could you tell?"

"Because you were as jumpy as a cat. We all were. You're always spouting off about catching your comet. The only difference between you and me, Margie Raines, is that when Glory Winslow finds the tail of her comet, she'll hang on to it and go for the ride. Yours will burn out while you're still thinking about it."

There was a long silence. Margie knew she should defend herself but what could she say? In Glory's shadow she dissolved into nothing.

"You've got what it takes, Margie," Glory repeated. "You appeal to men. Why don't you use it?"

Margie was the only one without a steady boyfriend, except for Glory, of course, who had plenty of offers but preferred men from outside the school because they were more exciting.

Margie took a deep breath and finally asked *the* question; "Have either of you ever done it? Really done it?"

Glory sat up, lifting her sunglasses from her face in frank surprise. The question was astonishing, and that someone had actually voiced it was even more so. That it had been Margie was unbelievable.

"You mean, like in going all the way?" Even Glory who normally liked to be shocking, had trouble finishing her own thought.

Susan blushed, and turned Sam's class ring round and round on her finger.

"Well," Margie finally answered. "Yes. That's what I mean. I know that men want you to. I know that it goes on, but I'm afraid. What if you actually let a boy and then something happened?"

Glory was searching her mind. She'd been talking about herself when she'd accused Margie of being jumpy. Glory was dead certain that Margie hadn't let any boy make love to her. The boys might joke about her, but Glory had it on good authority that Margie was just a tease. She'd neck with them all night, even let a guy get an accidental feel, but that was all, or had Sunday been different?

Susan frowned again, but she didn't change the subject. "I haven't. Sam has never tried. Around me he acts like he doesn't know how, or as if he's turned to steel. I mean, I know he's interested, but we just don't."

Glory stared at her two friends. "Didn't you two ever wonder what it would be like?"

"Sure," both Margie and Susan admitted quickly.

"But I'd be afraid to find out," Margie admitted in a low voice. "I mean, what if you got pregnant?"

"What if you *did?*" Glory asked recklessly. "I mean, you don't always, do you?"

"I don't think so, but I wouldn't want to take a chance," Susan answered. "Of course it's Sam who makes the decisions. Sam is very controlled."

Glory glared at Susan. "Really? That doesn't sound like the Sam I know. Have you ever touched him—his . . . ?"

"The only time I ever touched him was an accident and he slapped my hand away."

"Well, frankly, I intend to make love to a man and find out what all the mystery is about," Glory said sharply. "Then maybe I'll tell you two. Personally, I'm not sure it's worth the trouble. I don't know who wrote the rules that say men make the world go around anyway. I think it's the women and I, for one, intend to make the men do what I want," she added, bending her knees and lying back on her towel in a dramatic move that was pure Rita Hayworth.

"You're really going to let a man?" Margie asked.

"What makes you think I haven't already?"

Both friends were stunned into silence.

"Do you think that Frances is p.g.?" Glory changed the subject to the other girls' surprise and relief. "I mean, why else would she run away to get married and miss the church wedding and all the showers? She was already engaged to Preston, and her father liked him. Nobody would have objected."

Neither Susan nor Margie had an answer.

"Makes no sense to me," Glory said as she slipped her sunglasses back on her face and lay down on her towel. "Even if I was expecting, I wouldn't have missed having a wedding."

"Maybe," Margie suggested uncomfortably, "maybe she was throwing up and stuff. I've heard that you do."

"Maybe," Glory agreed, feeling an imaginary lurch in her stomach, and an ache between her legs. "Maybe we're the generation to change all that."

"I don't want to change anything," Susan said in a tight voice. "I like things to always stay the same."

Glory considered Susan's plea. Sweet, dull Susan, never willing to take a risk. Glory had always accused the others of being chicken. But she couldn't be sure. Maybe Susan was right. Maybe Glory had gone too far this time. For three days she'd tried unsuccessfully to keep her mind off what had happened on Sunday.

She'd been out with three different boys since the picnic and she'd disappointed them all by refusing them even so much as a good-night kiss. But revenge wasn't sweet. On the surface she was going through the motions, but, inside, very quietly, she felt as if she were going to explode. That desperate feeling was always there. And this time she couldn't quiet it.

Suddenly she stood and said in a quick, tight voice, "Let's get out of here. I don't think I'm going to like this summer if we can't find something fun to do."

The other two followed her, puzzled, yet not surprised. This was the way Glory was, quiet one minute, then wildly excited the next. There were times when they were forced to go along with her fast driving and daredevil antics because she didn't give them any choice. But mostly they participated because she gave them the courage to do the things they wouldn't have dared themselves. Her excitement was contagious.

"You're right, Glory," Margie admitted. "This summer is deadly dull. And vacation bible school is so juvenile, even if we're going to be full teachers this year. Making Jesus shoes out of cardboard and yarn is about as exciting as dirt."

"I have an idea." Glory stood up and gathered her towel and suntan lotion. She charged toward the car, leaving Susan and Margie to hurry behind her. They didn't ask where she was going.

When Glory pulled into her own driveway Susan and Margie gave a sigh of relief. When she was on one of her wild streaks they never knew what she'd do.

Mrs. Winslow was at work at the Georgia Power Company office where she held the title of office manager and bookkeeper. In reality, she was the only office employee and the title was self-chosen.

They lived in a small gray house which sat back from the road by a magnolia tree. With a screened-in porch and neat black shutters, it was quietly tasteful. Brightly colored cushions and pale-green carpet gave a *Better Homes and Gardens* decorated look to the house which was kept up by Sallie, the black woman who came in three days a week to clean and do the washing and ironing.

Glory walked into the dining room and opened the black Chinese cabinet where her mother kept the liquor.

"Let's have a drink, and celebrate our futures."

Without waiting for an answer, she took three glasses from the inner glass shelf and filled them with liquor. "Four Roses," she explained. "My mother's boyfriends keep her supplied with liquor. They think it makes her easier to sleep with. It doesn't. She'd do it without the booze. She doesn't think I know that, but I do."

Margie and Susan gasped and looked at each other in horror as Glory walked into the kitchen, filled their glasses with ice, opened a Coke and added it to the drink.

"What about *your* mother, Susan?" Glory asked. "She's divorced. Doesn't she have any boyfriends?"

Susan thought about her short, stout mother with the big bosom and slow way of speaking. She'd never thought about her being a woman with needs. Martha Miller have a boyfriend? Susan couldn't even imagine her mother being married to the tall, gruff man who had been her father. "No. Not since we came here when I was in the second grade."

"She must be frigid," Glory observed wisely.

"I still remember how scared you looked that first day, Susan," Margie said. "It was Christmastime and nobody knew you were going to be there, so you weren't getting any presents."

"But I did," Susan said thoughtfully. "I never understood that. I thought somebody must have told you I was coming."

"No, my grandmother and some of the others always sent extra gifts in case there were any students who weren't getting anything. And we just took the cards off some of our gifts and addressed them to you."

Susan looked at Margie in surprise. Her eyes glistened with wetness. "You've always been my friend, Margie, but I never knew about the gifts."

"So we'll drink to friendship. And sex," Glory said dramatically, then paused. "One night I woke up and heard my mother and her boyfriend," she said, her normally deep voice becoming suddenly high-pitched as she asked if her friends wanted her to tell them what she saw. She handed drinks to Susan and Margie, a smile breaking across her lips. "Of course you do. I know you do. You're just too silly to say so. Drink up, kiddies, Auntie Glory is about to tell you a bedtime story. Come into my bedroom."

She took a swallow of her drink, frowned, and picked up

the liquor bottle. "What the hell, let's empty the bottle." She added another inch of liquor to each glass, tasted it again, and nodded her approval.

Susan and Margie followed, each horrified at their actions, yet too afraid of being laughed at to refuse. Margie took a sip of her drink. Actually it was rather good—sweet, but good. Boldly she took another.

Susan looked at Margie. "For once I'm not going to be Miss Goody Two Shoes. After all, we're not in high school anymore. Sam and his friends drink bourbon and Coke. So can I."

"So? Drink up." Glory added more whiskey to her drink. "There's nobody here but best friends."

"That's right," Susan agreed. "Who'll ever know? Besides, I'm curious." Susan turned up her glass and drank. "Oh! It makes my stomach feel warm."

Margie followed suit, and nodded her agreement.

Glory swung around. "So, do you want to hear? You have to say it. I want to hear you say you do. Say that you want to know all the delicious details of my mother's private life."

"Yes," both Susan and Margie said in a whisper.

"Yes *what?*"

Margie looked at Susan and rehearsed her words. They'd been down this road before. Glory was going to make them repeat her own words. One way or another she would force them to say something shocking, just to prove that she could.

"We want you to tell us what your mother's boyfriend was doing to her."

"Okay, fine. But first, I'm going to take off this bathing suit." Glory put her drink down on her white wicker dressing table and peeled the suit off, dropping it into a sodden heap on the carpet. She walked back to the mirror, stared at herself critically, and lifted her glass.

"A toast," she declared, "a toast to breasts. I propose a toast to using our breasts to drive men crazy." She lifted her glass in a mock salute. "Go fuck yourselves, gentlemen—all of you."

A moment later she swung around, touching her glass to their glasses, leaning back so that her breasts seemed to jut forward in their faces.

Wordlessly the girls followed Glory's action and drank again. By this time the glasses were half empty and Glory filled them again.

"What do you think of my breasts? Honest opinion," she asked, turning as she cupped one in her free hand and held it up for examination. "Do you think men would want to suck them?"

Susan looked at Margie in surprise. What on earth was Glory up to now?

"They're nice," Margie managed to say.

"Take off your clothes," Glory directed. "Let's compare."

"Why?" Susan was beginning to have second thoughts about this. While they'd never been shy about changing clothes in front of each other, they'd never blatantly displayed themselves, either.

"Come on, drink up," Glory said. "I dare you. Let's examine each other. What's the matter, are you afraid? Of course it would be more fun if we had a couple of real men here," she said defiantly. "I like men. I like making them want me, and they like how I make them feel."

She leaned back on the dresser, posing like some garage mechanic's pin-up poster on a girlie calendar.

"Besides, it's appropriate that we be naked while I tell you what I saw."

Six months ago, Susan and Margie wouldn't have complied. Even a week ago they'd have found a way to giggle and laugh themselves out of Glory's idea. But they weren't children anymore and they were becoming deliciously tipsy and decidedly bold. Without looking at each other they began to remove their clothes.

"Great," Glory said with a laugh. "Now come over here and stand beside me. Let's look at each other in the mirror. We'll see what the men see when they look at us."

As Susan and Margie came to stand beside her, they had trouble looking in the mirror at first. Glory began to frown. "I look like a tiger down here," she said, her fingers combing the rust-colored mat between her legs.

"And Margie doesn't have much hair at all. Susan, you look the best." Glory's fingertips rimmed Susan's jet-black curls. "I'll bet Sam just loves the way you look."

Susan gasped. "I wish. Sam's never seen the way I look."

"I'll bet he's seen your breasts, though, hasn't he? Come on, admit it. You've been dating Sam for four years. You can't tell me that by now he hasn't seen them. Don't be a goose. I'll be honest about it. I've let plenty of boys look at me."

"I don't believe it," Margie said in a rush. "They would have bragged about it. You know how they are. Somebody would have said something."

"Not my boys, not if they wanted to look again. I made them swear on the Bible. Besides, why not let them look? You don't get pregnant that way and it drives them crazy."

Susan looked in the mirror curiously. Her breasts were small with little pink nipples. Margie's were large and lush, with light-colored nipples that seemed undersize in comparison to the size of her breasts. But Glory's breasts were beautiful. Not large, but with nipples that seemed almost voluptuous. A wide circle of bronze-colored skin was centered with a dark nipple that hardened into a ball the size of a small grape as she stroked herself.

A breathless feeling slid up Susan's backbone and jammed her throat. She wanted to turn and run. She wanted to cry and she didn't know why. She felt as if she had to go to the bathroom, and she tightened her muscles to hold it back.

"Okay, kiddies, it's story time," Glory said, breaking the tension by sitting down on the floor with her back against the bed. "Come on down." She patted the floor on either side of her and waited for the other two girls to comply.

They did.

"I always see people as things," Glory said. "We're flowers. Margie is a white rosebud, innocent, ready to open herself to the sun. JoEllen? She's a lily, proud and regal."

"And what am I?" Susan asked curiously, trying to see something about herself to suggest a blossom.

"Oh, that's easy. You're a gardenia, all velvety and pure. But you can't be touched, or you'll become discolored and die."

Susan winced. Maybe she'd already begun to turn brown. "And you, Glory, which flower are you?"

"A dahlia, a fire-colored dahlia. Don't you see? I'm lush and wild. I only have one bloom and then I die."

The girls looked at each other in the mirror, Glory's words echoing ominously in their ears. Margie considered Glory's descriptions, a lily, a gardenia, a rose, and a dahlia—all flowers that budded, and lived, replenishing themselves from their roots. She shivered.

"Drink up, girls," Glory said brightly. "Let's get in the mood."

They drank.

"Now, here's the story. You know my dad's been dead since I was five. I didn't know it when I was little, of course, but my mother, the luscious Adele, is a hot-blooded woman. She's always had lots of dates; she's always loved parties and dancing and men. She and her cousin Al always entered every dance contest in Augusta—and won them—until she married my dad. After Daddy got killed she'd go over to Augusta to meet her men. Now, I guess she's tired of going to that much trouble. She brings them here."

Susan tried not to look at Glory, but she felt almost hypnotized into watching. Glory held her drink in one hand and continued to play with her breast with the other. Susan had never sat on the floor naked before. The carpet felt strange. She twisted her bottom, trying to force the cramping feeling in her lower body to go away. She only succeeded in touching her hip to Glory's. The sensation of bare flesh against bare flesh was shocking. The urge to pee was growing stronger.

"All right," Margie said sharply, studying the size of her thighs compared to Glory's. "Get on with it."

"Well, the first time I saw her, Mother had been out with Fred and Daisy Wilson. Late that night I heard a noise. I thought she was crying, so I got up to see. Her door was cracked and the bathroom light was on, so I could see in her room. She was lying on the bed and Fred was—Fred was in bed with her."

Margie gasped. "You mean she was doing it with a married man?"

"Married, single, when you want a man, you don't care," Glory said in a strangled voice. "Anyway, this is the best part. She was playing with herself."

"Playing with herself?" Susan heard her own voice asking. She covered her confusion by taking another long swallow of her drink. She was beginning to feel uncomfortably hot.

"Yes, playing with herself. Like this . . ." Glory's hand left her nipple and slid down her body, disappearing between her legs into the russet tuft of hair in a slippery moist sound. She gave a little groan and caught her lower lip with her teeth.

"What was Fred doing?" Susan asked, all pretense at

embarrassment discarded. She focused her attention on Glory and the picture she was painting. Susan was certain that she was going to wet herself. Unconsciously her fingers slid down there, pressing against herself, trying to stop the flow.

"He was playing with himself, too. Then he straddled her and put his mouth on her—down here. That's when she really started to make a noise. Like this. Glory began to moan and arch her body. Her bottom lip was clamped between her teeth.

Glory's breathing was erratic. Margie gave up all pretense of disinterest and watched her hand touching herself.

"What happened?" Susan whispered from the other side.

"Then he put it in her and she wrapped her legs around his hips. She was saying, "Don't stop! Don't stop!""

Bounding to her feet, Glory paced rapidly back and forth as if she'd forgotten that Susan and Margie were there. She hadn't intended to touch herself like that in front of anyone. But she had. What the hell? She hadn't done anything they weren't doing, too. Susan, pure, angelic Susan was pressing against herself. Margie's eyes were closed. she was holding her breasts and making little jerky motions.

Glory knew both her cousins, Sam and Steven, did it. She'd heard them when they'd spent the night at her house. Sam would come home after a date with Susan and he'd do it to himself while he and Steven talked about sex. That's how she'd known what to do to all the boys who wanted her. She never worried about what her grandfather would say the way Sam did. It hadn't taken her long to understand that there was no reason why girls couldn't do it, too.

Glory glanced around at Susan and Margie. "Let's try it. Are you game?"

Susan opened her eyes. "What do you mean, try it?"

"We could use something—a bottle. Why not?" Glory started to go to the kitchen.

"No! No!" Susan stood up, and Margie followed suit.

"Hey, you guys. Why stop now? You're all ready. Let's get another drink and we'll do it to each other."

"No!" Susan began pulling on her clothes. She had to get out of there. Her head was pounding. Her body seemed to be on fire. Drinking might be normal for Glory, but it wasn't normal for her. It made her feel all funny inside. She was a

83

virgin. If she went along with Glory, Sam would know and be furious. She was sorry she'd taken that drink. She'd never have another drink around Glory as long as she lived.

"I have to go, too," Margie agreed. "My grandmother will be wondering where I am."

But Glory wasn't listening. "Please, Glory," Susan begged, "I want to go home."

"Ah, what's the matter with you two? Aren't we going to have any fun at all? Let's go somewhere, Florida maybe, alone, just the three of us. Remember that time my mother took us to the beach and we went to the amusement park?"

Margie remembered all right. She remembered that Glory had slipped out later that night to meet a college boy she'd met standing in the roller-coaster line. She and Margie had to stay up almost until morning to let her back in so that her mother wouldn't know.

"Yeah, and what about that Chinese restaurant?" Margie joined in, glad to change the subject.

Margie and Susan dressed as they relived the startled look on their waiters' faces when they realized that their guests didn't speak any Chinese and had no idea what they wanted.

Margie pulled on her wet swimsuit. "It was you, Susan, who came up with the answer. Just lay out the money we wanted to spend and let them bring what that amount would buy, you said."

"And we thought the first course was all we'd get and we ate every bite," Glory added.

Susan laughed lightly. "And they kept on bringing it out, seven courses, until we were about to pop."

"And when they brought out that ice boat with all that fresh fruit stuck in it, one of the guys said that it looked like Noah's Ark. That's when I knew I'd better find a ladies' room quick."

"Which is what I'd better do right now." Susan headed to the bathroom, pulled down her suit, and felt the welcome relief of letting go. She wasn't prepared for the ripple that swept over her when she wiped herself. The more she wiped, the more it came until she leaned back against the toilet in stunned amazement.

"Hey, Susan, are you okay in there?"

Susan quickly flushed the toilet and pulled up her suit. She didn't know how to answer.

Glory, suddenly ready to bring the afternoon to a close, was cleaning up the evidence of their raid on her mother's liquor cabinet. She donned clean shorts and shirt and drove the girls back to Galilee. They were halfway home when she gave out a cheer and proclaimed her latest idea.

"I know what. Let's go to Augusta this weekend and see JoEllen. We can spend the night with her and go shopping for school clothes."

"We can't do that," Susan began. "My mother would never agree. Besides, Sam will be home."

"I doubt they'd let us in the dorm," Margie added.

"Yes they will," Glory insisted. "JoEllen told me last weekend that she can have prospective nursing students come and spend the night. Wouldn't that be great? We could drive over on Saturday and come back on Sunday. I'm sure that my mother will let me drive."

"Well, maybe," Susan agreed doubtfully, "but . . ."

"No maybes. If your mother is going to let you go to Augusta to business school in less than two months, why will she say you can't go now? You'll see Sam the rest of your life, Susan, but this will be our last trip together, the four of us."

As usual, Glory's argument prevailed. By the time she let them out at their homes, both Margie and Susan had agreed to ask permission, without either being quite aware of how it happened. But that was always the way it was with Glory. Every day had to be an adventure.

But Augusta meant Camp Gordon—soldiers. And soldiers meant Roger Sasser, Joseph Cheatham II, and Nick Zambino.

Eight

On Saturday morning, Glory, Margie, and Susan were squeezed into the front seat of Glory's convertible for the forty-five-minute drive to Augusta. They tied scarves around their hair to keep it from blowing wild and donned white sunglasses, declaring that they looked exactly like college girls heading for Fort Lauderdale for spring break.

The convertible whizzed through the countryside as Glory recklessly passed slow-moving farm vehicles on the highway. They sang "How Much is that Doggie in the Window" and discussed Audrey Hepburn.

"I may be an actress," Glory said, "like Mary Martin. Did you know she actually washed her hair on stage in *South Pacific?*"

"You're kidding," Susan said.

Margie didn't comment. She only wished she'd been there to see the play. "Some Enchanted Evening" was one of her favorite songs. Someday . . .

JoEllen met them in the dorm lobby, hugging them enthusiastically.

"I'm so excited!" she exclaimed. "Bring your bags up to my room and then I'll take you on a tour of Lawton Memorial Hospital, my home for the next two years."

"Great," Glory declared, lifting her new tan Samsonite makeup case and following JoEllen up the steps. "Can we go over to Camp Gordon and see the base hospital, too?"

Base hospital? Margie felt her breath take a funny leap. Base meant Nick Zambino. She hadn't allowed herself to think about him. He hadn't written, though she hadn't expected him to. But visiting JoEllen wasn't supposed to bring her into contact with the Greek God of Love. Now Glory was changing directions. Margie took a deep breath. She wouldn't think about it. Just because he was a soldier didn't mean he'd be at the hospital. There were thousands of soldiers on the base. If they met it would be because they were supposed to. If they didn't, that was all right, too.

Susan looked at JoEllen. Now it was becoming clear. The only medical world that Glory was interested in was the world of Dr. Roger Sasser. All this "let's go visit JoEllen" was her way of seeing him again. Susan felt a lump in her throat when JoEllen nodded. "If you really want to."

Three hours later Margie was pleased that Glory's plan seemed to be disintegrating into failure. They'd seen JoEllen's classrooms, toured Lawton Memorial, and most of the base hospital as well. Glory's smile was growing tighter and tighter, her eyes more frantic.

"JoEllen," she said, in a tense voice, "this place is crazy. I've never seen a hospital that was all on the same floor and covered fifty miles. What exactly do you do around here?"

"I work in the lab, picking up the blood samples. It's so big that I actually ride a bicycle from one ward to the next."

"Was there a shortage of ladders and elevators when they built this place?"

"No, this is an army hospital, and they operate on the theory that the enemy will try to bomb it and if they spread it out, everybody won't die."

"Bomb it? In Augusta, Georgia?" Glory shook her head. "I want a cigarette. Isn't there a lounge or something where the doctors and nurses go for a break?"

"Well, yes, but student nurses aren't allowed in there. Maybe you can go to the therapy ward at the end of this hall."

"Fine. Lead on," Glory grumbled, ignoring the catcalls from the soldiers in the rooms they passed.

Glory was wearing lavender pedal pushers, red strap sandals, and a red print blouse over a red halter. Glory always wore red, and orange. *Vivid* was the word that came to Margie's mind . . .

Volatile was the word that came to Roger Sasser's mind when he moved out of the room and into step beside the very girl who had been driving him wild all week.

"Well, Dr. Sasser," Glory said, her voice changing instantly from irritation to soft as honey. "Fancy meeting you here."

"*Fancy* isn't quite the word I'd use," he admitted, "but it's all I can say in mixed company. What are you doing here?"

"We came to visit JoEllen. I wanted to go to the lounge for a cigarette, but she isn't allowed in the doctors' break room."

"*I* am," he answered, "and anyone with me is welcome, too."

"I accept."

Glory and Dr. Roger Sasser might as well have been the only people in the building. Susan and Margie looked at each other and shook their heads.

"But—" JoEllen started to protest.

"Fine. You go on," Margie said, anxious to be rid of Glory. She knew they weren't going to stop her and she was afraid that somehow Glory would get JoEllen into trouble. "But how do we get back to JoEllen's dorm? We're in your car, remember?"

"Here." She handed Margie her keys. "Don't wait up for me, kiddies. I'll catch up—sooner or later."

The three girls watched as the doctor and Glory walked down the hall.

"Don't wait up for her?" Susan said in disgust. "We'll be lucky to see her by breakfast."

The therapy ward's sunroom resembled a solarium with its potted trees and game tables. Men in wheelchairs and on crutches lounged around reading, playing cards, listening to the radio, or just staring out into the bright sunshine. JoEllen spoke to several of the patients she remembered from the picnic and introduced her friends to them. Susan and Margie chatted with the men who seemed glad to see a fresh face.

And then Susan saw him, Jody, sitting away from the others, just looking across the porch rail. He seemed so alone. She thought of Sam's order that she stay at home this weekend, then walked toward the slim young boy.

"Hello, Jody," she said softly. "What a nice view."

Jody glanced around in surprise. "Miss Susan! Golly! What are you doing at the hospital?"

"I'm just visiting a friend and I saw you sitting over here," she said.

"You did?" His voice cracked and he grimaced. "I mean, that's great."

"How's your leg?"

"Fine," he said. But Susan knew from the tight, wooden way he'd answer that he wasn't fine at all.

"Have you thought any more about going to school?"

"Yeah, I thought about it, but I don't know. My mama's coming to see me tomorrow." A quick smile broke his lips, then faded as he looked around at the patients staring at him. "Maybe you shouldn't talk to me."

"I'll do what I choose," she said, and caught the handles of his chair, turning him around. When she reached the table where Margie and JoEllen were standing, she paused. "You remember Jody," she said. "He was at the picnic."

"Well, sure," JoEllen agreed. "We were just going down to the cafeteria to get something to drink, Susan."

Another second and they would have been gone before the orderly came whistling into the room.

"Look, Margie," Susan whispered. "It's your guy—from the picnic."

It was. Margie took an involuntary step back. They hadn't talked about his assignment. She hadn't really expected him to be here. She'd hoped that he wouldn't, or maybe she'd hoped that he would. It was all a muddle. Now that she'd seen him, what would he say?

"God, he's good-looking, and he knows it," JoEllen said. Every nurse in the hospital drools over him. He's a medic, assigned to the orthopedic ward. Be careful, Margie, he's dangerous."

"Well, well, if it isn't my little Margie." Nick's smile filled his face. He greeted Susan and JoEllen and turned back toward Margie. "I'm surprised to see you girls here. Hi, Jody. Are you responsible for this?"

"Oh, no," Margie mumbled, then rolled her eyes in embarrassment. She glanced down at her ballerina slippers, white eyelet blouse gathered at the neck, and black-and-red print skirt. Pure teenager. And here she was facing a man who caused every female hospital employee they passed to take a second look.

"We're visiting JoEllen for the weekend," Susan explained.

"Great, JoEllen," he said, as if he'd never seen her before. "Just perfect. Let me take you girls to dinner. What about it?"

Margie shook her head. "No. I mean thank you, but we couldn't."

"Sure you can," Nick insisted, taking Margie's arm. "I'll find a couple of buddies and we'll all take you to a Greek restaurant, I'll show you some good eating."

He was ignoring Jody. Irrational as it was, Susan felt a burning resentment for the young boy who was so used to being insulted because of the color of his skin that he didn't even seem bothered. Yet she knew that was the way it had to be. She certainly couldn't imagine them going off base with a black boy.

"I don't think so," she heard herself saying, "but thanks anyway. We were just leaving, weren't we, girls?"

"Ladies, I insist. You have to eat. Okay, if you don't like Greek food, we'll have seafood. You treated us, now it's our turn. What about it?"

"I have to be back at eleven o'clock," JoEllen said. She moved away from Nick and out into the corridor. "Besides, what about Glory? She's gone with Dr. Sasser."

"If Glory's not back by the time we get ready to leave for dinner, we'll leave a note for her," Nick said as if it were already decided.

He leaned down and, under the guise of whispering in Margie's ear, planted a kiss behind it. "Don't turn me down, baby. I really want to see you again."

The moth to the flame. The forbidden apple. Margie felt like Eve in the Garden of Eden, all set to take a bite. Fate had stepped in. She didn't have to make a decision. She was being given a second chance. He wanted to be with her. She couldn't refuse. She wanted to be with him once more.

"All right," Margie agreed in a whisper. "Just dinner, that's all. That is, if Susan and JoEllen will go, too."

"Sam wouldn't like it," Susan said, knowing that it wasn't Sam's approval that was holding her back. She didn't want to go. It might be very well for Sam to go out with other girls when he was away at school, but it wouldn't feel right to her to go out with another boy. She'd never dated anybody but Sam, and this would be a date, even if Nick said it was only for dinner.

"And what about you, JoEllen?" Susan couldn't stop herself from asking. "What does Teddy think about you being in this hospital with all these soldiers?"

"It never occurs to Teddy that I wouldn't be true to him. He trusts me. Besides, he's gone to Texas for the summer, the whole summer, and you know Teddy the athlete, he's probably already found a—someone to take him around."

"Teddy and Sam's absence is the U.S. Army's gain," Nick said with a flourish. "Until tonight, ladies. Jody, I'll take you back to the ward. Girls, we'll pick you up at the dorm at seven."

He gave an elaborate bow, kissing Margie's hand like a knight taking leave of his queen, then turned and pushed Jody's chair back inside, whistling merrily.

Margie, with the help of JoEllen's directions, drove Glory's car back to the dorm. Now that the decision was made, Margie was worried. Sam and Teddy were one thing. But these were real men. Soldiers.

"It's not on account of Teddy, but I really don't think this is a good idea," JoEllen said. "I'm not supposed to go out with hospital personnel. The supervisor won't approve. They don't like us mixing with our superiors."

Susan cut her gaze to JoEllen. She seemed nervous, worried. That wasn't like JoEllen. She was always so sure of herself. Come to think of it, JoEllen had avoided contact with any of the men on Sunday. She'd been like a butterfly flittering around. Susan had assumed then it was because she was on duty, but this reaction seemed too intense.

"What's wrong, Jo? Are you and Teddy having trouble?"

"No. I mean I don't think so. But sometimes Teddy's so young. Everything is so *now* for him. He doesn't think much about the future, doesn't plan ahead. I mean he's still riding a *bicycle,* for God's sake. I know that I'm impatient, but sometimes—sometimes I wish I'd never graduated early."

"But I thought all that was so that you could get married as soon as he finished accounting school."

They walked across the dorm lobby and started up the steps.

"The truth is, accounting school is my idea. Teddy would rather go to work for his brother in the garage and race cars. I love Teddy, but being captain of the basketball team and the best dancer in school doesn't do a lot toward a secure future."

"No," Margie agreed, remembering the smooth way Teddy had of moving across the dance floor, "but he sure makes a girl feel good."

"Not always," JoEllen muttered under her breath. "Looks and smooth moves aren't all what they're cracked up to be."

Smooth moves? Margie glanced at her watch. Five o'clock. Two hours to go. She tightened her stomach muscles and remembered what had happened at Glory's house. She'd probably have something to drink tonight, too. Yes, she'd drink bourbon and Coke. She slid her hand inside her skirt pocket and pressed against herself. She felt very tight down there. Tight and shivery and good.

"Where is this break room?" Glory asked as they walked down the corridor and into the emergency exit stairwell.

"Do you really want a cigarette?" Roger leaned against the block wall and pulled her into his arms.

"No," she whispered. "No."

His kiss was as reckless as her response. When he finally pulled away, he let out a tight, desperate breath. "What have you done to me, witch? I haven't been able to get you out of my mind for one minute since Sunday."

"Good," she said with a satisfied purr. "I want you to want me and want me and want me." She spread his fingers and filled them with her breast.

Roger gasped. His head was whirling. His body was on fire. In another minute he'd rip her clothes off and take her right there in the fire escape.

"Not here," he groaned. "I'll find a place."

"Can you leave?"

"I was just going off duty."

Desperately he thought. Where? He couldn't take her to the officers' quarters where he spent his off-time. He couldn't take her to the doctors' room where he slept while on duty. Where?

There had to be a place. He'd drive her someplace, he decided. He touched his pocket, feeling the small package of rubbers he'd bought after he came back on Sunday. Next time he'd be prepared. He hadn't been on Sunday, and even

92

then he couldn't have stopped himself. But marriage and a wife at this stage of his career was one problem he didn't have time to deal with, and certainly not with a girl like Glory who reeked of money.

His car was a '50 Chevy, plain, battered, and nondescript. Glory was disappointed. Still, it was transportation and there were plenty of soldiers who had nothing. She slid inside and planted herself in the middle of the seat, watching as he peeled off his white coat and got in beside her. He kissed her once more, then pulled himself away and started the engine.

Glory laid her head on his shoulder and put her arm around his waist. She planted little kisses down his cheek and under his collar. He hand moved back across his chest and unbuttoned his shirt, working her fingers inside. She felt his heart thudding wildly.

"Your heart is beating," she said.

"Good. I thought I was dead and had gone to heaven."

"You think I'm an angel?"

"I don't know whether you're an angel or you're one of the devil's women. Which are you, Glory Winslow?"

She nipped at his earlobe with her teeth and reveled at the power she held over him. This time her hand moved lower, playing lightly across the hard protrusion at the vee of his legs.

"God, don't do that, woman. You'll make me have a wreck."

"Do you want me, Roger? Are you going crazy wanting me? Do you want to rip off my clothes and be inside me?"

"I think you know that, Glory," he managed to say. They came to a light and he had to stop. A car pulled up beside him. The occupant blew the horn, and yelled, "Wahoo!" Glory leaned in front of Roger and smiled, giving a wave with the hand now tapping the back of his neck.

She smiled broadly at the elderly couple in the car on the other side of them while she pulled Roger's zipper open and slipped her hand inside.

Roger gasped. She didn't know what she was doing. She was going to make him come right here, at a traffic light in downtown Augusta. The light changed and the car lurched forward as he let out the clutch and gave it gas.

"Damn it, Glory!" Between changing gears he managed to grab her hand. "Stop that!" But holding her hand against

93

him was all it took. "Ah—damn—Ahhhh!"

Glory looked at him, half in surprise and half in satisfaction. "Did you do it?"

"Hell, you know I did. Now I'm a mess." He let go of her hand, reached for the handkerchief in his back pocket, and handed it to her. "Clean your hand."

Glory took the handkerchief and wiped her fingertips. Then she slid it back inside his pants and began cleaning him off. The cleaning seemed to go on and on, until Roger felt himself begin to stir. He realized what she was doing and moved her hand away.

"Why did you do that?" he asked, picking up speed again. He glanced in the rearview mirror, checking the road behind him.

"Didn't you like it?" she asked innocently.

"I liked it," he admitted. "But we could have been seen."

"That's what makes it exciting," Glory said brightly. "Doing what you want to do, no matter what anybody thinks, no matter what the rules are. But if I bother you, I'll just sit over here." She slid across the seat and hugged the passenger door. "Where are we going?"

"I don't know. Maybe to the lake, or the park."

"Not this time, Roger," she said dramatically. "I want to do it in a bed, a real bed. Let's find a motel. Can you afford it?"

"Well, yes."

"That's what I want. Let's buy some liquor and find a motel, a seedy one with a squeaky mattress and roaches and a neon sign that flashes on and off."

Roger frowned. "Roaches?"

"Forget it. I was just kidding," she said with a light, nervous laugh.

But all the time Roger was buying the liquor and finding the motel, he thought about what she'd said and he wasn't at all sure she didn't mean it.

They used the rubbers, all of them. They drank the whiskey and made hot, sticky love for most of the night, stopping only to go out for hamburgers and fries. By morning Glory had done everything possible to erase Steven from her mind. She made Roger lie with his arm beneath his head. She'd aroused him and made a tent of the sheet to cover his erection. She'd pretended to wake him with her kisses, but even while she was replaying every second of the time she'd been with Steven, she knew that the man she was with wasn't the man she wanted.

The seafood Nick had promised Margie turned into catfish at a roadside juke joint with sawdust on the floor and a juke box that played Hank Williams songs over and over. They ate and danced. At least, Nick and Margie danced.

JoEllen was ill at ease and uncomfortable with her date. He seemed nice enough, but he expected her to respond like any other girl out on a date, and she could barely tolerate his innocent conversation. All she could think about was what had happened with Teddy. She was sorry that she'd come. She was comfortable with Teddy because she could be herself. They'd grown up together. They'd played the "going steady" game because it was expected. To him, JoEllen was older, smarter, and ambitious, everything he wasn't. To her, he was almost like a little brother, to be admired and protected. Or he had been, until the night before the picnic.

Susan's date was too old and too loud. After two beers he was ready to find a private corner of the restaurant and get serious. She quickly put him in his place by explaining that she was engaged and wasn't "that kind of girl." After a few complaints about how much the evening was costing, he gave up and turned his attention to the juke box and his beer.

After a few clumsy attempts on the dance floor, both girls gave up the pretense that they were enjoying themselves and waited for Nick to signal an end to the evening. Susan, always the peacemaker, politely carried the conversation, covering for all of them.

On the dance floor, with both hands clasped around Nick's neck, Margie let him pull her close and whisper in her ear. Being with the best-looking guy in the room, with the others watching his open courtship of her, was heady. If only Glory had been there to see her, the evening would have been truly complete.

All Margie would agree to was one stolen kiss in a dark corner, and the hand that crept finger-touching close to her breast. But there was no mistaking the evidence of his desire pressed against her, and both of them knew, when he told her he'd see her the next weekend, that she wouldn't refuse him again.

When Glory slipped in after breakfast she offered no explanation for her disappearance or where she'd been. She was ready to go then, immediately, and she didn't want to talk.

The trip back to Galilee was strained. Susan was tired and a bit angry at Glory's subterfuge, Margie was subdued, and Glory was depressed. She'd accomplished what she set out to do, to completely subjugate a man, but in doing so, she'd promised something she wasn't certain that she wanted to give—herself.

Margie and Susan agreed in advance to chip in and share the cost of the speeding ticket Glory almost got on the way home. But neither of them was surprised when she talked the officer into a warning instead.

"Are you seeing him again?" Susan asked Margie.

"Who?"

"The Greek god, who else could I be talking about?"

"Yes, next weekend. How'd you like your date?"

"He was forty years old, Margie. How would you like a man who's all hands and no brains? He certainly made me appreciate Sam. Oh, Lordy, I hope Sam never finds out about this. He'd kill me."

But nobody asked Glory about Dr. Sasser and she didn't comment on him.

The next weekend Nick hitched a ride to Galilee with a couple of other soldiers who were coming back to see girls they'd met at the picnic. Under her grandfather's disapproving frown, Margie borrowed his car and drove them to a place outside of town that sported a dance floor, a skating rink, a bowling alley, and a pool. The pool was open, but this time they didn't swim.

Margie was surprised to find that Nick was fun. She already knew he was a smooth dancer, but he proved to be an enthusiastic bowler, too. It was on roller skates where Margie outdid him. After Nick fell twice, laughed, and picked himself up for another try, Margie began to relax. When they got back into the car to leave, Nick slid across the seat and took Margie into his arms.

"This has been great, Margie. I'm not meeting the guys for another hour and a half. Can't we drive down under those trees and talk a while."

Walking on air, Margie didn't say no. When he kissed her, Margie knew that this time she wouldn't refuse him. She didn't want to. Nick took his time, touching her, kissing her, saying all the right words. By the time he unzipped his pants, Margie was so ready that he didn't have to beg. He surprised himself by using the rubber. She surprised him when he realized that he was the first. And he was even more surprised afterward when he felt a twinge of guilt.

For Margie, it was done. It was meant to be and it had happened. She'd been with a man. And it had been exciting. She'd worry tomorrow about the guilt she was sure to feel. Tonight, Nick loved her. He'd told her that and that was enough. He thought she was beautiful and smart and that they were great together. Nick promised her that the next time it would be even better for her. He'd make certain of it.

The guilt she expected didn't come. For the next week Margie floated on air and revised her plans for the future. She'd go on to college, of course, but married women could go to night school. If she and Nick were separated, they'd write every day and wait for each other. But she wouldn't live in Galilee. She'd get a job in Atlanta, or maybe even New York City. Nick was obviously not a small-town boy.

For the next week Margie made secret plans and waited for Nick to return.

The soldier who knocked on Margie's door the following Friday night wasn't Nick, but a stranger who seemed surprised when Margie refused to go out with him. After all, Nick had assured him that the girl was willing and ready. What other kind of girl goes out with a married man? the stranger asked.

A married man? Margie was devastated. Nick was married? Hot, wrenching humiliation replaced her euphoria. All this time she'd held back, protected herself, waited for the special man who would appreciate her. And she'd been betrayed.

Margie berated first him, then herself. But in the end she knew the choice had been hers. Nick hadn't promised her anything, except a next time. She'd given herself to a man who didn't even follow through on his plans. She'd let him make love to her. He was her first man, and it hadn't been important enough for him to come for a second date. Margie felt something shrivel up inside her. Maybe she wasn't so smart after all.

The important thing was that nobody else knew. She didn't totally regret what she'd done. The experience would prepare her for Atlanta and the future. But she decided that it would never happen again—not like that. Never. If she gave her body to a man, the next time she'd get something important in return.

The soldier who appeared the next weekend was welcomed into Mr. Jim's home for a meal, then sent on his way. He was the last one to come to see Margie.

Back in Augusta, Nick regretted what he'd done. That was rare. He liked women, but he usually picked the ones who knew the score. He found that he cared about Margie. She was fresh. And he'd been the first. That hadn't happened to him since he was thirteen. He decided to write her a letter, and enclosed the picture he'd been about to send to his wife. He thought about it a minute, then pulled the picture out and wrote across the bottom:

For a very special girl, I'll always remember.
With love, Nick

For JoEllen, the weekend with Glory, Susan, and Margie was unsettling. Where they'd once been close, the gossip now seemed childish, the giggling uneasy, and the conversations strained. She was the only girl on her floor who hadn't had visitors and she'd looked forward to having her dorm mates see her friends. Glory always impressed everybody, but Glory had disappeared, leaving JoEllen to explain. The weekend had been a disappointment.

JoEllen consoled herself by saying that it was because they'd barely seen each other in the last year. And she was different from them now.

The four friends had always let Glory lead the way. JoEllen had been careful to keep her insecurity hidden. That fear of failure had spurred her into getting a head start on her future by graduating early. Her three friends had been surprised, but impressed. But carrying that new-found determination into nursing school hadn't worked. JoEllen was no longer the oldest and the smartest. Here she was the youngest and least prepared.

The classroom part of nursing had been so much harder than she'd expected. Ashamed to admit that she'd had a biology teacher who was so unqualified to teach the subject that they never even lit their Bunsen burners, JoEllen struggled in silence.

Fear that she might fail almost paralyzed her. Nobody knew how many times she'd locked herself in the bathroom and cried so hard that she'd thrown up. In the dorm, there was no friendly foursome claiming JoEllen as a member. She hadn't grown up with her classmates and she couldn't seem to fit in with their easy lifestyles. She couldn't tell the other students how afraid she was. Everything seemed so easy for them.

Only on the hospital floor did she come alive. She liked the registered nurses who were her superiors and she was quick to volunteer to do more than was expected. On the wards she felt good about herself. Emptying bedpans and bathing patients was easy. There was something about walking into a room and having a patient glad to see you that made the lessons tolerable. Crisp white sheets, white walls, and whispered instructions gave JoEllen a sense of urgency. Here, she had something to give. Here, she was important. Here, she was respected.

Her high school friends seemed a world away. This weekend proved they no longer had anything in common. Their lives had moved too far apart. She wasn't sure she truly wanted to leave Galilee behind, but she didn't fit there anymore. She couldn't be one of them again. In her zeal to succeed, she'd outgrown her friends.

With certainty she understood that not only had she left Galilee behind, but Teddy was back there, too. With her past.

PART TWO

The End of Summer

"Hey there, you with the stars in your eyes."
— *The Pajama Game*, 1954

Nine

The week after the stranger came, Margie took the sleek new Nancy Hanks passenger train to Atlanta. She was leaving in September anyway, she explained to her grandfather, she might as well start a few weeks early so she could get a good job before the other students arrived. Besides, what was there for her to do for the rest of the summer?

Until Nick she'd been so sure about her future, not what it would be, but that it was out there—waiting. Now there was fear and guilt, and both were driving her crazy. She couldn't talk about the fear, and she couldn't forget the guilt. Nick had damaged her self-confidence.

The train moved swiftly on its daily trip from Savannah to Atlanta and back again. It was running late, slinging the walking passengers from one side of the aisle to the other, trying to make up time. Margie Raines sat at her table in the dining car and ordered lunch. She felt an unexpected charge of excitement. Something about the precise elegance of the servers and the table made her feel important. Her ham sandwich had little toothpicks in the middle with a red cellophane tassel at the top. A handful of potato chips and an olive completed her lunch plate. She ate slowly, allowing herself to savor the sensation of being alone and on her own.

Across the aisle were two blue-haired ladies, holding their purses with tiny white-gloved hands. They looked like statues of begging poodle dogs. They'd finished their meal and the waiter presented the bill on a small silver tray. One of the women reached inside her dress and removed a handkerchief. She unknotted the ties and fished out a neatly folded bill which she handed to the black man who was waiting. Afterward, both women stood and left the dining car, lurching forward, then waiting until the train steadied before moving again.

Margie calculated her own bill, then brashly reached back in her wallet for more money. The ladies hadn't left a tip. But they could be forgiven. They probably didn't know better. She'd leave a dollar. Somehow her tip was a symbol for her future, a down payment on what she intended to become. She'd gotten away. Galilee was eighty miles and a lifetime behind her.

When she stepped off the train in Atlanta, Margie felt a surge of excitement sweep over her. She claimed her suitcase from the porter and trudged up the stairs to the lobby. There was an energy about the terminal, with its cavernous ceilings and polished marble floors teeming with travelers.

Beyond the lobby was a circular drive lined with taxis. She stopped just outside the brass-framed glass doors and thought. She hadn't planned any further than this. Her mother's friend knew she was coming, but Margie had insisted that she didn't need to be met. Finding her own way had seemed important at the time. Now that she was really here, she wasn't sure what she wanted to do first.

Arriving in the early afternoon gave her enough time to check out the school's student employment office before she left the downtown area. Taking a deep breath, Margie stepped out to the curb.

"Taxi, lady?"

"Yes, please."

The cab driver opened the back door and Margie and her suitcase got in. "Where to?"

"The Atlanta Division of the University of Georgia."

"We're on the way."

In less than five minutes he stopped in front of a building that looked more like a parking garage, opened the taxi door, took Margie's money and waited for her to get out.

Inside, the building was almost vacant. On the right was a reception desk and switchboard where a young man sat studying what appeared to be a play script.

He directed Margie to the placement office and shook his

head as she carried her suitcase in one hand and her purse in the other. She wondered if her gray dress with its ballerina skirt and twenty-one buttons down the front might be too casual for her first interview, then decided it was too late to worry about that now.

As it turned out, it didn't matter. The office was vacant. The woman emptying the trash explained that nobody was there between quarters.

"Oh, but I hoped I could get a job this afternoon, before I went out to . . ."

The woman looked up and smiled. "Sorry, miss. There won't be anybody back until Monday. I answered the phone a few minutes ago. By mistake," she added quickly. "Didn't see no harm in taking the message about a job. I don't guess it would matter if I gave it to you."

"What kind of job?" Margie reached out and took the note.

"Don't know. Just said they wanted to interview a girl to work in the office. I wrote it down."

"It doesn't matter," Margie said. She lifted her suitcase once more and walked back down the ramp and out the front door. She could see up the street opposite the school. There were office buildings and banks and a hotel. She could find a taxi there.

Once more she started out, wishing she'd brought a smaller suitcase, or that she had some place to leave it. But her grandfather had bought this one for her graduation present, and she'd been so proud of it. Her arm was aching. She was the only woman she saw with luggage. A taxi pulled up beside her and the driver opened the door.

"I'd like to go to—" She glanced down at the note. "A place called Janco—Jano—" She finally spelled out, "Jancowoski's at 600 Peachtree Street."

Fifteen minutes later the driver stopped before a low, flat building without any windows. Only the name Jancowoski's spelled out in script over the door told Margie they had arrived at her destination. She paid the driver, realizing how much of her money she had already used up. Taxi fare was more expensive than she realized. She wondered how soon she'd get paid.

Inside the building her shoes sank into the thick burgundy carpeting that caught the sound and held it. Behind the slate-gray marble reception desk a red-haired woman looked up in surprise.

"May I help you?"

"Yes," Margie answered firmly. "I came about the job."

"Job?"

"Yes, ma'am. For the girl you want to work in the office."

"And you brought your suitcase?" the receptionist said in amusement.

"Well, yes. I just got to town, on the train. I need a job before I find a place to live."

"Let me call Mrs. Phillips. She's the office manager."

Margie found herself quickly herded through the reception area to the office, a crowded, noisy machine-filled room presided over by a thin woman with narrow black glasses and very red lips.

Mrs. Phillips listened to Margie's impassioned plea for a job. Yes, the interior decorating firm needed a part-time student, after school. The job would involve filing invoices into ledgers. "Why didn't the school call for an appointment?"

"Oh, I'm sorry. There was nobody in the office except the cleaning lady. She gave me your notice. I didn't think to call first. I'll take the job, thank you."

Mrs. Phillips's lips quivered for a moment before she let them spread into a wide smile. "That's fine, Margie. It's a bit unusual, but I believe that you will do very well. And if you'd like, you may work full-time until school starts. That would be a big help."

Linda Phillips walked Margie out a side door, explaining that employees didn't use the customer entrance. "When may I expect you to begin?"

"Would tomorrow be all right? I need to get out to the house where I'm going to stay tonight and find out about the bus schedule."

"Where are you staying?"

"My mother has a friend in Decatur who is going to rent me a room."

Linda Phillips frowned.

"Is there something wrong?"

"No, except transportation from Decatur to the office is going to be difficult. You might want to find a place farther out Peachtree later. There are several living facilities for girls

106

in the area."

"Where?"

Margie was already in love with Atlanta, with Peachtree Street, with the woman who'd just hired her. The moon wouldn't have been too far for her to commute, but she respected Mrs. Phillips's suggestion.

"Well, the Churches Homes for Business Girls comes to mind. I don't know too much about them, but I think you might be comfortable there, and I've been told the rates are reasonable."

Margie thanked Mrs. Phillips and left, promising to be at work at eight A.M. sharp.

At the corner she looked around for a taxi. She didn't see one, but a trolley bus stopped and the door opened.

"Do you go to a Churches Home for Business Girls?" she asked the driver.

"Last stop I make on Fourteenth Street before I turn around," the driver said. "Hop on."

Margie plopped her suitcase on the long bench behind the driver, fed the proper change into the box, and sat down, more than satisfied with her day's efforts. She was in Atlanta, on her own, and she had a job.

Peachtree Street was a lively avenue of office buildings, churches, and small businesses. Margie noted the flower shop with its baskets of fresh flowers spilling out onto the sidewalk. There was a blue-and-white diner, a woman's club with a sign proclaiming the little theater in the rear, and a motion picture house advertising a foreign film.

The driver turned down a street comprised of apartment buildings and on-the-street parking. Fourteenth Street ended at the entrance to a park. The bus stopped beside a Gothic stone structure complete with tower rooms on the corners. The building looked as if it had come straight off the cover of a book. All it needed was a light in the window.

"Here you are, lady," the driver said, indicating the stone building. "The Churches Home for Business Girls. Don't let the spooks get you in there."

Margie did feel a shiver of concern as she stood before the door. There were actually bars on the ground-floor windows. Back in Galilee there wasn't even a latch on their front door. Inside she heard the sound of a radio playing and hushed laughter through the open windows above. At the top of the three-step entrance was a foyer with a parlor on one side and an office with a reception area on the other. Behind the mahogany desk was a very small white-haired woman wearing a black dress.

Margie felt like whispering. "I've come about a room. Are you the person I'm supposed to see?"

"I'm Mrs. Brown, the housemother on duty, yes. Have you filled out an application?" The woman's voice was soft and very polished. She sounded like a nun, or like Margie thought a nun might sound.

"No, ma'am. I just arrived in town from Galilee, Georgia. I'm going to the Atlanta Division of the University of Georgia."

"Oh, dear, I'm very sorry, but the policy of the home is that we do not accept students, only working girls with references."

"Oh, but I already have a job. I start work in the morning at Jancowoski's on Peachtree Street. I go to school at night."

"I see. And how did you find us?"

"The lady who hired me thought it would be more convenient for me to live here than in Decatur, which I had planned."

"She's right about that. But I'll still have to have you approved by the board. Fill out this form, please."

By the time Margie completed the form, the girls in the house had begun arriving home from work. They came noisily through the door, caught sight of the housemother, and hushed as they disappeared up the stairs and out of sight.

Mrs. Brown looked over the application and Margie once more, then excused herself, disappearing into the quarters behind the desk. After a long time she reappeared and studied Margie again.

"It will be difficult for you to get across town in the rush-hour traffic without a car if you don't know where you're going. The other housemothers and I have agreed that it would be best to let you stay the night, if you wish, while we get formal approval. I'll take you to a room."

Margie gave a big smile. "Thank you, Mrs. Brown. I'm very grateful." Fate, Margie thought.

The idea of living on her own, working, and earning a

salary was overwhelming. After calling her mother's friend, Margie followed the housemother up the stairs to what was once a four-room apartment. The other girls were all identified as employees of Southern Bell Telephone Company.

By the next week Margie had answered the pay phone outside the door and received her first obscene phone call, and she'd decided that filing invoices for an interior decorating firm whose records were at least a year out-of-date was not the way she wanted to earn a living. After another week she understood there was a reason that the home didn't cater to college girls. Small-town working girls and girls who dreamed of New York and being on Broadway had little in common. The other members of her section were trying to save money to work their way back to the rural towns they'd come from whereas Margie was working herself away.

Every weekend the apartment cleared out completely as the residents went home—except for the Beavers sisters who shared the best room on their wing. They were both in their late twenties and had been there longer than anyone else. Something about them bothered Margie, and she finally realized that it was because they were so much like the women in Galilee. They'd lived in Atlanta forever, but they fiercely fought taking on any big-city ways.

Such a waste, Margie thought, and avoided them.

In the beginning Margie did try to fit in with the girls. They went to the park together and took in an occasional movie. Next door to the Churches Home there was a neighborhood tavern which had been declared off limits to the girls. After Margie suggested that they get a hamburger there, her suitemates suddenly became very busy whenever she came around.

There were times when Margie wondered how smart she'd been to leave Galilee early. At least there she'd had Glory and Susan. Here she was totally alone and out of place. Then one day she got a letter from Nick, sent to her in Galilee and forwarded by her grandfather. She was surprised to see the return address and even more surprised to find his picture inside. For a moment she thought about answering it. Her roommates thought he was handsome and the idea was terribly romantic. But she could still remember opening the door and finding a stranger—the stranger who had been given her name by Nick.

Nick was being transferred to Virginia and she'd never see him again. In the meantime, her status in the apartment was raised considerably by the picture of the handsome man pasted on the mirror of her dressing table. But she never answered his letter.

Ten

Susan couldn't understand Margie's sudden decision to leave for Atlanta early. With Teddy gone, JoEllen away, and Glory behaving so strangely, she felt as if she'd been deserted.

"I think I might go on up to Augusta, Sam," she said the next weekend. "Maybe I could get a temporary job before business school begins in September."

"Absolutely not. What would people think?"

"People might think it was a smart idea."

"No. I need you to stay here, Susan, with me. You can't go."

"Why? You're away at college, except for the weekends."

"Because—because—I just do."

"And when you're home you're so busy with your grandfather that I hardly see you."

Sam took Susan's hand and held it tightly. "Everything I do is for us, Susan, for our future, just like we planned. I'll tell you what. You're always wanting to have a picnic. We'll go out to the lake Saturday afternoon, I promise."

"A picnic? Really? Maybe we should ask Glory and Dr. Sasser to go with us."

"No!"

There was something unusually intense about Sam tonight, something Susan didn't understand. "Why not? Glory's your cousin and she's my friend. With everybody leaving Galilee, I'm lonesome."

Susan knew that it was more than just being lonesome that was bothering her. She'd planned three years for this future, but she hadn't counted on the big hole that had been left

111

when Margie went away. She was used to Sam being gone, but she hadn't expected to miss her friends so much. The heat was unbearable and the days long and empty. There were no more gossipy gab sessions, no more trips to the pool. Glory didn't even call. Susan felt left out.

Until today. She'd gotten a letter, an unexpected letter from the last person on earth she'd imagined would write to her—Joseph Cheatham. It simply said that he'd been transferred to another hospital and was doing well. He'd made an appointment to talk with an officer about applying for the G.I. Bill and he wanted to thank her for encouraging him to do it.

At first Susan felt guilty, as if Mr. Larson, the postmaster, knew who Jody was and was telling everybody in town about the letter. Later she allowed her guilt to change to something like pride. She'd done a Christian thing and, as long as no one knew, she could recall the afternoon with a certain amount of pleasure. Jody hadn't felt out of place and nobody else had seemed to mind his presence. Mrs. Green was just being hateful later during bible school when she told Susan what the town was thinking. She wanted to make Susan regret her kindness.

Then, when Sam came over tonight, he'd been so angry. But a picnic? That showed he was sorry. Maybe he'd relax and they'd have fun.

When Saturday arrived, Susan packed a picnic lunch and dressed in her favorite pedal pushers and blouse with her new two-piece Jantzen swimsuit underneath. She tied a silk scarf around her neck, allowing the corners to peek out from beneath the collar of her blouse. The color of the scarf matched her fingernail polish and her lipstick. Sam would notice. Sam liked her fingernails.

When he picked her up, she felt a tremor of pleasure at the appreciative look he gave her. Maybe the afternoon would be fun. She was glad they'd be alone. Folding a blanket over her arm, Susan watched him pick up the basket and put it in his truck. He gave the blanket a quick frown, but didn't refuse to take it.

But the day was spoiled as soon as they pulled down the dirt road leading to the lake. There was already a car parked

112

there, a bedraggled automobile they soon found out belonged to Dr. Sasser. He and Glory were cavorting in the water on the other side.

"Let's go," Sam said with a growl.

"How would that look, Sam? Of course we won't go. There's enough lunch to share with them. Besides, it'll be fun with the four of us."

Sam unpacked the truck, but Susan knew that the pleasure of the day was gone. She undressed, emerging from the truck wearing her swimsuit.

"Did you have to wear that suit?"

"It's new. Don't you like it?"

Sam was already wearing his swim trunks. He glared at Susan as if she were indecently dressed. She glanced down at her new two-piece suit and cringed. Maybe it *was* cut a little low, but it was certainly stylish and respectable.

Susan held her retort and plunged into the warm water. With long firm strides she made her way across the lake toward Glory and her doctor.

Sam, clearly unsettled, walked across the dam before diving into the water. He would never admit that Susan was the better swimmer. He simply pretended that he wasn't as fond of the water as she.

It wasn't until Susan reached Glory and Roger that she realized they weren't wearing swimsuits. Glory pulled herself out of the water across her inner tube, exposing her bare backside to the world.

"Hi, Susan . . . Sam. God, it's hot, isn't it? Even this water isn't cold. Did you know it hit a hundred and seven this morning?"

Dr. Sasser hovered at the side of the inner tube, keeping Glory between him and the two newcomers.

"For Gods sake, Glory. You're naked as a jaybird. What would Grandfather say?"

"Who cares? Roger likes it. Why don't you try it, Susan. I'll bet Sam would like it, too."

Susan felt Sam's censure.

"Susan has more morals than that, Glory. Put your clothes on right now or we'll leave."

"Oh, all right, if you insist. Party pooper!" She slid from the tube, disappearing into the water.

Susan, treading water, let out a sigh of relief. She knew

113

how vocal Sam was on the subject of his cousin, and this was the first afternoon he'd reserved for Susan in nearly a week. She didn't want it to end so soon.

Sam, watching the shoreline with a frown, suddenly gave a strangled cry and disappeared from the surface in a splash of water. Moments later he shot to the surface, chest-to-chest with Glory.

"What in hell do you think you're doing, Glory Winslow?"

"Playing with you, Cousin Sam. Don't you ever just relax and let go? I'll bet Susan is the most frustrated woman in the county. And we already know *your* condition, don't we?"

She gave one last splash of water and turned toward shore. "Come on, Roger. Let's put our clothes on before Sam decides to offer a sermon and baptize us."

"But, Glory . . ." Roger began. "I'm—"

"Oh, fudge, Roger, Susan doesn't care if you're naked, too. Give her a thrill. Sam sure isn't planning to."

Susan and Sam watched in stunned silence as Glory reached the bank and walked slowly into the trees. Roger Sasser was obviously chagrined and showed his discomfort by dashing from bush to bush to conceal his nudity. Finally Susan swam toward Sam. She laid her hand on his shoulder.

"I'm sorry, Sam. But you know Glory. She just likes to shock you."

"Shock isn't the word I'd use," Sam said.

"Would you really like to go?"

"And leave her with him? Like that?"

"Well, we could always take off our suits and join them. I'm willing if you are." Susan unbuttoned the strap holding her suit top around her neck. Before Sam could stop her, it fell foward, exposing her breasts.

"Susan—" Sam's voice was meant to be hard, but it sounded more hoarse. "You mustn't do that."

"Why not? If Glory and her doctor can swim nude, why can't I? At least we're engaged. Aren't we, Sam? Aren't we going to be married? Don't you want to see my body?"

"Of course I do. But it isn't right."

"Right! Wrong! I'm getting a little tired of you making all the rules, Sam. I'm the one who goes to church every Sunday, not you. You've already lost your place in heaven. Why fight it?" Susan moved closer, allowing her bare breasts to skim Sam's chest.

114

"Hey, you two," Glory called out from the trees. "If you're going to fool around, you'd better get out of the water before Sam drowns. Why don't you join us in here? We have an extra blanket."

Sam whirled around and struck out across the lake. He almost made it all the way before he began to falter. Susan, swimming behind him, had to catch his arm and try to hold him up when he went under. But he was too heavy and pulled her down for a moment.

"Turn on your back, Sam. Float."

"No way," he sputtered.

"You're going under," Susan shouted. "Stop fighting me before you drown us both. I know how to do this. I learned at School Girl Patrol camp."

"I won't!"

He went under again and Susan was forced to grab his chin and tow him to shore. She pulled him onto the bank behind a spit of land that hid them from Glory's view. Once on land, she understood Sam's reluctance to turn over. His erection was still firm, even as he choked and coughed up water from his lungs.

Once he was breathing easy, Sam opened his eyes and groaned. Susan was staring at his cock, staring with a look that said she wasn't going to scream and back away. Her suit top still lay around her waist. Her breasts were more beautiful than he'd imagined. All he wanted to do was reach up and take them inside his mouth. Then she was leaning forward, her hand almost touching him. If she went any further he'd be lost.

"Damn. Glory!" he whispered.

"Forget Glory," Susan said, and caught him with her fingers.

What might have happened then was forever lost as the crashing sound behind them forced Sam frantically to his feet.

"Sam, boy, are you there?"

"Grandfather! Oh, God, Susan, fix yourself. He'll kill me!"

The old man pushed through the brush, glared at Susan who was adjusting her top and turned his fury to Sam who'd turned over and was lying on his stomach. "You said you were going fishing. Thought I'd join you."

115

"Where's your pole, Granddaddy?" Glory appeared from the woods, dragging a red-faced Roger Sasser with her.

"Afternoon, Dr. Sasser. I didn't expect you, but then I know my granddaughter. Sooner or later, you will, too. My pole is back in the truck, Glory. What are you supposed to be doing here?"

"We're having a picnic. Would you like to join us?"

"Yes," Susan agreed. "There's plenty of food."

"I think not. Sam, boy, I'd like to see you later. Please stop by the house when you're finished with—whatever it was you were about to do."

But the afternoon was spoiled for Sam. As soon as his grandfather left, he herded Susan to the truck and drove silently back to Galilee.

"I'm sorry, Sam," Susan said when he walked her to the door. "But we weren't doing anything wrong."

"Not yet, but in another minute we might have been. And it's all that little witch's fault."

"Glory? You mean she's the one who caused you to—"

"Yes! I mean no, of course not. It was seeing your breasts. We can't let that happen again, Susan. It would be sinful."

"Of course not. It would be sinful." But she was simply mouthing the words. Seeing Sam *like that* had set her on edge. She recognized those urges and she fought them back. She had to be strong, for Sam.

She opened the door and Sam brought the still-full picnic basket into the dark hallway.

"Mother? We're home." Sam followed her down the hall to the kitchen and put the basket on the table.

"Mother?" There was no answer. They were alone.

Susan began to unbutton her shirt. "Would you do something for me, Sam? If I asked you to? Just once?"

Sam watched her slide the damp blouse off her shoulder as she untied the straps to her swimsuit top.

"What?"

"Look at me, Sam, and touch me, just once."

He moistened his lips.

"Please, Sam."

"Grandfather is expecting me," he finally said, backing slowly out of the kitchen like one of those wind-up toy soldiers.

The following Monday Sam went back to school. He wouldn't be home next weekend, he explained when he called to say goodbye.

Susan had known that her friends were going off in different directions, but she'd never really thought about what that meant. Galilee had always meant home, family, security for her. Suddenly Susan felt as if she were seven years old again. She'd been abandoned by everyone, except her mother. It was almost as if she were starting over in Galilee again.

For the first time, she resented Margie, Glory, and JoEllen. She'd always considered Margie her champion, but Margie never had any intention of staying in Galilee. It was JoEllen's defection that bothered Susan, because she didn't understand it. JoEllen was most like her. JoEllen's father had abandoned her, leaving her and her mother and little brother struggling to survive. After graduation she and Teddy had planned to be married. JoEllen's life was to be a normal one, like hers and Sam's.

Then suddenly JoEllen had decided to go to summer school and graduate early. Now Teddy was in Texas, and JoEllen had become a stranger. Susan had always expected that the four friends would be there for each other, no matter what. But they were all taking different directions, as if they didn't need each other anymore. Without Sam and her friends nothing felt right.

Eleven

JoEllen came home once more that summer, in August, when her mother went to Lynville to be with Aunt Rose who was having surgery. JoEllen would stay with her brother and keep him out of trouble while her mother was away overnight.

From the time JoEllen arrived on Friday afternoon, Skip acted as if he had a secret. He took long, sly looks at her, marching around the apartment, bragging about the girls in his class, about how immature they were, how they tried to get the boys' attention with their tight sweaters and skirts, and how they pretended they didn't know what they were doing to the boys with their flirting.

Since the Fourth of July, JoEllen's schedule and part-time job had taken its toll. She was tired, her nerves were stretched to the breaking point, and Skip wasn't helping. Finally she sent him outside to mow the lawn.

Complying sullenly, he changed from his jeans and T-shirt into swim trunks and used the push mower to cut the lawn as he had a hundred times in the past. But this time JoEllen was constantly aware of him.

Her little brother had grown up. His muscular chest was covered with a mat of thick dark hair, his long legs were bunched with muscles from riding his bicycle, and he needed a shave.

He made her think of Teddy. Like Teddy, Skip was a child in a man's body. She dealt with men daily at the hospital. She had to touch them intimately, bathe them, clean their wounds. Sometimes they responded to her touch and she had to look away until they were able to compose themselves. That didn't bother her, it was her job, but Skip, the small house, and coming home to the same room where she'd spend most of her life seemed to close in on her. There was a sweet, sick taste in her mouth that filled her nostrils and made her stomach turn over. She recognized all too well what was bothering her. It was the smell of sex.

And it came from Skip.

He finished mowing the lawn and turned the water hose on himself to wash the grass clippings and the sweat from his body. The water made his white trunks transparent. The shadow of the dark mass of hair beneath it was obvious, as was the shape of his body. She had the feeling that he knew she was watching as he continued to hose himself. Once he pulled the waistband out and turned the hose inside his trunks. She could hear his groan through the open window. Then he turned off the hose, began squeezing the water from his wet trunks and, when he was finished, stepped onto the back porch and closed the screen door behind him.

JoEllen turned to the food she was cooking, ignoring him until he reached the mat inside the kitchen door. As she glanced up, he was peeling his wet bathing trunks from his body, slinging them back to the porch behind him.

"Skip, what are you doing?"

"Don't want to drip on the floor," he said with a grin as he stood there, blatantly exposing himself.

"Cover yourself! You shouldn't walk around like that in front of me."

"Why not? We're family. We even slept together until I was ten, or don't you remember."

She remembered. She remembered all too well their childish exploration of each other's bodies.

"We aren't children anymore."

"Boy, that's the truth, Jo. You're a woman. And I'm practically a man, or haven't you noticed?" He wrapped a towel around his lower body. "Sorry if I turned you on."

He dried his feet on the mat and walked casually through the kitchen and down the hall.

JoEllen took a deep breath and faced the fact that her younger brother was deliberately showing himself to her. He was swaggering around like an oversexed teenager, which was exactly what he was. Hormones, she decided. Nothing unusual. He couldn't get his way with the girls in town, so he

119

was like a rooster in the henhouse, trying to impress her with his masculinity.

She wanted to throw up. It seemed like a hundred years ago that Teddy had been like Skip and she'd been one of the girls he'd tried to impress. Teddy. Thank God he was still in Texas. She pushed the thought of Teddy from her mind as she had since that night. She didn't think about Teddy anymore. He was her childhood and she felt she'd left that behind this summer.

After supper, Skip left to drive around with some of his friends. When he returned, JoEllen was already in bed. She listened as he undressed, as the toilet flushed in the bathroom between their rooms.

JoEllen finally fell asleep. She might be able to close out Teddy in the daytime, when she was awake, but at night he invaded her dreams. They were back in that motel. He was kissing her, touching her with his mouth, his hands. Except tonight, in this dream, Teddy was Skip and she could hear his excitement.

Suddenly she was awake and Skip's voice was no dream. She could clearly hear his sexual excitement.

JoEllen slid from the bed, through the connecting bath, and pushed open the door to her brother's room. He was there, in his bed, with a girl. JoEllen could hear her moaning.

At that moment JoEllen did get sick. It was happening to the girl beneath Skip, but JoEllen was back in that motel room and it was happening to her. She slammed the door, ran for the bathroom, and threw up, again and again. Finally, exhausted, she slipped to the floor and leaned back against the wall.

The next thing she was conscious of was a cool, wet cloth being applied to her face.

"Are you okay, JoEllen?"

"JoEllen kept her eyes closed. She couldn't stop herself from shaking. As Skip wiped her face, she began to cry.

"I'm sorry," he said, "I didn't mean to upset you. I thought you'd understand. I mean—you and Teddy . . . I thought you must have . . ." Skip sat beside her, pulling her into his arms and comforting her as if he were the adult and she the child.

120

"No. And *you* mustn't do that again, Skip."

"Don't worry, I'm careful. I always use a rubber."

JoEllen didn't believe him. She remembered Teddy's haste and his carelessness. "You can't be sure. You could ruin your life."

"What life, Jo? This is as good as it gets."

"You can get out of here, Skip. Make something of yourself."

"I don't think so, Sis. I'm not smart like you. I'm more like Teddy. I don't have any great ambition. Life here in Galilee is all I'll ever have. I wouldn't know how to get out."

JoEllen felt Skip's calm acceptance of his situation. Sometime during the time Skip was holding her, JoEllen heard a car leave. The girl had gone home. They were alone, just as they'd been for most of their lives. She wanted to argue, but she was too tired. Finally Skip helped her to bed and sat beside her until she fell asleep.

Come morning, JoEllen wanted to die. The apartment was quiet. Skip must have already left for work at Granger's where he weighed produce and cleaned up the store.

She lay in bed, facing the enormity of Skip's behavior. She'd been such a fool. She was responsible for her brother and she'd been so caught up in her own dreams and her own future that she'd lost track of him. She foolishly thought that he'd follow the example she was setting. Except it wasn't her example Skip was following, it was Teddy's.

When her mother came home that night, JoEllen explained her nervous stomach as something she'd eaten.

When Skip came to her room later that night, she forced herself to put aside her preaching and talk to him as an equal.

"I know how powerful the sex drive is, Skip. I can't say I don't. But you know there are other ways. Use them."

"And go blind? Why, JoEllen, I'm surprised at you."

"That's an old wives tale, Skip. And you won't grow hair on the palm of your hand, either."

"So that's what nurses learn."

"Don't be silly. I'm serious. You never had anybody to look up to, but there's a whole world out there. Don't cheat yourself by having to get married and being forced to work in the shirt factory."

"Why not. That's what happened to Dad."

"And look what he did. He ran away. It doesn't have to happen to us, Skip. There's more to life than sex and Galilee."

"Maybe, but from where I stand, that's about the best thing going for me. Don't worry, JoEllen, I'll manage."

"Just don't do anything foolish, please. In two years I'll be a registered nurse. Then you can come to Augusta and you'll go to school and—"

"Sure, JoEllen," he agreed.

But JoEllen knew that he didn't believe anything she said.

When she left on Sunday afternoon, she reassured her mother she was all right but that she wouldn't be home for a while. She was going to sign up for extra weekend work in the lab over at the base and more hospital duty so she could make faster progress.

She didn't count on being so sick. The emotional upheaval of the weekend interfered with her eating, and she slept poorly.

Three weeks later she stopped fooling herself and faced the inevitable truth: she was pregnant. The sins of the father, she thought with a grim laugh. Or maybe, in this case, the mother.

No, the sin was hers.

The morning sickness didn't go away. She lost weight, but still she pushed herself. When her roommate asked her if she was pregnant, she denied it, just as she'd denied it to herself. There were days when she decided it couldn't be true. She'd heard about women who caused their periods to be late because they were worried. But not this time. All the other signs were present; tender breasts and nausea and mood swings.

What would she do? How would she face Skip, her mother, her supervisor? All her plans were ruined. After all her warnings to her brother, she'd been the one caught in Galilee's trap. She could just hear Glory: "Life won't let you escape. Tradition, that's the god of our future. It's already been determined what we'll be and nothing we can do will change it."

Teddy would marry her, but he was only a senior in high

school. What kind of life would they have?

No. Glory was wrong. JoEllen wouldn't give up her dreams. She couldn't let Skip down. She couldn't do that to Teddy, either. And she wouldn't do it to herself. She'd have to find a way to get rid of it. She wouldn't think of it as a baby. It was just another problem in her life, a setback that she'd find a way to get through. There were ways. She'd heard whispers about how a woman could do it to herself. She'd find out how, and do it. Whatever happened she wouldn't be pregnant.

But she *was* pregnant. She couldn't pretend anymore.

When Teddy returned to Galilee the week before Labor Day he expected JoEllen to come home for the holiday weekend. She didn't. He considered driving over to see her, until he found out that there was a drag race over at Lynville that gave money to the winners.

Teddy borrowed his brother's car and won his first trophy and his first money that weekend, racing stock. He'd found the kind of excitement in winning a race that he used to find on the ballfield. Besides, the girls at the dragstrip were willing, and after a summer of experimenting, he'd learned enough to make them very happy.

If JoEllen didn't appreciate him enough to welcome him back, he'd just let her find out what she was missing. It was nice not to be nagged about his grades and his ambition. He liked working in the garage; he was good with his hands. He'd learned this summer that he was good at other things as well.

JoEllen was his future, but he had another year to get there. The present was just about as much fun as he'd ever wanted. Teddy didn't want to own the world, just his little corner of it—eventually.

For the girls, Labor Day of 1954 came and went. JoEllen studied the newspaper article about the Senate voting to censure Senator Joseph McCarthy for conduct unbecoming a senator. Margie read the script of the Pulitzer prize-winning play *The Teahouse of the August Moon*. Susan listened to Sam grouse over the winning of the All-Star baseball game by the American League, and Glory spent the weekend in Augusta with Roger, where she amused herself by watching one of the new country club television sets and picking Lee Meriweather to become Miss America of 1954.

At the hospital, JoEllen's schedule was three hours of classroom instruction, three hours of on-the-floor clinics, and two hours of assisting on the wards. Since the Fourth of July, she had volunteered for extra night duty in addition to her work at the Camp Gordon lab on Sundays. She was learning fast.

As a second-year nursing student she had graduated from full-time bedmaking and bathing of the patients. And her supervisors were beginning to rely on her. Occasionally she crossed paths with Roger Sasser at the base hospital. He was friendly, but nothing more. No mention was made of Glory.

At Lawton Memorial the holiday brought in the usual number of boating accidents and near drownings. A couple of fans who got in a fight at the final Sally League baseball game of the year between the Macon Peaches and the Augusta Tigers had to be stitched up.

JoEllen kept up her hectic schedule, refusing to dwell on her troubles. Her meals were taken catch as catch can, and her study hours too few, with too much to learn and too little time to do it. She was always tired, and her strength seemed to be waning. But she'd satisfied herself that it was because of stress and worry, not her problem. She was eight weeks pregnant now and still had no solution.

Her training would end if they found out about her pregnancy, and, Jo wanted to cram as much learning in as she could before that happened.

The hospital recovery room nursing station was in an uproar when JoEllen reported in for the three-to-eleven shift. Martha Fenell, the head nurse, wasn't wearing her cap for the first time since JoEllen had been assigned to her floor.

"Jo," she said with a sigh of relief. "We've had quite an evening. Every bed is taken and we're short a staff nurse. You're going to have to fill in tonight."

"Yes, ma'am," JoEllen agreed with forced cheerfulness. So many of the head nurses continued to treat student nurses as maids. It was exciting to be looked on as someone who could actually help. "What can I do?"

The petite dark-haired woman who'd become JoEllen's mentor and idol glanced at the charts she was writing up and handed three of them to JoEllen.

"Read these records. I'd like you to monitor these three women. The first one is suffering from severe depression. It seems that she locked herself in the family's new bomb shelter and refused to come out.

"Bomb shelter?"

"I know. The world's going crazy building bomb shelters in their yards. When her husband broke the door down, she had a rope around her neck and jumped from the center beam. He managed to save her, but there was so much trauma that a tracheotomy had to be performed so she could breathe. She's been sedated and the airway is open now, but, the doctor is concerned about her mental condition. Don't let her pull the breathing tube out."

JoEllen clasped the charts and tried hard to concentrate on what her supervisor was saying. That a woman would try to kill herself in a bomb shelter seemed the height of irony.

"The second woman," Nurse Fenell went on, "is recovering from a heart attack. It's just a matter of monitoring her heart rate and keeping the fluids dripping.

"The third one is the really touchy situation. She's just a kid. She took herself to one of those back-street butchers who nearly killed her with an abortion."

"Abortion?" JoEllen felt the air fly out of her lungs.

"I don't know what the quack used, but he put her out on the hospital steps, and she nearly bled to death before we got her inside. They had to remove her uterus and transfuse her. She's had four pints of blood, but she's still risky."

"What should I watch for?"

"Blood pressure, pulse, vital signs. Keep the kinks out of the tubes in her arm as she wakes up. Keep a close watch on her temperature. Infection is a definite possibility in spite of the antibiotics she's on. Just let me know if there is any change. You never know what these kids will do when they wake up and realize what's happened."

JoEllen could identify with that. "What does her family say?"

"They're on the way. When they get here, you know who'll have to talk to them. The doctor will be too busy."

"Yes, ma'am, and you'll do it well. You have a way about you, Mrs. Fenell. People have confidence in you."

"You handle people well, too, Jo. I've noticed how patients respond to you. That's why I'm making you responsible for this section tonight." She started to walk away, then stopped. "You look tired. Are you all right?"

"Yes, ma'am. I'm just working hard."

The critical-patient wing was actually one long room. In the center was the nurses' station. There was a nurse assigned to each section with one roving nurse moving back and forth between and one nurse always at the station itself. JoEllen straightened her cap and took the charts to her section to read through them. She didn't want to think about the abortion patient, but she couldn't stop.

There was a soft quietness about the room, with the sounds of the machines and the hushed whisper of the nurses' shoes scurrying back and forth. Occasionally a patient would cry out or moan as they began to wake from anesthesia, but there was little talking.

The heart patient was sleeping quietly. She looked like somebody's grandmother with salt-and-pepper hair and a soft, wrinkled face. The machine recording her heart rate seemed to be functioning properly and the sound of it humming was reassuring.

The woman from the bomb shelter was awake. She was staring at JoEllen warily. A tall, thin woman with long arms and a bony chin, she looked as if she was trying to hide in the bedclothes.

JoEllen glanced at the chart. "I'm JoEllen Dixon. I'll be sitting with you for a while. If you need anything, please tell me."

"Don't bother. Armageddon is at hand. Those fools and their bomb shelters. Won't nothing stop the evil of men."

Jo shivered. There were many kinds of evil, and she suspected that women could claim responsibility for a great deal of it.

After checking the patient's tubes and tucking the blanket around her, JoEllen moved on to the last patient. Cindy Stewart, the back-street abortion case, was in the most critical condition. She was younger than Jo, with blond hair and skin as pale as moonlight on fresh concrete. Her eyes were closed, but tears trickled down from the corners.

"Are you okay?" Jo whispered softly.

"No, but that doesn't matter anymore."

"Of course it does. We're going to have you up and out of here in no time."

"Why bother?"

"I know how awful you must feel, but—" Jo's voice broke off.

"How? How could you possibly know?"

Because I'm pregnant, Jo wanted to say. *I know how it feels to be desperate. What I don't know is what to do about it.*

"Because I'm a nurse," she finally answered. "Or at least I will be someday."

"Then tell me, why won't they let real doctors help you, so nobody would ever have to go through this awful thing?"

"I don't know. I truly wish they would."

"I never thought I'd get pregnant. I thought he loved me, but when he found out I was—you know, he got mad. There was someone else he was going to marry. The wedding was already planned. He forced me to go to that terrible place." She was whispering, almost to herself.

"Your boyfriend?" JoEllen asked.

"No, not my boyfriend, not anymore." She turned her face to the wall, took a deep breath, and said, "But it wasn't my boyfriend who took me to get rid of the baby, it was my—my own daddy. He said that I couldn't have a baby, that it would kill my mother if she found out."

"Your own father arranged your abortion?"

"Sure, my father, the mayor's personal assistant, the pillar of the community. The deacon in the church. It hurt. It hurt so bad, and my baby's dead."

She began to cry harder and JoEllen was forced to call Nurse Fenell, who gave the girl a sedative to quiet her before JoEllen could question her further.

JoEllen couldn't get the girl's desperation out of her mind. Sixteen, terribly unhappy, and afraid of her own father. JoEllen's father wasn't her problem, it was her brother. And it wasn't fear she felt, but desperation. After all her warnings to Skip, *she'd* been the one to fail. She'd let him down. And she'd made all her mother's hard work a lie.

Yes, she understood how Cindy felt about going home. JoEllen wouldn't go home again, either.

127

During the late hours of the night, the woman with the heart condition stabilized enough to be out of danger. The patient who hid in the bomb shelter was taken to the psychiatric ward for evaluation. Cindy was moved to a private room.

It was four o'clock in the morning before JoEllen was relieved. She went down to the cafeteria for a snack. Martha Fenell was there, drinking coffee and pushing the pieces of a doughnut around the saucer.

"JoEllen, come and sit with me. You did very well tonight, particularly with the abortion patient."

JoEllen put her Bireley's orange drink and ham sandwich on the table and sat down. "I—why did it happen? Other women have abortions without bleeding to death. I've heard some women even do it to themselves. Is that true?"

"Yes, it's possible, if they know what they're doing. A back-street abortion is simply doing something to interrupt the cycle. Then left alone, nature takes care of the problem. Women use everything from coat hangers to cooking spoons. But you see what can happen when the job is botched."

"Yes, it seems a shame, doesn't it?"

"I've been watching you, JoEllen. You're going to make a splendid nurse. Even the doctors are impressed. Do you plan to stay on here at University Hospital after you graduate?"

"I wish I could, but I'm not sure that I'm going to be able to graduate," she said softly.

"Not graduate? Why? JoEllen you're the best student I've seen in four years. You have good grades. You work hard and you love what you're doing. In fact I see a lot of myself in you."

"You do?" *But I'll bet you never were pregnant and not married,* she wanted to add.

"I hadn't intended to tell you, but if there's a chance that you're about to drop out, I'm going to do something totally against the rules. You're not supposed to find out until spring, but you're going to get the second-year nursing award and be given a scholarship for your last year."

"A scholarship?" JoEllen wanted to cry. She wanted to scream. It wasn't fair.

She'd thought that she'd faced the worst that could happen, until now. A scholarship. Her whole life had

128

changed this summer. Marriage to Teddy was no longer what she wanted. Maybe it never had been. She just hadn't known it until the night in that motel.

Teddy was her alternative to failure. She cared about him, she really did. He was a part of her life. But being a nurse was all she ever really wanted—what she still wanted. Now she could lose it all.

But she couldn't blame it on Teddy. He hadn't forced her to go to bed with him. Maybe she'd subconsciously wanted to test herself. If making love to Teddy had been as wonderful for her as it had been for him, then she could live with failure if it came. But it hadn't been. She hadn't expected to get pregnant. What a fool she'd been.

"What's wrong, JoEllen? Can't you tell me?"

"Nothing, nothing's wrong," she said. "I'm just tired. "I've got to get back to the floor." She stood up. "Thank you, Mrs. Fenell. I'll try not to disappoint you. I—I'll work it out."

"I'm sure you will," Martha said, and watched the girl as she left the cafeteria. She made a mental note to talk to JoEllen's adviser. There was something wrong here and this was one girl she didn't plan to lose. Probably the boy back home. That was usually the trouble. Sooner or later JoEllen would realize that marriage and nursing were two separate careers, and there were not many women who could combine them.

JoEllen Dixon had the brains and the drive. Martha Fenell would bet her bottom dollar that she'd work out whatever her problem was.

Twelve

A possible solution to her problem came to JoEllen the morning after she'd been assigned to care for Cindy. Cindy had had an abortion. She knew what to do. She could tell her. JoEllen stopped by Cindy's room, knocked, then stuck her head through the open door. The girl was lying with her back to JoEllen. She didn't turn.

"Are you feeling better?" JoEllen walked around the bed so that Cindy could see her.

There were dark circles beneath Cindy's eyes and a wild, desperate look in them that gave JoEllen a moment of panic.

"You were there last night, weren't you? It was you who I—talked to?"

"Yes."

"But you aren't my nurse any longer, are you?"

"No. I was worried about you. I'm going off duty now and I stopped by to talk—to make sure you're okay.

"You're the one I spilled my guts to. Promise me you won't say anything to my mother. Promise me. Daddy doesn't want her to know how it really happened."

How did it happen? Telll me. I'm the one who needs to know. JoEllen wanted to say. But Cindy's fragile state of mind wouldn't let her ask. JoEllen was a nurse. Her responsibility was to soothe the patient. "But, Cindy, don't you think you'd better tell her the truth before you go back home?"

"I won't go back home," she said defiantly.

"Why? Your mother must be very worried about you."

"She'll be ashamed. Then she'll pretend it isn't true."

"But she's your mother. She loves you, I'm sure. Go home,

Cindy, and talk to her." *I can't tell my mother, but you can talk to yours.*

"I can't. She'd never believe anything bad about my father. And he'll never let me forget what I did. There's nothing anybody can do."

"I think you ought to give her a chance," JoEllen argued. "Our mothers love us, no matter what. Maybe she's stronger than you think."

"No," Cindy said in resignation. "My mother has never been able to stand up to my father. She surely won't now. They sent a counselor up here. He told me that Mother came alone. My loving father was suddenly called out of town. She can't even handle taking me home. She wants me to stay here until he gets back."

JoEllen felt very old. "You're only sixteen," she began. "And you have your whole life ahead of you. Maybe staying here and talking to Dr. Willis is a good idea. When you do go home, things won't be nearly so bad as they look, I promise you."

"No, I'll never go home."

JoEllen felt Cindy's hopelessness and she knew that the girl meant what she was saying. She understood that talking to her mother was no better solution for Cindy than it was for herself. What had happened was so awful that it couldn't be brought out in the light of day by *anybody*. Her own guilt lay like a heavy weight around her heart, filling the space with dark, impenetrable gloom. She couldn't bring herself to ask what she most needed to know: where she could go to get help for herself.

On the way out JoEllen stopped by the counselor's office. She wanted to hear Dr. Willis say that Cindy was going to be all right. Somehow knowing that Cindy would make it was important.

In the waiting room, JoEllen flipped through a new *Life* magazine for a moment, then dropped it in her lap. Somehow the Korean War seemed a million miles away. It didn't matter that Swanson had come out with a frozen dinner that could be taken right out of the refrigerator freezer and heated. It didn't matter that Coco Chanel's new dress designs were all the rage. All that seemed like another world.

A wave of lightheadedness swept over JoEllen and she felt

131

an all-too-familiar rumbling in her stomach. She was going to throw up. The bathroom opened into the waiting area, but JoEllen barely made it in time. After washing her face and taking a deep breath, she made her way back to the waiting area. Maybe she'd talk to Dr. Willis about her problem.

Still dizzy, she put her head between her legs and took long, even breaths until it passed. What in God's name was she going to do? Suppose something like that happened while she was on duty. Already she had great difficulty in concealing her morning sickness from her roommates. She let out a deep sigh.

The counselor's assistant picked that minute to step into the waiting room and address JoEllen. "Can I help you, dear?"

"I—I—" She couldn't do it. "I was just worried about the patient in 302. She had an abortion last night and nearly died. Dr. Willis spoke with her earlier and I think she needs to talk with someone again."

"I'll tell Dr. Willis for you. He's busy, busy, busy. But thanks for stopping by."

Using her concern about Cindy as the reason for her curiosity, JoEllen spent the next two days asking questions about abortions. With the proper medical knowledge there had to be a way out, one that wouldn't bring her to the same end as Cindy. She couldn't afford to wait any longer. One nurse finally explained a way that seemed to make sense, a way a woman could do it to herself and nobody would ever know about it.

Three days later, JoEllen stole a piece of rubber tubing and a box of cotton pads from the supply room and started the procedure that would abort her child and change her life.

The tube was supposed to be inserted into the uterus and packed in place with the cotton. But she couldn't force it inside her. It was too limp, too stubborn. Finally, in desperation she threaded a bent coat hanger into the tube and pushed. This time it went in. This time it hurt.

JoEllen hadn't expected it to hurt like that. But it was in place. She refused to think what was happening as she forced the cotton pads inside her and around the tube to hold it in place. Then she pulled out the coat hanger and stood.

132

Not too bad. She could bear it.

Six to eight hours, the nurse who'd explained the procedure had said. Then the cramps would start and she'd lose the baby. It would be just like having her period, maybe a little heavier.

But nothing happened. Between class time and floor duty she decided that perhaps the tube had gotten kinked. She went back to her room and inserted the coat hanger again. The pads were bloody, but that was all.

It wasn't working. She'd done something wrong. She wasn't even cramping. JoEllen glanced at her watch. She had to get to the floor. She removed the coat hanger, afraid that she might poke a hole in something and do permanent damage to herself.

She'd go back to work and wait. That was the only choice she had.

JoEllen was walking down the corridor to take some ice water to a patient when the cramp hit her, doubling her in half. Before she could move, she felt the blood gush out and run down her legs. There was a swishing feeling. The cramp immobilized her. She couldn't move. Beneath her feet was a puddle of blood and one soggy cotton pad.

A resident suddenly stepped out of the room opposite where she was standing. He took one look at JoEllen's expression and the floor. He pulled out a sheet from a laundry cart nearby and swept the mess up inside it. Then he lifted JoEllen into his arms and stepped back into an empty room behind him. He'd moved so quickly that nobody witnessed what had happened.

"Is this what I think?"

JoEllen nodded helplessly.

"Damn! Do I help you and keep quiet or do I send you down to Emergency?"

"Help me, please."

He laid her on a gurney, covered her body with a sheet, and lifted her skirt. With a groan he removed her underpants, separated the tube away from the cotton, and flushed it all down the toilet.

"You little fool. Why didn't you ask somebody for help?"

"Ask for help? Who?" JoEllen began to laugh hysterically. The last thing she remembered was feeling the blood flowing out of her into the bed beneath her.

When she opened her eyes she was in the recovery room. Except this time she was the patient and Martha Fenell was standing beside the bed.

"Why didn't you tell me?" the woman asked softly.

JoEllen's throat was dry and it was hard for her to talk. "What could you have done?"

"Nothing, perhaps. But you might have died. There was a rupture in the uterus and you hemorrhaged. Dr. Brooks is attributing the rupture to an ulcer. I went against my better judgment, JoEllen, and assisted in the surgery. You owe him your life. He took a real chance in helping you and nobody will ever learn the truth. You just get well and don't do anything so foolish again."

"I won't," she said. "I'll never let another man touch me, I swear."

But she did.

It was eight weeks before Dr. Thomas Brooks invited her out. The Augusta merchants sponsored a Harvest Festival on the Broad Street green. He asked if she'd like to go and, though she knew it was against hospital regulations for a student nurse to date one of the doctors, she felt obligated to say yes.

The green was an expanse of land that ran down the middle of Broad Street. In the 1700's, cows grazed on the green, peddlers offered their wares, and people took their nightly promenades. It was still beautiful, especially in spring, with its mulberry trees and flowers.

Now local merchants were offering their winter harvest—sugarcane and syrup, dried corn and peppers, pumpkins and gourds. The stores were running special sidewalk sales and vendors were hawking pralines and cotton candy.

JoEllen forced herself to relax as they walked about, enjoying the warm fall night and listening to a band playing in the center of the promenade.

As much as she appreciated what Dr. Brooks had done for her, JoEllen was embarrassed. He was making her feel uneasy. He was going through the motions, but his mind obviously wasn't on the festival. There was something unnaturally possessive about his solicitude that made her uncomfortable.

He seemed very pleased that she had accepted his invitation, complimenting her on her navy suit and matching shoes and the way she'd styled her hair. But something about his mannerisms reminded her of Glory when she was trying to convince her friends to follow her latest scheme.

"I know how good you are as a nurse, JoEllen. And I understand your desperation. I've had a rough time, too. I've been thinking that maybe we could help each other," he said, taking her arm and folding his hand over it possessively.

"I plan to be a very good nurse," she answered, trying gently to put some distance between them.

"Oh, I don't mean that. I know how dedicated you are. I mean, you'd be an asset to a doctor who was ambitious, a doctor who needed money to set up an office. I have a feeling that you could use a little extra money. I think we would make a very good team."

"Perhaps. But I don't think the hospital encourages that kind of—fraternization."

"Oh, I didn't mean social. This would be more of a business arrangement, that and an exchange of other—services."

"I don't understand."

"JoEllen, I don't plan to stay on at the hospital. I'll go into private practice next year. Gynecology. Women always have problems. And I can help them, like I helped you. No one needs to know. I already have an offer, back home in Glyndale, but I don't want to practice in some little hole-in-the-road podunk town. I have to be in the city where women can find me. If I had enough money I could open an office right here in Augusta."

She didn't ask what he meant by "helping women the way he'd helped her." The desperation she'd felt was a permanent part of her every waking moment, that and the sight of her blood puddling on the white linoleum of that hospital corridor. "Thank you, Dr. Brooks, but I'm going to stay on at University Hospital when I graduate."

"Don't say no," Tom pleaded. "I'm offering you a job working for me, part-time now, until you graduate, and full-time later. I'll share our special income with you. Nobody will know about it but us."

"But suppose you get caught? Why would you take such a risk, Dr. Brooks?"

"There was someone I cared about—my little sister. She died from a botched abortion. I'd like to keep that from ever happening again. And, if I can find enough money to open up my own office, I can make sure that it doesn't."

JoEllen tried not to reveal her revulsion to what he was suggesting. She'd prayed for somebody like him when she was in trouble, but now that he was offering himself for that purpose she had as much guilt over the idea of participating. The truth was, she believed that abortion was morally wrong . . . unless the unwanted pregnancy happened to you.

"I can't, Dr. Brooks. I've already told Mrs. Fenell I will stay at University. She's grooming me for emergency-room duty. It's been decided." JoEllen was beginning to feel very uneasy. She was very sorry she'd agreed to go out with him.

"I think we'd better go, Dr. Brooks," JoEllen suggested. "I'm afraid someone from the hospital will see us."

"You're right." He agreed much more easily than JoEllen had expected. He walked her back to the car he'd borrowed. A short time later, when he stopped in front of an apartment building in a strange section of town, she knew she'd made a mistake.

Even then, JoEllen never suspected what he was going to do. He'd put his career on the line for her. He'd seemed concerned about her, checking on her two or three times a day until she was released. Afterward he'd been friendly, stopping by to have coffee with her, just to talk about the patients, even helping her catch up on her classwork. She'd believed that he was trying to be her friend.

"Who lives here?" she asked, trying to keep her voice casual. She was certain that it would only make things worse if she allowed him to see how upset she was.

"Another resident and his wife. I promised you a relaxing evening away from the hospital, remember? And I'm going to supply it."

"But, really, I ought to get back." She looked around in alarm. "Where are your friends?"

"Oh, they're away. They gave me a key so we wouldn't have to hurry back. We'll just have a drink and talk and unwind. We're both pretty tense, don't you think?"

He unlocked the door, switched on a lamp in the living room, turned on the record player and put on a stack of records.

136

"Please, Dr. Brooks. I don't feel right about this."

"I think it's time you called me Tom. After all, we know each other very well, don't we?"

"I'd like to go home, please, Tom. I'm very grateful to you, but I don't feel—like that about you."

"I know you don't, JoEllen. But having sex doesn't require love, does it? We're both two adults who know the score. Why not enjoy what we can give to each other?"

"You mean you expect me to have sex with you?"

"Well, if you want to be that blunt about it, yes."

"No! I mean, I can't. I mean, I thought we were—friends."

"JoEllen, darling, men and women are never friends. They work together. They have sex together. And sometimes they marry and make a life together. But friends? I don't think so."

She tried to pull away. "But I don't love you, Dr. Brooks. And I'm not the kind of person who can just have sex with a man, not like—like this."

"Were you raped, JoEllen?"

"No, of course not."

"And was it being in love that got you pregnant?"

"Yes. No. Not exactly. It was all a terrible mistake. It never should have happened."

"Well, you don't have to worry about me, JoEllen. I won't make you pregnant. That's the last thing I need."

"Please. Please let me go! I won't let you do this."

"Oh, yes you will."

And then she understood. "That's why you helped me isn't it? You had this in mind all along, forcing me . . ."

"No, actually that idea came along a little later. What I had in mind for now was having you assist me occasionally, and later, when I'm set up, having you run my office for me. I thought you'd understand."

"If you don't take me home I'll report you to the hospital."

Tom allowed a hint of hesitation to slow his movements. "I took a big risk for you, JoEllen. Now you're threatening me?"

"I certainly am!"

"That's not playing fair. What will you say when I tell everybody that you attempted to abort your child and that Martha Fenell helped conceal it. Your career will be ended. So will hers."

"So will yours."

"I don't think either of us is willing to take that chance. JoEllen, I know it's hard to take that first step, but this will work out for both of us, if you just take a moment to see the advantages. Why be poor and lonely? I understand you. Nobody else will."

She knew then that she had no choice. While she might be willing to tell her story, she couldn't do anything to hurt Martha Fenell. Martha had helped her. Martha knew her terrible secret. And how could she deliberately keep Dr. Brooks from helping women who truly needed help after what she'd done to herself?

She wiped the tears from her cheeks and began to remove her clothes. She had no choice.

But as she lay down on the bed, she listened to its creak and swore to herself that never again would a man control her body for any reason. After tonight she would do the using, any way, any time she chose. Two men had wanted her, and both of them had used her. This man would be the last.

She looked up at the doctor who'd saved her life, the man who knew her most terrible secret. He could influence her hospital record. A good record meant good advancement. Advancement meant control. Control meant change and choices. She had no intention of ever allowing him control over her future, but for now, he needn't know that.

JoEllen Dixon opened her arms.

Thirteen

Glory pretended much longer than JoEllen had before she accepted the truth, but the outcome was the same.

A week after she pledged Delta Delta Delta, her mother's old sorority, she started feeling uneasy. It was the late hours and the drinking, she told herself. She'd cut back on the partying and get more sleep. The next week Roger finally got a long weekend and she took him home to meet her family. By that time she knew she was in trouble.

The following Wednesday she made an appointment with a doctor away from the campus.

The doctor glanced across the top of his glasses and said, "Mrs. Wilson, is it? How come you're here in Maysville instead of seeing your regular family doctor?"

"He's out of town," Glory said smoothly, repeating the story she'd fabricated while she fingered the class ring she'd turned backward on her finger to simulate a wedding band. "My husband is so excited that we just couldn't wait until he gets back to know."

"Well, I can't be positive, of course. These tests have been known to be wrong. But going from the dates and your symptoms, I suspect that it's a good possibility that you're pregnant. I'll have to examine you to be sure."

Pregnant? People didn't even say that word. "Expecting," maybe, or "that way," but "pregnant" was so final. Then she realized what he'd said. "Examine me?"

"Yes, please lie back on the table and put your feet in the stirrups. I'll have to do a vaginal examination."

"Isn't there some other way?" Glory was beginning to be concerned. Something about the look in his eyes and the

139

bulge in his pants told her he was reacting to her as a man, not as a doctor. She began to feel sick to her stomach and started to get up from the table.

"No. I've changed my mind."

"Stay put, girl. I know you're lying about being married. I get a steady stream of college girls in here, but you're the first this quarter. School's just started. What'd you do, give him an early going-away present?"

"I don't have to listen to this," Glory said, and clamped her legs together.

"No, you don't. But you're here and you need to know. You might as well let me find out. What difference does it make now?"

He was right. She couldn't face taking off her clothes and lying on that cold examining table again. And she had to know. Not that she was pregnant. She was already sure of that. What she had to know was, how long?

She leaned back on the table and closed her eyes. He lifted her legs and fitted her heels into the metal cups that extended from the ends of the table. She felt him lift the sheet covering her lower body as his fingers parted her, sliding inside. The cream he'd spread on his finger was cold.

"I'm going to put something inside to open you up enough for me to examine you. It will hurt a little, but not for long."

She sniffed.

"For God's sake, girl, don't cry."

It was awful. She felt as if she were being torn apart. His fingers probed and mashed. Just as she thought she would die, she felt him taking out the metal piece. She let out a sigh of relief. Then she heard him. Opening her eyes, she saw that he was playing with himself as he leaned forward. Without removing his clothes, he covered her mouth with his hand and stuck himself inside her. Only a few plunges and a grunt and he was done.

He stood up, zipped up his pants, and turned away. "Clean yourself up, girl," he instructed, and handed her a tissue.

She followed his directions. What else could she do? He knew she wasn't married. She couldn't even report him, and he knew it.

Later, when she was dressed and sitting in his office, he confirmed what she already knew. She was pregnant. About three months if his examination was right.

"How many weeks, exactly?" she asked.

"No way to be that precise now. All I can tell you is that you are. Won't your husband be pleased?" he said with a leer. "No? That's what I thought. Well, there are ways, you know, around the situation. I've been known to be very helpful to wealthy young women who are nice to me. All you have to do is come up with the cash."

Nice to him? Glory came to her feet. "You dirty old man. After what you just did I could report you."

"Fine," he said. "Do it. Of course, you're probably already too far along to get rid of it anyway. Who'd believe you? I'm a respected member of the community."

Glory let out a cry of anguish and ran out of the doctor's office, throwing a twenty-dollar bill on the receptionist's desk as she left.

The old lecher. What she had needed to know was how long? It might not have happened with Steven. If she were only two months along, it would be Roger's. If it had happened on that Sunday with Steven, then she didn't know. She'd never know. But then, neither would Steven.

And suddenly she was calm.

Steven wouldn't know.

She was pregnant and he'd made love to her. Steven would have to marry her. She was pregnant with his child. Nobody could keep them apart now. All she had to do was tell him.

But telling him wasn't going to be easy. She knew that her mother wouldn't tell her how to reach Steven. She tried to call the law firm where he'd interned, but he'd been sent to a special school for training. No, they weren't allowed to give out phone numbers. They referred Glory to Steven's fiancée. Glory didn't call. She wrote a letter, in care of the firm, telling Steven it was urgent that she talk to him immediately.

Steven's future father-in-law intercepted the letter and destroyed it.

In the meantime, Roger came up to Athens and they went to their first college football game together. She pretended that she was still wildly in love with him. For another two weeks of school, and Roger's lovemaking, she waited.

Steven didn't answer. Her second letter told him that it was a matter of life and death. When another two weeks passed, she began to panic. She was beginning to show. Her clothes didn't fit. She couldn't understand why Roger didn't notice. Finally she couldn't wait any longer.

At Thanksgiving, Glory went home. She'd go see Aunt Evelyn and tell her the truth. She would send for Steven and everything would be all right.

"Great news, darling," her own mother said as Glory was unloading her car and bringing her dirty clothes into the house. "Evelyn called today. Steven got married last week. Of course he was engaged, but nobody expected this . . . Are you all right?"

The walls were swaying. Glory crumpled in a heap on the floor at her mother's feet.

When she came to, her mother was wiping her face with a wet cloth. "What's wrong, darling?"

There was no answer except the truth. Glory stared stonily at her mother and said, "I'm pregnant. I'm going to have a baby."

"You can't be," her mother said. "What will people say?"

"They'll say a great deal, I expect."

"How far?"

"Four months."

"Are you sure?"

"I'm sure."

"Too late to get rid of it." Adele Winslow didn't rant and rave. Instead she took Glory's hand. "Roger will have to marry you. It won't stop the gossip when the baby comes, but nobody will dare say anything if you're married."

"But Mother . . ." *it isn't Roger's* she wanted to say. But she didn't. The truth was, she didn't know whose baby she was carrying. The truth was, she'd lost Steven. Nothing mattered anymore.

In a matter of seconds her whole life had changed.

Fourteen

Change was slow in coming for Margie.

One of her suitemates moved out of the Churches Home, leaving vacant a small, windowed tower room only big enough for a bed and chest. But there was a curtain strung across the open doorway that could be pulled closed, and claiming that she needed to study now that school was about to begin, Margie petitioned for and was granted the private room. At last she could separate herself from the others.

Though her life was following the course she'd set, her future was still hazy. She'd hoped for so much, and the truth was, she'd just exchanged one place for another. After one letter to Glory about her new life, she hadn't written another, and Glory hadn't answered. Susan only talked about Sam and that made Margie's loneliness worse. JoEllen had already left the group, and with summer's end, Galilee was no longer a part of Margie's life.

There was no way Margie could translate the energy of the city into words on paper anyhow. Nobody in Galilee would have understood. But Margie felt it, in the air, beneath her feet, and she knew that somewhere out there in the future was fame and success. And sooner or later, she'd find a way to become part of it.

As she moved her things into the new room, an odd memory of Mr. Sims filtered through her mind, of how out of place he'd been in Galilee. She'd certainly learned what it meant to have nothing in common with the people she spent her time with and no way to find the kind of friends she longed for. She wondered if Mr. Sims had found a place for himself.

At fall quarter registration, she stood in long lines, made X's in blocks on perforated cards, and bought her books and supplies. College didn't seem real until then. She'd thought she was finally ready to get on with her life, but it hadn't worked out that way. Again, she had nothing in common with either the women where she worked, or the day students in her classes. Most of them were local girls who still lived at home. They all knew each other and stuck together much as Glory and her group had done.

Margie was the only one who had gone away to school at a downtown college where classes were little more than an extension of high school and where the curriculum was so heavily influenced by local businesses that other than the journalism department, the school paid no attention to the humanities.

Margie had no car. Her clothes were wrong and, worse, she had an inflexible curfew at the Churches home. Having to sign out every morning and sign in every night was like having Mr. Jim wait up for her. The grand plan to change into a new person wasn't working. She was an outsider.

In desperation, she used most of the money she'd saved during her weeks of filing to purchase stylish new clothes. With the rest she went to a beauty shop and had her hair styled in a French twist. She wrote checks for emergency cash on her grandfather's account, knowing the bank back home would honor them. She cut her work hours so she could join the drama club, the newspaper staff, and attend the rush functions given by all three of the local sororities on campus.

In two weeks time, using Glory as her model, she'd out-danced, out-drunk, and out-flirted every girl being considered. She quickly realized that being in demand by the boys translated into being in demand by the girls. After rush week she received bids from all three sororities. She didn't have the money to join, but she'd accomplished her goal: She'd been asked.

From then on, Margie Raines began to make her mark. She was beginning to make her presence known on downtown Ivy Street. And sooner or later she'd find her niche.

*   *   *

For Susan, change came too swiftly. Business school wasn't fun. It was just what it said it was: business. Margie and JoEllen might like living in the city, but Susan felt out of place and lonely. She went to school, back to the boardinghouse, and to bed. Soon her classmates stopped asking her to join them. Susan was lonely. Occasionally she talked to JoEllen, but her schedule seldom matched Susan's and, when it did, Susan found that she had nothing in common with JoEllen's frantic dedication to her career. As for fitting into Glory's new life, Susan might as well have been on another planet.

Some girls had boyfriends back home who came to see them, but Sam never came. There was nothing in Augusta that interested him, and, according to his grandfather, no point in wasting money. So Susan went home on the weekends, as did Sam, and life went on as usual. Sometimes, in the living room, sitting on the couch with Sam, Susan had the feeling that nothing had changed at all. But that was what she'd wanted, wasn't it?

JoEllen's life changed forever the night she took Tom Brooks into her bed. She learned that sex didn't have to come from love, or from lust. With the right teacher it could become a kind of release without emotional commitment.

Assisting Dr. Brooks in his private practice was never easy. One day she was certain that she was doomed to hell, the next, she was sure that she was part of a special calling. She put herself into the shoes of every patient he aborted, and each time she had to wrestle her way through her moral dilemma. But, little by little, she came to understand that she was fulfilling a need that nobody else could. Her only inflexible rule was that every case had either to be one of desperation—resulting from rape or incest—or one that could ruin the life of the woman.

The change occurred slowly and painfully, but little by little she and Tom Brooks became more than criminals, more than saviors. They became friends.

Everything changed for Glory. From the day her mother learned of her pregnancy and arranged the wedding for

145

Glory and Roger, Glory felt as if she had lost control of her life. She never went back to the university. Her mother and her aunt salvaged enough furniture to fill a tiny three-room apartment which Roger insisted was all he could afford. That the Sasser apartment was still more elegantly furnished than any of the other residents' was a fact that Glory accepted readily. After all, she was a Winslow and she'd never known anything but comfort.

The relationship was strained from the beginning. Roger felt pressured into a marriage which, though not unwelcome, was taking place much earlier than he'd planned. He was both infatuated with Glory and dismayed by her selfishness. He was proud, and, at the same time, scared of her way of overwhelming him.

Glory was ill during the entire pregnancy, and they found out quickly that they had little in common except sex. Roger filled his days and most of his evenings with work.

Having Roger gone suited Glory. But she hadn't expected the loneliness. Never before had she had to fill her day. The other wives were either hardworking and dedicated to their husbands' careers or suspicious of the woman who spent her time sunbathing on her patio or going out to the club for lunch. Though Susan and JoEllen were both in Augusta, everything had changed. They weren't high school girls anymore. Glory tried to continue the friendship. She needed the security of maintaining her position as leader of the pack, but they no longer needed it. Each had an agenda and neither seemed interested in anything not connected with their own lives. Glory soon assigned them to the past and forgot their former friendship.

Without focus for her energy, Glory grew more and more restless. Roger was busy, completing his internship as a surgeon. With his schedule of seven days on duty and two days off, she rarely saw him. When she did, he was so exhausted that all he wanted to do was make love and sleep. The lovemaking was still new, and for a while Glory closed her eyes and pretended it was Steven holding her. It wasn't hard to convince Roger that her excitement was genuine.

But the heavier she grew, the more unsettled she became and the more she complained. The one thing Glory had always been able to count on was her beauty. Now her face was swollen, her trim figure disappeared into a huge, round

146

bulk, and her hair hung lifeless and damp on her shoulders. Only the sure knowledge that the child she was carrying belonged to Steven kept her from complete collapse.

Twice a week either Adele or Evelyn Winslow would drive over to Augusta to comfort and care for Glory, cooking several meals, cleaning, and doing the laundry. If the path Glory had chosen hadn't taken her where she wanted to go, her family was willing to make some order in the direction she'd taken.

Glory became a little girl again and submerged herself in their care, fantasizing that the baby would be born and Steven would leave his wife and come to her. Adele Winslow was pleased. Eventually Glory's unhappiness would end. Her son-in-law would soon provide exactly the future Adele had envisioned for her daughter. And she'd be safe.

Away from Winslow and the Winslow influence.

Fifteen

Joining the drama club brought Victoria Lansing into Margie's life. Victoria was a real actress. She'd been the star of every play presented by the University of Georgia in Athens for the five years she'd attended, gaining a reputation that should have guaranteed her a chance at stardom. But that hadn't happened.

Living on coffee and cigarettes for five years had taken a toll on Victoria, and her first step to fame, a stint at the prestigious Scarsdale Playhouse, had ended in a physical breakdown that brought her back home to Atlanta to stay.

The Atlanta Division's funds were allotted to establish insurance and accounting departments, offering just enough general studies for a student to graduate with sufficient credits. A full-time staff position as director of the fledgling drama department was out of the question. Victoria Lansing was a local star, and she worked cheap. When Victoria was hired as the director for the school's first serious play, Margie became her most ardent admirer. She could overlook the fact that Victoria often wore the same dress for two or three days in a row, that it was spotted with coffee stains, that she was a nervous chain-smoker who stuttered during a normal conversation.

With Glory gone, Margie had been without a mentor. Now she didn't need Glory as her inspiration anymore. Victoria was everything Margie wanted to be. A month later Victoria offered to rent Margie half of her two-room apartment for the same amount of money she was paying to live in the Churches Home. Margie didn't even stop to consider her answer; she accepted. She didn't stop to think that the Churches Home also offered three meals a day. Margie was finally on her own—no curfews, no housemothers, and nobody to tell her no or chastise her if she didn't live up to somebody else's expectations.

The week after Margie moved in, Victoria took her to meet Luther at the theatrical studio where Victoria worked, and Margie said goodbye forever to filing invoices. Being paid to paint sets and sew costumes was heaven, and the hours could be adjusted.

When Victoria didn't cast Margie in the college play, Margie put aside her disappointment and built sets and designed costumes with boundless enthusiasm. Luther listened to Margie's dreams when Victoria was too busy, and, like Margie, turned a blind eye to the fact that Margie was doing a good part of Victoria's work at the studio.

When Victoria landed the role of Maggie in *Cat on a Hot Tin Roof* at the local community theater, Margie was content to be the gofer, sitting in the audience and watching her new mentor become the woman who desperately wanted to be loved.

Margie could identify with the character. She remembered Glory's intensity when she had played that same kind of frustrated woman in Mr. Sims's play on the Galilee High School stage. She felt a twinge of guilt for not having written to her friends back home. But Glory had abdicated. Victoria reigned.

The actor who took the role of Brick was Arthur Noland, a solemn soldier stationed at Fort Mac, just outside Atlanta. He was serious and abrupt, staying to himself offstage, spurning the invitations of the cast members to go for coffee after rehearsal. Margie never admitted it to herself, but she fell madly in love with Arthur and became his willing slave. She never thought he'd notice her, until one night he asked her to stay after rehearsal and help him with his lines.

Margie agreed, her heart in her throat that he'd chosen her. But it wasn't her help he wanted, it was her adoration. When he kissed her and told her nobody understood how difficult it was to deal with the emotions that built up on stage, she told herself that she understood. Arthur was nothing like Nick. Arthur was a part of the theater and represented the kind of life that Margie wanted desperately. When he wanted more than her kisses, she tried to say no,

149

but Arthur didn't listen. They were alone in the theater, and he was masterful.

When he told her how she was driving him crazy, how much he wanted—no, needed her—she let herself believe it. There was something wild about him, like Glory when she'd talked about her mother and her lover—something that Margie recognized and responded to. When Arthur took off her clothes on the stage, amid the smell of greasepaint and canvas, she told herself that this was the life experience on which real actors drew, that Arthur was what she'd been waiting for—a lover who shared her dreams.

If she couldn't share the stage, she'd be the inspiration for the man who was destined for greatness. He was dramatic, masterful, and quick. Afterward, he dressed and abruptly walked away, turning off the stage lights almost before Margie was dressed. The next day his wife came to rehearsal, and Margie knew that Arthur was just another soldier.

Teddy didn't understand JoEllen's sudden coldness. He'd never really understood her ambition, and now, being a senior, he didn't have much time to wonder. With football practice in the afternoons and helping his brother in the garage, his plate was full.

When the mayor offered him a job driving his Cadillac for his wife and running errands, he quickly accepted. It was early October before he had time to drive over to Augusta to confront JoEllen. He dropped the mayor's wife off on Broad Street for some shopping and headed for the hospital. JoEllen had to be impressed with the car. He'd take her for a drive.

But she didn't even see the car.

By then JoEllen was a patient in her own hospital, pale and shaken, and he didn't know why. A nurse took him aside and talked to him before he was allowed to go in.

"She's just had surgery, a perforated ulcer," the nurse explained. "She lost a lot of blood. We almost lost her. She doesn't want to see you."

"Doesn't want to see me? But she's my girl. I've got to see her."

"All right, but just for a short time."

White-faced and worried, Teddy entered the hospital

room and sat in a chair beside JoEllen's bed.

"Are you all right?"

"I'm very tired, Teddy. That's all."

"I drove up in the mayor's car. I planned to take you for a drive."

"The mayor's car?"

"Yes, I'm driving for him now, saving up for my own car. I'm getting a Chevy two-door hardtop."

"That's nice. How's school?"

Teddy carried on small talk for a while, but he could tell that JoEllen was only going through the motions. She was tired, but more than that, she'd changed. Teddy had always known that JoEllen was older, but now he felt as if he was still the child and she an adult. Their paths had separated.

"What's wrong, JoEllen?" he finally asked. "Is there someone else?"

At that moment Dr. Brooks entered the room and JoEllen looked up at the man with obvious relief in her eyes. She gave the doctor a look of gratitude.

"Tom," she said, and held out her hand. "Teddy, this is— my doctor, Dr. Thomas Brooks."

Even Teddy didn't miss the bond that existed between them. After a moment, Tom leaned down and kissed her on the forehead.

"JoEllen, darling, are you feeling better?"

"Yes, thank you. I'd like you to meet an old high school friend of mine, Theodore Wallace."

"Ted," Teddy corrected as he stood. "Pleased to meet you, sir. Are you JoEllen's doctor?"

"Well, yes, that, too. I'm afraid that she's not up to having visitors for too long at a time. She needs her rest."

Before Teddy knew what was happening, he was being ushered to the door. Before he left, he glanced back. Tom Brooks was holding JoEllen's hand. JoEllen gave Tom an intimate look that answered Teddy's unasked question.

"Was he the one?" Tom Brooks asked as the door closed.

"Yes."

"He's too young for you."

"I know." There was a sadness about her flat reponse that said she understood and she regretted that understanding.

Teddy drove the big black car back downtown. He knew then that he wouldn't be back again.

151

But he'd learned something. He'd learned that whether or not he ever intended to leave Galilee, he'd do well to expand his horizons. If he were going to live with JoEllen, ever, he'd have to learn about her world. He'd back off for now, but JoEllen was his girl, and one day he'd claim her again. Teddy might not be smart, but he understood JoEllen better than she knew, and once he made his decision he never changed his mind.

After that, Teddy spent all his free time observing how the mayor handled his contacts with the business world and dealt with the employees of his road construction firm.

The mayor's wife was very willing to teach him how to be worldly and Teddy never stinted in paying for her tutoring. He figured that sex was a fair exchange for sophistication. They were both pleased with their bargain. Teddy might never have an occasion to need his newfound worldliness, but if he did, he was ready. He might never wear a Brooks Brothers suit, but he knew how to buy one and how to wear it. And before he was done, he'd know what to say when he put it on.

His mechanical ability at the garage was more immediately valuable, and by graduation time, Teddy was not the same boy who'd made crude jokes a year ago about naming his son Dick Tracy.

In June, Margie's mother died and Margie went home for the funeral. In her first year of college she'd failed French and Algebra. Her grandfather, though disappointed, sent her back with his promise to help her if she needed him. By this time, Margie had fallen in love with writing and decided to concentrate on journalism and political science. If she couldn't be an actress, she'd be a reporter.

The next time Margie fell in love it was with Richard, a science-fiction addict who listened to jazz and understood the deep secrets of the universe.

Sixteen

Glory's baby was born in April of 1955, exactly nine months after the Fourth of July celebration during the summer of the soldiers.

The baby was long and thin, with dark hair and eyes.

Like Steven.

Glory knew immediately, and she was glad. She'd had Steven's child and he was all right. Roger thought he had a son. The dark hair and eyes could have come from Glory's father. Glory wondered if her mother might have guessed the truth, but if she did, she never said anything. Her mother never mentioned Steven at all. And neither did Glory.

Glory named her son Damon, because she liked the name and because she knew no one who shared that name. Damon was her child, a part of herself and Steven. She'd love him the way she loved his father.

Damon soon became the focus of her world. She liked the way his great dark eyes watched her. She liked the way his mouth felt on her nipples, hurting her with his tugging and demands. She kissed him, touched him, bathed him. At eight weeks his eyes seemed to deepen when she spoke, as if he shared her secret and knew that they were very special to each other.

Glory made certain that Steven knew about the baby, but he didn't come to her. She began to doubt that he'd gotten her announcement until she received the gift with a card signed *Elizabeth and Steven*. The handwriting was Steven's.

Roger didn't understand her obsession with the baby. He hadn't expected it. They'd only been married four months when Damon was born and Roger was still in love with his green-eyed wife. But once the child came, Glory seemed to have lost all desire for her husband.

"Don't worry," his cohorts advised smugly. "Women get that way with a baby. It'll pass."

But it didn't.

June came and Roger announced his plans. "We're moving to Savannah in September, Glory. I've accepted a staff position with Family Practice."

"Savannah? You decided on a job in Savannah without even talking to me? I wanted to go to Atlanta."

"I'm sorry, Glory, but it's Savannah. I think you'll like it there, and the opportunity for me to have both a private practice and share hospital surgical duties will be just what I've worked for."

"Well, it isn't what I worked for, Roger. I want to go to the theater, to the symphony, to be where the excitement is. Savannah is still a backwater town. I won't go!"

"Yes you will, Glory. You're my wife," he snapped in a rare show of temper. "Now get dressed, we're going out to celebrate."

Roger hadn't made love to Glory in nearly three months. He'd expected her to be pleased with a future even more prestigious than he'd dared hope for. He'd looked forward to tonight for three days. For the last week he'd walked around semihard. Simply examining a female patient threatened to cause the one thing a doctor was never allowed—a full erection.

He'd resorted to cold showers, jacking off. Once he'd even found a willing nurse and made use of Nick Zambino's old supply room on the therapy ward.

Roger had become addicted to Glory and he'd tried everything to reach her: flowers, candy, a sexy new nightgown. Finally, this afternoon he'd asked a student nurse to babysit so he could take Glory out to one of the expensive restaurants she liked so much.

"You did what?" Glory whirled around, the swirl of her skirt revealing the top of her stockings and stirring Roger's already heated desire.

"I'm taking you out to dinner to celebrate the beginning of our new life. It's the Bellaire for us tonight, Mrs. Sasser, and a room in the hotel afterward. Just me and my beautiful wife."

154

"You expect me to leave the baby alone?"

"Not alone, darling. Marcia is a nurse. She's assigned to the baby ward. She can take care of Damon. If anything happens she can get in touch with us."

"I don't believe you." Glory's face was white. Her eyes widened in disbelief. For a moment Roger thought she was about to slap him.

"Believe me, darling," he said, his voice softening. "You're my wife. I know that Damon is our son and he needs you. But I need you, too."

"Damon is my life," she said with an earnestness that belied contradiction. "There is nothing in the world more important than my son."

"Don't I mean anything to you, Glory?"

"I don't know, Roger. I really don't know anymore. Everything has changed." Her voice trailed off and she walked dramatically across the room and pulled open the drapes, staring out into the summer night. She let out a little-girl sob and realized that her answer was an honest one.

When Roger took her in his arms, she resisted. But this time he didn't back off but jerked her forward and forced her arms around his neck. He pulled her against him, grinding his body into her, allowing her to feel his erection as he took her lips savagely.

When he finally pulled away, he said in a voice that dared her to disagree. "No more, Glory. You're my wife and I intend to make love to you. I can do it forcefully, right here in the middle of the floor with the babysitter in the other room, or we can do it in a romantic way with dinner and a fancy hotel. Either way, it's going to happen."

Glory leaned her head against his chest and thought about what he'd said. She believed him and she noted the reaction of her body as it responded to his touch. At that moment she knew that she was going to let him love her. She was a Winslow woman and she knew what was expected of her. But she'd never give him the pleasure of her enjoyment. She'd do it on her terms, in her own time.

Glory began to cry. The tears that came were tears of relief and defeat, and finally tears of triumph. She couldn't have cried in front of her mother or her friends, but Roger didn't matter, so she could unburden herself to him. She and Roger were like ships passing in the night. She could take what she needed from him without diminishing herself.

Tonight Roger wanted her, and Glory needed to be wanted.

They left Damon with the nurse and went out to dinner. Afterward, they made love for most of the night. When Roger left for the hospital the next morning, Glory packed her clothes and the baby's things and went home to Winslow.

"I'm leaving Roger," she announced to her shocked mother. "I don't love him. I never did."

"That doesn't matter," her mother said matter-of-factly. "You're his wife and you're going to stay his wife."

Glory looked at her mother in amazement. "What?"

"I mean, my darling girl, that I have no intention of having you live the kind of life I've had to live. Do you know what it means to lose the man you love and have to get up and go to some lousy job day after day, to long for a real life and see it become dimmer and dimmer with each passing year?"

"But, Mother—"

"No, of course you don't. You've been raised to expect the best and to get it. Well, let me tell you, Glory, it doesn't always happen. Your grandfather controls the Winslow money, dribbling it out, like Scrooge. I have enough to support myself but not you and your child. Just how do you plan to make a living without Roger?"

"I'll get a job."

"Where?"

"I don't know. Here. Augusta, Atlanta. Somewhere."

"Doing what?"

"I'm not sure, but I'll find something."

"And what will you do with Damon?"

"I'll find a sitter."

"And how will you pay for it? I know, you'll manage. But it will take another man to do it for you, and what makes you think you won't get an even worse one the next time? Or that you can get a man at all, Glory? Men don't like women with children. I know."

Glory hoped her surprise didn't show. This was a conversation between two women, not between mother and her child. She didn't want this. She wanted her mother to take her in her arms and say everything would be all right. She wanted to go back and do it all over again. She wanted Steven.

156

"I don't need a man," she protested.

"Oh yes you do. You don't fool me. You never did. You're just like me, Glory. You fell in love with a man you can never have and you learned what love is. You can't do without a man. If you come back here, what do you think your prospects will be?"

"I don't know. I haven't thought about it. But I have a good mind. I can get along without a man."

"The world won't let you. I know. And there are no good men available. The nice ones are married. The rest have something wrong with them, and the men you end up with are never what you want. You just keep on hoping. Sooner or later you find out there are no Prince Charmings out there and you take what you can get. It's better to have a husband, even if you don't love him. It might even be better if you don't. Then you don't feel guilty."

"You make it sound like there is nothing else to life except sex. I don't believe that."

"Believe it, darling. After all, isn't that what got you into all this?"

And Glory began to understand.

Her mother knew the truth. She was right. Everything came down to sex. Those who had it and those who wanted it and those who knew how to use it to get them what they wanted. Yet nobody talked about it. Nobody acknowledged its secret power.

What Glory wanted was Steven. And the world wouldn't let that happen. Just having his son wasn't enough. There had to be a way to have more. Maybe she'd found it. Roger was her husband. She didn't love him, but when she considered what she might have chosen, he wasn't bad.

Glory turned around and drove her convertible back to Augusta. When Roger came home that night, Glory welcomed him with open arms. She could play the game as long as she made the rules. She didn't have to enjoy it.

157

Seventeen

In June, Susan finished her business course and started work in the Bank of Galilee. She liked the old building with its oiled plank floor, the swishing sound of the blades of the ceiling fans over her head, and the brass railing around the teller's cage that had to be polished once a week. Every payday she dutifully deposited her check in the account that would pay for the house she and Sam would build when they got married.

Once, she got a note from her father. He was getting married again, for the third time, and moving to Denver. She looked at the scrawling handwriting on the letter and didn't even recognize it. She didn't answer.

On July 24, 1955, Sam's grandfather died, and Sam learned that the farm had been left to him. The money had been divided between Glory and Steven, and his grandfather's insurance policy went to Sam's father who used it as a one-way ticket out of town.

The funeral was the largest the Winslow Baptist Church had ever seen. The mourners came back to the house from the cemetery and lingered long enough to be respectful—everyone except Glory and Steven, who, at the last minute, didn't come. Everyone commented on how strange it was that they didn't show respect for their grandfather, but Susan thought about her father in Denver and forgave them.

After the mourners had gone, Sam and Susan sat at the kitchen table in the farmhouse and drank from icy bottles of Coca-Cola.

"I've decided not to go back to school, Susan."

Susan leaned forward and took Sam's hand. "Your grandfather wouldn't have wanted you to drop out."

"I know, but he left the farm to me, and I have to look after it. My daddy isn't interested in the farm, or me." His voice trailed off, so Susan barely heard the end of the sentence. He was hurting so bad. Losing his mother when he was a baby and his grandmother when he was only ten, his grandfather had been the driving force in his life. Now that force was gone, and Susan couldn't think what to say.

And then she knew.

"We'll get married now, Sam. And I'll help you."

He looked up, the confusion fading from his face as her words registered. "Now?"

"Well, as soon as we can arrange the wedding. You'll finish fall quarter while I make my dress. The wedding has been planned for years. All I have to do is contact everybody and make the arrangements."

"Yes. That will work out. And we'll live here in Granddaddy's house."

"But what about our plan to build our own little house next door?" Susan looked around the kitchen with its old-fashioned gas stove and refrigerator. There was no shower in the bathroom, no washing machine, no rugs on the floor. Sam's grandmother had been dead for years and Granddaddy Winslow hadn't seen the need to do anything to the house. The part that was seen by the outside world was judged to be grand, but inside, it was just old.

But Sam wasn't listening. He was staring across the fields, shoulder-high in early corn. "We don't need to do that now, Susan. This is mine. Ours."

Susan walked over and stood beside him. What did it matter where they lived as long as they were together? They would live here forever. Sam would never send his children away because his wife was short and stout and didn't fit into his lifestyle anymore. There'd be no marrying a new young wife and moving to Denver.

Sam would always be here. At last they were about to be together as husband and wife. Her mind was whirling with plans. She'd call JoEllen and Margie; they'd have to arrange time off from work. Glory had had her baby so she wouldn't be a pregnant bridesmaid. Susan's heart sang. She pictured

159

the bridesmaids' dresses and how her friends would look walking down the aisle. She'd make their dresses, too. Her wedding—her wedding to Sam. She'd be the first one to have a real wedding. Glory's didn't count because nobody was there to see it.

And then she realized that tears were filling Sam's eyes. Sam Winslow was silently crying.

"Oh, Sam darling. Don't worry. Everything will be fine. It's just what we always planned. We're only moving the schedule up a bit."

Sam continued to look out the window. Susan was right. Everything was happening just as they'd always planned. But he hadn't planned on it happening so soon. He was only twenty and he was scared.

Susan burrowed against his shoulder, pulling his arm around her. "Sam, Sam, please, don't. Sam?" In the fading twilight she pulled his face down for a gentle kiss. Wiping the moisture away from his eyes, she kissed his lips, his chin, his neck.

Then, with slow, deliberate motions, she began to unbutton his shirt.

"What are you doing, Susan?"

"You always said that I was going to be your wife. You respected me. You wouldn't soil me. Well, Sam, the time has come to stop waiting. I'm giving myself to you, here, now, forever."

She unknotted his tie and pulled it off, unbuttoned his waistband and unzipped his pants, boldly sliding her hand inside. Sam gasped and caught her shoulders as if he were about to shake her. She hadn't expected him to tremble beneath her touch.

"Susan, this isn't a good idea," he gasped. "I'm not prepared."

"What do you have to do to get prepared, Sam?" With her free hand she pried his fingers from her shoulder and placed them on her breasts. "Don't you want to touch me, Sam? I want you to touch me."

Sam was breathing hard and moving against her hand. He let go of her breasts and pushed her against the table, pulling her skirt up as he leaned against her.

"Sam! What are you doing?"

But he didn't hear her. He didn't see her. His eyes were closed, pain etched across his face as he pressed himself against her. But there were barriers. Her panties kept him from penetrating, though he didn't seem to notice. Susan stopped struggling. She'd never seen Sam like this, hurting, losing control. But she loved him, and if this was what he needed, she'd not refuse him.

And then he groaned and twisted away.

"Oh, Susan, God, I'm sorry. I should never have touched you. That was wrong. I didn't mean to do it."

Susan pulled her dress down and stood up, more uncertain than ever of what her response should be. "I'm sorry, Sam. I wanted to be with you, to let you . . ."

"I did, Susan. Do you understand, I did, all over you? Here, in Granddaddy's house."

"It's your house now, Sam, and it will soon be mine. There's nothing wrong with two people loving each other. Your grandfather wouldn't mind."

"You don't understand, Susan. Granddaddy would kill me if he knew. Go home and clean yourself. I'll see you tomorrow."

But he didn't see her the next day. He called. "I'm going back to school. Daddy will stay here until I finish fall quarter. Plan the wedding, Susan. Whatever you want."

"But when will I see you, Sam. I don't understand."

"In two weeks—just like always."

Like always. That wasn't what she wanted. She wanted to rail out at Sam. But she didn't. She would be his wife before Christmas. Then things would change. Mrs. Sam Winslow. The very thought made her shiver.

That and the fact that she was touching herself.

Margie was first on Susan's list. A man answered her phone.

"Who's the sexy voice?" Susan asked her.

"Sexy voice? Leonard?" Margie studied Leonard as he went back to his sketching. "He's the man I work for." She never thought about Leonard as being sexy, though his Russian accent did make him interesting.

"Sounds like he's straight out of an Ingrid Bergman

161

movie. Does he look as good as he sounds?"

"I don't know, I never thought about it." But he did, Margie admitted to herself as she listened to Susan's invitation to be in her wedding.

"I don't know, Susan," Margie said. "I'm not sure I can afford to buy a bridesmaid dress. I mean, I don't make much money and school is pretty expensive."

"Don't worry, I'm going to make the dresses myself. I have plenty of time. All I'll need are your measurements."

Next Susan called JoEllen, who sounded very distant, agreeing to take part in the wedding but without the excitement Susan had expected.

Glory was the only one who seemed enthusiastic. She apologized for missing the funeral, "but Damon was sick and I was afraid to bring him. Besides, Granddaddy would probably have risen from the coffin and told me I was dressed wrong. Did anybody ask about me?"

"Ask about you? Well, yes, everybody wondered where you were, until Adele explained about the baby."

"I suppose, since I'm a Winslow, I'll be expected to be the maid of honor. What color are we wearing?"

Maid of honor? Susan had always thought that one of her own sisters would come, but this made sense and Glory was excited, so she didn't argue. "Green. It will be a Christmas wedding."

"Perfect. Who—who will be Sam's best man?"

"His cousin, Steven, I suppose," Susan answered, remembering the plans they'd made so long ago.

There was a long silence before Glory finally answered. "That's what I thought. Of course I'll be there. I wouldn't miss your wedding for anything, Susan."

In October, Susan got a letter, postmarked Detroit. It was addressed to Miss Susan Miller, General Delivery, Galilee, Georgia.

I thought you'd like to know that I'm in Detroit, working in a restaurant, and I'll be going to night school on the G.I. Bill. Thanks for your kindness at a time I needed to believe.

162

The letter was signed *Joseph Cheatham.*

Susan battled with herself for weeks whether or not to respond to his letter. In September she finally answered.

I'm so happy for you. Sam and I are getting married in December. I'll finally have what I've always wanted, too, a home of my own, and a place to belong.

Your friend, Susan

Eighteen

By the fall of 1955, parents were protesting the influence of Elvis Presley, a singer from Memphis whose hip gyrations on stage were corrupting young people's morals. *Peyton Place* was published and *On the Waterfront* was named outstanding movie of the year. Racial segregation in public schools was officially banned by the Supreme Court and Dr. Jonas Salk invented a vaccine for polio.

Teddy Wallace was working in the garage full-time and driving for the mayor in his off hours. Little by little he was learning how a small-town businessman could be successful in the outside world.

Glory Winslow Sasser moved to Savannah in August, the hottest month of the year. She was nineteen years old, married with a four-month-old baby. But there was no fine house, no prestige, no housekeeper. Her mother was wrong. A Winslow woman wasn't always rewarded for her efforts.

Glory looked around the new apartment, stacked with boxes, and furniture that was sadly worn. What they'd had more than filled their apartment in Augusta and would have been called luxurious compared to the other students' furnishings. Here, it was shabby and embarrassing.

Damon squirmed in her arms and began to cry. He was tired and hot and probably wet. Glory watched Roger and the son of the apartment superintendent bring in the last chair. She sighed. Her husband was a doctor. That should have meant luxury, not this dump. She felt betrayed.

Damon began to cry in earnest.

Roger looked at Glory, waiting for her to direct their placement of the chair.

"I don't care, Roger. Just put the damned thing down and help me find Damon's diapers."

"Thanks, Bill," Roger said, with a frown for Glory. He pulled his wallet from his pants and peeled off two bills that the burly young helper accepted and tucked inside his shorts. He gave Glory a long last look as he left the room.

"Glory, I wish you wouldn't run around half dressed in front of strangers. That kid nearly split his eyeballs looking at you."

Glory looked down at the halter and shorts she was wearing and back at Roger. "Balls? Yes. Eyes? No, I don't think that was what he was worrying about. Besides, it's hot, Roger. The temperature must be ninety degrees in this sweat box. Turn on the fan."

"There is no fan."

She could only stare in disbelief.

"Then you can just be prepared for me to go without any clothes at all." Glory gave a tug to the tie behind her neck and let the handkerchief halter fall forward. Another tug and the garment floated to the floor, exposing her bare, milk-filled breasts. In another minute her shorts followed, leaving her wearing only her lace panties.

"Glory!"

Roger's eyes revealed her mistake. He started toward her. Damon began to scream and nuzzle her breast angrily.

"Don't you dare touch me, Roger Sasser. You find those diapers and start putting this stuff away. I may have to live in this dump for now, but I won't do it for long."

"Don't touch you? Of course not. You're either too sore, too tired, or too sleepy for me to touch you, unless you decide to give me a reward. Well, you can find the diapers yourself, Mrs. Sasser," Roger shot back. "I have to get to the hospital to check in with Dr. Fincher. At least *he* needs my services."

Roger looked around until he spotted the box marked "Roger's Junk" and dug inside. A moment later he'd pulled out a pair of trousers and a wrinkled but clean shirt. Glory was left standing in the middle of the floor listening to the sound of the shower running and Damon squalling.

She sank to the floor, tears rolling down her face. She didn't want to be here. She'd dreamed of a life with Steven, an exciting life of travel and the theater and— But she'd lost that. Instead of living in a sorority house and being a college student, she was in a hot, sticky apartment in Savannah, Georgia.

"Oh, Steven, it wasn't supposed to be like this."

Damon hushed momentarily, focusing his huge, dark eyes on his mother's face in a kind of awe. He made a sound and touched her bare breast with his tiny fist.

Glory looked down at her son, her beautiful son, the child who would never know his father. She kissed him on his forehead and felt him claim her breast again. No matter how bad things were, Glory could always gain some kind of peace when she held Damon. For a moment she closed her eyes and pretended that it was Steven sucking, Steven with his mouth on her, Steven here in this awful hot place.

Then Roger moved back through the room, pausing briefly to plant a kiss on her cheek.

"I'll try not to be gone long, Glory. And I'll pick up a fan on the way back. It won't be so bad, I promise."

"You'd better pick up some food, too. I have no intention of making this hellhole any hotter than it already is."

"I'm truly sorry, darling," he said softly. "We won't have to stay here long. Just until I get a couple of checks so we'll have enough rent money for something nicer."

"If you'd let us use Grandfather's money—"

"I said no, Glory. That money will belong to Damon. I'll take care of my wife and family. Until I can provide better, this is where we'll live."

The door slammed.

The heat shimmered in the stillness.

Damon, tired and fussy, was half sleep in Glory's arms. She reached behind her, pulled the cushion from the couch and laid him on it, then struggled to her feet. With the other cushions she walled off an area where he could be contained without touching the floor. She wished she had Sallie, their old maid. She wished she had her mother. She wished she had Margie and Susan. She wished last summer had never been.

Thirty minutes later she'd been through two cartons and still hadn't found the diapers. What had been a jumble of boxes was now a hodgepodge of clothing. If Glory had a telephone, she'd have called her mother to come and get her. If Roger hadn't driven her car, she'd have packed up and left.

Finally, in self-defense she'd pinned a towel on Damon's bottom and turned to survey the mess she'd made. It wasn't fair. A Winslow woman was supposed to have wealth, position, and servants. She didn't know how to cope with all this. She shouldn't be expected to.

The doorbell rang. Without a thought for her nudity, Glory strode across the room, stumbling over the mess, and flung the door open. Bill, the high school kid, was standing there. His mouth fell open and his Adam's apple quivered like a turkey about to let out a gobble.

"I—I saw Dr. Sasser leave and I came back to see if you might need my help."

"You're just what I need, Bill. Come in."

Glory jerked the startled boy inside and slammed the door. "Do you think you can help me put all this stuff away."

"Uh, yes. I guess so." But he couldn't move. He couldn't pry his gaze away from Glory's full breasts and from the sight of her pubic hair peeking through the lace of her underwear.

"Oh, I'm sorry. I forgot I wasn't dressed. It's so hot in here. I was only trying to get cool."

She was too late. Bill was already hard. His skimpy shorts were pulled tight against his erection. Glory, who could barely tolerate her husband's touch, connected with the boy's desire and felt her body respond. Maybe it was thinking of Steven. Maybe it was punishment for Roger. Whatever the reason, Glory's reaction surprised even her. She'd thought she'd never want to have sex again.

"It *is* hot." His voice was gravely. "I'm sorry, but you—you're so beautiful. I've never seen—" He blushed. "I'm sorry, Mrs. Sasser. I didn't mean."

She took a step closer. "You've never seen a woman's breasts when she was nursing her baby?"

"No, ma'am."

Glory ran her fingertips underneath her rib cage, touching herself lightly. "They're very tight, and full." Her eyes dropped to the front of his shorts. "Just like you."

"Oh, gosh. I mean, I'm sorry." He tried to cover himself with his hands. "I keep saying that, don't I? I'll be glad to help you put this stuff away." He started to turn away.

167

"I can't pay you."

"That doesn't matter. I mean, I wouldn't charge you."

"That wouldn't be right, would it? Maybe we can think of something." She walked across the floor and came to a stop and turned. "Do you think we can put up the bed first."

Bill didn't answer. He tried to cover himself as he started toward the bedroom. Between the two of them they erected the frame, and placed the mattress and springs on the slats. The dressing table was rolled into place, along with the only other piece of furniture—a battered chest that would hold Roger's clothes.

Glory mopped her face with one of Roger's T-shirts. A bead of perspiration rolled down her cheek, fell into the vee between her breasts and puddled in the waistband of her panties.

"I ought to put on some clothes," she said. "I'm tormenting you."

"Oh, don't worry about it." He cleared his throat. "I'll manage."

"You're a fine boy, Bill. No, that's wrong. You're a *man*, not a kid."

"Yes, ma'am." Bill gave up all pretense of being busy and stared openly at her breasts. There was a bubble of milk beneath one nipple.

"Have you ever touched a woman, Bill?"

"No, ma'am. I mean, well, I've touched Sherry's— She's my girlfriend. But that's all. I mean she's not built like you. Nobody's built like you." He was breathing so hard that he could hardly speak.

"Just a minute, Bill. You just stand there."

Glory left the bedroom. Damon was asleep now in his makeshift crib. There was the beginning of an open path across the living-room floor. And the late-afternoon heat was beginning to let up. There was still a lot to do and she knew that no matter what Roger's intentions, she wouldn't see him until much later. He'd get involved in the hospital and forget all about her.

Roger wouldn't expect her to have the apartment in order when he returned. He'd already learned that being a housewife wasn't her talent. This time she'd surprise him. If she had to live in this place, she'd do it on her own terms . . . and she'd punish him in her own way. Glory stepped out of her panties and padded back to the bedroom.

"Bill, would you like to touch a real woman?"

He was more than she'd expected. Young and eager, yet ready to follow instructions. The first time was quick and rough. Once he'd climaxed she started him over again. The second time, when he lowered himself over her, she was ready. When she felt her own shuddering release, she smiled. Roger would never know the reality of her passion. This was private. He had no idea of the lust she was capable of feeling. He didn't arouse it and he would never be the recipient of it. But she knew it was there and that she could give it whenever she chose.

Bill would be handy to have around. He was built like a stocky young bull, and he'd always be ready. Yes, for now, this arrangement would work out very nicely. What she hadn't counted on was the boy's guilt. When he finally fell back on the unmade bed, he was very quiet.

"What's wrong, Bill?"

"Oh, Mrs. Sasser. I'm sorry. I—I mean, we shouldn't have done that."

"Why not?"

"Well, you're a married woman."

"You mean you could have fucked me if I were single?"

"Well, maybe. No, of course not. I mean, it's disrespectful. It's wrong."

Glory rolled over and leaned over him, allowing her nipples to graze his chest. "Are you a Boy Scout, Bill?"

"Yes, ma'am." He squirmed, trying to arrange his body so his new erection wouldn't be obvious.

"And aren't Boy Scouts supposed to offer aid and assistance to women in distress?"

"Yes."

"Well, you just did. I was in great distress and you came to my aid. I'm simply saying thank you in the best way I know."

"But—but—"

Glory kissed him, smothering his concern.

He never mentioned regret again.

When Roger returned, the apartment was tidy. The clothes were put away and the kitchen things had been

169

arranged. Glory had showered and was wearing a loose, cool-looking shift. The fan Roger brought would do temporarily, but one of those new room window air-conditioning units would have to be their first purchase.

"I'll be the junior man on the staff. There will be four of us, plus the interns and residents. Dr. Fincher is the chief. We all share in the private practice, according to our seniority, and we are responsible for overseeing the residents and interns on the staff. As the junior man I'll catch all the bad shifts and cases."

"Of course," Glory agreed. She would see little of him. That was one part of his job she could deal with. Leaning back against the front of the couch, she watched him as he talked. There was a fire in his eyes. Whatever else Roger was, he loved his work. Roger was a good doctor, and for that, Glory was proud.

Glory wished she loved him. She should. He cared about her. He was her husband. Sooner or later, he'd give her the kind of life she was brought up to expect. But there was nothing else for her—not even desire. For most of the afternoon she'd made passionate love to a stranger. But there was nothing there for her husband.

Glory listened halfheartedly. The second thing she intended to buy was a television set. She was missing the Miss America contest. They ate sandwiches on the floor and Roger told her more about his new job. All she could think about was that this was the year she would have been Miss Pine Tree Festival. And after that, her dramatic reading would cinch the title of Miss Georgia in 1956.

"Glory?" Roger's voice had trailed off and she realized that she hadn't been listening to him. "I know hearing about my work is boring. I don't think I told you, but the place looks nice. You must be exhausted."

"I am."

"Let's go to bed."

"You go on. I have to feed the baby."

She picked up Damon and unbuttoned her dress, allowing him to grasp her nipple. For a moment Roger stood and watched, then turned to the bedroom. Glory heard the shower running and the bed creak as Roger sat on it. When she'd delayed as long as she could, she put the baby in his crib right outside the bedroom door. Inside, Roger was snoring

170

quietly, just as she planned.

When she slid into the bed he came awake and turned to her, just as *he'd* planned.

"Glory, it's been so long. I want you. You're my wife."

"Yes," she managed to say. When he moved over her and plunged inside, she winced and held herself stiff.

"Relax! Good heavens, you're as tight as a tick. I can't even get inside you." He rolled off and opened the night-table drawer.

Glory knew that he was getting the Vaseline and a rubber. Roger wasn't even that big, but except for that first day at the lake, when she'd come to him from Steven's bed, she'd never been wet and ready for him. Now he'd be greasy and when he was done she'd have to take a shower.

"Ah, that's better."

For a moment, Glory let herself respond, willed herself to respond, planted her legs around him in response. But it was all a lie. All her action did was make him finish sooner. But he didn't know that.

"I hope you used a rubber, Roger."

"Yes. I did." He was very tired.

"You'd better have. The last thing I want is to be pregnant again." She loved Damon fiercely, but he was the only child she ever intended to have. She might have to be married to a man she didn't love, but she didn't intend to be anybody's brood mare. Being pregnant was sick and unpleasant, and having a baby hurt. Her breasts hurt, though tonight she couldn't be sure whether it was from Damon's greedy little mouth, or Bill's.

Bill. Sixteen, sexy, and insatiable. At least Bill was going to make living in this dump bearable.

The next week her period began and she learned that sixteen-year-olds are interested in everything about a woman. Bill was hornier than he was squeamish, and Glory had found a willing slave. Still she knew that she had to be more careful. She didn't want to have Roger's child and she didn't want to have Bill's, either. She preached repeatedly that he had to use a rubber, that no matter how aroused he was, he should never take any chances when making love to his girlfriend.

171

"There is no girlfriend anymore," he swore. "Nobody but you."

"But won't your mother get suspicious when you're here all the time?"

"Don't have one. She ran off when I was a kid."

"What about your father?"

"When he ain't—"

"Isn't."

"Isn't drunk, he's gone, or he's with Mrs. Landry on the fourth floor. They have something going. He doesn't know what I do—or care. So long as I stay out of his way and don't ask for money, he doesn't know I exist."

"I'm sorry, Bill. That must be hard."

"I think I'm a chip off the old block. When the old man gets within ten feet of the widow, he gets that way. Once, I borrowed his super's key and let myself inside the apartment. They were going at it so hot and heavy that they didn't even know I was there."

"And now, you have something going with the lady on the third floor."

"That I do, ma'am. And you're right, it's hard, it's very hard. Want me to show you?"

Nineteen

The move to Savannah quickly brought Glory face-to-face with her first rejection. The Family Medical Practice wives had no intention of welcoming her into their circle. She might have handled it more gracefully, certainly with more efficiency, if it hadn't been for the second revelation: She was pregnant again. It didn't matter whether the baby was Roger's or Bill's. Being pregnant threw her into such a depression that she could barely function. She had to find a way out.

To Roger's surprise, Glory hadn't returned to Winslow for her grandfather's funeral, which made her decision to go home six weeks later a mystery. It took three days of tears before a confused Roger reluctantly approved her plea for a visit home.

When she arrived in Winslow, she left Damon with her mother while she went to Augusta to ask JoEllen for help with her problem.

"I want an abortion, JoEllen, and I knew you must know someone, a doctor who will do it."

Glory's request shocked JoEllen. She'd made certain nobody knew that she worked with Tom Brooks. Now Glory was changing that. This was the first time JoEllen had come face-to-face with making the decision about performing an abortion. Glory didn't fit into any of the categories of patients of whom JoEllen approved. But Glory was a friend. Glory needed help and she'd come to JoEllen.

"You're married, Glory. You weren't raped, and another baby won't ruin your life. If you want an abortion, why don't you get Roger to do it? He's a doctor."

"Roger? He's an old stick in the mud. He'd insist that I have the baby."

"Why don't you?"

"I have a five-month-old and I'm living in a dump. I'm going crazy, JoEllen. I won't be pregnant again. If you don't help me, I'll go out on the street and keep asking until I find someone who will." Glory's voice had been deceptively calm when she started. Now it was shrill and desperate. "I absolutely will not have Roger's child."

"Glory, calm down."

"I will not calm down, JoEllen. I may well start screaming. Will they put me in a straitjacket and lock me away if I scream? At least in an insane aslymn I wouldn't be ignored, would I? They don't let the patients have babies there, do they? Maybe Roger could have me committed."

Glory was shrieking. This was no hare-brained scheme to her. For whatever reason, Glory meant what she said. She'd do something crazy.

"Besides," Glory went on, "I don't have any money. Do you realize how humiliating it is for me to have to ask for something I can't pay for? Roger handles the money and how would I explain? You must know a way, JoEllen. You must!"

JoEllen wasn't certain she could bring herself to admit that she knew from firsthand experience how such things were done, but she couldn't refuse to help Glory. Eventually, as Glory had predicted, JoEllen did just as she'd always done, as she and Susan and Margie had always done. She agreed to Glory's plan.

But it wasn't easy. JoEllen hated to ask Tom to help a friend when she'd refused to consider assisting others in Glory's situation. Not only did it force her to reconsider her own reservations, but it put her even more in his debt.

In the end, with JoEllen assisting, Tom Brooks performed Glory's abortion in his apartment, on the kitchen table.

Glory had herself fitted with a diaphragm and bought a year's supply of rubbers. Roger didn't need to know about the diaphragm, and by using both methods she would never, ever get pregnant again.

She'd learned once again that sex meant power and power

meant control. Returning to Savannah, Glory swore that if she couldn't have the man she wanted, she'd make the one she had into someone so important that nobody would dare turn their back on her. And she'd be just as important.

Damon was six months old when Glory decided she'd been rebuffed by the medical elite long enough. She was a Winslow and her lineage went back as far as that of the women who were looking down at her.

The wives of the other hospital staff doctors dutifully invited her and Roger to their homes, to their clubs, but they disregarded their husbands' request and ignored Glory, just as the practice wives did. New doctors' wives were always examined, put on trial and judged. Glory was too vivid, too dramatic, too sensual. The other wives didn't know why they didn't like her, but it was obvious they didn't. And they were jealous of the ease with which she joined into their husbands' discussions. It never occurred to them that if they'd welcomed her, Glory would never have forced herself where she didn't belong.

"Mrs. Sasser," Dr. Fincher began one evening as he led her to one of the small tables that curved around the country-club dance floor, "the annual hospital fund-raiser takes place in January, just in time to collect all those nice end-of-the-year tax deductions. I hope you're planning to give our ladies a hand."

"Fund-raiser? What do you do?"

"We have a dinner dance for charity. Boring, but everybody attends out of duty."

"Charity I understand." Glory grinned, sliding forward in her chair so she was leaning closer to the silver-haired man who was the senior partner in her husband's firm and the chairman of the hospital board. "It's the boring I can't abide."

She could see his gaze fall to her breasts. They were covered, Roger insisted on that, but the soft jersey dress she was wearing outlined her body seductively. The low-cut bra beneath made her breasts spill over the edge and she knew that the good Dr. Fincher was visualizing what he couldn't actually see.

Dr. Fincher was at least sixty, but nothing about his body reflected his age. With a great mass of silver hair and a physique that was trim and beautifully exhibited by his

175

imported silk suit, he was an impressive figure.

"Well, perhaps you could help the wives find a way to liven up the evening."

"I'm sure I could, Dr. Fincher, if they'd let me and if it doesn't conflict with a wedding I have to be in."

"If they'd let you? I don't understand what you mean."

"I know, and it's so noisy in here that I can't think. Do you suppose we could find a place where we can talk? I'd like to discuss the project with you."

For a moment Lawrence Fincher wasn't sure he was following her. Then, as she moistened her lips and smiled at him, he understood. An eagerness he hadn't felt in years drew him to his feet. He glanced around to see if anyone was watching and was dismayed to see his wife's frown from across the room where she'd been talking to the pharmacist's wife.

"Would you like a fresh drink, Mrs.—Glory?" he asked, feeling his body deflate under his wife's withering gaze.

"I suppose," Glory said. "But that isn't very exciting, is it?"

There was no mistaking her invitation now. There was no holding his reaction back, either. "Meet me on the patio, by the pool, in about ten minutes," he said. "I'll get the drinks."

With a leisurely movement that came as easily as if she'd always done it, Glory moved around the room speaking to everyone, including the silently furious Mrs. Fincher, then made her way to the ladies' room. Ten minutes later, she was in the garden, beneath a tree by the pool.

Lawrence Fincher was less comfortable. He stood in the light spilling out from the clubhouse and peered nervously about. The liquid in one of the glasses he was holding spilled down his trousers and he swore.

She wasn't coming. She'd made a fool of him, this beautiful young woman who was forty years younger than he; she was playing with him. He sighed. It was disappointing. For the last ten years he'd found his sexual desire and his ability to perform disintegrating. He and his wife had ceased sleeping together almost that long ago. The few times he'd had sex since had been quick and without memory. He hadn't even felt real desire.

But now he felt his body throb to life. Damn her! His wife had complained when they'd hired Roger Sasser. Roger's wife was too lush, too outspoken, too alive, she'd said. The

176

wives had decided the first week that Glory would never fit in, and they'd made certain that she knew it.

Roger was a good doctor. And what was even better, he took all the bad hours and difficult cases without complaint. All in all, the staff was pleased with Dr. Sasser, and Dr. Fincher, Chairman of the Board, was delighted. Now he had another reason to be grateful: Roger's wife.

"Dr. Fincher? I'm over here."

She was standing in the shadows beneath a tall moss-hung live oak. Once he stepped into the darkness beneath its limbs, they were both hidden from the eyes of the world. They didn't drink the drinks. She didn't even play games. The moment he drew her into his arms and she felt his erection, she unzipped his trousers, knelt down, and took him into her mouth.

It was incredible. He felt twenty-one again. She never mussed her hair and never wrinkled her dress. In less than five minutes they were done and she was straightening his clothes.

"Why?" he asked.

"Because I need something from you. And I can give you something in return."

"Name your price."

"I want those bitches back there to accept me. I have to live here and raise my son here. I won't be kept out."

"What can I do?"

"That, my dear Dr. Fincher, is your problem. My problem is making you happy. I think that's a mutually acceptable exchange."

"When—when can I see you again?"

"When your wife appoints me to a committee to work on the charity ball. Call me," she said, taking his hand and filling it with her breast for a moment as she slid by. "I'm in the book."

The next week Glory Sasser was appointed to chair a new committee to plan the auction to be held before the dinner. When Dr. Fincher called the next morning, Glory gave him her apartment number and told him where to park his car.

Glory couldn't have taken a sixty-year-old man as a lover if he hadn't been a man of iron. Lawrence Fincher was hard

177

and virile. His silver hair had been that color since his early thirties and his reawakened staying power was more than adequate.

Roger was an earnest lover, easily satisfied and grateful. Bill was vigorous and gave Glory the satisfaction she needed. But Lawrence was a man of patience and experience. Where Glory plunged headlong into satisfying each of her partners, only Lawrence seemed to care little for his own gratification. Almost from the beginning he realized that loving Glory and teaching her how to enjoy their being together was the single most rewarding thing in his life.

When Mrs. Fincher threatened her husband with divorce, he told her quite simply to go ahead. She would then lose her status as wife of the chairman of the board and the enviable lifestyle she enjoyed. He had no intention of giving Glory up, and any attempt on his wife's part to injure Glory in any way would be a serious error.

Mrs. Fincher dropped her threat immediately.

Glory decided that her mother was right. Going back to Winslow was impossible. She could never be Glory Winslow again. She had her son, a husband, and position. And more than ever, sex was the tool she wielded. Marriage was the safety net and the world was hers for the taking. Within a year, Glory intended to be living in a fine new home in the most exclusive section of Savannah. She would have a maid, a nanny, and a gardener who grew dahlias the likes of which nobody had ever seen.

In the first year of her marriage, Glory had taken two lovers. Now she was going home to be a bridesmaid in Susan's wedding. She had skipped her grandfather's funeral because Steven was out of the country and hadn't been able to get back. But Steven would be home for the wedding.

"Teddy, do you think you could take care of a little problem for me?" The mayor propped his wing-tipped cordovan on the edge of the tire rim and watched Teddy as he tightened the lug nuts on the new tire for the Caddy.

"Sure, Mr. Mayor. What do you need?"

"I need you to go fetch Claude. Seems he fell off the wagon and is causing a little disturbance."

Teddy tightened the last nut and leaned back on his heels.

Claude was the mayor's thirty-five-year-old son who'd fallen off more wagons than were owned by farmers in Beaumont County. "Where?"

"Augusta. The Blue Light Club. The manager put him in his office to let him sleep it off. But if he's not gone by morning, he'll call the law. Bring him home, Teddy."

"What makes you think he'll come with me?"

"Because he's out of money and that's the only way he'll get more liquor. I've put out the word to refuse him service."

Teddy came to his feet and wiped a spot of grease from the fender where he'd rested his hand. "You realize, Mayor, I'm only twenty. Are they going to let me in?"

The mayor handed Teddy a role of folded bills. "This ought to get you anywhere you want to go, and out again. Whatever's left is yours."

An hour later Teddy was on his way to Augusta, leaving his brother to close up the garage and the mayor to wait for his call.

Driving the Cadillac was nothing new now and Teddy found himself pressing on the gas pedal more often than usual. He toyed with driving by the hospital first, just to say hello to JoEllen, but he didn't. She'd probably be with that doctor, and even if she wasn't, Teddy didn't know what he'd say to her.

The Blue Light Club wasn't a high-class establishment. Claude must have thought that by slumming he'd run less chance of being recognized. Then again, he probably didn't care. Claude's idea of success was having a bankroll that would choke a horse and buying drinks for everybody in the club.

It was after midnight when Teddy arrived. He knocked on the door and waited for an invitation to enter. Richmond County wasn't dry, but since the club ran a high-stakes game in the back room, just anybody didn't come in. A slot in the door slid open.

"Who're you, kid?"

"Ted Wallace. I've come to pick up Claude Jordan."

"Don't know any Claude Jordan."

Teddy pulled the roll of bills from his pocket, peeled one off the top, and held it out. The door opened into a smoke-filled room. A jukebox was playing "Blue Christmas" while a few couples danced slowly around the floor.

179

"Where is he?"

"In the back room, playing poker. Don't think he's quite ready to go."

Teddy hadn't counted on that. Claude passed out was bad enough, but three sheets in the wind was trouble. He wasn't going to be interested in coming home. Teddy nodded and followed the doorman.

What Teddy found was worse than he'd expected. Claude was down to his last stack of chips and still drunk enough to want to fight.

"Evening, Claude. Your daddy sent me for you."

"And who're you?"

"Ted Wallace. I do some driving for your daddy."

"Fine, you just drive on back and tell Daddy that I'll be home when I'm ready."

Teddy took a few steps into the light, sizing up the men at the table. Strangers. That was good. Intimidating someone he knew would be harder.

"I'll do that Claude, later. Think I'll just watch for a minute, if you fellows don't mind?"

"Hell, do what you want!" Claude threw out a chip. "See you and raise you one."

Two more rounds and only Claude and the dealer were left. Claude, and no more chips.

"I believe it's up to you, Claude," the dealer said.

"I'll see you and call."

"See me? With what? You're all out of money, Claude."

"No problem, my daddy will take care of my I.O.U."

"I don't think so," Teddy observed. "He's put out the word, Claude. You've been cut off. No gambling. No drinking. And no bribes. Guess you're ready to go after all."

Claude turned the table over as he stood and lunged at Teddy. But Teddy was prepared. He hadn't played four years of football, basketball, and baseball to let himself get out of shape in one year. He simply lowered his shoulder and caught Claude in the stomach, folding him neatly over Teddy's shoulder. Before Claude knew what was happening, he was on the backseat of the Cadillac and Teddy was turning up the volume on the country music playing on the radio.

"I'll fix you for this, Teddy," Claude swore. "You'll be sorry you ever laid a hand on me!"

"Let me know if you're going to throw up, Claude. I'll stop the car. Don't want to soil your daddy's upholstery, do we?"

Teddy didn't hear an answer, for Claude had passed out.

"Blue Christmas" played over and over on the trip home, reminding Teddy that he was probably the only boy in Galilee not buying a present for his girl. And this Christmas he had the money to buy something special.

After he'd delivered Claude to the mayor's back door, Teddy walked home. In his room he unfolded the roll of bills the mayor had handed him and counted out three hundred dollars in twenty-dollar bills.

Added to the money he already had, his savings amounted to over a thousand dollars, just enough to make a down payment on the '55 Chevy over at the dealership in Lynville. His first car. And it was practically new. But there was nobody he wanted to take for a ride in it.

The '55 would be his first car, but it wouldn't be his last. And the job for the mayor wouldn't be his last job, either.

Teddy looked after Claude and Mrs. Jordan. He took care of problems for the mayor and ran errands for his business. Teddy was becoming the son the mayor never had, and Claude, sleeping off a hangover, woke up one morning to learn that this time his father hadn't sent Teddy after him.

Teddy and the mayor were in Savannah at the mayor's convention. And Claude hadn't even been invited.

Twenty

JoEllen stood inside the hospital nursery and studied the babies. Most of them were sleeping, but it was time for the four o'clock feeding when the infants would be taken to their mothers. She felt vaguely uncomfortable. The nursery was the duty that most of the student nurses like best. But not JoEllen. There was something about holding a newborn in her arms that disturbed her. They automatically turned their little heads toward her breasts and tried to nuzzle her. Once, in the dark, when she was alone, she'd unbuttoned her uniform and let the little mouth fasten onto her empty nipple. But the baby had quickly let go, disappointed that she had nothing to offer.

Being rejected had hurt and she'd decided that the baby wing was the place she liked least in the hospital. Even before Glory had moved away from Augusta, JoEllen had rejected Glory's plans to spend time with her. There'd been something about watching her with her son that made JoEllen feel guilty. She didn't like that, and she was glad that Glory had moved to Savannah.

She'd never expected Glory to return. She still couldn't believe she'd allowed herself to be drawn into an action that made her more vulnerable. Not only did Thomas Brooks have control over her now, so did Glory. JoEllen still hated the idea of abortion and yet she could not bring herself to leave Dr. Brooks.

Her attachment to him wasn't just friendship, though there was certainly that. It was a bonding of ambition, dreams, and respect. He was doing what he could to help

182

women who needed help at great risk, even as he understood the two-sided coin of JoEllen's secret.

Each case was a battle on JoEllen's part. She was torn. Rationally she understood the medical and emotional need for what the two of them were doing; morally she still had doubts. And with each new patient her guilt grew. It became entwined with her guilt over what she'd done to her own baby, and many times she didn't sleep after they'd performed their little service. Only the relief and gratitude of the women whose lives would be ruined made any of it acceptable.

Tonight JoEllen was unusually depressed. Susan's wedding was tomorrow and she had agreed to be a bridesmaid, providing she didn't have to come for the rehearsal. Returning to Galilee for any reason would be a strain, but a wedding would be even more difficult.

In June, she'd been forced to attend the graduation exercises for the Galilee High School class of 1955. Her mother would never have understood if she'd refused and she wanted to be there for her brother. He deserved her support and congratulations. Teddy had graduated, too. She'd thought that she was prepared to meet him, but she wasn't. After the ceremony, he'd fallen in step between her and her mother as they walked to the car.

"Go for a drive with me, JoEllen," he'd said. "I'd like to talk to you."

"It's late."

"Nonsense," her mother had intervened. "Go with Teddy. Skip will be out all night celebrating. I'll be fine. Enjoy yourself."

JoEllen had been forced to agree, delaying their leaving by looking around at all the students hugging each other, greeting families she'd known all her life, classmates. But there'd been an awkwardness. She didn't belong anymore. Many of the members of her own class already had babies and were beginning to look like housewives and mothers.

Skip walked over to the car and caught JoEllen in his arms. "Thanks for coming. Did Mother tell you the good news?"

"No, what news?" She'd carefully timed her arrival so her bus dropped her off at the intersection just in time for her to walk through Church Square to the high school auditorium. She'd catch a bus back first thing the next morning.

"I'm going into the Navy, Jo."

"Oh, Skip. I'm so glad. You don't know how exciting it's going to be for you." She gave him a hug. It wasn't college, but it *was* an opportunity for him to see the world.

"No job in the shirt factory for me. And look." He held out his hand, palm up.

"What am I supposed to see?"

He grinned broadly. "That's it. Nothing. No hair," he whispered in her ear. "And my eyesight is pretty good, too. Remember what you told me? It was hard, but I took your advice."

She remembered. That weekend, that summer, that part of her life would be with her forever. "Good for you, Skip. I'm proud of you."

Then Teddy took her arm. "See you later, Mrs. Dixon," he said, directing JoEllen to his brother's car which he'd borrowed for the evening, just in case . . . "You okay, JoEllen?"

"Yes. No. I'm just very tired, Teddy. Hospital hours are long. I had to work two shifts straight to get the time to come."

"You must do that often."

"Yes, we're short-handed. Teddy, I'm sorry. I'm not very good company. Do you think you could drive me back to Augusta tonight?"

He'd looked startled, but nodded his agreement, watching while JoEllen explained to her surprised mother what she was doing. Mrs. Dixon had looked from Teddy to JoEllen and back again before she seemed to agree. Teddy didn't know what JoEllen was up to, but he was more than willing to be alone with her. It had been nearly a year since they'd been together. He'd never understood what had happened, or why JoEllen hadn't come back home for a visit.

Until he'd gone to the hospital that night.

"Are you and the doctor still friends?" His question had been casual and reasonable.

"We still work together."

"Oh?"

"He has his own practice now, and he uses Lawton

184

Memorial for his patients. I do some private-duty work for him on the side."

"I see."

Teddy helped her into the car, closed the door, then got in and drove away. He was taller now, and quieter. There was something about him that was comforting. On the way out of town she braced herself for what was sure to come. She'd expected recriminations, questions, accusations. Instead, he talked about life in Galilee.

"You know they're planning to integrate the schools. The parents are working on a way to pull their children out if that happens."

"Oh? Why?"

He frowned at JoEllen. "Do you realize that so many of our people have moved away that the ratio of blacks to whites is three to one. We already have a hard time getting teachers. Remember what happened to Mr. Sims. They're afraid there won't be any learning."

"But that will correct itself in time."

"Maybe, and we'd have a monster ball team. But would you want your children to lose two or three years of learning while the blacks catch up? By that time the standards will be so low that even the whites will end up working in a gas station like me."

Teddy sounded like a parent himself, like an adult member of the community. "So, what are the parents going to do?"

"The mayor and some of the citizens are putting up the money for a private school, with tuition and volunteer teachers."

"Really? Where?"

"The old Winslow High School. It's still in the planning stages, but the whole county will pitch in to rebuild the classrooms and set up a staff. Want to nail some nails for the cause?"

JoEllen laughed. "You must be kidding. I'm just about to start drawing a real paycheck. I can hardly afford to pay off my education; paying for someone else's would be a joke. Are you sure you don't mind driving me back?"

"JoEllen, I don't mind at all."

The car windows were open. The soft night air caught

JoEllen's hair and tousled it wildly. Teddy made no effort to turn the evening personal and JoEllen began to relax. She'd never known Teddy to be so relaxed. The ex-star athlete and acknowledged stud was gone. He was just a nice guy taking someone for a drive.

"How are Susan and Sam?"

"Doing fine. Susan finished her business course. She's working in the bank."

"I know. And Glory's living in Savannah with her surgeon."

"Does anybody ever hear from Margie?"

"I saw her a few months back when she buried her mother. She looked pretty good. She's lost a lot of weight since she left Galilee."

JoEllen gradually relaxed. She had been surprised, for being with Teddy in the past had been exciting, energetic, but never relaxing. He'd finally learned to be still. JoEllen was almost asleep when the car stopped and Teddy spoke.

"JoEllen, I told myself I wouldn't ask, but what happened? I have to know. Was it my fault?"

She'd known that the question would come. It was just as well. They had needed to get it said and behind them. When she was in the hospital she'd sent him away because she couldn't talk about it. He deserved more.

"Your fault? No, Teddy. It wasn't your fault."

"Was it the motel room? I know I was clumsy. I thought I was being so smart, so tough. I didn't know anything about making love to a woman. I was just a kid."

"No, it wasn't the motel room. Not entirely. Though I was, I suppose, more shocked than I knew. But truthfully, Teddy, that wasn't it."

"Then what? What happened? We'd made so many plans. And suddenly they were all gone. I have to know, JoEllen. It's driving me crazy. Was it that doctor?"

JoEllen sat in the darkness thinking. He was right. He had to know. He deserved the truth, but what was the point? What would it accomplish, telling him that she'd aborted a child, his child? What would he think about her? About what she thought of herself, probably. But she couldn't change anything, even if she wanted to. She'd made a choice then, a choice to become a nurse. And that was what she was. Better

186

that she take the blame.

"No, Teddy. It wasn't the doctor, and it wasn't the motel. It was time and reality. We both grew up with one set of values. We thought we'd live the same kind of life as our parents, that's all we knew. We would finish school, get an education, and get married. That was supposed to make our lives work when our parents' lives hadn't. We never considered anything different."

"Why should we have?"

"Because there's a whole world out there, Teddy. I'm only just now discovering that. I still don't know what I'm going to do, but I'll find it."

"What about me, JoEllen. Isn't there room for me?"

She turned and looked at Teddy in the darkness. He'd stopped by the side of the road. For one brief moment she wanted to hurl herself back in his arms and be safe. The past was a framework with which she was familiar. There was a time when Teddy and nursing had been the whole of her dreams for the future. No longer.

She didn't answer.

Teddy finally drove slowly away. He wanted to prolong the trip, for he knew this might be his only time with the woman he would always love. He belonged in Galilee, at the service station with his brother, but JoEllen belonged to another life, another time. He'd blown it that summer, as surely as if she'd known about the women he'd slept with in Texas. They hadn't meant anything to him, but he'd been young and he'd discovered sex. JoEllen had been the last thing on his mind. He hadn't even written to her.

JoEllen had welcomed the silence. Had she ever loved Teddy? Or had he merely represented the security she needed? She had barely thought about him that summer. In her mind she'd said that he'd never walk away like her father had. But he *had* walked away. For the summer. And when he returned, it was too late. What she and Teddy had shared had ended with the season. The summer of the soldiers had changed everything.

Teddy had driven JoEllen back to her dormitory and left the motor running. "I'll be here, JoEllen," he said softly as she was getting out of the car. "If you ever need me, just call."

"I will. Thank you, Teddy." She'd leaned over and kissed

187

him one last time.

Teddy watched her go inside. He felt his eyes fill with moisture as she disappeared from sight. He hadn't meant it to happen, but that summer had changed every part of their lives. He'd made love to JoEllen for the first time and he'd lost her because of it.

A year later Teddy still wished he could relive the summer of '54.

Twenty-One

Glory wasn't returning to Winslow to be in Susan and Sam's wedding. She was returning to see Steven.

And she did, the moment she left the small commuter plane she had flown from Savannah and entered the Augusta airport. Her eyes were drawn to the tall figure like a magnet. He was standing at the car rental counter, his garment bag slung over his shoulder. He'd just finished signing something and the clerk was handing him a key.

"Steven."

She hadn't considered the possibility that their paths would cross before the wedding, though she should have guessed it might happen. Obviously he'd fly into Atlanta from New York and on down to Augusta. Adele had been vague about whether or not Steven was coming, but Glory knew that, as Sam's cousin, he would be expected to serve as a groomsman. Susan had confirmed that when she'd called to discuss Glory's bridesmaid dress.

Leaving Damon behind was hard because Glory wanted Steven to see his son, but she didn't want anything to interfere with their meeting. That Steven and she were in the same place at the same time, seemed a sign that her plan was meant to be.

Glory stopped where she stood and drank in the sight of him. She hadn't seen him in over a year, except when she held Damon in her arms and looked down at the father when she held the child. And yet it was as if they'd never been apart.

Steven turned slowly, as if the force of her gaze called out to him. She saw him frown and take a step forward, then stop. He wasn't going to come to her, but he wanted to. There was no denying the connection between them. It was up to her, just as it had always been.

Glory walked toward him.

"Hello, Steven. Are you going to the wedding?"

"Yes."

"Can you give me a ride?"

"Isn't Adele meeting you?"

"No, I told her I'd rent a car and drive down."

"That's what I'm doing, too."

"I know."

They were saying the proper words, but their eyes and their bodies were speaking a different language.

I still want you, Steven.

I know. I want you, too.

Where?

How?

Glory took the final step that brought her to Steven. She touched his cheek and was rewarded with a ripple of response and a clenched jaw.

"Let's go, Steven. Let's get out of here before I forget to worry about whether or not somebody might be here to see me kiss you."

The rental car was big and black, an automatic with no gear shift to interfere with Steven sliding in behind her and covering her body with his as their lips met.

"Ah, Glory, this isn't a good idea."

"This may be the only good idea I've had in a year," she managed to say as her lips devoured the man she still loved. "Take me somewhere, Steven, or I'll rip off your clothes right here in this parking lot."

Steven sat up and took a long, shuddering breath. "I didn't intend this to happen, Glory. I'm married. You're married. You have a child."

"It doesn't matter. Nothing matters but us. That's why I came. That's why you came. Admit it. For God's sake, admit it, Steven Winslow."

"Yes. You're the reason I came."

"Then find us a place to be together—before I die from wanting you."

The Heart of Dixie Motel Steven took them to was on the outskirts of Augusta. He registered while Glory stood by.

190

For the first time in her life, she watched the man she loved sign the register *Mr. and Mrs. Steven Winslow.*

"That's what I'll always be," she whispered to Steven as he unlocked the room door, "Mrs. Steven Winslow. No matter what my name legally is. No matter how many women you marry, Steven, I'll always be your wife."

Their baggage never left the car that night. Their clothes were wildly discarded as they fell across the bed in a frenzy of desire. It was nearly midnight when they were finally exhausted. Glory lay in Steven's arms, willing her eyes to remain open. She had the rest of her life to sleep. She didn't intend to waste a minute of her time with Steven.

"Why did you marry her?"

"Because it was best, Glory. We could never have been together."

"We could have gone someplace where nobody knew us. We could have lied. We should be together, Steven. Nobody else is like us—like this. Admit it."

"Yes. There is nothing that compares to this, Glory. I love you. I'll always love you. But our families would never have allowed it to work."

"So what do we do with the rest of our lives?"

"First, we have to call and let them know that we're going to be late."

"We aren't going to be late, Steven. We aren't going at all. I've waited for this, and I'm not giving up a minute of it."

But it wasn't easy. When her mother answered the phone, Glory told her she wasn't coming. "What do you mean, you aren't coming? Where are you?"

"I'm at the Heart of Dixie Motel in Augusta, with Steven. And I'm going to stay right here with him, so don't try to stop me."

"What do I tell Roger if he calls?"

"Tell him whatever you like, Mother, I don't care."

"Oh, Glory, I thought that was over."

"It will never be over. I love Steven. I always will."

"But you're married to Roger."

"I'll tell him the truth."

"No you won't, Glory. Steven won't let you. It would ruin his career and he would never allow that to happen."

"You're wrong, Mother."

"No I'm not. You'll see."

191

Steven was less honest when he called his mother. Glory listened as he explained that a crisis at the office was the reason for his absence.

"Why didn't you tell her the truth?"

"I don't think that would be wise, Glory."

"She'll have to know, sooner or later."

Glory caught Steven's expression.

"What's wrong?"

"Glory. No matter what we feel for each other, nobody can ever know. There's my career, my wife. She's expecting a baby. I couldn't leave her now."

Glory slid out of bed and walked toward the bathroom. The heavy scent of lovemaking permeated the air. Her body felt heavy, sated. She felt Steven watching her, just as he had that Sunday morning when he'd announced his wedding and she'd left his bed and walked away.

This time she went into the bathroom and turned on the shower. She didn't know what to say. She felt as if some shield had slid down over her, separating her present from that past summer of her innocence. For Glory, nothing had changed, nothing would ever change.

"Tell me about her, Steven. Tell me about your wife."

"You want to know about Elizabeth?"

"Yes. I need to know about this woman who is more important than me . . . than this, than us."

As she stepped into the shower, Steven followed her. As she washed his smell from her body, he replaced it with his touch. They stood, entwined, the hot cleansing water sloshing over their bodies, and each knew that nothing would take the imprint of the other away.

"She is tall, rather thin, and nice."

"Tall and nice. Is that what she's like?"

"Yes, I think so."

They dried each other with the cheap towels provided by the motel, dried and touched and started the slow melting process all over again.

"You've lived with her, made love to her, given her a child, and all you can say is that she's tall and nice?"

"Tell me about your husband."

"Roger is the salt of the earth, I think. He's kind and caring. He loves me, no matter what terrible thing I do to hurt him."

"And do you hurt him?"

"Constantly. I don't mean to, but I do. I punish him because he's not you." Glory laughed and kissed Steven lightly. "Roger and I made love in a motel room once, but not like this one. I made him find a seedy, ratty little room, with roaches."

Steven narrowed his gaze. "Why?"

"Because I didn't want it to be nice. I wanted it to be dirty and wicked. I never wanted to be with him like I'd been with you. I never have."

"Poor Roger."

"Poor Elizabeth."

"I'm never cruel to her," Steven protested.

"Yes you are. I heard how you described her. Tall and nice? That's cruel. How would you describe me?"

Steven leaned back against the bathroom door and studied her. "You make everything more vivid. You're exotic, exciting, and intoxicating. You're irresistible."

"You see, Steven? That's very different. You'll always be drunk with love for me."

"And me? Describe me, Glory?"

"Oh, that's easy, Steven. I've always known how to describe you. You're my soul."

Steven let out a deep, long breath. "I know. I go for days without thinking about you. But you're always there. You're in my blood. I never touch another woman that I don't want it to be you." He grazed her nipples with his fingertips, then clasped her possessively, pulling her closer.

"Are there many women?"

"Yes."

"Doesn't your wife mind? If you were mine, I'd kill anybody who touched you?"

"I don't think she knows, and if she does, she doesn't say anything. What about you—and Roger?"

"Roger tries, Steven. But he doesn't satisfy me. Nobody really satisfies me, except you. I just get through one day at a time. Except for Damon, my life is one big void. I know now that I can't live the rest of my life that way."

"Damon. I—we got the birth announcement . . ." Steven hesitated. "How old is he now?"

"He was born April 2, 1955." *You know,* she wanted to say. *You sent a blue blanket from Elizabeth and Steven.*

193

"I see."

Glory felt Steven's heart beat steady and strong beneath her hand. "He has dark eyes and dark hair. He's a tall, serious little boy. He looks just like his father. Like you."

"Oh, Glory." Steven groaned, lifting her in his arms. He carried her back to the bed and laid her down, falling across her, burying his head between her breasts. She'd expected him to show his pleasure, his excitement, but the wetness that seeped down her stomach was a surprise. "I'm so sorry I couldn't be there. Is he—all right?"

"Our son is very much all right, Steven. They were wrong when they said those awful things. They were all wrong, your mother and mine. We had a child and he is perfect."

"Does Roger know?"

"No. I'd never hurt him like that."

"Will you tell Damon?"

"Perhaps, someday, if he needs to know. What do we do now, Steven?"

"We just love each other, for now. But this can't happen again. We can't take a chance, Glory. We've been lucky so far. We have this moment, but we dare not tempt fate."

When Steven entered her again, Glory gave herself over to the joy of his touch and the wonder of their loving. The future was now. Tomorrow was somewhere out there. She'd worry about it when it came. Steven was all that mattered, and they were joined together for all time.

Later, as Glory slept, Steven faced the situation and took blame for what they'd done. He should have refused to give in to Glory. In every other way, he'd always considered himself strong, except for Glory.

From the time he'd stumbled on her in the hallway of his grandfather's house the day of her father's funeral, he'd felt responsible for her, responsible and connected. She'd looked up at him with those big green eyes and made him a king. Except, somewhere along the line, the king had become a slave. Glory, without trying, without making demands, was worshiped, followed, and protected.

Until this weekend when Steven hadn't been able to protect her from himself.

Twenty-Two

"After tonight you can't see me until the wedding ceremony."

Susan lay against Sam's arm in the dark living room. All afternoon they'd put away Susan's clothes and their wedding gifts and made Sam's house ready for Susan to move into when they returned from their honeymoon. Now they were sitting on the couch enjoying the moment.

Through the curtains, the moon rose full and yellow from behind the trees. It was a winter moon, not the June moondaisies and forget-me-nots she'd always planned, but they were getting married and that was all that mattered.

Until now, the house had been off limits. Susan hadn't understood why, only that Sam said it was.

"Why can't I see you before the wedding?"

"It's bad luck for the groom to see the bride on their wedding day until she comes to him at the altar. Besides, I have a hundred things to do tomorrow."

"Like what?"

"Like getting my hair done. Glory will be coming in to try on her dress. I may have to make some adjustments—just wedding things."

The couch creaked as Sam pulled her closer. His hand was resting near, but not touching her breast. After the funeral, when he'd almost made love to her on the kitchen table, he hadn't allowed himself to touch her again. It was his fault that she'd lost her inhibitions, his fault that she seemed to be inviting him to go further. Occasionally in the past, in spite of his best intentions, he'd gone too far, but he'd stopped just short of taking advantage of her. It didn't matter about other

195

women, but Susan was to be respected, his grandfather had made that clear to him a long time ago. Now that he was gone, it was even more important for Sam to show that his confidence was not misplaced.

Susan hadn't understood. She'd asked what she was doing wrong, but night after night Susan had groaned in frustration as Sam stumbled out into the darkness to get himself under control. After tomorrow there would be no more waiting.

"I'd better take you home, Susan. It's late."

"No. If I can't see you tomorrow, I want to stay a little longer now." She lifted her lips for another kiss. "I can't wait until tomorrow when we can—be together. I want to see you, Sam, all of you."

Sam became tense. "You *are* seeing me. I'm right here."

"That's not what I mean. Besides, it's dark. I want the light on."

"Sorry. The only light here is from the moon."

Susan remembered other nights, when Sam had parked his truck by the lake and kissed her. She was never entirely comfortable about being at the lake with Sam. It was private and beautiful, but there was never a time she didn't remember last summer, after graduation, when she'd sat on the park bench with Joseph Cheatham. She finally asked Sam to park somewhere else.

She didn't know whether it was guilt over being nice to Jody that bothered her or guilt over the forbidden pleasure she'd had in their friendship. Susan loved Sam; she always had. But he rarely asked her opinion. They rarely talked. Sam talked and she listened. That was the way it would be, she knew, but she wished he'd listen to her. Sam would never understand her private correspondence with Jody, the exchange of letters that she'd ended with her last letter, in which she had told Jody she was getting married. She knew he'd understand their letters had to stop.

"Sam, are you going to be happy?"

"Of course. Why would you ask a thing like that?"

"I don't know. This. You . . . us, it's what I've always wanted. But do you ever wonder if there's something else out there."

Sam raised up. "What do you mean by that? Do you mean another man?"

"No, though I have wondered about other men. You're the only man I've ever been with, Sam, the only one who's ever kissed me, touched me."

"So? What does that mean?" Sam was beginning to fidget, revealing his discomfort with Susan's conversation, just as he always did when she raised questions about tradition.

"You know, don't you, Sam. You know what it feels like with another woman. You've kissed other women, touched them, gone all the way?" She felt him stiffen even more.

"I'm not criticizing you. That's not what I meant. I always knew that you did. But I never have. You've never done that to me. But you have with someone else, haven't you? Tell me the truth, Sam. I need to know."

"Why do you want to talk about that? It isn't proper."

"I want to know, Sam. Tell me the truth."

"Yes. I have. But it didn't mean anything, Susan. You're the woman I love, the woman I've always loved. The others don't count."

"But they let you do it to them. Did they think you loved them? Did you tell them you did?"

"No, of course not. Susan, you wouldn't understand about this, but there are girls who get just as excited as men. They want it just as bad as we do. But that isn't love, it's just sex."

"That's what Glory said. She made the boys hot, but I don't think she ever let them go any further. I think she did things to herself, like you do."

"Don't talk about Glory," Sam said gruffly. "Glory has the morals of an alley cat. Hell, she even came on to me, and I'm her cousin."

Glory was the last woman Sam wanted to think about while he was holding Susan. Glory had tormented Sam for most of his life. Until she was twelve he'd thought it was just innocent child's play. It was later when she'd let him kiss her, let him feel her budding breasts, and touch her down there . . . Sam groaned and tried to close off the remembering.

But it was there. Glory was always there, smiling at him, daring him to touch her, touching him. Provoking him to the point of insanity, then dancing away with a laugh. Glory was the dark side of his life. Susan was the sunshine.

"I know, Sam. She told us what she used to do. But I don't

197

understand *us,* Sam. I love you and that love ought to make it all right for us to—I mean, for me to do it, too."

"Susan!"

Susan raised up. "I want to touch you, Sam. I need to touch you. You only let me touch you that once, in the kitchen, when you . . ."

She slid to the floor in front of the couch and knelt beside him, pushing him back against the arm of the couch as she ran her fingers down his stomach, feeling the tensing of his muscles as she traveled lower. Clumsily she unbuckled his belt and unzipped his pants. She heard him take a sudden breath as her fingertips found what she was looking for.

Sam lay there, holding himself still with superhuman control. Susan didn't know what she was doing. She couldn't know what she was starting.

"Don't do that, Susan. It's wrong. If you don't stop, I don't know what I'll do to you."

"You'll do nothing, Sam. You never do, remember? I'm the woman you're going to marry. Men don't dishonor their future wives, remember? You just leave me crazy. This time I'm not going to let you stop."

Susan's blouse was gone. Her bra was gone. She'd removed both before she moved over Sam. Now she stood up and peeled off Sam's slacks and shorts and stretched his long, lean legs out on the couch. Still standing, she slid out of her skirt, underpants and all. When she lay back down, it was on top of Sam.

"Ah, no, Susan. Stop moving."

But Susan didn't. She slid up and down, catching Sam's penis between her legs so that it slid back and forth, giving delicious strokes inside the valley of her desire.

"Susan, you're going to make me come."

"What does that mean, Sam? What happens then? Will I feel the same thing? What makes a woman come, Sam?"

But she didn't have to be told, for on one downward thrust she caught him at just the right angle and he was inside her.

"Oh!" It was her voice moaning. It was her body that began to vibrate. But it was Sam's hands that caught her bare bottom and began to move her up and down. Then suddenly Sam slipped to the floor and she was on her back. Sam, still inside her, had stopped moving.

"Susan, I don't have anything on. If I don't stop, you

198

could get pregnant. Let me get a rubber."

"You have a rubber?"

"Of course. For tomorrow night. For our wedding night, Susan."

But for Susan, the words came too late. She felt the tidal wave of heat begin its vibration. She clamped her muscles tight and thrust herself against him. "Oh, Sam. Ohhhhh! Don't stop. It's—it's—something's happening."

It was too late for Sam, too. He slid his hands beneath her and gave her what he'd withheld for so long. Even Sam was astonished at the height of his release, at the wildness of her response. He hadn't made love to many women in his life, but this was the first time that the woman's climax and his own had been simultaneous. It was an explosion beyond anything he'd expected.

"Oh, Sam. Why did you make us wait?"

"Susan, I'm sorry, so sorry. But—you—you didn't act as if you'd never done it before," he said, unable to conceal the tiny seed of doubt in his mind.

Susan was supposed to be a lady, subdued and unemotional. His grandfather had explained it all to him. The woman a man married wasn't expected to respond like one of those girls at Rosey's Lucky Slipper who did this kind of thing for a living. But Sam had never had a woman in Rosey's who matched what he'd just shared with Susan.

The best sex he'd ever had was also the most confusing.

Sam rolled over, feeling himself pull out of her with a sucking motion. She groaned and slipped back across him as if she didn't want to be separated. He drew her close and they lay there together on the bare floor in what would soon be their new home.

Later that night Susan lay in her own bed, smiling. Everything was going to be wonderful. Loving Sam was going to be wonderful. She squirmed, pulling the sheet between her legs and reveling at the feeling that its rough cotton texture set off. Once before she'd set off that sensation, at Glory's house that afternoon when they'd had too much to drink. But now she knew what could happen with Sam. Now she knew what she had to look forward to. She couldn't wait.

It was ten o'clock the next morning when Susan flung herself back across the same bed and cried, "How could Glory do this to me? Why isn't she coming? She's one of the bridesmaids and now everything will be out of kilter."

"No," Mrs. Miller said. "It won't be uneven. Steven isn't coming, either. Some kind of crisis on Wall Street, he told his mother. Personally I think you're just as well off without them. I never did trust that girl. She was always wild."

"But I counted on her. I wanted my three best friends to be in my wedding. I always planned for it to be like that. How dare Glory not come?"

"She might have been one of your closest friends, but how many times have you heard from her since you graduated from high school?"

"None, but you know Glory. She's been busy, having a baby, moving to Savannah, and setting up her new house. Mrs. Winslow says she even has a maid and a nanny now. I don't see why she couldn't come."

"Some kind of virus," Adele said.

Susan cried briefly, then allowed herself to be coaxed out of her hurt. This was her wedding day and she didn't want her face to be puffy. She would never forgive Glory Sasser for not being in her wedding, but JoEllen and Margie would be there and she would still have the wedding she'd always dreamed about. And then there'd be the honeymoon. Susan smiled and looked at her watch. The hands seemed to be creeping instead of flying.

Later, when Sam heard about Glory's defection, he breathed a sigh of relief. When he heard that Steven wasn't coming, either, he wondered briefly at the coincidence, then forgot about it as he anticipated the night to come.

The house was ready. There was a new tractor in the barn and his fields were already plowed under and ready for planting in the spring. Everything had come to pass just as he'd always planned. He couldn't understand why he was afraid.

Today was his wedding day. At least Glory wouldn't be there to torment him. He'd tried all day not to think about what had happened between him and Susan last night, but it was like the fear, it stayed with him. He worried briefly about not using a rubber, then decided that it didn't matter. They'd planned to wait two years before starting a family, but if it happened sooner, so be it. None of the present-day Winslow cousins had any brothers and sisters. He knew that Steven and Glory's fathers had been killed in the war, and his own father had never married again. Sam had worked up enough courage once to ask his father why. He'd just looked at Sam with a pained expression on his face and said, "Ask your grandfather. He always had all the answers."

But Granddaddy growled his refusal to discuss the topic, saying only that the Lord decided those things in his own time, that Sam should visit Rosey's until he got married.

If the Lord decided, Sam didn't know why he bothered to buy the box of Trojans in the first place. There was certainly no reason for him to worry about that tonight. He felt himself harden. After tonight he'd never have to worry about that again. After tonight he'd have a wife.

Six hours later, Sam stood in the little hallway off the sanctuary listening to the organist play. He could see the candles glowing warmly behind the pulpit, which had been disguised by a fan-shaped spray of smilax and chrysanthemums. Susan had wanted a candlelight wedding. It wouldn't have been dark enough in June. In December it was perfect.

Standing in the vestibule, Susan surveyed the little church with pride. She'd planned this wedding in the eighth grade, right after she'd had her first date with Sam. All the way through four years of home economics, she'd studied cooking, sewing, and budget management to reach this point in her life.

"You look beautiful," JoEllen said.

"I love these green satin dresses," Margie commented for the tenth time. "It's a good thing you made them for us or I couldn't have afforded it."

Susan's brother stood awkwardly by, pressed into giving the bride away in the absence of the father she hadn't seen in over ten years. Her mother was being seated. Her dusty rose dress was already too tight and Susan had given up on talking her into cutting her hair and having it curled. Instead, she had braided it and folded it across the top of her head as she'd always done. Susan realized how dowdy she really was.

"Wonder what happened to Glory?" JoEllen whispered under her breath to Margie.

"Who knows? She's probably run off with the Fuller Brush Man for a weekend at Daytona Beach."

The procession began and JoEllen made her way down the aisle, followed by a groomsman, Margie, and the final groomsman. The church was full.

Afterward, there was a reception in the Sunday School rooms. Little finger sandwiches, nuts and mints, punch and wedding cake were served while the men decorated Sam's truck with shaving cream and streamers.

After the service Susan changed into a smart little navy-blue dress and navy pumps. Sam wore his new brown double-breasted suit and loafers that squeaked. They made a mad dash through a cordon of rice throwers to Sam's truck and roared off toward Augusta with the rest of the wedding party blowing their car horns and racing along behind.

Somewhere on the other side of the county line, the cars dropped off and let the newlyweds drive away.

Later, Sam pulled into the motel, parking his decorated truck in a space beside a big black rental car.

"We're here," Sam announced. "Do you want to get something to eat before we—before we check in?"

"Couldn't we wait until later? I mean, we have the goodie box that Mother packed."

"And I have a bottle of champagne that Teddy slipped behind the seat."

Susan tried to quell her excitement by gathering up the box of reception treats and her purse while Sam went inside and registered.

He came back to the car and opened the door, clasping one bag under his arm and carrying the other, leaving one hand free to open the door. "Wait right there, Susan," he said in a low voice as he dropped the cases inside the door and turned back.

Susan complied, smiling as he lifted her and stepped inside. "Mrs. Sam Winslow," she said in a dreamy voice.

"Yes," Sam responded sternly, "my wife."

Twenty-Three

Steven and Glory missed their return flights. For two days they never left the motel room, except for food. On the sixth day there was a knock on the door. Steven stepped into his pants and pulled on a shirt before he opened the door.

The stony-faced, angry woman standing there was Adele Winslow.

Glory, in bed with the sheet pulled up to cover her breasts, gasped.

Adele didn't move out of the doorway. "Glory, get dressed. Steven, put on your shoes and go outside. I want to talk to you."

Steven stared at the floor. "I'm sorry you came, Aunt Adele. I don't know what to say, except that Glory and I—"

"Don't say anything. Just go to the car and wait. I thought we'd explained, but it's obvious what we said wasn't enough. There is something you have to know. As for you . . ." She turned toward Glory. "Get dressed. You're going back to your husband if I have to drag you."

Glory let the sheet drop. "Steven belongs to me. He always has. He always will. Nothing you can do will change that."

"And what about your son? *Roger's* child?"

"Steven's son. I'll handle that, Mother."

Mrs. Winslow gasped.

"It's true, Adele," Steven began. "I'm sorry, but Glory is right. I love her. I always have. I won't lie about it anymore. Glory is the woman I love."

"I know. I've always known. But you're a Winslow, Steven, and I think that what I'm going to tell you will change your mind. Now put on your clothes and go to the car."

Glory started to protest. She wouldn't allow Steven to go. He'd walked away from her once, but he wouldn't do it again, not even to protect his family name. He gave her a little shake of the head that said he wouldn't let anything come between them and fastened his shirt. Glory let out a sigh of relief. He wouldn't leave.

Her mother turned and followed Steven, closing the door. Glory dressed quickly. She wanted to be ready to leave with Steven. They'd go to Savannah and get Damon. Roger couldn't stop them. Damon wasn't his child. She didn't care where she and Steven lived, just as long as they were together.

But when the door opened again, Adele was alone. Steven had gone. Steven had left her. And Adele refused to explain why. It didn't matter, she said. Steven was married, and so was Glory. Nobody knew that they'd been together, and nobody ever would. Steven was out of her life forever.

Glory screamed and raged and threatened, but in the end, without Steven beside her, she was forced to comply. Worn out and so distraught that she couldn't think, she packed her clothes to go home. She'd lost Steven and she didn't know why. He'd promised and he'd abandoned her, as he'd always done.

"What do you expect me to do, Mother?"

"I expect you to make damned sure that Roger never finds out about this. You do whatever it takes to keep him from ever being suspicious."

Glory didn't answer. She knew what that would be. She'd go along with her mother's orders until she could talk to Steven.

Roger didn't know what brought on Glory's sudden desire, but he attributed it to the wedding and enjoyed it until it passed. In return, Glory got a new house and the vice-presidency of the hospital Ladies' Auxiliary. The move left young Bill behind, but by this time his girlfriend was reaping the benefits of Glory's tutoring.

Talking to Steven proved to be impossible. He refused her

calls and her letters were returned unopened. When, with uncharacteristic pleasure, Glory announced her pregnancy three months later, Roger was puzzled but delighted. Glory hadn't wanted another child—until now.

This child was Steven's, too, and Glory would have walked on hot coals before she'd let anything happen to it. She took care of herself: no drinking, no emotional tirades, no more Dr. Fincher.

Still, the baby came early. In two years of marriage Glory had been pregnant with three children: Damon, the child she'd aborted, and Stephanie—the little girl with lungs that weren't fully developed and a physical deformity of the skull. Roger forbade her to see the child.

In spite of her physical appearance, from the moment Glory bribed the nurse to let her hold the child, Glory loved her daughter fiercely. Roger never knew that she'd been there, watching, when the baby took her last breath. Glory carried Stephanie back to Winslow to be buried in a private ceremony. The funeral left Glory silent and depressed for months.

The medical staff said that without a history of heredity as an explanation, it was just a freak occurrence. Glory and Roger didn't have to worry about future children. The chances were that they would be fine.

Adele wasn't so kind. "The child was deformed because she was Steven's," she said coldly and with no compassion. "I tried to warn you, Glory. That's what happens when . . . cousins marry. They make babies who are freaks."

Glory, still grieving for her daughter, finally understood what Adele and Evelyn had tried to explain that summer of '54. She refused to listen to reason or to put her irrational anger behind her.

She clung to Damon. He was fine. Even more than before, she devoted herself completely to him, fiercely closing out everything and everybody but her son. And Roger tried not to be jealous. After all, this was his offspring, though he never felt the slightest connection to the serious, dark-eyed child.

Glory's unaccountable spells of depression occurred more and more frequently.

"The next baby will be fine," Roger assured her, accepting

her despondency as the normal result of losing a baby.

"There won't be another child. I'm moving into the other bedroom, Roger."

He didn't argue. Avoiding her hair-trigger fits of temper would be a relief. The separate bedroom would pass. But three months later she was still there. On the occasions when Roger insisted on claiming his marital rights, she complied. Otherwise, Glory appeared to have lost all interest in the physical side of their relationship.

When Glory got a thank-you note from Steven's wife for the baby gift Adele had sent in Glory's name, Glory took an overdose of sleeping pills.

"Accidental," Roger said.

"Depression," Lawrence Fincher said, and prescribed a tranquilizer.

"Intentional," Glory said, and in a desperate attempt to forget, swallowed a tranquilizer with a shot of straight vodka.

But the memories were stronger than the medication and the liquor, and Glory needed to find ways to get more. The surest way was Lawrence Fincher and he was more than happy to prescribe them to bring Glory back to him.

Only when she was floating in a haze of forgetfulness could she get through her day. The days got longer and the medication stronger.

Two years and two months had passed since Glory had dramatically decided that Margie was a rose, JoEllen a lily, Susan a gardenia and she a dahlia. But she'd been only partially right. Not a lush single blossom, Margie was more like the wild rose that curled its tendrils across the dirt of a city lot. JoEllen, like the regal lily, opened herself to the sun, bloomed briefly, and closed herself away in the darkness. Susan's beauty, like that of the gardenia, was still pure, giving off the faint sweet scent of promise that would intensify as life's bruising began. Only Glory's own blossom, the fiery, vibrant dahlia, had begun to droop, its bold bid for the sun weighing heavily on the delicate stem that struggled to hold the bloom aloft.

Three of the friends had fled the place of their birth; one in fear, one in anticipation, one in defiance. Only Susan, who'd come from the outside world seeking haven, still remained. Susan stayed and waited for life to come to her. The summer of '54 was gone, but the four women's lives had been forever changed.

Twenty-Four

"But Mayor, I don't know anything about construction. Why would I want to go to work for you full-time?"

"Because you're dependable. You have a talent for dealing with people and I like you, Teddy. Don't you want to get ahead?"

Teddy looked at the man who'd given him a part-time job nearly three years ago and thought about the question. "I'm not sure that I do. I like living in Galilee and working with my hands. I can control what I do and why I do it."

"But you're never going to make any money here, Teddy. Unless you own land or some kind of manufacturing business, you'll live from payday to payday."

"That's true. I know it looks like I don't have much ambition, and maybe I don't. But if I decide to go fishing I can always find an hour or two to do it."

"Hell, boy, come to work for me and you can buy the whole lake. Somebody has to be ready to take over what I have when I get ready to step down."

"What about Claude?"

Ed Jordan gave a painful laugh. "Claude's in Mobile, in one of them drying-out places. When he gets out, he's going to New York. Always wanted to go there, you know, but I wouldn't have it. The doctors think that might be why he drinks. Can you imagine that?"

Teddy thought about his own father's drinking. That summer he'd spent in Texas, they'd talked. Teddy still didn't understand his father's need to keep moving, but he had learned that he was a man who was always searching for something and never finding it. Maybe that's why Teddy had been able to deal with Claude; he could see the same pain.

He could see Ed Jordan's pain, too, and he couldn't add to it. Teddy had never thought that much about his future. He'd just gone through one sports season to the next, with a generous amount of fishing, hunting, and raising hell along the way. But his friends were off in the Army now, or getting married. Even his brother had gotten married. Now they were expecting a baby and money at the garage was tighter.

Teddy hadn't told anyone, but he'd tried to join the Army. They'd turned him down because he hadn't passed the physical. For an athlete, failing a physical was an emotional blow that had been hard to handle. So he did have flat feet and had hurt his knee playing sports, that didn't mean he couldn't be a soldier. But they'd refused to take him. Maybe this was his answer.

"All right, Mayor Jordan. I'll come to work for you, providing I don't have to leave Galilee. Also, I want to keep working part-time at the garage. My brother Ben needs me and I've been fooling around with a little idea that would mean better gas mileage."

"Done. First thing I want you to do is take over the new school-site selection. The old Winslow High School is fine for now, but it's going to be too small eventually. If we can locate the school out in the county, we can draw from a much larger area."

"Why would we want to do that?"

"Money, Ted. Without more students paying more tuition, we can't buy the fancy equipment we need to have for accreditation as a Christian School. See if you can find somebody who wants to donate us a few acres."

"Yes, sir. I'll get to work on it."

"And Ted, do you have a girl?"

That stopped Teddy for a moment. "No, nobody special. Why?"

"Find one. People like having a mayor who's married."

"Mayor? What's that got to do with me?"

"I told you. Sooner or later, I'm retiring. Need to start getting you ready."

This time it was Teddy's turn to laugh. "That's a long way

209

off, Mayor. Besides, how can you be sure anybody would want me?"

"Doesn't matter. Those things can be arranged. Are you interested?"

"One thing at a time, Mayor."

"That's what I like about you, Son, you have your priorities. Aren't you going to ask how much I'm going to pay you?"

"Nope. I don't work cheap, and if it's not enough, I can always quit."

There were times when Susan despaired of ever getting past Sam's peculiar notions of propriety. She'd thought that once they were married things would change. He loved her, she knew he did. And she loved him. They'd made a life together and worked hard to build a future.

They'd been married two years when Jennifer was born and Susan had left her job to stay at home. But even in a time when women were pushing for equality, Sam still insisted that Susan undress in the bathroom every night and close the bedroom door if they were going to make love.

He turned out all the lights and often simply pushed up her nightgown without even undressing. There was never a question of Susan's not giving herself openly and fully to Sam. Nor did he hold back once he was aroused. But she sensed that he was never truly comfortable with her abandon, and little by little she learned that he preferred her to be quiet and still. When she became pregnant, he rarely reached for her, and by the time the baby came, he was often so tense and surly that he left early and stayed in the fields until well after dark.

Once when Jennifer cried out and Susan rushed to her bedside without stopping to pull on a robe, he'd been horrified.

"But Sam, she's just a baby. Besides, it's dark. Why should I cover my body?"

"You're my wife. You should conduct yourself properly."

Susan wished there was someone she could talk to. It had to be her fault. She didn't know how husbands were expected to feel, but she knew that Sam's actions were . . .

different. Maybe there was something unnatural about her. She liked sex. She liked touching and being touched by Sam. She always responded, and he always seemed surprised by the depth of her climax.

In every other way their lives seemed to move along just as they'd both planned. Sam was active in the Farm Bureau and took his position as a member of the community seriously. When the first rumblings of real trouble over desegregation started, Sam took a firm stand: his children would never go to school with blacks. Susan tried to suggest that maybe they weren't being fair with their separate but equal arrangements, but Sam wouldn't listen. Remembering her relationship with Jody, Susan held her tongue.

On a small black-and-white television that Sam's father provided on a rare visit home, Susan watched Marilyn Van Derbur become Miss America of 1957. She played Pat Boone's latest hit song, "Love Letters in the Sand" on the piano and wished they could afford to get the upright tuned. If her life hadn't turned out exactly as she'd envisioned yet, Susan was willing to wait. They had little money, but they had each other, and the farm and a baby. If they were very careful, and the rain came next spring, they'd finally begin to see a few more extras. If not, she might even consider going back to work, though she hadn't mentioned that to Sam yet.

Susan put a load of diapers in the washtub to soak and thought about Glory. She probably had a washing machine. No, Glory probably had someone who did her laundry and cooked. But Susan wouldn't change places with Glory for anything. Susan was where she belonged.

The rains didn't come. Sam's crops struggled and his temper shortened. By the following June a Georgia girl, Joanne Woodward had won an Oscar for her role in *The Three Faces of Eve*. And Sam was trying to rig up some kind of irrigation system to save his corn.

Susan, standing at the receptionist's desk in the doctor's office, studied the balance in the checking account and sighed. She'd never done it before, but she'd had to ask the doctor to let her pay him on the first of next month instead of today, though she wasn't certain that the balance would look

211

any different then.

When she stepped outside, the heat seemed to envelop her, sapping the last of her energy. With uncharacteristic dread she cranked the truck engine and started toward her mother's to pick up the baby. Scheduling her doctor's appointments on her mother's lunch hour required cooperation from Dr. Bailey's staff.

Glancing in the mirror, Susan felt tears well up in her eyes. She was three months pregnant. She hadn't had to go to the doctor again to know, but she'd hoped against hope that she was wrong. Guilt assailed her. She and Sam had planned to have two children. They just hadn't planned to have the second one so soon. Susan couldn't imagine how the pregnancy had happened. Sam had made love to her so seldom in the last few months, and when he had, it was without words and was over almost before it began.

Nobody ever told her in home economics class that being married would be so lonely. Jennifer was supposed to be a joy, the culmination of Susan's every dream of being a wife and mother. In the beginning, when she and Sam still talked, they'd planned out her pregnancy just as they'd done their lives. But Jennifer was an irritable, cross child who at nine months still wasn't sleeping through the night.

And Sam was working so hard that he seemed eternally exhausted, often falling asleep at the supper table in the middle of a meal. Susan glanced down at her chipped fingernail polish and sighed. She loved Jennifer and she loved Sam, but she was only twenty-two. Before she'd even learned how to be a proper wife and mother, she was pregnant again.

She didn't know how she'd tell Sam. He had so much responsibility now. As Winslows they were considered well off. And they were, but their wealth was in land and equipment. Cash was almost nonexistent. Sam could buy seed and fertilizer on credit, but if he hadn't taken on some outside work they couldn't have bought groceries.

If only it would rain. But the sun beat down unmercifully, sucking up every drop of moisture in the air and shriveling the corn in the fields. The drought, coming on the heels of a winter freeze that had meant replacing every pipe in the house, and a March-wind-induced fire that burned the hay

Sam had put away to feed the stock till spring, had been a disaster. She didn't know how he'd feel about another baby coming.

Susan drove slowly up the quiet street. It was too hot for anybody to be outside in the middle of the day. Even her mother was sitting in her bedroom, in the dark with the fan blowing hot air on her and Jennifer.

"Well?" her mother said quietly as she picked up her purse and followed Susan to the door.

"I'm pregnant. I don't know how I'm going to tell Sam. He's got so much on his mind. He'll be angry."

"Humph! Just remind him what he had on his mind to get you this way," Mrs. Miller said sharply. "If he kept his self on his side of the bed you wouldn't have to worry. That's the way with men. Never worrying about anybody's wants but their own. At least you picked out a man who knows how to stay where he belongs."

Susan glanced at her mother in surprise. She'd never heard her make that kind of personal remark before, and never with such venom. She wanted to ask if she'd regretted her pregnancies, but Lillian Miller had never discussed either her marriage or the divorce she'd gotten in a time when few women did.

"But Mother," Susan protested, "Sam and I want children."

"It wasn't the children I was speaking of, Susan, it's the getting of them. Women have to tolerate that, and having them, too. The men get all the pleasure and leave the women to pay for it. It don't seem fair."

Susan settled Jennifer on the seat and was glad that she dozed off before they reached Winslow Road. Her mother's words stayed with her all the way home. *Women have to tolerate that.* Susan had never looked on making love as something to be tolerated, at least not until lately. It seemed the more she enjoyed their making love, the quicker it was over. She tried to force herself to keep still and quiet, but the minute Sam touched her she seemed to turn into someone else.

There was something wrong when girls were taught everything about making a good home except how to live with a man. And the myth was perpetuated, with every

213

generation convincing their daughters that if they learned to cook and sew and rear the children properly they'd be rewarded with a beautiful life and a husband who appreciated them.

It was all a lie, a hypocritical lie. They should have known that, the four of them: she, Glory, JoEllen, and Margie. Margie's father dumped her with her grandparents. Glory's father was killed, leaving Glory's mother alone. JoEllen's father deserted her, too; just left one day and never came home. And her own father? The missing figure in a family that ceased to exist the day a little girl and an overweight, uneducated woman took a train to the past.

Get married and life will be fulfilling. The four friends had bought the dream for a while, though the other three had escaped the very thing she'd longed for: roots and tradition. They'd pursued their own special dreams, but more and more Susan wondered if her own dream was a lie.

A line from Mr. Sims's play suddenly came to her: "Life keeps on making faces at you and you're never sure whether it's laughing with you or at you." She hadn't understood what that meant, until now.

Jennifer fretted in a restless sleep. She was probably wet and hungry. Susan sighed. Sam would be ready for dinner, which was to be served at one o'clock every day. He lived by a strict routine and anything that disrupted it brought silent frowns and under-the-breath grumbling. This morning she'd prepared a cold lunch and left it wrapped in waxed paper in the refrigerator so it would be ready for him. With any luck Sam would have read her note about his lunch and would already be gone.

She wasn't lucky. Sam was slamming cabinet doors when she walked into the kitchen.

"Where have you been?"

"I had to go to town," she said, and moved past him down the hallway. "Your dinner is in the refrigerator, Sam. Let me change Jennifer, and I'll get it for you."

"You couldn't get back early enough to get dinner on the table?"

Susan tried not to snap at her husband. It wasn't his fault things weren't working out as they'd planned. The pictures they'd drawn in her parlor hadn't included debts and heat

214

and unending hours of work that rolled over from one day into the next. Sam's grandfather had had years of experience and enough money to carry him through the bad times. All Sam had was a dream that had shriveled and died with the corn in the field.

Susan closed out the sound of Sam's complaints as she changed Jennifer and prepared a bottle of juice to occupy her until after Sam had gone back to the fields. She thought longingly of Margie in Atlanta, working in an air-conditioned office and going to college. Glory was in Savannah, a doctor's wife, with someone to look after her baby and clean her house and cook. She probably had an air-conditioning unit in every window. JoEllen surely did at the hospital, and she had fresh white uniforms to wear and a cafeteria where she could eat whatever she wanted without having to cook every day.

What Susan had was a kitchen that was hot enough to cook food in without using the stove, water that barely trickled, and a house that still needed new rugs. Maybe now wasn't a good time to tell Sam her news, but there was nobody else she could tell, nobody to talk to.

From out of the blue came the unwelcome memory of Jody, who had nobody to talk to, either. Jody would understand, Jody who'd found a way to escape the kind of life she'd so carefully planned for herself. Susan sighed; life's dreams were just that. Reality was the living of them, and the pain of learning that dreams were fairy tales for children. Being an adult wasn't what she'd expected.

First Mr. Sims, now Jody. But she couldn't discuss Jody with Sam. "Sam, do you remember Mr. Sims?"

Susan unwrapped the sandwiches she'd prepared earlier and took the trays from the freezer and pulled the lever loosening the ice so she could fill their glasses.

"You mean the English teacher they fired?"

"Yes. I always felt sorry for him. It must have been awful not to have anything in common with the people he worked with."

"Why are you thinking about him?" Sam picked up a sandwich and took a bite. "Baloney? You expect me to put in a full day's work on baloney sandwiches?"

"I'm sorry, Sam, it's all I have. There's fried chicken for

215

supper, but it's just too hot to cook it now."

"Too hot, or did it interfere with your going to town? What's so important about going to town, anyway? You certainly weren't going to the grocery store."

"I couldn't have gone to the grocery store if I wanted to, Sam. There isn't enough money in the bank to shop, or do you expect me to become Jesus Christ and turn twelve dollars into twelve hundred!"

Sam put down his sandwich and stared at Susan in surprise. He'd never heard her talk like that. Something about her was different this morning. She was angry, really angry, and she was staring at him as if she'd like to do to him what she'd done to the chicken yesterday.

Sam rubbed the sweat from his forehead with his shirt sleeve. He had no right to complain about the baloney. In fact, he liked baloney. It was the heat, and the expression on Susan's face that had gotten to him. What had happened to all their dreams? Their life together wasn't working out as he'd expected. And it must be his fault because it was the man who was responsible. But no matter how hard he tried, the crops never quite made what they should have, the full litter of new pigs never survived, and the last two calves had been stillborn.

Worse than his knowledge of failure was knowing that his grandfather would be disappointed. All his life Sam had patterned his future according to his grandfather's wishes, confident that someday he'd measure up to the Winslow standards. But it wasn't happening. By now, all his hunting buddies were either graduating from college and beginning new careers in the cities, or they were in the Army and traveling around the world. His world was Susan and their daughter and the farm.

He wouldn't have it any other way. But he'd never imagined that his world would be so small, or that it would be so hard, and he couldn't bear the censure in Susan's eyes.

He wished that his grandfather was there to tell him what to do. But, he knew what his grandfather would say. He had a problem and he was a Winslow. A Winslow would solve it.

"Don't be irreverent, Susan," he snapped.

Be irreverent? That was too much. Susan pushed her chair back from the table and stood up slowly. "Don't be

216

irreverent? Don't march around in your nightgown, Susan. Don't make so much noise when I touch you, Susan. Don't bother me, Susan. I'm tired. I've got too much to do to stop and have a picnic with you. Stop carrying on like Glory. Now that we're married we don't have time for that kind of foolishness."

She turned and raced out the door, across the field, and into the stand of pine trees at the lake, frantically peeling her sweaty clothes from her body and dropping them as she ran. She hesitated at the water's edge, then plunged in. If she didn't cool off she'd explode. It never occurred to her that, without a thought, she'd left Jennifer behind. Frantically she swam across the narrow end of the lake with a strength she didn't know she had.

On the far side she waded through the squishy mud to the bank and collapsed, gasping for breath on the pine needles beneath the trees. A peaceful silence gradually swept over her as she lay there in the shade allowing the hot air to dry her.

All this was her father's fault. If he had loved her and her mother she'd never have come to Galilee and she'd never have met Sam. But her father had abandoned her, and Sam had loved her in his place. She wasn't sure she knew what love was anymore, but just lying there, thinking about Sam's lean, strong body made her ache.

A gardenia, Glory had called her, pure and white and easily bruised. She'd been right. Somehow Glory had found a way to reach that forbidden secret part of Susan Miller and to know her thoughts were tarnished. She remembered Glory touching herself. She remembered touching her own body that first time and the unexpected jolt of sensation.

And then she realized that she was touching herself now, and that she was beginning to respond. With a cry of dismay Susan sprang to her feet and looked down at herself. Her breasts had never fully regained their shape from nursing Jennifer, and now there was a new baby waiting to suckle. Her stomach was already taking on a round shape that would expand and sap her energy. And Sam would stay away. She'd never realized how her having a baby would affect Sam. He had seemed pleased over the first pregnancy, but once her body began to change, so had Sam.

217

Now she was pregnant again, and she needed Sam's comfort, Sam's closeness. Instead, she was afraid that she'd lose it. Susan slid back into the water and started across the lake. Sooner or later she'd have to tell Sam, but not yet. Tonight she'd make him love her like he did that first time. She needed her man and it was her turn to have her needs answered.

Susan took the fried chicken from the iron skillet and laid it on newspaper to soak up the grease. Creamed corn was bubbling in the other skillet and cornbread was browning in the oven. Jennifer had already been fed, bathed, and dressed in her nightgown.

Susan glanced at the clock. It was past time for Sam to open the screen door, unlace his work shoes, and leave them on the porch. Next would come the work pants and long-sleeved shirt which he'd thrown on top of the second-hand washing machine that had been a gift from her mother. She'd watched him do that for two summers—walk into the kitchen in his underwear, his bronzed face, neck, and arms making his pale skin look like the chicken she'd fried.

She'd never understood his lack of modesty, when he insisted that she cover herself completely if she made even one step outside their bedroom. She'd bet her last twelve dollars that Glory never worried about that around her husband.

Glory. Susan had learned early on not to mention her name around Sam. Glory was his cousin, but something about her filled him with anger. Sometimes he acted as if he was sorry she was his cousin. Steven was rarely mentioned, either. Susan had the feeling that as far as Sam was concerned, they were a part of his family he'd put behind him when his grandfather died and left Sam the farm. Most of the money had gone to Steven and Glory, which had put a hardship on Sam from the beginning.

Susan understood, but there were times she was tempted to ask Sam to sell the farm and use the money to make a new start somewhere else. Maybe tonight, if things worked out, she'd mention that to him.

At nine o'clock Susan put the food away and exchanged

218

her slinky nightgown for a more practical one. When she heard Sam's stumbling step on the porch she pretended to be asleep. When he crawled into bed with her and rolled over her, Susan cringed at the smell of alcohol on his breath. Pretending to be asleep, she allowed him access to her body without responding. After a few fruitless moments of awkward attempts at penetration, when his body refused to cooperate, he swore and slid away.

Moments later he was snoring.

The next morning Sam ate his breakfast in silence and left the kitchen without mentioning where he'd been or what had happened. That night he dressed and attended a rare Wednesday-night prayer meeting with her and she knew that was his way of apologizing. After Jennifer was asleep he made love to her, more slowly and more tenderly than he had in a long time.

Later, he lay with his head on her breasts, as if he were the child. She felt a wetness on his cheek, and like a mother, she began to caress his forehead and his back. "It's all right, Sam. I know how hard it is. I'm sorry. I wish I could make it easier."

"You do, Susan. I couldn't do it without you. I'm tired and cranky and you're always so good to me. There are times when I don't understand why I treat you so badly. Granddaddy taught me to respect my wife, to take care of her, to remember she's a lady. I'm a failure. He'd be disappointed in me."

"Oh, Sam. Sometimes I think your granddaddy didn't know much about women. I don't want to be a lady, I want to be your partner. Your grandmother must have been a very lonely woman."

"I don't guess I know," he said. "She was just Grandmother." He began to nuzzle her body, tasting her cautiously, as if he were afraid he'd be rejected.

"Well, I'm not just Susan. I'm learning a lot about myself, Sam. I'm not a girl anymore. I'm a woman and I need you Sam, the way a woman needs a man." She shifted so her nipple was pressed against Sam's mouth. With a groan he took it between his lips.

She gave him a few minutes, then turned him to his back and let him have the other nipple, all the time rubbing the vee between her legs against his awakening penis. Drawing herself to her knees, she pulled her nipple from his mouth and replaced it with her tongue.

"Susan—Susan—what are you doing, Susan?" His question lost its intensity as she covered his mouth so completely that he could no longer speak. Then, lifting herself, she reached beneath her and held his penis so she could direct it inside her as she lowered her body.

"I'm loving my husband, Sam. I'm making love to you. Don't talk. Just lie there and let me do it. Oh, Sam, you make me feel so good." And she stopped worrying about how much noise she was making or how wanton her actions were.

Sam's protest were cut short as his body was caught up in Susan's passion. He tried to hold back, tried to tell her that she shouldn't be on top, that he was the man and the man always got on top. But this time all his preconceived ideas of sex between a man and his wife disappeared in the hot, throbbing passion of the woman riding him.

Afterward, he lay silent, stunned. When Susan let out a deep sigh of contentment and rolled away, he felt the sticky aftermath of their lovemaking between his legs. Finally he sat up, walked to the bathroom, and closed the door.

Lust like that was wrong. He wouldn't call it a sin because he wasn't a man to do much churchgoing, but he felt guilty, and he told himself that Susan's behavior was somehow his fault. He knew that only loose women did things like that. He tried not to remember how good it had been. It had been his fault for losing control.

He ought never to have gone to the juke joint just over the county line, but sometimes his feelings built up until he thought he would explode. There were always women there, women who appealed to his baser nature. Not women like Susan. But somehow she'd known the evil desires he'd had and she'd responded. Yes, that was it. What had happened was his fault. He was being punished. He'd just put it out of his mind and make certain that neither he nor Susan ever lost control like that again.

He made his way back to bed, content that he'd worked out an answer. He'd just stay away from bars and liquor and women who visited places like that. Sam lay down and let out a deep sigh.

"Sam? Are you all right?"

"I'm fine, Susan. Go to sleep."

"Sam, we need to talk."

"Not tonight, Susan. We need to sleep. I have a hard day tomorrow."

"That's what I wanted to talk about, Sam. I hate to see you work so hard. Have you ever thought about—about selling the farm?"

If Sam had been surprised at Susan's abandon earlier, he was stunned now. "Sell the farm?"

"Yes, maybe move up to Augusta or down to Savannah. You could get a job and we could go to movies and—"

"I don't know what you think you're saying, Susan, but I'll never sell this farm. It's the Winslow legacy. What could you possibly want that you don't have here?"

"Hot water and a bathtub for one thing, and to have our baby delivered in a real hospital!"

"Jennifer got here fine. She was born in this very bed, just like all the Winslow children."

"Not Jennifer, Sam. The new baby. I'm pregnant."

Sam wanted to say that he was happy about the new baby, but all he could think about was Susan riding him like some loose woman. All he could feel was the sweet taste of her breast in his mouth. All he could see was the round little pooch of a stomach bloated again and blue-veined and ugly. He felt himself shrivel up as he bit back the rising threat of nausea.

"How? How could you allow that to happen?"

"Sam, you should be able to answer that. You come in at night after I'm asleep and wake me up ramming yourself inside me. Do you put a rubber on before you start?"

"Of course not. You bought one of those things, didn't you?"

"A diaphragm? Yes, but it has to be inserted. It doesn't work very well in the night-table drawer."

"But I expected you to take care of it," he protested stubbornly, knowing all the time that she was right.

"Sam, you don't expect me to do anything that you don't tell me to do. It's time you learned that I have thoughts and

221

needs, and I expect you to listen to them. Oh, Sam," she said, sliding her leg across his thigh, "we used to talk about dreams, our future. Now we just live together. Don't you care about how I feel?"

"Feelings aren't important, Susan. We have made a life together and we both have certain responsibilities. Talk is foolish now. Besides, it never works out like you want it to."

"I'm sorry I'm pregnant, Sam. I don't look forward to throwing up and getting fat. I don't look forward to having another baby in diapers when I'm just about to start potty training Jennifer. But most of all, I don't want you to shut me out of your bed like there's something wrong with me."

"It isn't you, Susan. It's me. I just don't feel right about making love to you when you're pregnant. I mean, I know that a baby doesn't know what we're doing, but I feel like it's there, listening, watching."

Susan took Sam's hand and laid it on her stomach. "Sam, there's a child there, a child that came from you fucking me, from you coming inside me and filling me with sperm. Those sperm went after what they wanted and we've made a baby, but it was the wanting each other that made it happen, the wanting and the good feelings that wanting made. That's the way it's supposed to be, Sam. That's the way God made it. You want me, Sam, and I want you!"

She slid his fingers down her body, through the hair, until she found the course of the moisture already seeping onto Sam's leg. "This is what you do to me, Sam." She pushed his finger inside and thrust herself against him. "And this is what *I* do to *you*." She moved her hand away from his and clasped his hardening penis, moving the sheath up and down in matching movements to her thrusting. "And I won't spend the next seven months doing without it."

In spite of the horror he felt, Sam gave up his protest, allowing himself to explore her body in a way that he never had. When he moved over her he wasn't fucking his wife; his wife didn't talk like that. The woman beneath him was one of those women back in the bar. When he allowed himself to say all the words he'd always held back, it wasn't Susan hearing them. When she gave herself fully to his needs, matching them with her own, he refused to acknowledge his awareness. Then he was coming again. It wasn't until he

222

heard Jennifer cry out that he realized how quickly he'd lost his resolve, or how Susan's response had made him behave so crudely.

His grandfather would be horrified.

But his grandfather had made a mistake. He'd made two mistakes. First he'd been convinced that Sam could take his place. And he'd chosen Susan as Sam's wife because Susan was a good girl, a real lady, a perfect Winslow woman.

Now Susan wanted to sell the farm.

Twenty-Five

While Susan stayed in Winslow and listened to Pat Boone on the radio, Margie was at the Fabulous Fox movie theater in Atlanta watching Yul Brynner weave his magic in *The King and I*. She was also building sets for a local production of *Bus Stop* and taking part in "intellectual" debates with her college friends at night.

"I have the answer," Richard said one night.

Margie lit a Pall Mall and leaned back waiting for whatever new pearl of wisdom he was ready to release.

"What if, on coming of age, every person in the world was given one nickel? And everything in the world was priced at a nickel."

"Doesn't sound too prosperous to me," Paul, another friend, observed. "You could never buy but one thing."

"No, that's the beauty of my theory," Richard said dramatically. "The nickel is actually worth ten cents. Every time you buy something that costs a nickel, you get a nickel back. That nickel is worth ten cents."

Margie sighed and blew out a long stream of white smoke. Richard. Even if she didn't know what he was saying half the time, she liked listening to him. He was smart and he forced her to ask questions and learn. And it was nice, being a pair. If Richard seemed less than enamored of her philosophical contributions, he didn't feel the same way about her body. If she wasn't as excited about having sex as she was with having Richard as her tutor, it seemed an even exchange.

By the time she'd completed her sophomore year of college, Eisenhower was beginning his second term as President, Richard had transferred to the university, and

224

Margie realized that she was still where she'd always been, on the outside looking in. Being Victoria's roommate made her Victoria's willing shadow. Being president of the drama club didn't bring her the prestige she'd expected, it just brought her all the work.

Margie built sets and painted scenery for the drama department, then went to the studio with Victoria and did the same thing again for Leonard, often doing her work and Victoria's, too. It was becoming obvious that covering for Victoria was the price she paid for being allowed into the inner circle.

Between projects she read history and current events, explored the art museum and the downtown Atlanta library. Margie was becoming a well-informed person, but her fingernails were permanently paint-stained whereas the beautiful, well-dressed day students still caught the tails of their comets. She was beginning to believe that she was holding on to a meteor that was falling to earth instead of aiming for the stars.

"What's wrong with me, Leonard? Why can't I get one lucky break? No, don't answer that. I love what I'm doing. I shouldn't complain."

Leonard looked up from the order sheet he was working on and sighed. Margie had so much potential, but she never really worked at anything hard enough. She latched onto people who had what she wanted, then depended on luck and consoled herself by calling it fate. If a thing was to happen, it would. If it didn't, it wasn't supposed to. That philosophy kept her going, but there were times when she let down her guard and allowed her pain to show.

"Why do you put yourself down, Margie? You're pretty and smart, and you're talented enough to do whatever you want if you really set your mind to it."

"Oh, Leonard. You're sweet, but I know the truth about myself. I'm not smart, I just parrot what I hear. I'm not pretty, I'm . . ." She remembered what Glory had said about her; "You have what men like and you don't even use it."

"The truth is, Leonard, I'm almost a lot of things. But the only thing I've ever been good at is letting myself fall for the wrong men. But no more. I'm finished with men. If I can't succeed by myself, I'll just be a failure."

One thing had become painfully clear. Nick, Arthur, and

225

Richard had taught her that she didn't even have the kind of talent to keep a man. It was time for her to rethink her plan and start again on the campaign she'd abandoned when she'd met Victoria. She was tired of living in someone else's shadow. She wanted her own success.

"I'll never be a great actress, Leonard."

"My mother wanted me to be a concert pianist like she was. But I wanted—well, I thought I could take short cuts to being famous. So now I build sets for other famous people. Maybe the stage isn't where you ought to be. There are other ways, Margie."

"What? I'll never lose my southern accent. I can't ever land a local role worth having, so I'll never get to New York. Even if I could type well, and spell, which I can't, I can't write a straight news story for the college newspaper. My editor rewrites every word I turn in. So what do I do?"

Leonard had no answer for her. He put down his paperwork and poured a cup of the coffee he kept brewing in his office. What he wanted to do was put his arms around her and shake her. She was so busy trying to be like the people she admired, she never saw herself for what she was.

"I wish I could tell you, Margie. But we all have to find our own way."

"Sure, but how do I do that? Maybe I've been kidding myself. Maybe I should never have left Galilee. I could have taken a business course like Susan and gotten married and—"

"Why do you do that, Margie?"

"Do what?"

"You meet Victoria and move in with her. She's involved in the little theater groups, so you become their gofer. She works here, so you work here."

"Oh, no, Leonard. You don't understand. Victoria is what I've always wanted to be. I love the theater. I love working here. If it weren't for Victoria I wouldn't have any of this."

"Victoria is a failure, Margie. She draws her strength from the people around her. She becomes whatever and whoever she needs to be at the time. Inside, she's a big open space, a blank. You can't be somebody else until you know who *you* are."

"I know who I am, Leonard. And don't talk like that about Victoria. She's an artist. She's sensitive and she cares

226

about me."

Leonard was unusually quiet for the next few days, then they were back to their old relationship. She could talk to Leonard. He let her be herself and she let him be her balancing rod.

Nothing changed until Victoria brought home another protégée, a black girl who had dreams of being the first Negro student to enter a white university. The militant young woman moved into Victoria's tiny apartment, sleeping on the floor. Victoria left her job at Leonard's studio and went to work in the office of a group actively planning the desegregation of Atlanta. They'd already taken on the public library and were involved in a campaign to open the city parks to blacks. Next they would take on the churches.

Margie wasn't asked to move, but she no longer blindly respected her roommate. She listened to their heated arguments, but Margie had a hard time seeing Victoria in church. As far as Margie could tell, Victoria didn't believe in anything but herself, but she knew how single-minded Victoria could be about her latest cause.

Having attended services at the black churches back home, Margie loved the freedom of their worship. Why they'd want to change that for the stiffness of the First Baptist Church in Atlanta was hard for Margie to understand. But that opinion was small-town and diverged from the intellectual climate of which Margie considered herself a part, so she kept it to herself.

Margie failed French for the second time and decided that she was wasting her time and money in night school. She had to stop fooling herself about what she wanted and do something productive. Leonard was right. She wasn't going to be rich and successful like Glory. She wasn't going to get married and be a wife like Susan. She wasn't smart enough to graduate from college like JoEllen and she'd taken the same road as Victoria long enough.

Margie severed her connections with Victoria by finding a job with a publishing company as a typist and moving into a one-room efficiency apartment. It wasn't until she started to work that she found out the company published banking regulations and the job was almost as bad as filing invoices. But what was worse was that she'd left Leonard behind, and

227

of all the people in her life, she missed him.

Margie Raines had been in Atlanta for four years and she hadn't even seen her comet. The summer of 1954 seemed like a long-ago dream. She'd stopped believing in fate. Glory had been wrong when she said Margie was a rosebud, waiting to open. The petals had opened wide. Now they were falling off and drying up.

Twenty-Six

Susan Hayworth won an Oscar as Best Actress for her role in *I Want To Live* in January of 1959 and Sydney Poitier starred in *A Raisin in the Sun* the following March.

In a last desperate attempt to do something at least marginally creative, Margie applied for a job with the leading advertising firm in town. Neither her schooling nor her theatrical experience qualified her for the copywriting job she'd hoped for, but her deliberate seduction of the personnel director got her a job as a typist in the pool, which she hoped might lead to something better.

For the first time in her life, Margie was reasonably secure; a real job with benefits, an efficiency apartment that was all hers, and a chance at a career. Every day for the next two and a half years she carefully dressed in one of her two business suits, a pert black hat, gloves, and high-heeled black pumps, and rode the trolley downtown to her office at Five Points.

Then one day the black cobweb of trolley lines were removed and diesel buses belching gray smoke took their place . . .

If Margie was overdressed for her job in the typing pool, she didn't let that faze her. She had ambition and ideas, and she knew there was opportunity somewhere. She just had to find it and be ready when she did. She continued to polish the copy she'd been given to type, but her boss pretended not to notice. Every time she asked for an opportunity to submit an idea on her own, he gave her a raise and patted her on the back. She needed the money, but she needed the chance to prove her worth even more.

229

It took another seduction, that of an account executive, before she was promoted into a full secretarial position.

To save her salary to pay her rent and add to her business wardrobe, Margie often went across the street to the low-priced Krystal at lunch and ordered two hamburgers and a Coca-Cola, being careful to brush her teeth afterward to remove the odor of onions before returning to the tiny desk outside her boss's office.

It was June of 1963, and the sidewalks were teeming with lunch-hour workers. The day was hot and she hurried the last few steps past the newsstand to the burger restaurant. Inside the door the smell of onions and frying meat assaulted her. She stepped up to the counter and got in line to place her take-out order.

"Margie?"

She turned. It was Victoria, rumpled and thin, her hair flying across her face, her yellow-stained fingers holding the usual cigarette. "Victoria! Hello. How are you?"

"Oh, I'm—I'm fine. Say, I wonder—I wonder if you'd do something for me." Victoria always spoke in an apologetic voice, as if she was unsure of her status. On stage she portrayed her character with more heightened realism, but in person, talking with someone she knew, she was all hesitation.

"Sure," Margie said. She hadn't remembered Victoria being quite so seedy-looking. She'd changed in the last few years, or maybe Margie had. They didn't share the same philosophy of life any longer. Margie was firmly committed to finding her way to the top, and Victoria was traveling a strange path. "What do you need, Victoria?"

"Would you place my order for me. I'd like to sit down. I—I don't feel . . . well."

"Sure." That was simple enough, and probably the truth. Victoria didn't look well. "I'd be glad to order for you. What do you want?"

At that moment the man in line ahead of Margie picked up his order and left and the counter clerk called out, "Next?"

Margie stepped up to the counter. "I'd like two hamburgers and a small Coke. Oh, and . . ." She turned to Victoria who was standing beside her. "What do you want?"

"Ten burgers and ten small Cokes" was her answer. "Here's the money. I'll wait over there."

Margie took the money and added, "Make that twelve burgers and eleven small Cokes."

The waitress raised her eyes from the pad she was checking, gave Margie a long, hard look, and said sharply, "I'm afraid not. You can't fool me. We don't serve niggers in here."

Margie looked around. Behind her, snaking out the door, were nine black students following Victoria to the booth.

"But I'm not with them," she protested.

"But you're with *her,*" the waitress said, "And she's with *them.*"

There was an explosion of a flash from a camera and Margie gasped. Someone had taken her picture. Someone who thought she was with them. She looked around in a panic. What had Victoria done?

"Why?" she asked Victoria, mouthing the word that never became audible.

"Excuse me, miss?" A woman standing in the doorway holding a pad and pencil was looking at Margie. "May I have your name?"

"My name? Why?"

"I'd like a quote, please. Did you expect to trick the restaurant into serving blacks?"

"I—I don't even know these people," Margie managed to say as she looked around, trying to find a way to escape. But the reporter and her cameraman blocked the door. To make matters worse the blacks gathering outside the restaurant began to call out ugly comments.

Margie wanted to die. Victoria had used her. It wasn't as if she didn't have sympathy for the Negroes' cause; she truly did. A person ought to be able to go inside a restaurant and be served, but for her to be used by someone she'd thought was her friend was such a shock that she froze where she stood.

Then, from the cluster of blacks gathered around Victoria, a man with a limp stepped forward. "She didn't have anything to do with this. But I think I can give you the answer to that question if you'll step outside with me."

In a few minutes the reporter and photographer emptied the doorway and Margie fled into the crowd, her face burning, her breath a painful throb in her throat. It wasn't until she reached her office that she realized how familiar the

231

black man had looked. She'd seen him somewhere before, but when or where eluded her.

Lunch she could skip, she decided, but when her picture made the front page of the late-afternoon edition of the *Atlanta Journal,* she found that job security was a fleeting thing. The world might not know the name of the woman in the black suit who tried to trick the restaurant into serving blacks, but the advertising firm for whom she worked did. She also learned that the black man with the limp was Joseph Cheatham, Jr., a political activist and budding movie script writer from California.

Suddenly she had no job, no future, and no efficiency apartment. Everything was lost in that one short moment. Margie Raines was finally somebody—somebody even Margie didn't want to be. An integrationist.

All the philosophical discussions she'd had with her friends over late-night coffee, all the brave proclamations that they wouldn't mind going to classes with blacks, all the wicked secret speculations about the physical prowess of the dark-skinned men who'd been such a part of the southern woman's past evaporated in that public moment.

No matter what Margie might have said, she was still a white, small-town southern girl who'd been taught to call the woman across the road who came in to iron Aunt Liza, at the same time she'd been cautioned not to be too familiar with the children. She had her place and role to play, as did they.

Now the mold was broken and Margie was terrified.

Thank God nobody in Galilee read the Atlanta papers. Thank God for her old friend Leonard, who took her in, gave her a place to live in his theatrical studio and her old job back, even if he had to let another student go. Thank God her grandfather hadn't lived to see her disgrace. She felt tears of self-pity welling up in her eyes.

Then, out of nowhere, she remembered Susan's courage. Susan, who'd come to the aid of a black boy on a Sunday afternoon nine years ago, in Galilee during the summer of 1954.

Twenty-Seven

"Don't you think it's time you gave up your racing, Ted? It's the wrong image for a future politician."

The mayor was studying his assistant with narrowed eyes. Behind him, heavy equipment was ripping into the earth, excavating the foundations for the new school. It had taken five years to find the land and even longer to raise the money to begin building. But Teddy had pulled it off, just as Ed Jordan had expected.

Everything was proceeding just the way Ed had envisioned, everything except for Claude. But that was something he couldn't change and he tried not to think about the forty-three-year-old son he was still supporting up there in New York City. Except for Teddy's interest in drag racing, Ed was content. Teddy didn't drive the cars anymore, but he still built them in his brother Ben's garage.

"That's just a hobby, Mr. Jordan. I can't see how it's a problem. I like working with my hands."

One of the machines made a bobble and the sound of spinning tires sent out the smell of burnt rubber. "Damn, Ted. I'm already donating most of the cost of this work, I can't afford to lose a piece of equipment."

Teddy was already halfway to the site. What he saw was a puzzle. They'd dug down about three feet. Now the back left tire of the motorgrader was mired in what looked like white mud.

"What is it, Mo?" Mayor Jordan asked.

"Don't know, boss. Looks like wet kaolin."

"But kaolin isn't gooey," one of the other men commented. "Must be something else in there with it. Never saw

233

anything quite like it."

"Somebody get over here and pull me out," Ed said.

By the time they rescued the machine and revised the plans for the building site, Teddy had the soft white clay all over his shoes, his hands and arms. He headed back to the construction office to clean up.

After a couple of comments about making mud pies, he got past the secretary and into the bathroom, where he turned on the water, hoping the hardened clay would dissolve. To his surprise it became moist and even softer as he wet it. Its consistency was almost like hand cream. Not only did it wash off but it removed all the oil stains left over from working on the dragster's engine the night before, and soothed the cuts on his hands at the same time.

If his white mud would do that, it ought to do a job on those pistons and nicked cylinders he was cleaning. Wouldn't hurt to try; they were too burned to use like they were. Following a hunch, he drove back to the school site and did some calculating. One of the reasons they'd managed to get this land so cheap was because it had never produced well and there was a swampy area joining the section. Teddy strolled down to the bog and took a look.

No doubt about it. The ground was white and gooey. There was apparently a large area of the white mud, and somewhere out there was a spring. The combination had left the area desolate and unstable. Back at the building site, Teddy scooped up an empty oil can full of the clay.

Later that night, he leaned back and surveyed the pistons. Slick as a whistle. Maybe he was on to something. If it worked, he'd found a real short cut to cleaning automobile parts.

It didn't immediatley occur to him that the clay might have contributed to the engine's performance the next Saturday night at the tracks, but the car outran the nearest local competitor easily. He knew he had to get another supply of the white mud before the workers covered up his source. But how would he keep it from drying up?

Teddy finally decided that he didn't have to worry about that; he'd buy the swamp. He'd saved his money and he was certain that old man Jones wouldn't mind parting with another unproductive section of land.

The mayor didn't understand why Teddy would buy a section of swamp land and insisted that if he wanted to invest in land, he ought to at least buy some good acreage along with the swamp. A quiet word to the bank and Teddy suddenly owned a hundred acres of farm land. He then leased it back to Mr. Jones, who kept on doing what he'd been doing for forty years, planting corn, and shook his head at the foolishness of the young.

Susan and Sam had been married seven years. Jennifer was almost six, Marcie was four, and their son Mark two and a half. By the time Jennifer and Marcie were Mark's age they'd begun following Sam around the farm. Not only was Mark still in diapers, but he still tried to nurse whenever Susan lifted him.

Sam wouldn't have approved, but Susan never refused her son. He seemed to need her much more than either of the girls and sometimes, she thought perversely, more than her own husband. Susan loved Mark with all the affection she couldn't give to the man she married.

That was the spring Sam hired eighteen-year-old Bud Screws, a college student, to work on the farm so he could take a job driving the school bus. By working for the county Sam got benefits that his family badly needed. Bud lived nearby, so he went home every night, but Susan was expected to provide his dinner. Sam had hoped that Bud would make his workload easier. Instead, he planted an extra field and, in the end, started earlier and finished later.

Bud had fought against the snide remarks over his name for most of his life. Finally he decided to forget the comments and live up to the name. The first time he saw Susan Winslow he was shocked by her earthy sexuality. Sam was known as a hardworking, fair-minded man of few words. He seemed to ignore the woman who scurried around the kitchen like some servant charged to be efficient and quiet.

Once, when he realized that she was staring at his bare chest showing between the edges of his open shirt, Bud felt a response that embarrassed him. Susan was a small woman, with a sun-kissed face and soft, curly black hair that hung

235

limply against her forehead in the heat. Perspiration had dampened her blouse, outlining full breasts and a wide pelvis that would hold a man just right.

"Eat you food, Bud," Sam had said. "My wife's a good cook, but she has work to do, so we don't tie up her time by dawdling at the table."

Once Sam sent him to the house for ice water and to call the county agent to set up a time for him to come to the farm and examine a problem with the pine trees. The acres of pine trees Granddaddy Winslow had planted in the 'fifties were ten years old now and threatened with an outbreak of new insects determined to halt their growth. Sam was worried. Those trees were to pay for the children's education.

Bud had stepped up on the porch, catching sight of Susan through the open window. He'd felt himself harden at the sight of her full breasts beneath the halter she was wearing with her shorts. For a moment he'd just stood there, watching. He let out a sigh, and she looked up and saw him.

She met his gaze head on, simply staring for a long minute before opening the door. There was a tension there so palpable he could taste it. She'd seen his desire.

"I—I need to use the phone. Sam wants me to call someone for him."

She stepped aside and pointed to the phone, standing in the open doorway while he made the call. Bud tried not to look, but with the light behind her, her body was outlined against it like a silhouette.

He thanked her and started back through the door. When she moved to allow him to pass, he adjusted his direction and they met, body to body, in the heat of the afternoon. She gasped and looked up at him, her eyes dark and hot.

"I'm sorry," she said.

"I'm sorry," he echoed.

But neither moved.

After a long moment she let go of the screen door. It slammed shut behind them. "You ought to go," she whispered.

"Yes."

One of the children called out and Susan moved quickly past him and out of sight down the hall. Bud walked out the door and slowly across the field. When Sam asked him where the cold water was, Bud endured his displeasure and

236

said he had forgotten it.

But he didn't forget Susan Winslow. For the next three weeks he camped outside Sam and Susan's bedroom window watching and listening, knowing that what he was doing was wrong, but unable to stop. Bud learned that Sam was a man of few words in bed as he was everywhere else.

Bud stopped trying to hide his interest in his employer's wife. Blatantly he followed her with his gaze at the dinner table, finding ways to accidentally touch her, drawing her out in conversation until Sam would cut him down with a glance that said he'd heard enough talk. Only with the children did Sam really let go. Sam often allowed the little girls to tag along with him, on the tractors, in the fields. They adored their father and followed his every command.

Through the summer Bud watched. Susan often held the boy, straddling him across her hip, watching with sadness in her eyes as Sam ignored his son. The child, Mark, seemed content to have all his mother's attention. He fondled her openly, hiding behind her legs when he was on the floor and climbing into her lap whenever she sat. It was hard for Bud to understand a man who spent more time with his daughters than his son.

Sam attended two meetings each month: he went to the private school board meeting with Teddy, who'd surprised everyone by accepting the job of heading up the committee, and he went to the farm bureau meeting, alone. He'd stop early, clean himself up and drive off in the truck, leaving instructions for Bud to finish the chores and put the tractor in the barn.

It was late August and the hottest day they'd had when Bud decided to take a swim in Sam's lake before he headed home for the night.

He'd just climbed from the water when he heard someone coming toward the lake. Quickly stepping into the trees, Bud waited. It was Mrs. Winslow hurrying down the path, shedding her clothes as she ran. By the time she reached the water she was completely nude. Before she jumped in Bud was already hard. He watched as she swam around, torn between joining her and watching her white body in the dusky light. Then she stopped moving and turned toward the shore, stopping her gaze at the spot where Bud stood watching.

237

He stepped into the path and waited, without speaking.

For a long moment she treaded water, then started toward the bank and held out her hand. He pulled her up and into his erection, capturing her breast in his free hand.

"We can't stay here," she said. "I can't hear the children."

She wasn't sending him away. Instead, she pressed herself against him hard. Then she pulled away and led him down the path, stopping only to pick up her clothes as they moved.

"Where?" he said in a voice so hoarse that he didn't recognize himself.

"On the porch."

"What if . . . ?"

"We'll hear."

Susan felt her heart pounding. She moved as if in a dream, across the yard and onto the porch. She lay down on the rag rug and pulled the boy on top of her, taking him inside her and giving in to the hot pulsing of her instant response. Clasping him inside her legs she met his young body thrust for thrust, feeling the approaching climax before he'd half begun.

"Wow! I never had anything like that," he gasped, still inside her, feeling the moisture trickling out and matting the hair between them. "You're wild. You're—you're something. I didn't know you felt like that about me."

"I don't, Bud." Susan was beginning to have grave doubts about what she'd done. She'd thought only a husband and wife could experience that kind of earth-shattering release. It was disconcerting to find that it could happen with somebody other than Sam.

"Then why did you let me?"

Susan lay, clamping her muscles around the boy who was still hard inside her. She tried to answer his question, as much for herself as for him. "I needed to be wanted, Bud, me—the woman I am. And you did."

"Yes, ma'am, I did—do." And he forgot any other questions he might have asked.

For the rest of that summer Susan and the young student found ways to be together. He liked it when she yelled, when she found different ways to make love, when she showed her intense pleasure. He didn't like using rubbers, and he had to deal with a guilty conscience when he was with Sam, and pain when he stood beneath Sam's window and listened to

Susan's silence when Sam occasionally made love to her.

Summer ended. The school building was going up. Bud went back to college and life moved on, stopping only momentarily in November when President John Kennedy was assassinated. Susan mourned. Sam never seemed to notice. He never knew about the note she got from Jody, who felt Kennedy's loss deeply.

The next summer Susan was disappointed when Sam hired an older man to help out. She decided to let her mother keep her children while she took a part-time job. Her income would help ease their financial burdens and the mayor, for whom she worked, had an office with very thick walls.

Susan loved Sam with all her heart, but she'd learned that there were two Susans, the one Sam wanted and the secret one who Sam would never understand. She thought of Glory and that first afternoon when Glory had made the four friends see one another as sexual beings. She wondered what might have happened if that summer had taken a different turn: if Sam had made love to her then, if Jody hadn't written letters of longing and dreams, if Glory and the others hadn't moved away.

But that summer *had* happened. The innocent gardenia was beginning to bruise and she didn't know how to stop it. There was no one for her to talk to, and, besides, talk wasn't what she needed.

Twenty-Eight

Glory Sasser studied herself in the mirror and frowned. At twenty-seven she was getting little lines at the corners of her eyes, age lines. And she'd noticed a perceptible sag to her breasts when she'd dressed tonight. Age. Glory had never thought she'd grow old.

Doug Masters could take care of that. He'd promised her that she would never have to age, not as long as he could keep her beautiful. He was only a fair lover, but he was kind, and there were times when Glory needed kindness. And Doug was the best plastic surgeon in Savannah. Maybe a few sessions at the gym would be in order, too. She'd never had a weight problem, but a few extra pounds here and there were beginning to creep up in spite of the diet pills she ate like M & M's.

She reached for her lipstick and swore. The red one, the new one, was the one she wanted, but it wasn't there. After rummaging in the mass of cosmetics strewn across the top of her dressing table she swept them to the floor and let out a yell. "Letisha!"

The door opened and a uniformed maid appeared. "Don't be yelling at me, Miss Glory. What you doing throwing all that stuff on the carpet?"

"Where is it, you thieving bitch, my new Elizabeth Arden lipstick?"

"Now you know that I don't wear none of that stuff, and I ain't now and never have been no bitch. You just watch your tongue, missy, or I'll lock up your medicine and call Dr. Roger."

Glory gasped. She knew that Letisha was only making an

240

idle threat, but she couldn't afford to push her too far. Her nerves were drawn tight and she was running low on Valium. Getting more prescriptions was becoming difficult. Even Fincher was beginning to caution her about overuse. But they didn't understand. Nobody did. There were times when it was only the pills that kept her from getting in her car and driving off the nearest bridge.

She took a deep breath. "I'm sorry, Tish. I must have put it in one of my purses. I'm just on edge tonight. This will be my first time as chairman of the Winter Ball. I'm—I'm nervous."

"Of course you are, baby. Now, just let Letishia look for that lipstick. You put your dress on. Dr. Roger will be sticking his head in here any minute, impatient to go, and you don't want him to see you screaming like some fishwife."

Tish was right. Roger would glare at her and then he'd ask her what she'd taken. He'd stopped bringing his medical bag into the house after he discovered her riffling in it one night when she couldn't sleep. Roger hadn't mentioned what she was doing: the bag just disappeared. Confrontation wasn't something Roger could handle. If he had, perhaps their lives would have been different. But the Winslow women always married weak men. The strong ones they took as lovers.

Glory needed tonight to be a success. Tonight she wanted to be perfect—not just for herself, but for Roger. She turned to her closet and slipped the dress from beneath its wrapper. Nobody had yet seen what she was going to wear. She'd planned her dress very carefully to match the decorations. Having selected them, she had the advantage over the other doctors' wives. Of course that would have made little difference. Glory always outshone them, to their dismay and her triumph.

The dress was midnight blue, with silver threads woven through the fabric. It was short, showing a scandalous amount of black-stockinged leg. Over the dress she wore a silver jacket, sheer enough to tantalize but opaque enough to be considered tasteful.

She clamped great rhinestone earrings around the lobes of her ears. By the next ball she intended the rhinestones to be diamonds. Her hair, made even fuller by the addition of a hairpiece, had been piled high on her head in a modified French twist. She'd seen Mrs. Kennedy's sister wearing the same style in *Life* magazine last week.

241

By the time she'd clasped the matching rhinestone bracelet around her waist, Letisha had found the lipstick. Glory applied the red color to her lips and added a touch of dark-blue mascara to her eyelashes. She leaned back and decided that the look was perfect. Ice and fire. With the blue of her dress against the icy-white background of the decorations of the hotel, she'd be the only one any man at the dance would see.

"My, God, Glory. Surely you aren't going to wear that!" Roger was standing wide-eyed in the doorway.

Letisha made a quick exit, closing the door behind her.

"Don't you like it?" Automatically Glory assumed a vampish pose as she leaned back against her dressing table, allowing the jacket to fall away, exposing her body provocatively.

"Damn it, Glory." Roger voiced his usual argument, feeling the telltale tightening of his body even as he spoke. "What will the other women say?"

"It doesn't matter what the women say, does it, darling? The men are the ones who will vote on the next chief of surgery, aren't they?"

"I've told you before, Glory, I'll get that job, but I'll get it on my ability—not through politics."

"Bullshit! Nobody ever gets anything because of ability. It's who you know and what you're willing to do that gets you where you want to go. Right now, you do all the dirty work and that's just where they want you to stay." Glory hadn't missed the extension of his trousers when he'd caught sight of her dress, and for just a moment she'd felt a response in her own body. But when he started that whining about his honesty, her desire had vanished.

Roger glared at her, his beautiful wife who had been sleeping with the hospital Chief of Staff since the first year they'd come to Savannah. He knew it, though he pretended he didn't, and he suspected that the others knew as well. Roger cringed every time he thought about her beneath that old man. But he'd kept quiet, because to admit his knowledge would also admit his inability to stop her.

"Glory, I've closed my eyes to the things you've done to 'help me,' but I won't have you buy the chief's job for me. I'm the logical person for the job and I expect to get it—without your help. I deserve it. I've earned it."

242

Glory picked up her evening bag and checked the contents to make certain that it contained both her cigarettes and her pills.

"Roger Sasser, when is it going to sink into that thick, stupid head of yours? You aren't automatically going to get that job. They're considering bringing in a man from Emory, a man who has grant money that the hospital needs. We've got to do something. Not just me this time, but you, too."

Roger gasped. "How do you know that?" He'd heard gossip, of course, about their interviews, but until now he hadn't given it much credence. Leave it to Glory to know more about what was going on with his work than he did.

"I—I just heard it somewhere," Glory said lamely. "Some of the other wives were gossiping." But she knew that Roger wouldn't believe that. The doctors didn't discuss internal procedure with their wives, only their mistresses.

"Then I'll just have to go back into private practice. That's what I'd planned to do all along. I'm a good doctor, Glory. I can make it."

"Don't be foolish, Roger. Who'd go to a doctor who was passed over for promotion by the hospital authority? All you'd get would be the charity cases and the dregs. I have no intention of being married to a failure."

"Is that what you think of me?" Roger turned white and sagged to a sitting position on the bed. Belatedly Glory realized that letting Roger know was a mistake. Lately he'd seemed more and more defeated. Roger was a good doctor. He was a good man, but he'd never learned to play the game. Glory sighed. Tonight was too important to let him blow it. She'd have to find a way to fix the damage she'd done.

"Roger, you're a very fine doctor. This has nothing to do with ability."

He didn't even hear her.

"Roger? Roger, look at me," she said, letting her jacket fall to the floor.

He glanced up as Glory unzipped the dress and stepped out of it, wearing only a black lace garter belt with long black straps hooked to the black stockings.

"Stand up, darling. I want you to see us, together. We're a team—remember? I make you strong. Come over here."

As if sleepwalking, Roger stood up and walked toward the closet where Glory was standing before the full-length

243

mirror on the door. He could see himself in the mirror, and Glory's bottom, white and plump and bare.

"Glory! You aren't wearing panties?"

"No," she admitted in a low voice. "Just watch, Roger. Don't look at me, look at the mirror."

Kneeling down, she unzipped his trousers and pulled his penis through the opening. Already half hard, it quickly stiffened. "Roger, you'll get the job. Don't ever worry about anything. I'll take care of you as I always do. I'll make you strong."

She took him into her mouth, and he watched, feeling the rising roar of power that she always gave him. This woman was his. She loved him. She wanted him. She was all that counted. As he spilled into her mouth he forgot whatever he might have said and let her take him wherever she wanted to go, just as he always did.

Later at the party, the sense of power lingered. When Mike Littlejohn's wife got a bit overheated, Roger was more than willing to take her out on the balcony for a breath of fresh air. With her, he was in charge. The element of danger didn't matter, he could give to her what he could never give to Glory. He could plunge inside her and know that he was the force that brought her to her knees.

He knew as he slammed into her what he's always known. Glory was like a drug. She was the source of his power. She instilled it in him and fanned it to a peak. Only when he'd made love to her could he claim that dominance that made him a man. No matter what she did, or who she did it with, he'd never be able to say no to her.

The only thing he couldn't accept was Glory's refusal to have more children. Nine-year-old Damon was his son, but Roger never felt comfortable with the quiet, brooding boy. He wanted a girl, a girl with blond hair and blue eyes like the Sasser women, a girl to replace the one they'd lost.

They didn't talk about the deformed baby born eight years ago, but he knew that Glory had been as deeply affected as he. She would never have anything less than perfect. When he tried to explain that the child's genetic flaws were merely a freak occurrence, that it was unlikely that they'd have another deformed child, she wouldn't believe him.

Across the ballroom, Glory was dancing with Greg Fuller, the hospital pharmacist. "But Greg," she was saying, "I don't see why you can't refill my prescription without my having to get another one. All you have to do is say that my husband called it in."

She pressed herself against him, knowing that he understood what she was promising in return, knowing, too, that she was running the risk of being gossiped about. But she couldn't stop herself. She'd think of a way to cover any anxiety. After all, her husband was going to be the Chief of Surgery.

"I can't sleep, Greg. Then when I finally get to sleep, I can't wake up. I need the pills to keep my weight down and keep going. Everybody is taking diet pills, what's so wrong with that?"

"Nothing is wrong, Glory, if they're prescribed. It's just that if you are supposed to take one, you automatically take two. Look at yourself. Your pupils are dilated, you're high as a kite, and you're drinking straight vodka. Your body can't take that kind of stimulation."

"You're right, Greg. That's why you're going to take care of my body. Why don't we go down to the garage to my car? I need you, Greg. See how much I need you?"

Glory maneuvered Greg behind a potted palm and slid his hand beneath her dress, between her legs. She was sloppy wet. She knew he felt her rippling to his touch.

"God, Glory!"

"I'll meet you downstairs in the garage," she purred. "Look for Roger's Lincoln, in the corner. Hurry!"

Lawrence Fincher was the only one who saw what was happening. Glory started to head toward the ladies' room, veered off, and at the last minute stepped into the elevator. Shortly afterward, Greg Fuller started casually in the same direction. At the elevator, Fincher intercepted him.

"Where, Fuller?"

"Where what?"

"Where are you meeting her?"

"I don't know what you mean, Dr. Fincher."

"Yes you do. You're meeting Glory Sasser and I want to know why and where."

"What if I am, what are you going to do?"

"I'm going to meet her instead."

245

"But, Dr. Fincher. You don't have to do this. Everybody knows that you can meet her whenever you want anyway."

Fincher's eyes narrowed dangerously. "I trust that you will never repeat that, anywhere, anytime, Mr. Fuller, if you expect to keep your job in this hospital."

"Eh, no, of course not. She wants more pills. I'm meeting her in the garage, at her car, that's all."

"What kind of pills?"

"Uppers, downers, Valium. Surely you know that she's an addict. Everybody—"

"Everybody?"

Greg Fuller stopped himself. "I mean that everybody prescribes them for her. At least they used to. Lately they've been backing off, and she wants me to give them to her."

"Do it," Fincher said.

"How?"

"Under my name."

The elevator door opened, and Fincher stepped inside. He thought about what he was going to do as the elevator plunged to the parking area below the hospital. More and more he'd become completely infatuated by Glory Sasser. She made him feel young again. In ways that he'd never dreamed, he needed her. Until now, he'd been able to deal with the fact that there were other men, but no longer. Fincher would share her with her husband, but nobody else.

He stepped into the garage and found Roger's car in the far corner, the dark corner. Keeping to the shadows he circled the area until he reached the silver Lincoln. He opened the door and slid into the backseat.

She was lying across the seat, her legs spread. She was hot and ready. It didn't matter when she realized that it was Fincher instead of Greg. The whole incident was over in a matter of minutes.

Afterward, she sat up, smoothed the wrinkles from her dress, and reached for her purse.

"Where's Greg?"

"He won't be coming."

"But I need Greg, Fincher."

"No, you don't need anybody but me. I'll take care of you, darling. I'll see that you have anything you want. From now on, I'm the only man you sleep with."

"What about Roger?"

"I don't care about him. Just stay away from the others."

"On one condition, Fincher."

"What's that?"

"Roger gets the job as Chief of Surgery."

"Done."

Roger Sasser took over as Chief of Surgery and Damon was sent away to boarding school. To cut down on her drinking and her need for prescription drugs, Dr. Fincher gave Glory her first injection of his own special ingredients designed to make her totally dependent on him.

For the next three years Glory alternated between being the most powerful woman in Savannah and a woman with an addiction so powerful she had to be secretly admitted to every drug and alcohol treatment facility in the South. After her latest release, Roger sent her home for a Thanksgiving visit, hoping that Adele could handle her increasing irrationality.

Glory hadn't known that Steven would be there with Elizabeth, pregnant for the second time. This time the Valium didn't work, neither did the combination of pills Glory took that resulted in a midnight trip to the hospital to have her stomach pumped out.

She had really wanted to die. Steven's wife was having another child. She could see them together, this tall, thin woman beneath Steven as he spilled himself into her, giving her what Glory wanted so badly.

The child should have been hers. Nobody could ever know how badly Glory wanted to be with Steven, have his child at any cost. Lately she'd had difficulty separating the dark, intense dreams of Steven from reality, and Roger. There were times when she knew that she was deluding herself into believing that she and Steven could have another normal child. They'd had Damon. Then she remembered their daughter.

Her daughter. It was those memories that forced her to retreat into that dark place where nobody could reach her. Roger had tried everything: doctors, long stays in private facilities that pretended to be health spas but were in fact designed to wean her away from pills and alcohol. But nothing helped. And she couldn't stop.

247

*   *   *

Roger hoped that if Glory became pregnant she would come to her senses. Lately he'd taken to piercing the condoms she always insisted he wear. And last month, in desperation, he'd substituted identical tablets for the as-yet-unmarketed samples of birth-control pills she was taking.

So far he didn't know how much he'd accomplished. And even if she did become pregnant, could he be certain that the baby was his? In the end, he decided he didn't care. He wanted another child and he intended, for once, to overrule Glory and make her pregnant. Then he'd hire a full-time nurse to make certain that she remained free of drugs and drink. To that end he'd made love to her almost every night for the three weeks before she left.

Glory finally pulled herself together, determined to find a way to be alone with Steven, but her mother seemed equally determined that the meeting not happen. After suffering through the last family dinner where Steven's wife made repeated attempts at conversation, Glory excused herself to go for a walk. She ended up in the cemetery where her baby daughter was buried and collapsed across the grave. When Steven appeared in the darkness it was as if she'd willed him there. He tried to comfort her, knowing as he put his arms around her that he wouldn't be able to let her go.

Three months later she learned that she was pregnant again—for the fourth time in her life. She threw up every morning for a week before Roger ambled into the bathroom with a big smile on his face.

"Looks like we're pregnant again, Glory."

"We are not. We can't be. I've taken my pill every day—no matter what," she said, making no reference to the fact that, in addition, she'd made certain that he used a condom.

"Doesn't matter."

Roger was too smug, too pleased. She felt too awful. She *was* pregnant again, and as much as she wanted the child to be Steven's, she knew it couldn't be. Though she hadn't used her diaphragm, she'd taken her birth control pills without fail. How could she be pregnant?

She stood up and wiped her face, leaning over the sink to wait for the next wave of nausea to pass. "Roger, how could this happen?"

248

"I'll tell you how, Glory." Roger stepped up behind her, reaching forward to clasp her breast with his hands as he pressed his erection against her. "I did it."

"You didn't. There's no way," she said, trying to move away from him.

"Oh yes I did, my loving wife. I substituted a placebo for your pills and my condoms were . . . altered slightly."

More and more often now she had blackout spells, and there were times when she had great blank spaces of time that she couldn't remember. She knew that Roger had been attentive both before she went to Winslow and since she'd returned, coming to her bed with increasing frequency. But after several double vodkas at night, she was only half awake when he rolled over on top of her.

"You bastard! You know I don't want to have any more children!"

"I know. What I don't know is *why*." For the first time, Roger felt a power of his own, coming from the knowledge that, for once, he'd bested Glory.

By this time he'd lifted her nightgown and was sliding himself between her thighs. Glory whirled around, felt herself go dizzy, turned, and caught the toilet seat to steady herself. That was all it took. Roger slid inside her, catching her waist to hold her up as she leaned forward.

"Why, Glory? Why? Because I want you pregnant. I want you fat. I want every man who looks at you to know that you belong to me. I want them to know that you're carrying my child. Damon is thirteen years old. It's like he isn't here and never was. Maybe if we have another child you can forget whatever it is that's driving you crazy."

Glory gritted her teeth and endured being taken. She'd never known Roger to be so aggressive. From the first time they'd made love she was the one who called the shots. She'd invited him into her bed until she'd tired of it. Then she'd turned him away until she'd finally reached the point that it didn't matter. He'd always accepted her wishes. But this was unlike him. Under other conditions she might even have been turned on. But now she was angry and she was scared.

Crazy? She'd been with Steven. She'd been with Fincher. She'd been with Roger. And now she was pregnant. Whose child was she carrying?

It was Steven's. Somehow she knew. And there was

249

something wrong. As sick as she'd been before, she'd never felt like this.

When Roger finally groaned and let her go, she slumped down onto the toilet. "Did that make you feel like a big man?"

His answer was strange. "I always feel like a big man when we make love, Glory. You make a man feel that way. You know it and you use it. You've always known that whatever else you are, you're the best fuck a man ever had. But now you're caught."

He'd done this to her on purpose. Roger had wanted her pregnant, and now that she was, he'd taken control. Glory didn't know what had happened and she was afraid. Brashly she railed out, "Roger Sasser, has it ever occurred to you that the child might not be yours?"

He looked at her for a very long time before he gave his deadly answer. "Has it ever occurred to you that it doesn't matter?"

Roger was wrong. It mattered. Glory still had nightmares about her little girl. Roger never knew that she'd held her baby, seen her terribly misshapen little body, suffered with her as she tried desperately to live. She'd never do that to a child again. She wouldn't.

Twenty-Nine

JoEllen glanced around the ward, grateful for the late-night quiet. On the surgery wing nurses had to deal with postoperative pain and uncertainties. The emergency room was fraught with tension and constant pressure, but here, on the late shift in the psychiatric ward, most of the patients had been sedated for the night.

The charts had been written up, the medications dispensed, and now, after midnight, the nurses' station was empty. The only other two attendants were making coffee in the lounge and talking in low voices.

JoEllen glanced at the chart on top and winced. A lobotomy. Thank God they didn't do that procedure anymore. Once, it had been the last resort for the worst mental cases. At last, medical science was learning more about the brain. Still, even now among the staff members there was a raging difference of opinion on how to handle violent cases.

This patient, a man who'd been brought in for treatment, had once had a streak so violent that contact with him was forbidden except by a full medical team. A single doctor or nurse didn't dare be alone with him. No longer. Now he shuffled along like some horror movie Zombie. Tomorrow he would be transferred back to a mental facility where he'd spend the rest of his life.

"Want coffee, JoEllen?"

Bobby Jones held out a thick white cup filled with steaming liquid. "JoEllen?" He tapped her on the shoulder. She reacted with a jerk so unexpected that the coffee splashed over the edge of the cup and spilled to the scuffed white shoes he was wearing.

"Hey, careful."

"Sorry, Bobby, you startled me."

"Yeah, you were standing there like that Williford kid in 321. At least you weren't holding your arm up in the air like the Statue of Liberty. He's been doing that for the past three hours. The kid's a real nut case."

JoEllen took the cup and frowned. "Don't say that. He can't help it. He's suffering from catatonic schizophrenia. He's in the rigid stage."

"Yeah," Peggy Porter, the other ward nurse, agreed. "If you don't believe it, try lifting the sheet."

"That's better than the other side of the problem." JoEllen took a sip of the coffee and grimaced. "What did you put in this?"

Bobby grinned. "Nothing that you want to know about. What's the other side of the kid's problem?"

"Destructive, hard to control excitement."

Peggy rolled her eyes upward. "Yeah. Like I said folks, look under the sheet. He's a man. Excitement is all the same, whether it's stationary or moving. Too bad—such a waste. I have it! Why don't we put him in with the sex addict. She'd love this guy."

"Why don't you put old Bob in with her? At least I could appreciate her."

"Bobby, I wish you'd be more respectful of our patients. Lorraine doesn't know what she's doing. One minute she's a Haight-Ashbury love child in a sexual frenzy and the next she's hiding under her bed. Until they find some medication to maintain her on an even keel she'll be kept sedated."

Bobby shook his head. "Like Peggy said, such a waste."

JoEllen joined in the conversation as she always did, keeping just enough distance between herself and the other two to avoid giving approval to the baser elements of their conversation. She didn't like this ward. She'd never been comfortable with extreme emotions. As often as she could, she found somebody else to cover the shortages of personnel she was responsible for. But there were times when she had no choice but to step in and fill a shift herself.

Lorraine Lindsey made her uneasy. There was something

252

about her furtive gaze and fluttering hands that set JoEllen on edge. Bobby might call her a hippie, but to JoEllen she was very ill. Her extreme mood swings unnerved JoEllen. Earlier tonight, as Lorraine waited for her evening medication, she'd begun to move about her room in fast, jerking little movements, singing, laughing, and talking rapidly under her breath.

JoEllen listened through the intercom as she became more and more agitated. When JoEllen entered the room, Lorraine had removed her hospital gown and was caressing her breasts.

For a moment JoEllen's mind flashed back to that afternoon in Glory's bedroom. There was something in Lorraine's expression that, just for a moment, reminded JoEllen of Glory then, and even more of the way she'd looked a few weeks ago when she'd driven all night from Savannah for the second time since JoEllen had been at Lawton General.

Glory had the hospital operator page JoEllen and they'd met in the corridor, just outside the children's ward where JoEllen was on duty. Glory looked tired. There were dark circles around her eyes and she was smoking intensely, holding her cigarette between her lips in that tight, determined way she had.

"JoEllen, I need to talk to you."

"Glory? Why didn't you let me know you were coming?" JoEllen felt uneasy. After the first year Glory had moved to Savannah, no one heard from her. She had cut herself off from her old friends completely, except for an occasional visit to her mother. Even Susan didn't see her, and Susan was family. But then, JoEllen didn't see either of them, either.

There were times when JoEllen felt as if Galilee were some great eye, focused on all of them, judging, waiting. If they came too close to the eye they'd all be destroyed. She shook off her thought. They were simply busy adults now, all leading different lives. But this was Glory and she needed JoEllen's help.

"Is there somewhere we can go?" Glory asked.

"Sure, in here." JoEllen led her into the lounge.

"God, what an awful place."

JoEllen glanced around. She was so used to it that she

253

hadn't noticed how tired it looked. There was a long, stained wooden table covered with half-empty coffee cups and soft drink bottles, a couch, springs broken from too many nights of too many interns grabbing some desperately needed minutes of sleep, and a few dog-eared magazines.

"Yeah. Well, it doesn't matter. We don't get to spend too much time in here anyway. What's wrong, Glory?"

"Everything. It's February and everything is brown and dead. I hate my life. I hate my husband. I hate myself the most." Glory laughed. "Do you realize that we're thirty-one years old and I'll never—I'll never again look like Twiggy in a miniskirt."

JoEllen didn't interrupt. It didn't take much to figure out that Glory was on the edge of hysteria.

After a long minute filled with deep breathing and darting glances, Glory announced, "I'm pregnant, JoEllen."

JoEllen felt as if she'd been kicked in the stomach. She didn't want to hear what Glory was about to say. "Well, that's wonderful, Glory."

"No, that's hell. I came to you for help once because I didn't want to have a baby. This time I *can't* have it, JoEllen. Nobody, not even my mother can make me have this child. I'll kill myself before I'll have it."

"Why, Glory? What's wrong?"

Glory stubbed out the cigarette she was smoking and immediately lit another.

"It isn't Roger's."

"Oh."

"I don't give a flying fuck about that. It's just that— You can't possibly understand and I can't explain, but I don't dare have the baby."

"Glory, I know this might sound crass, but how will Roger know?"

"He won't. But I will."

"How could you let something like this happen, Glory? How did you get pregnant?"

"I wasn't careful enough. If I'd known, I might have— No, that's a lie, I wouldn't have changed anything."

For a moment, a look of pure fulfillment washed over Glory's face. But the moment passed and Glory whirled around, desperation filling her eyes.

"What could possibly be so awful? Whose baby is it, Glory?"

Glory wasn't about to answer. She'd never talked about the men in her life except to say that what she did was her business and this would be no exception.

"You don't understand, JoEllen. It isn't that I don't want this child. I do. God knows, I want it so bad I hurt. But I can't. Never again. You must help me. You must!"

JoEllen glanced toward the door. Glory's voice was rising. Sooner or later someone on the staff would come into the lounge. She had to get Glory calm to be able to help her.

"Wait, Glory, wait. You stay right here for a minute. I'm going to get something to relax you."

"Not necessary, JoEllen. What shall I take? Pick out something." She opened her John Romaine bag and emptied it of the prescription bottles she had inside.

JoEllen lifted her eyebrows in amazement. Four different kinds of tranquilizers had been prescribed by four different doctors—the most recent one dated 1/18/68, just weeks ago. And none of the doctors was Glory's husband.

"Where did you get all this?"

"Let's just say that I have my sources. I'm a doctor's wife, remember. My husband's associates are . . . very helpful."

JoEllen selected a tablet and handed it to Glory. She poured a cup of water and watched her swallow it down. After a few minutes Glory seemed back in control.

"Why did you come to me, Glory?"

"I want you to help me get rid of it, like you did before. I trust you. Is that Dr. Brooks still here?"

"Glory, wouldn't one of those associates who gave you the pills help you? They're doctors."

"Only if they thought it was theirs. Making babies with my husband's associates would never happen. They're not above a little fooling around, but they're very careful. They'd know the baby wasn't theirs. I can't tell them any more than I can tell Roger. No, it has to be an outsider, someone who doesn't know me."

Helping unmarried women who stood to have their lives ruined was one thing, but Glory was married. Helping her the first time had been something that JoEllen had to live

255

with ever since. Since that time, JoEllen had drawn the line at emotional blackmail.

"Let me get you a room, Glory, and call Roger. I'm certain we can find an answer." What she wasn't saying was that *she* had to find an answer as well. All she'd ever wanted to do was be a good nurse. Playing God wasn't right. Yet, she looked at the women who came to see Tom Brooks and she couldn't understand why God piled such burdens on women.

"You're refusing me? Fine. Then I'll find Dr. Brooks myself." She turned around. "No. Forget that I asked you, JoEllen, that's okay. I'll find another way."

It had to be the pills giving that deadly edge to Glory's already volatile nature. "No, wait."

Glory stopped, intentionally calming herself, but that very control was out of character. JoEllen had known Glory too long to trust her composure. Glory would do something stupid. Whether it was the medication or her state of mind, Glory was in danger and she was desperate. JoEllen had been there once and, no matter how hard she tried, she'd never forgotten.

Still, this situation was different. JoEllen had been single and just starting her career. For Glory, the first abortion had been understandable. She was scared. She had a baby and a new husband and she was trying to learn to be a mother and a wife. But this was different. Glory was not behaving rationally. JoEllen wondered if her state of mind was entirely a result of the pregnancy.

"Glory, let's not panic." JoEllen didn't want to call Thomas Brooks again. So far she'd managed to keep their working together to a minimum, only when she was convinced that an abortion was the woman's only solution. His great plan to prevent women from dying of abortions performed by quacks had become a reality.

Glory caught the hesitation in JoEllen's voice and that hesitation seemed to answer her question. "But you will help me, won't you, JoEllen? Please!"

"Glory, are you sure? Things don't always work out perfectly, even when a doctor is doing the procedure. You've already had one abortion. You could become sterile."

"All the better."

"There could be complications. How far along are you?"

256

"Three months."

"You're sure?"

"I know exactly when it happened. I live my life around— Let's just say I'm sure. Just know, JoEllen, that I can't have this child. I don't dare take a chance."

"Every man you've been around adores you, Glory. I'm sure that Roger is no exception." JoEllen had to try one last time. "Why don't you go home and have a talk with him? He might not like it, but surely he'd understand."

"No, he wouldn't understand. Besides, it really doesn't have anything to do with Roger. It's the baby. It will have something dreadful wrong with it."

"How can you know that. You have a son who is all right, don't you?"

"Yes, Damon's perfect. But . . ." She moved away and stared out into the crisp February night, "Eleven years ago I had another baby—a little girl. She was beautiful, but she was—she wasn't *right*. Oh, JoEllen, she was deformed, all wrong inside. She died. I can't go through that again. Look at me. I'm a wreck. There's something wrong with this baby—I know it."

And JoEllen understood that Glory was right. Somehow she knew that her child was flawed. And JoEllen knew, too, that there was something wrong with Glory. After studying and learning about illnesses, she finally understood that there was some tiny, secret part of Glory that was flawed, too.

"Just tell me how to find him, JoEllen. You don't have to be involved. Tell me!"

"No, Glory. You can't do that. I'll arrange it—something. Where are you staying?"

"I don't know. I hadn't thought."

"Go to the Richmond, check in and wait. I'll call you."

Glory had left, strangely calm at the assurance of JoEllen's help.

For the first time in her nursing career, JoEllen filched a patient's tranquilizer and took it herself, pretending that the patient had destroyed the tablet in an attempt not to swallow it.

With a little checking she found out that Tom Brooks was assisting in surgery. When he had completed the operation

257

and was showered and dressed, JoEllen was waiting at the door.

He gave a puzzled smile. "Are you by any chance looking for me?"

JoEllen took a deep breath and gave an answer that she never thought she'd give.

"Yes. Do you have time to talk?"

"Talk? I thought you might have something more personal in mind."

"No, not personal, Tom. This is business."

She explained the situation. But when they arrived at the hotel, Glory was gone. There was just a note: she'd changed her mind and gone back to Savannah.

Glory called Steven at his office.

"Glory? What's wrong?"

"Steven," she fought to get her voice under control, "I'm pregnant."

"Oh, God. How?"

"I think that's fairly obvious, my darling Steven. We made love in a cemetery. Now I'm pregnant. It's yours. No matter what happens—I want you, here, beside me. I won't have this child alone."

"Glory, I can't come there. You have a husband. I have a wife."

"Divorce her."

"Glory, I can't. I won't. I don't want to hear this kind of talk from you."

"You won't come?"

"I can't. You're behaving irrationally."

"That's what Roger said. Maybe he's right."

"Glory, what will you do?"

"Do? I guess I'll do what I have to. One thing, Steven, just one last time, tell me that you love me."

"Glory, this is crazy. I—"

"Say it, Steven. Tell me you want me—you love me. You'll always love me."

"I want you, Glory. I love you. I'll always love you, but this is all we can ever have."

Glory took a shower . . . and the rest of her bottle of

258

Valium. She crawled into bed. She knew that she was hallucinating when she saw Roger standing in the doorway laughing at her. But she was deadly sober when she turned off the light.

Steven was right. Nothing could ever change. She finally understood.

All her life she'd wanted Steven. She could never have him and she couldn't live without him.

PART THREE

The Reunion

"You've come a long way, baby."
—Virginia Slim's Advertisement

Thirty

Roger Sasser stood beside his car and looked at the mound of earth and the green funeral tent. He felt such pain that he couldn't hear the words being spoken by the minister. He'd loved Glory not just as his wife, but as the very air he breathed. She'd been the driving force in his career, her smile a measure of his success and her frown a censure of his failure.

How had it gone so wrong? Glory had come into his life and infused it with fire. That fire carried over into his practice, it nurtured the image he had of himself both as a doctor and a man.

Now that fire was gone. And he felt cold and empty.

On the car radio, as he and Damon had driven to Winslow from Savannah, he'd heard every goodbye song anybody had ever written. One singer was asking the way to San Jose. Another left the earth entirely with Up, Up and Away—in a balloon. Even the news broadcaster told of the launching of Mariner 6 on its way to Mars. As he turned off the radio, Glen Campbell was singing his latest hit, "By the Time I Get to Phoenix," singing about leaving his lover, like Glory had left him. But Glory had always come back—until now.

The sky was dark. A light mist began to fall. The temperature, hovering at the freezing point since mid-morning, began to drop in the early February afternoon. By the time the hearse arrived at the cemetery, the ground was crackling beneath the footsteps of the mourners.

The hump of gray dirt lifted from the earth to make room for the vault was obscene, made even more so as the attendants covered it with artificial green carpet and sprays of flowers. On the signal from the undertaker Roger took Damon's hand and stepped forward, followed by Glory's family, up the slight hill, leaning backward against the wind as if they were being blown where they didn't want to go. One by one they took their seats beneath the green tent covering the gravesite.

Adele Winslow, dry-eyed and stiff, held tight to the hand of the thin, dark-eyed boy who was her grandson, and stared straight ahead as she leaned on her son-in-law, Roger. Evelyn Winslow followed, gripping her son Steven's arm. Last to take their seats were Sam and Susan with their daughters.

"They have a little boy, too," JoEllen whispered to Margie, "but he's not a strong child. They must have left him at home."

The rain changed into tiny pellets of ice that clattered against the canvas cover like giant grains of salt flung from some unseen shaker. The wind picked up, rushing through the branches of the pine trees that bordered the cemetery in a low, painful sigh.

"She couldn't have a funeral like anybody else," Margie grumbled under her breath. "She doesn't even have a church service. That would be too ordinary. Hers has to have sound effects and hollow-eyed mourners. And do you see what kind of flowers they used to make the casket blanket? Dahlias! Red-orange dahlias!"

"Margie! Shh! Glory's dead."

"I know she's dead. I got up at the crack of dawn to drive down here because she's dead. I'm going to lose two days' pay because she's dead. What I don't understand is, why? Why the hell is Glory dead?"

Margie was angry, dangerously angry. How dare Glory be dead? She'd always had everything. She was beautiful, smart, talented. Life came to her with no effort on her part. From the time Margie had first seen Glory she'd been the yardstick by which Margie had measured her accomplishments. Now, suddenly she was gone. There was nobody to be better than.

Margie glanced around at the mourners, standing like

264

statues planted in the dead grass surrounding the gravesite. She wondered how many of the class of '54 would be here to mourn its most—most whatever it was they'd elected Glory. Margie's gaze moved down to the family section and Susan. Her face was swollen and pale and she was mauling a handkerchief. Margie had the absurd thought that Susan's long red fingernails looked like drops of blood against the white fabric.

Susan didn't know that she was being watched. Her gaze never left the dahlias. All she could think about was Glory's cataloging them that summer afternoon. She'd been a white gardenia, Margie the white rose, and JoEllen the white lily. White, pure—silent—death. Except it was Glory who was dead. Her thoughts were so painful that she could only hold on to her daughters and wish that the service would end quickly.

Susan didn't understand her pain. She'd been Glory's friend, yet she never thought about what that meant. In some way, Glory's death made her understand that nothing in life was permanent. Like her father, people came into your life and disappeared. Glory had changed Susan's future simply by being a part of her past. Like Mr. Sims who'd come to Galilee briefly, brought in the outside world, and then been sent away. Like Jody, who shared her dream for a moment and vanished before he could damage her safe haven. Like that summer of the soldiers when everyone's life had changed.

In ways Susan couldn't understand, Glory had helped shape the direction of their lives, beginning with Sam. Sam was holding himself so still that Susan feared he'd crack from the strain.

Now he was looking at the ground, his mouth drawn into a grim line that seemed to be more anger than grief. Their daughters, Jennifer and Marcie, too young to understand what had happened, were staring at Glory's son, Damon, a thin, intense child who showed no sign of grief. Susan felt the same intensity of the connection between the children when they'd all been together on special family occasions. She finally decided that it was Damon. He had that same kind of aura of control about him that Glory had had.

Margie pulled the fur collar of her suede coat closer, and

tried to shake off the tension that grew with every word the preacher spoke. She wished she'd worn her black all-purpose raincoat instead. At the time she'd dressed for the trip, looking successful had seemed more desirable than comfort, but that had turned out to be dumb. She might look great, but nobody was interested in anybody except Glory, and Margie was freezing.

The crowd was large. This funeral was an event. If they were asked, every person in attendance would have said that they knew Glory well. But outside of Margie, Susan, and JoEllen, no other members of their class had braved the weather and the group was composed mostly of strangers to Glory.

Neither Winslow nor Galilee had experienced a suicide for more than fifty years. Nobody could understand or answer the burning question. Why?

Why, on the morning of her thirty-first birthday, had Glory Winslow Sasser, the girl who had it all, taken a deliberate overdose of medication and killed herself?

"JoEllen, God damn her," Margie said. "Why'd she do it? Of the four of us, Glory should have been the one to be happy. She had a husband, a child, position, money. She was always somebody."

But JoEllen couldn't answer that question, not any more than she could answer the question of why she felt responsible, not just for Glory's death, but because she was alive and Glory was gone. JoEllen knew that it could have been she in that coffin. She kept waiting for Teddy to appear at the funeral, to tell her everything was all right. In her heart she knew he wasn't coming because she would be there, and she wouldn't have known what to say if he had come.

Ever since she'd gotten the call from Susan, JoEllen had felt as if her life was tearing apart. Glory had come to her for help and she'd hesitated. Knowing Glory's mental state, she'd let her own chaotic uncertainty make Glory run away. Even now, JoEllen wasn't certain whether it was guilt, or her submerged anger at Glory's refusal to have her baby when she had no valid reason not to. The inescapable truth was that JoEllen was a nurse who could have saved two lives and didn't.

If she'd helped Glory willingly, would Glory still be alive?

Was Glory's death her fault? She stared at the red-orange flowers and felt the great weight of her guilt. She'd never know.

"Why?" Margie whispered again.

"How can we know, Margie?" JoEllen asked as they walked back toward the car, the grass crunching beneath their feet as it began to freeze. "How can we ever really know the right thing to do?"

"Well, killing yourself sure isn't it."

"I wonder if it isn't partly our fault. After all, what did we really know about Glory's life?"

They stopped at JoEllen's car hugging old friends, murmuring condolences as expected to those who voiced their own dismay. JoEllen went on. "I mean, how many times have you heard from Glory since she got married?"

"Not once," Margie admitted. "Of course, there was no reason. Why would she call me? Glory was a member of the Savannah upper crust. We didn't have a great deal in common."

"Why do you say that? She often shopped in Atlanta and you were her friend. Why didn't she call you? The measure of our success, or the lack of it, shouldn't have changed that."

Margie knew there was something wrong with JoEllen's argument, but she couldn't verbalize the flaw. She only knew that success and position drew people together, and without it, someone like her was always on the outside looking in.

"Maybe," Margie agreed. "But the only time I've seen you was at Susan and Sam's wedding twelve years ago, and Glory didn't show up there, remember?"

"She was supposed to be one of the bridesmaids. She was flying from Savannah to Augusta. Susan said that she'd already arranged for a rental car, but at the last minute Glory called Adele and said she couldn't make it. I don't even think she's been back home but two or three times since then. Mrs. Winslow always went to Savannah to see her."

The crowd was beginning to disperse. Most of the mourners had dropped by the house or the funeral home last night or during the morning. Now the event was over, except for the immediate family and a few close friends who would be expected to go to the house and share a meal before leaving.

267

Susan and Sam directed their children to their car and walked over to speak with JoEllen and Margie. "You are coming to the house, aren't you?" Susan asked, the unexpected sharpness of her tone revealing how tired she was.

"Do we have to?" Margie knew that she was behaving badly. She couldn't forget the shock she'd felt when she heard the news.

Conflicting emotions had plagued Margie all the way from Atlanta. She'd been alternately grief-stricken and horrified at a secret part of her that said that she'd finally bested Glory, by survival if not accomplishment.

Then, somewhere just outside of Galilee, Margie was struck with another emotion: fear. She understood how a person could be desperate. She'd understood how death as an avenue of escape was always out there, she just refused to admit that final acknowledgment of failure. She hadn't decided yet whether it was courage or weakness that made suicide possible. But Glory knew. Glory was the reflection of all their mortality. Glory, who had it all, was dead.

"Of course we'll come by the house," JoEllen answered for them both. "It's archaic, but we have to do it. I guess I've lost touch with the customs, dealing with life and death on a daily basis. I suppose they still sit up with the body the night before the funeral."

"Certainly," Sam said sharply.

Certainly. Margie remembered the torture of sitting up with the body, first at her grandmother's funeral, then later at her grandfather's. By the time she buried her mother, the custom had finally been abolished and she'd been able to attend the service and drive back to Atlanta the same day. Burying her grandparents had been hard. Burying her mother had left her filled with overwhelming guilt.

"And the neighbors still bring in enough food to supply a division of Marines," JoEllen observed. "And we have to go through the motions of being the grieving friends."

"But we *are* her friends," Susan said softly. "And I, for one, *am* grieving for her."

"I don't know if we should grieve. Glory made her own choices," JoEllen said, more to herself than to the others. "She always did."

268

"Are we sure about that?" Susan asked, not expecting an answer.

Sam didn't join the conversation. He glanced over his shoulder as the cars carrying the family began to drive away. "I think Roger and Steven would appreciate your coming by. Aunt Adele insists that Glory would want you there," he said, adding under his breath, "and Susan would like it, too."

"Roger and *Steven?* Why do you suppose Sam said that?" Margie asked once she and JoEllen were in the car. "I don't even know Steven. He was older than Glory and always away at boarding school. I think he graduated before she started high school in Galilee."

JoEllen pulled in behind Sam and Susan. "I don't know. I don't even remember hearing Glory talk about him. Susan said that Glory and Sam and Steven all grew up together, before we knew Glory, before they came to Galilee to high school." She changed the subject. "Are you going to spend the night, Margie?"

"No. Where would I stay? I just realized that the only relative I have left in Galilee is a cousin, and I was never close to her when I lived here. What about you?"

"My mother's still here. Skip is in the Navy, on a ship in the Mediterranean."

Margie sighed and stared out the window at all the old white mansions that dated back to the Civil War and before. She'd never been in any of them, other than Glory's house, which didn't qualify because it had been built in the forties, just after World War II, before everything began to change. "Skip the hunk. Is your little brother still the ladies' man?"

"What do you mean by that?" JoEllen heard her voice sharpen.

"Whoa! I didn't mean anything bad, JoEllen. Didn't you know? All the girls drooled after your little brother, including those old enough to be ashamed of fantasizing about a kid? If I'd been sixteen when he was sixteen I might not have waited for a summer soldier to take my virginity."

"A soldier?"

"Yeah, you remember. Nick the Magnificent. The Greek god. He was my first."

"Is there someone special now, Margie?"

"Special?" Margie laughed, a dry, bitter laugh. "They're

269

all special at the time. But they're just passing through. What about you?"

"Me? No, there's nobody special. I'm much too busy for any kind of relationship. Besides, the men I know are users, all of them. Except for Sam. Susan doesn't know how lucky she is."

"JoEllen, what about Teddy? Do you ever see him anymore?"

"No."

"Is he married?"

"No. He never married. And no, there's no one else."

"What happened between the two of you?"

"What happened to any of us? We change, find out that nothing is like we've been taught to expect. We get away from our past and find we want different things from what we thought. You were going to leave Galilee and be somebody. Are you?"

Margie sighed. "No, not yet, but I haven't given up."

"What exactly are you doing in Atlanta?"

"I work for a Russian immigrant who owns a studio that builds sets for theatrical productions, television commercials and trade shows. And I model on the side. I've given up on ever making it to the New York stage. I do some local theater and an occasional commercial, but that's as far as I'll ever go."

JoEllen shook her head in disbelief. "You're a model and an actress? We always thought that Glory would be in the theater."

"A kick in the pants, isn't it? When I left Galilee, I didn't have any idea what I'd do. I just knew I was going to go where the action was, get away from here. Can you believe I actually ended up living in the Churches Home for Business Girls?"

JoEllen laughed. "You lived in a Churches Home? For how long?"

"Until they threatened to kick me out for being late for curfew. About the same time, I met someone, someone I thought was like Glory. She took me in. God, that seems like a hundred years ago. She turned out to be a lot like Glory. In the end we had different goals."

Margie could have said that Victoria had completely left

the theater, taking on the desegregation movement with the same zeal she'd approached her acting. And she was becoming almost as successful. Margie wondered how long it would take her to burn herself out this time?

There was a long silence as JoEllen turned into Glory's drive. The house still looked the same—set back from the road, neat and private. JoEllen parked the car at the end of a line of automobiles. She opened the door and straightened up, jutting her chin forward as if she expected the worst.

"I'm a nurse, Margie, and I deal with death all the time, but I admit, I'm having trouble accepting this. Do you realize that this is the first time we've all been together since the weekend you all came to Augusta? Nothing has worked out like we'd planned, has it?"

Nothing has worked out like we'd planned. JoEllen felt herself looking over her shoulder, admitting that the assault of memories had gotten to her. She'd stopped looking for Teddy. On the few occasions when she returned to Galilee, she'd avoided anyplace where Teddy might be.

And yet she'd watched for him today, not expecting so much as hoping that he'd come. Everything and everybody else in JoEllen's life seemed to be slipping away. Skip was still in the Navy, her mother was moving to Lynville to live with her sister. Now Glory was gone. And Teddy had stayed away.

Standing there watching the casket being lowered into the ground brought death to a personal level for JoEllen. Where had she expected her life to be fourteen years after graduation? When she'd left Galilee, she'd left without a thought about the people she was leaving behind, except perhaps for Skip. Had she been the selfish one? Could she have changed anything that had happened?

JoEllen knew that she should have called Glory to check on her. She was ashamed to admit her relief when they'd found her gone from the hotel. She'd never dreamed that she would do such a terrible thing. All she'd known was that she wouldn't have to make a stand.

Now she wished she had. Now she wanted to rail out at Glory.

How dare you kill yourself? You're playing some kind of cruel joke. This person they'd just buried wasn't Glory. She

271

was punishing them by playing a horrible joke. Any minute Glory would walk through that door, give a mocking laugh, and swish her red hair like some twenties flapper as she made one of her outlandish statements.

But it *was* Glory, and Glory was dead. And JoEllen felt a great hurting anger at the waste.

In the end nothing had worked out as they'd planned. Her goal had been to get out of school quick so that she and Teddy could get married. Glory would go on the stage and be famous. Margie was going to Atlanta and "be somebody." Susan was going to take a business course and marry Sam. Susan seemed to be the only one whose expectations had been realized.

JoEllen sighed. There was no going back, and dwelling over what had happened wouldn't change it. Teddy had gotten lost along the way. Now her work was the most important thing in her life, for it was the *only* thing. Margie was the actress, and Glory was dead.

Steven stood in the doorway of Glory's room and watched her friends talking in low voices. Roger, looking confused and uncomfortable, was sitting beside Glory's mother. Steven had gone to his aunt Adele as soon as he'd arrived and put his arms around her. She'd drawn back and with a look of pure hatred, said, "Don't you touch me, Steven Winslow! This is your fault, all your fault."

He'd been shocked. Then he realized he had to force himself to contain his feelings about Glory, his grief. His own mother had been just as distant and stiff. As for Sam, there was a moment when Steven thought that Sam was going to hit him. Nobody seemed to know or care that he, too, was hurting.

Steven had been operating on an automatic control ever since he'd gotten Glory's frantic telephone call demanding that he come to her. Then, before he'd been able to find a solution, Sam had called.

He'd been wrong. He should have gone to her, found a way to help her live the life she was being forced to lead, just as he'd had to live his.

Glory was dead. She'd killed herself. And it was all

because of him. He could neither vent his rage nor share the depths of his grief. He couldn't, for if he did, he'd disintegrate.

Steven couldn't stay there any longer. He had to get away. He was becoming angry, angrier than he'd ever been in his life. He felt a deep, violent, burning anger inside. There was no way to let it go. Glory shouldn't be dead. She *couldn't* be dead. Adele was right. Only he knew how right she was. This was his fault.

Glory had been desperate. Even when he wasn't with her, he could always feel her depression. She hadn't needed to tell him. It had become more and more obvious every time they'd been together. Perhaps if he'd been stronger, if he'd been able to refuse her, if he'd sent her away that first morning. But he hadn't. In every other part of his life he was considered a tyrant in his determination to be in charge. It was as if he had to make up for his weakness for Glory.

Life and joy and every beautiful thing that existed was what Glory had been to him. Steven never touched a woman that he wasn't making love to Glory. He never heard a piece of music that she wasn't the inspiration for its emotion. She'd made the colors of Steven's life brilliant. Though great chunks of time passed between the times they met, they were always connected. Quickly, urgently, they'd renew that commitment, and their sense of belonging together never faltered. Now that connection was broken.

Steven couldn't bear to look at Damon. Seeing him was seeing Glory, and the boy's pain was so intense that Steven felt his insides twist in sympathy. Damon was Steven's child, yet he couldn't comfort him. Finally, Steven turned and made his way around the room and out the back door. His cashmere jacket was little protection against the raw wind and cold that had set in. He welcomed the cold and the pain.

His steps carried him across the yard, through the woods, and down the road to the cemetery. By the time he reached the plot, the workers had filled in the hole and were gone. The rain, freezing as it fell, made jagged ice patches on the frozen earth. The blossoms of the roses he'd sent were already frozen. They'd remain just as they looked now until they thawed.

There was a sterile quiet about the scene, as if it weren't

real. Then came the sound of rain and wind, the feel of moisture on his face, moisture that didn't come from the elements but from his tears.

Glory was in the ground, but he was the one who was dead. He blamed the people in the house behind him for setting impossible rules, for not knowing what was happening. He blamed his grandfather, and his father's flawed blood flowing in his veins.

He blamed Glory for making him love her and then leaving him this way. But most of all, he blamed himself for his weakness, for knowing and not finding a way to prevent her death. Steven Winslow folded his arms across an ancient tree limb, slumped against them, and wept.

Thirty-One

Teddy had watched the services from a distance, which, he decided, was appropriate, for that's where he'd always been as far as JoEllen, Margie, Susan and Sam, and Glory were concerned.

JoEllen stood ramrod straight, her eyes on the casket, seemingly unaware of Margie holding onto her arm or Susan's distraught tears. Strong, invincible, that was Jo-Ellen. Teddy wished she did need someone to lean on.

After the services he drove back to the garage he'd built on his property near the school. He'd changed from building cars for the drag strip to building automobiles for oval track racing. Without the backing of a major automobile company he was forced to take a slower route to racing, but he was slowly gaining recognition as his one-man owner cars were beginning to be noticed.

His crews were loyal. They were sworn to secrecy about the special lubricant Teddy used to clean and coat the inner working parts of the engine. But even Teddy knew that it was only a matter of time before somebody would begin to ask questions.

Ed Jordan was waiting for Teddy. Ed was showing his age now, and depending heavily on Teddy to oversee his road construction business. Teddy didn't know that much about building roads, but he knew how to deal with men, and in the last five years, Ed had pulled together a reliable crew.

"Hello, Mayor, what's up?"

"It's Claude. I'm afraid you're going to have to go to New York and bring him home. This will be the last time I'll ask it of you, Teddy."

"What's happened?"

"He's dead—killed—in his own apartment in that place called the Village."

"I'm sorry, Ed. I'm very sorry. Seems like this is a bad time for all of us."

"Not those of us who stayed home where we belong. Just the ones who wanted too much and gave so little in return."

Claude Jordan was buried three days after Glory Winslow. The funeral was as large, the foral display even larger. This time Teddy was there, standing beside Ed Jordan, supporting the man who'd become so important in his life.

He looked at the houses along the route from the cemetery as he drove back to the Jordans' house, and wondered about Ed's words. When Teddy was a boy there was always something wonderful happening on Main Street. Jobe, the town's crazy man, walked the streets talking to the imaginary people who accompanied him. Miss Colleen Baker could be found sitting in her wrought-iron chair overseeing the hoard of black women she called on to pull the weeds from her grass. Mrs. Lem Lester always had a traveling salesman staying at her boardinghouse, and the railroad men would be sitting on the front porch talking about the hobos. This afternoon he didn't see anybody as he drove down the street. It was as if they'd all gone inside and closed the shades.

The Vietnam War had ended. Jimmy Hoffa was going to prison for jury tampering. Ronald Reagan had been elected governor of California. A Louisiana Grand Jury was investigating the possibility that conspiracy had led to the assassination of President John F. Kennedy. And the Dixie Theater had closed.

Teddy didn't know, but he suspected that the closing of the theater might have more of an effect on his life than any of the other events. It was another reminder of what once was, and what might have been.

In April, Teddy's car, the green Pine Tree Ford, was running second on the dirt track in Savannah just behind

276

Richard Petty's Plymouth, when he blew a tire. But he'd made his mark. And the next week a team of racing specialists from Ford appeared in Galilee to talk to the young unknown whose car and driver had burst onto the scene from nowhere.

But Teddy turned down their offer to join the team. He was happy where he was and with what he was doing. And he never told them about the white mud that was his secret.

Thirty-Two

From the time Mark was born, he was Susan's baby.
While the girls toddled along behind their father, going to
the fields, fishing, riding horses, Mark was content to stay
inside with his mother.

Sam was faintly disturbed over the reversal of roles. He
had two girls who worked in the fields and a son who worked
in the house. But he couldn't find a way to reach out to the
boy. He always felt uneasy around him and, even as a baby,
Mark sensed it.

A thin, quiet child, Mark was never as sturdy as the girls.
Father and son quickly fell into a pattern of separation that
they never recognized and wouldn't have known how to
correct if they had. The girls, still babies themselves when
Mark came, were pushed aside by Susan in order to look
after her son. He needed her, and they never seemed to.

Early on, Sam knew his life might have turned out
differently except for two Christmases. The first was the
Christmas before Mark was born. Jennifer was almost two
and Marcie only six months. Until Jennifer's birth, Susan
always played the piano for the junior choir and the pageant.
The regular church organist didn't have the patience to work
with the children and Susan loved it. She willingly made
angel wings, gathered bathrobes for the shepherds, and took
care of any problems before the children could be
embarrassed.

That Christmas of 1959, Susan was pressed into service
again. Adele had agreed to look after the little ones, which
meant that Glory's unexpected pre-Christmas visit presented a problem of logistics. Adele couldn't drive Glory

back to the airport in Augusta and keep the babies at the same time.

"Don't worry," Susan had assured her aunt, "Sam will drive Glory. He doesn't care for pageants anyway and this will give him a reason not to be there."

And so it was settled. Sam was less cooperative than Susan expected. He even tried to find another solution, but short of babysitting himself, which he didn't consider to be his job, he couldn't come up with anything.

The weather was unusually mild that week before Christmas. It seemed strange to be listening to Christmas carols about snow when he wasn't even wearing a jacket. He gassed up the truck and drove over to Aunt Adele's. Glory was strung higher than a balloon caught on a telephone wire in a windstorm. From the moment she crawled into the car, Sam feared what was going to happen.

But twenty miles outside Augusta he began to relax. He was going to make it. Glory was not coming on to him. She wasn't teasing or tempting him. After a quick greeting, she'd hovered in the corner of the front seat with no attempt at conversation. He felt like Adam in the Garden of Eden, expecting the snake to curl around him any minute.

Being in the truck with Glory was like being left in a room with a lot of money when nobody else knew it was there. He didn't dare take it, but he couldn't leave it alone, either. Morally he knew his feelings for Glory had always been wrong, but he couldn't stop them. He was startled when she began to cry.

"What's wrong, Glory?"

"You mean, what's wrong right this minute, or with the world in general?" Her tears were silent, steady without being hard. There as a hopelessness in her tears that Sam didn't know how to deal with. Her voice slowed even more and she took deep, long breaths.

"I'm not much into the world-in-general kind of discussions," Sam said. "I never could keep up with you and Steven there. I'm a pretty simple fellow. Try starting with what's wrong right now."

"Now? This minute . . ." She sat up straight and considered his question. "This minute, I have to pee. I think you'd better find a place to stop."

"Glory, there isn't a service station that's open for at least

279

ten miles, maybe more."

"Then you'd better find a dirt road, unless you intend to lend me your cap."

Sam sighed. He'd been wrong. He wasn't going to make it to Augusta. The next dirt road he came to he turned in, drove until he found a road bordered by a field on one side and a dark patch of trees on the other. It was late afternoon and the sky was cloudy, but Glory was in plain view when she hopped out and started into the woods.

"Come with me, Sam. I'm afraid of snakes."

"Glory, just do it and come back."

She stumbled and sobbed softly.

A crying Glory was new. He'd seen her scream. He'd seen her yell. He'd seen her pull a tantrum that brought her mother and her aunt to their knees. He'd seen her take off her clothes and parade around before him until he was almost crazy with wanting her and still not let him touch her. But this was different. This was a subdued, overwhelming kind of despair that wouldn't let go.

Sam finally gave a snort of resignation and crawled out of the car. He took her hand and held it until they were away from the car and under a tree, where she would be hidden from sight in case anybody drove by. In a moment he heard the sound of her relieving herself. He felt a tightening in his lower body. Maybe he ought to go, too. He unzipped his pants and tried, except he was half hard and nothing would come out. The more he strained, the harder he got. And it wasn't helping any that he heard Glory moving up behind him.

"You can turn around now, Sam."

"No I can't. Go back to the car, Glory."

"What's the matter, Sam?" Her voice got all soft and throaty.

"I thought I might as well go, too, while we're stopped, and you're making that impossible."

"Oh? Why?"

"Go away, Glory."

"Ah, Sam, you want me to take care of the problem?" Her arms slipped around him and she took hold of his cock. "Hmm, that's what I thought. I always did make you horny, didn't I, Sam?"

"Glory, stop playing games. I don't want this to happen."

280

"I think you do. The saintly Sam, dear old Granddad's favorite grandchild—hot for his cousin."

"I'm married. I don't fool around, Glory. You don't want me. I'm always a stand-in for somebody else."

"But that doesn't stop you from wanting me, does it, Sam? You just never wanted to admit that I got you all hot and hard and won't let you do anything about it except look, would I? It drives you crazy when I touch you, doesn't it?"

Sam only groaned.

"And you always pretend you're so pure. Sam Winslow doesn't have wicked thoughts, does he? Of course, you and I know that this wouldn't be the first time for you and me, Sam. Or have you forgotten?"

"I haven't forgotten." Glory was always hovering in the periphery of his mind. Oh, yes. His thoughts of Glory came hurtling back to haunt him every time he touched Susan, sweet Susan whom he loved but who never turned him on nearly as much as Glory did.

"Then why are you being so cold."

"Cut it out. I'm married, Glory. You're family."

"Fine, this time you touch me, and I'll look." And suddenly she was standing in front of him and he was touching her. And then they weren't standing any more. Sam groaned. For the second time in his life, Sam was being unfaithful to Susan—with Glory.

After he'd put Glory on her plane he'd gotten drunk and nearly raped his wife, all because of a residual desire that hadn't been satisfied. Glory had a way of feeding the flame, of making a man want more and more, of making him believe that he was strong enough to get it.

That night, after the Christmas pageant, Sam took what he needed from Susan, silently restoring order in his life with the reticence and decorum she'd finally learned, and in return he gave her Mark. But he never looked at Mark without seeing Glory.

The second Christmas that sealed forever the path they would follow was the Christmas of 1967 when each of the three children got a horse. The girls, already experienced from riding with Sam, were on the horses and riding them around the barnyard at daylight.

Susan had known the horses were a mistake and she'd tried to dissuade Sam, but she didn't know how to insist.

In a rare fit of exasperation, she'd told her mother that she felt as if she'd laid out the pattern for her life, cut it out, and sewed herself up in it.

"That's what a woman does," Mrs. Miller had answered. "At least you chose a man who appreciates you."

But Susan wondered about that. Sam appreciated what he expected of her, but if she strayed from his path, he became taciturn and stubborn. And this Christmas Sam was stubborn.

Mark was his son and his son wasn't too young to ride. Every farm kid in America could ride a horse. His grandfather had taught Sam to ride when Sam was six years old and Mark was already seven. This would be the means of building a proper father-son relationship.

Mark tried, but he was terrified. Susan bit her tongue as Sam lifted Mark onto the horse. Mark, big-eyed and frozen with fear, wanted badly to please his father.

"Sit up tall, like a man, Mark. You're not afraid of a horse, are you?"

"No, sir."

Mark sat there with a smile pasted on his face and allowed Sam to lead the horse around and around the paddock. But when Sam handed Mark the reins and waited for him to take them, Mark didn't move. Instead, a telltale trail of moisture made a dark stain on Mark's blue jeans and ran down the horse's side.

"Damn! Susan, this boy's just wet his pants! What kind of sissy have you raised?"

Susan cut off the girls' snickers with a look as she pushed Sam aside and lifted Mark to the ground. "Come inside, Mark. Don't worry."

Susan was seven again, and standing in the dark yard outside her great-aunt's house. As if it were actually happening, she remembered the feeling of urine running down her legs and puddling in her shoes. And her fury toward Sam's callous behavior began to grow.

Mark never got on the horse again and Sam, as if he knew how angry Susan was, never made another attempt to reach out to his son.

It was the next Christmas when Mark was given a role in

the pageant that Susan discovered the incredible talent her son had been given. When Mark sang the role of the child in *The Little Drummer Boy,* there wasn't a dry eye in the house, Mark had found his direction in life: music.

Jen and Marcie became Sam's sons, and Mark forever forfeited his place in his father's life.

Thirty-Three

Margie felt as if she'd lost everyone long ago. The only person in the world she could depend on was Leonard, and he was neither family nor lover. After all their time together, she didn't even know how old he was. Tall, thin, and serious, he still looked exactly the same as he had when she first came to work for him almost fifteen years ago.

Margie felt old. She couldn't even garner any real interest in going out with Richard, who'd suddenly turned up—a ghost from her past—inviting her to let it all hang out and come along with him. He planned to stop off for a few weeks with some friends in New York City, Greenwich Village, to be precise, then later they'd go to a happening. A happening, Richard explained, was a rock concert.

"Who's the Count?" Richard asked, sounding crude, not scholarly as Margie had once thought.

"He's Russian," Margie explained, "and he's my boss." Leonard wouldn't have stopped her from going; she did that herself. Later, after Richard accused her of selling out to the Establishment and left, Margie thought about Leonard.

He could be a count, if they had counts in Russia. He had that mysterious, royal manner. His mother had been honored almost like royalty because of her musical ability. Margie wondered why Leonard didn't play the piano. But perhaps he did. Leonard never talked about himself.

He still spoke with an accent. It helped his business, he was fond of saying. Theatrical people were expected to be eccentric. There were times when Margie would look up and see him watching her, but he never made an attempt to take

284

their relationship beyond that of employer and employee. He was better than family or lover. Leonard was probably the only real friend Margie had ever had.

Margie was glad Richard was gone. She'd been in *Ghosts* until two nights ago and she was tired. She was becoming one of Atlanta's oldest little-theater actresses, in longevity, if not age.

She thought of Richard, still chasing the elusive dream of free love and freedom to drop out of the race for success, and wondered if they were so different. Both seemed to be stuck in the middle of the road and no closer to finding what they wanted than they were in college.

There were times she was willing to concede that she was never going to find her comet and, even if she did, she'd probably be too tired to hold on to its tail.

The project she and Leonard were working on was a huge shoe for Mother Goose, Channel 8's children's program. Leonard had always done special work for the television station, and Mallory Madorn, the aging actress who played Mother Goose, was an old friend. He never talked about her, but apparently they'd known each other before either came to Atlanta, and his patience with the woman who'd become increasingly difficult to work with was a puzzle.

The shoe was almost finished when Richard had appeared at the studio. Margie wasn't certain how he'd found her until he explained that he'd been in the audience for the last performance of *Ghosts*. Leonard left the two of them alone.

Later, Susan heard him stumble through the doorway.

"Leonard?"

He was standing very straight, holding himself upright through sheer willpower. Then he grimaced. "I didn't know you'd still be here," he said. "I thought that you would go with your—friend."

"I couldn't leave you, Leonard."

He looked as if he didn't quite believe her, and Margie couldn't blame him. After all, she'd left before, without a thought for how Leonard might feel about her choices.

"I'm glad you're still here, but I believe that I've had too much to drink. Would you assist me, Marjorie?"

Margie put down her paintbrush and went immediately to Leonard's side. She slid her arms around his waist and together they walked to the area behind the studio where he had his living quarters. The feeling was strange, being close to Leonard. Always before he'd just been Leonard, her boss, or Leonard, her friend. But in that short walk, he became a man.

In the bedroom, he walked to the bed and stopped. "Thank you, Marjorie. I appreciate your decision to stay. I shall manage now." He attempted to pull the turtleneck sweater over his head.

Marjorie realized that he wasn't going to be able to get the garment off. With a tight sigh she reached up and pulled the sweater from his surprisingly muscular chest, but he was too tall and, in the process of stripping the sweater from his arms, she lost her balance. Before either knew what was happening, Leonard was lying on his bed and she was sprawled on top of him.

Leonard's expression was incredulous.

Margie knew that he'd had too much to drink. But she couldn't mistake the erection pressing insistently against her, nor could she erase the astonishing awareness of her own response.

"Leonard?"

"Go away, Marjorie!"

"But Leonard—"

"Now. Please, Margie. I apologize."

"I never knew . . ."

"Well, now you do. Get out of here before I do something that will ruin our friendship forever."

"Suppose I don't want to go?"

"I'm old enough to be your father, Marjorie."

"But you're not. I've slept with men for a lot of different reasons, but none of the men ever meant half as much to me as you."

"What are you saying?"

"I'm saying I care about you, Leonard." Margie raised up and peeled her sweatshirt from her body.

Leonard's eyes went involuntarily to her breasts. He let out a cry of anguish and pulled her down so he could touch her. "I would never have done this, Marjorie, but I cannot refuse that which I've coveted forever. Just once—no more."

"Just shut up and love me, Leonard," she whispered as he

286

claimed her lips with fierceness.

Margie learned that night that she'd never been loved by a man. Leonard gave her passion, pleasure, and finally tenderness. He taught her in one night that making love was more than two bodies seeking release. Later as he slept, cradling her in his arms, Margie faced the fact that she'd changed the course of direction of her life again, though she had no idea where this new relationship would take her.

Leonard was already up and dressed the next morning when she awoke. "Margie," he said stiffly, "you're going to have to finish Mother Hubbard's shoe and deliver it to Channel 8 this afternoon. Woody will help you. I have something I must do."

Margie hadn't known what to expect from Leonard, but business-as-usual was a surprise. She was disappointed that he was already up and dressed. She watched him leave, without even kissing her goodbye, then finished up the final trim work on the shoe. Leonard wasn't leaving her like the others had done. He'd be back.

By early afternoon Woody reported in and helped her load the shoe on the truck. She took a quick shower and dressed, wondering where Leonard had gone. Admitting that she was a bit worried, she consoled herself by remembering Leonard's private intensity. His disappearances weren't unusual, but something about this one bothered Margie.

Still, she felt good about herself this afternoon. Maybe she'd been wrong about her future. She suddenly had a good feeling about her life. Channel 8 was one of the television stations for which she'd done a couple of local commercials, maybe she'd get something today.

The upstairs apartment Leonard had provided as part of her salary was simple and sparsely furnished, but it had served her well. She hadn't realized until now how much influence Leonard had had on her. If she'd been asked, she'd have said that Leonard never talked. But he had, about history, and books and art. Gradually, without knowing, she'd learned to hold her own with the more literary members of her theatrical world.

They'd accepted her into the inner circles and, because of her dependability and love of theater, if not her talent, she'd managed to remain a part of Atlanta's stage world. But her

287

acting wouldn't even pay her grocery bill. When she finally understood the truth, she couldn't seem to give up, even knowing that she'd be disappointed.

As they drove to the television station this afternoon, Margie looked at the boarded-up buildings. For a time she'd fit right in with the flower children who'd moved into Atlanta's Tenth Street area. But once the Haight-Ashbury lifestyle spilled over the neighborhood, all the old familiar places began to disappear.

The tourists moved in, driving slowly down Peachtree watching the miniskirted runaways and the drug dealers. They supported rebellion with their curiosity by buying the underground newspaper, *The Great Speckled Bird*. Fast-food restaurants were replaced by vegetarian offerings and coffee houses where long-haired, gaunt singers made statements as they accompanied themselves on their guitars.

And finally Margie saw the street people for what they were: failures, people who turned their backs on life. Once they'd represented her every secret dream. But at thirty-four, she felt out of place. She decried the waste and she was furious that they'd killed the very thing they'd thought they were creating.

A wonderful part of the city and its past was gone forever, destroyed by free love and misplaced intellectual protests. Until last night, Margie had mourned what had been. There was the Margie of her childhood, the Margie of her "be somebody" phase, and this new Margie who was traveling in uncharted waters.

The truck pulled into the television studio and unloaded the set into the wide doors at the back. The temperature in the Channel 8 studio was always freezing. Margie, wearing leotards beneath her skirt, rubbed her hands together and shivered. It was the lights. The newscasters and announcers kept the heat off so they wouldn't perspire under the lights. She wondered why the children didn't turn blue.

Mother Goose was a bold new concept in local programming. A live children's show for the preschoolers. Cheap and easy to produce, it was designed to bring in local sponsors whose revenue allowed them to invest in a real set, beginning with a forest scene, and now Leonard's Old Mother Hubbard's shoe.

"Hey, Gus, you seen Madam Goose today?" Denny St. Claire, the producer of the show, asked as he wandered into the studio.

"Not yet."

Denny was the wonder boy of local television, an artist with a title: producer-director. Which, Leonard had once explained to Margie, meant that, as part of management, Denny gave directions to the union engineers who made twice as much money as he did. But he was the first local artist and had great ambition.

"Well, the goose is late again," Denny said. "Hello, Margie. The shoe looks great."

"Thanks. All I have to do is anchor it where you want it and I'll be out of here."

A few early-arriving children were filing in and taking their places at the fairy toadstool desks in front of the forest waterfall.

"Denny, telephone, in the control room."

Margie instructed Woody to secure the large screws that held the shoe to the floor.

"Where is Mother Hubbard?" a bright-eyed little girl with blond-hair asked.

A believer, Margie decided. "She's shopping."

"Does she have a dog?"

"I don't know, why?"

"Mother Hubbard's dog gets a bone."

"No way, the cupboard is bare" spoke the skeptic. He had a cowlick and a frown. "Besides, what kind of creep lives in a shoe anyway?"

"Mother Hubbard, Sammy. You bad boy, you just stop talking like that. Of course she has a dog."

"Oh, sure," the skeptic agreed. "And he has big teeth and he bites."

Margie almost smiled. He was putting the little girl on, a five-year-old con artist. "No, he doesn't," she corrected, "but he has a very long tongue. It can reach from the window all the way to the ground."

She had him there.

"Why?"

"Well," Margie thought for a moment. "He's Mother Hubbard's sliding board. All the children who eat their

289

supper and go to bed get to slide down the dog's tongue."

"Ah, I don't believe that."

"Well, I do," the believer said. "And I'm going to be the first to slide down it."

Denny returned and stood listening to the exchange between Margie and the children. "Margie, can I see you for a minute."

"Sure." She followed Denny out of the lighted area and into the corner.

"I have a problem. A great big problem. Leonard called. He thinks maybe you can save my life. What do you say?"

"Leonard? I don't know—maybe."

"I was listening to you out there talking to the little monsters. Mallory Madorn won't be in today. I want you to fill in for her."

"Mother Goose? Denny, I don't know anything about doing a children's show. God, I've never even watched one."

"Doesn't matter. You can fake it. Just let the kids talk. We'll throw in a few records and let them dance. Gus, Mother's helper, can handle that. A dozen commercials and it'll be over."

Margie's mind was racng. Could she do it? Yes, she could, and what's more she could do a better job than the insipid, overblown bimbo who was doing the show now. Mother Goose didn't even like children. Margie had lied to Denny; she'd watched the show a couple of times and wondered how much the kids got paid to suffer through it.

"What happened to Mother?"

"Politely speaking, according to Leonard, Mother is ill. She's been warned about her drinking and this may be the straw that breaks the camel's back. Even Leonard can't save her this time. Come on, Margie, give me a break and help me out."

"According to Leonard?" Margie was beginning to have an odd feeling about this. Did Leonard have anything to do with the state of Mother Goose's health? He had come home half drunk the night before. Could he have been with the actress? Leonard kept his private life very private.

Margie didn't even want to think that Leonard had come to her from another woman. She'd been so sure that Leonard genuinely cared for her. Had she done it again? Slept with a man who was only using her? Still, the opportunity to be on television was being offered to her and she'd be a fool to let her uncertainty cost her this chance.

"What's in it for me?" she stalled.

"Dinner and—who knows, we'll think of something."

"Professionally, I mean."

"Well, I don't know about that. I'll put in a good word with the station manager. Maybe a commercial or two?"

By the time the fairy music signaled the opening of the show, Margie had fashioned a leprechaun costume from felt, a pair of tights, some glue and glitter. Not a finished product, but without camera closeups it would pass.

"And Mother Goose had to go and visit the King of Hearts today," Gus was saying. "She left me in charge, and to begin the show today, we're going to do the hokey-pokey."

"Ohhhhh!" The children were not happy with Gus. They wanted Mother Goose. Even the presence of the outrageous hats they donned for their dance wasn't going to soothe their dismay. The show was heading for the toilet.

"But wait," Gus said, adding in desperation, "she sent someone very special to play with you, someone magical—"

The children grew quiet. Skeptical, but interested.

"She sent—Lacy the Magic Fairy, keeper of the Unicorn."

Margie took a deep breath and darted into the fairy ring. A bell tied about her ankle tinkled as she ran. "Please, tell me that he isn't here." She looked frantically around.

The children, caught up in the question, began to look around, too.

"Who?"

Margie recognized the skeptic. "The Pirate King and his wicked alligator. They were right behind me. Where did they go? Oh? I'm so afraid."

"Ah, there's no such things as fairies and pirates. And alligators don't live in the forest."

"They can, too," the believer argued.

"I don't know what to do. Will you be my friends and help me?" Margie turned a frantic look on the children and held out her arms.

In a moment they were all around her, wide-eyed, nodding

their heads.

The children bent their heads close to Margie and began to whisper. At that moment the director cut to the commercial. The timing couldn't have been better if he'd written and rehearsed the script.

Denny shook his head. The girl was a natural. In just a few minutes she'd accomplished something that Mother Goose hadn't done in four weeks: the children had become involved. Denny might be a minor director on a minor television station, but he knew magic when he saw it. Margie Raines was magic.

By the end of the show, the children had turned the pirate into the guardian of the fairy forest and the phone was ringing off the hook. Every mother who watched wanted to know how her child could get on the show. A bakery offered birthday cakes to celebrate the children's birthdays, and one of the local department stores wanted Lacy to appear in a fashion show for kids.

Neil Armstrong became the first man to walk on the moon at the same time Margie became Mother Goose. Neil's famous statement, "That's one small step for man, one giant leap for mankind," could have been just as easily spoken about Margie, for her television show would one day be known as the start of local live programing in Atlanta, Georgia.

Margie's television career was an instant success; her love affair with Leonard died a painful death. Night after night he went out and didn't return until after she was in bed.

"Leonard, I don't understand. I thought we had something special. What's wrong?"

"My darling Margie, don't be a silly chit. Why do you suppose I've never married?"

"I don't know. Until we made love, I never thought about it. Are you saying it didn't mean anything to you?"

"Of course it did. You're a wonderful lover and a very special girl. But I'm too old for you. You've got your comet, now grab on."

"What about us, Leonard?"

"There is no us, Margie. Mallory needs me, you don't. Go for the stars, little one."

Margie felt her heart twist. "I don't believe you. I refuse to believe that you don't want me. Somehow you got that part for me, Leonard, and I'm not going to leave you."

But Leonard was adamant. It was the hardest thing he ever had to do in his life, but he kept himself from taking Margie in his arms. He refused to meet her eyes, to share their meals, to come to her bed. Instead, he spent all his time with Mallory. She'd been the oldest child, looking after him when they had fled Russia as children. If it hadn't been for Mallory having a job they might have starved. Now she was in trouble, he had to protect her. After all, she was his sister. Margie was only the woman he loved.

It took Margie weeks to believe that she was finally a success. Leonard never admitted to having suggested Margie as a fill-in for Mother Goose, and he never came to her bed again. Leaving her apartment in Leonard's studio was like leaving home. It was very hard, but Leonard wouldn't hear of anything else.

Lacy the Magic Fairy was a small comet, but a comet all the same. With Denny as her coach and cheerleader, Margie Raines was at last on her way to being somebody.

For Denny, the show was the vehicle he intended to use to make it to the networks. As the success of the show grew, he tightened his control by initiating legal contracts to protect his ownership of the concept and by courting Margie to make certain she was committed to him.

At the end of their first three months on the air, Denny invited Margie out to dinner to celebrate. She'd splurged on a smart new black dress and heels, a trip to the beauty parlor for a stylish upswept hairstyle, and a bottle of expensive perfume.

Margie met Denny at the television station, testing her newly polished look on the crew before Denny arrived. He was late, and by the time he arrived, Margie was already floating on a cloud of male appreciation.

Denny was surprised. He'd seen Margie every day, on camera, in wardrobe and makeup, but he'd only seen her as a property. Tonight she was a woman and she was a knockout.

At the studio Denny wore black pants and black turtleneck shirts. Tonight he was dressed for public display;

he'd added a black collarless jacket and changed the turtleneck to red. He looked wicked.

"Wow, lady, do I know you?"

"I don't think so. Would you like to?"

That set the tone for the evening. The Coach and Six restaurant was crowded, but Denny moved past the line of diners and whispered in the ear of the hostess. Moments later they were shown to a table which was obviously being held for a VIP.

Denny ordered wine, sniffed the cork, and nodded his approval of his selection. He studied the menu. "What would you like, Margie?"

"I'd like to freeze this moment and keep it always. You order for me."

She was conscious of the other diners staring at her and Denny and whispering about them. When the waiter asked for her autograph for his daughter, Margie knew she'd arrived.

The waiter was attentive. The food was wonderful. The conversation soft and suggestive. The music quietly elegant. By the time they finished their dessert, Margie was floating. Glory had been wrong. Everything had come together for her. She'd found her comet and she hadn't needed to use herself to attract the man who was inviting her back to his apartment for a nightcap.

"Come home with me, Margie."

"I don't know, Denny. Having dinner was wonderful, but we have to work together, tomorrow, early."

"So, we'll leave from my place," he whispered, pulling her close as they waited for the valet to bring the car. "We're a team now, Margie. Just me and you. Let's see how high we can go."

As they climbed the steps to Denny's Piedmont Road apartment, Margie allowed herself a silent smile. The third floor was as high as they were going tonight. And Denny might be the hottest television director in Atlanta, but his apartment was not in the same league as the Corvette he drove. It didn't need to be; nobody important saw it. His furnishings were typical bachelor-sparse: a living room with wooden floors that creaked and a bedroom with an unmade bed.

And Margie didn't have a nightcap. She didn't even see the kitchen that night. The next morning she moved in with Denny. But she never could bring herself to stop helping Leonard. Leonard was family, and more. He was security, and no matter how well the show did, she didn't trust success. It could disappear as quickly as it had come.

In the third year of Lacy the Magic Fairy, the advertising agency writing the commercials for Lacy's primary sponsor never knew that the woman they were writing for was the same one they'd fired for having her picture on the front page of the *Atlanta Journal* during the desegregation of downtown Atlanta. But Margie knew, and if she made an occasional mistake reading the copy, she felt that it was only just deserts for the pompous idiots who never knew what they'd lost. Margie was suddenly in control. Or she thought she was.

One afternoon Denny suddenly had business downtown, business that he didn't explain. She knew that he was up to something and went home without him. It wouldn't be the first time he'd been unfaithful, but this time he seemed particularly nervous. When he finally did come home he was very tense.

"All right, out with it, Den. What's going on?"

"I—I don't know how to tell you, Margie."

"Just one word at a time will do."

He was taking off his gray buttonless Nehru jacket, hanging it on the back of the chair. Next came the pencil-slim gray flannel trousers that hugged his long legs, followed by the red turtleneck sweater that had become his signature as an "artist."

"The show has been syndicated."

"We're going national?" Margie was astonished. "I don't believe it! We're going national?"

"Not exactly. The concept has been sold. It'll be produced by ABC."

"So, where? Where will we do it?"

Denny sat on the edge of the bed and glared at the floor. "Not *we*, Margie. They're going to use Josie Carmichael as Lacy."

295

"Josie Carmichael? But they can't. That's my role. I don't care if she has been on television forever. I created Lacy. She's mine."

But Denny only shook his head. "Legally the show belongs to me. At the time that was the only way the station would accept you. But we never, I mean you never, insisted on a specific contract, Margie. The show belongs to me. ABC bought the show, but they didn't buy you."

Margie stood up. She stared at this man who'd shared her little moment of stardom. He was no different than any of the others.

When Denny left, Margie retained their apartment. She might not have a contract for the role of Lacy, but she did have a contract with Channel 8 that she had no intention of allowing them to break. Still, she'd better have something specific to sell or they'd put her in the prop department.

"What am I going to do, Leonard?" Margie was spattered with paint as she and her old friend repaired the set for the final production of the Metropolitan Opera.

"What do you want to do?"

"Well, I'm no stage actress. And there's not a big market for women on local television."

"What about another children's program. Couldn't you come up with an idea?"

"I could, but I don't want to dance around in leotards and fairy shoes for the rest of my life. I don't want to end up like—" She didn't say it, but Leonard knew she was thinking about Mallory.

"She's better, Margie," he answered her unasked question. "I don't know if she'll ever make it back as an actress, but she's started to paint again and she'll be fine."

"I'm glad. But I still don't have a clue what I'm going to do. The station has to pay me and they're doing it, but what they really want is to buy out my contract."

"Is that what you want?"

"No. I like television. There has to be something serious I can do, where it doesn't matter if I sound like Dorothy Kilgallen."

296

Leonard put down his brush and turned toward Margie. "Listen to me, Marjorie Raines. You've managed to get where you are through little effort. It's time you set your own course and worked for it. Go home and think about what you want, develop the idea, and present it to the station. You're smarter than you've ever given yourself credit for and you're in the driver's seat."

That was the longest speech she'd ever heard from Leonard, and the sternest. She shook her head in agreement, but she didn't believe a word he said, not really, not deep down.

But the Coming Events section of the *Atlanta Journal* gave her the answer. After a stiff pep talk and a long, careful handwritten plan, Margie was ready. The next day, she called Arthur Noland who was in town with his rock star wife, Noelle, who was appearing at Chastain Park with the Theater Under the Stars Summer Concert Series.

Margie, wearing her smart black dress with its matching jacket, met Arthur for lunch. She applied a little blackmail by reminding him of their inspirational meeting on the stage of the Woman's Club Theater during the run of *Cat on a Hot Tin Roof,* and how she'd helped him get over his nervous condition. Arthur knew how to play the game. He agreed to give Margie an on-camera interview. Noelle, who never gave interviews, was persuaded to join him.

The Channel 8 program director also knew how to take advantage of a situation, and when Margie Raines offered an interview with the hottest celebrity couple in Hollywood, he quickly agreed to allow her to do her first feature.

Margie never made it as an actress. She could never write a news story. But to her surprise, she found the transition from children's shows to interviewing celebrities and covering local human interest stories a natural. And by year's end, "A Chat with Margie Raines" became a regular Friday segment on the six and eleven o'clock news.

Soon she was making personal appearances on behalf of the television station as well. The contract ended and she was offered another with more money and more perks. Margie signed without hesitation.

Margie's guests were always interesting because she expected them to be. Susan and JoEllen would have under-

297

stood if she'd told them that every celebrity she interviewed was Glory. She always waited for Glory to shake her head and divulge some intimate, scandalous bit of gossip. And not once did her subject fail her.

Finally, after eighteen years, Margie Raines, at thirty-six, was on her way.

Thirty-Four

While Richard Nixon was gearing up for the final weeks of campaigning for reelection as President of the United States, JoEllen Dixon was made assistant administrator of Lawton General Hospital.

In order to become hospital director, JoEllen needed additional training and she was on her way over to the college to talk about taking classes in business. The on-campus protest against the war in Vietnam that she had to plow her way through brought her into the present with a resounding smack as she looked at the long-haired women and men with shaven heads sitting in a circle in the middle of the road.

JoEllen had lived through the sexual revolution, the struggle for desegregation of the schools, and the era of the flower children. She'd seen a President, a presidential candidate, and a civil rights leader assassinated, but nothing had prepared her for the stubborn resistance of the protestors or the brutality of their removal by the Augusta police department.

When one obviously pregnant young woman was shoved to the concrete, JoEllen charged into the fray, trying to help protect her from the billy clubs.

In a matter of minutes, JoEllen, along with the others, was herded into the paddy wagon and booked for disturbing the peace, demonstrating without a permit, and obstructing the flow of traffic.

JoEllen was horrified. What would the hospital board think? When the girl went into labor in the cell, JoEllen sent for a doctor. When he didn't arrive in time, she delivered the child herself, a child who seemed reluctant to take her first breath. The mother held the baby in her arms listlessly and sat, waiting for her "family" to come for her and take it away.

"Don't you want your baby?" JoEllen asked.

"Yeah, I guess."

"But why would you take part in a demonstration when you're about to deliver a child? Does the father know?"

"Who knows who he is?" one of the others answered for her. "She sleeps with a different guy every night."

"Don't worry," the new mother said. "Somebody will take care of the baby. They always do. I'm not very good at it."

"How many children do you have?" JoEllen asked.

"Three or four, I think."

JoEllen saw red. *Somebody would take care of her child? Three or four, she didn't remember?*

JoEllen was struck with total horror. For years she'd vacillated between firm opposition to abortion and the need for women to have a choice. Then the pill came and, with it, another set of doubts. There were other means of birth control, and using abortion to get rid of unwanted children because the parents weren't responsible became unacceptable.

Her anguish was always tied in with her own child, the only child she might ever have, the child she'd gotten rid of, the secret pain she lived with. She'd given up her child and Glory had died rather than have hers. Now this—this *child* was having babies indiscriminately. "Why do you let this happen? Why didn't you use birth control?"

But as she asked the question she knew that the confused expression would be her answer. "Birth control," JoEllen went on vehemently. "If not that, why don't you give the child up for adoption?"

"Give up my baby?" The girl turned a look of horror on JoEllen. "I could never do that. I believe in love for all mankind."

"Yeah" came a comment from another cell, "especially the ones who provide you with drugs. Don't worry, lady, the kid will probably get left somewhere along the way."

"But—but wouldn't an abortion be better than this?" Though JoEllen hadn't assisted in an abortion since Dr.

300

Brooks left Augusta, she had never forgotten the last time she'd been asked for help—by Glory. JoEllen hadn't forgotten her refusal to help her friend, either, or the results. JoEllen looked around the holding tank at the women there. Not only the protesters but the others, all sad, washed-out, some pregnant.

"Maybe," one of the women admitted. "But what can we do? One of our friends died when she tried to do it to herself."

"Sooner or later, abortion will be legalized, I'm sure. The next time, come and see me. Perhaps I can help you." She gave them her name and telephone number.

The woman and her child were taken to the hospital and JoEllen was released from jail. She couldn't erase from her mind the picture of the girl demonstrating for peace being clubbed by the police. Nor could she forget the unwanted child being born in a jail cell.

And suddenly JoEllen was jolted by understanding. Caring for people, that was why she'd become a nurse, not to handle personnel and payrolls. Those who knew what to do and could afford to pay for it didn't need her help. Somewhere along the way she'd let ambition blind her to her mission in life.

Glory had said it, a long time ago. "I always know what I want, and it doesn't matter what I do to get it. It's the end results that count. But no matter how hard you try, a woman can't accomplish a damned thing without a man."

Glory's man had let her down. Just as JoEllen had. JoEllen shuddered and made herself a promise to find a way to change that—all of it. She'd never had the opportunity to make a statement, and if she had, it wouldn't have involved a war on the other side of the world, it would have dealt with what she was seeing here. Sex, drugs, and women who couldn't make choices about their own bodies.

A woman deserved to make her own decisions, so long as they were made with pride, not because of which man provided the drugs or what the law dictated.

Two weeks later the girl from the jail appeared at JoEllen's apartment, her child clasped in her arms.

"You said to come if I needed help. I do. Someplace to stay

301

for a while," she said. "I hope you meant it."

JoEllen quickly ran through her options. She'd spoken from the heart, not from the mind. Taking a stranger into her home wasn't what she'd meant. She couldn't turn the girl away, but what would she do with her?

A moment later she opened the door and let her in. After a bath and a good meal, JoEllen put the girl, who called herself Morningstar, to bed, and left to work the eleven-to-seven shift. When she returned the next morning the girl, JoEllen's new red dress, and a jar of loose change were gone. JoEllen sighed and went to bed.

When the baby began to cry, she was shocked. When she opened the bureau drawer and the child focused frightened black eyes on her, she was captured instantly. There was a note.

I'm sorry. I can't keep her. I'm giving her to you. Her name is Teresa. Love her, please.

Dr. Thomas Brooks had been right all along, but he'd been right for the wrong reasons. He'd helped women get illegal abortions, because that was the only choice they had. JoEllen always thought having an abortion took courage. That was true, for some. For others, keeping the child was the courageous thing to do. She hadn't kept her baby, and she'd helped Glory get rid of hers. Neither of them had ever gotten over it.

JoEllen held the baby and felt a swell of peace rush through her, as if she'd been given a second chance. She'd keep Teresa and give her all the love that was bottled up inside her. And she'd find a way to help other women who were faced with the same problem.

In June of 1972, JoEllen resigned her position at the hospital, took Teresa, and moved to Atlanta to start a search for the baby's mother. She took over the running of Thomas Brooks's office and became his clinic director. Brooks Medical Center was part of a national network of clinics that handled women's procedures quietly and confidentially. Clients were referred there by a special women's network and a host of clandestine helpers across the country.

The Brooks Center soon had a reputation so sterling that the local doctors quietly referred special cases to Dr. Brooks. The only concession that he was forced to make in order to keep JoEllen satisfied was to offer a percentage of his work to charity. He also tolerated the times that JoEllen listened to her conscience and helped a woman who decided to keep her baby.

The remaining flower children, the runaways, and the street people learned about JoEllen and came to her with their problems. Through her underground contacts JoEllen finally located Morningstar and obtained both her signature and that of the father on Teresa's private adoption papers.

Though JoEllen was in Atlanta, she avoided Margie, for Margie was a reporter and reporters believed in the public's right to know. JoEllen had no agrument with that, but until abortion was made legal, she had no intention of having the spotlight on her. She worked long hours and took on the problems of all the women who came to her. Jobs, living quarters, counseling all became a part of JoEllen's duties.

There was no time for a personal life.

Occasionally she saw Teddy's name in the newspaper. His race cars continued to dominate the NASCAR circuit, astounding the other mechanics, not because he won, for he didn't always, but that a small-town guy would refuse the offers he'd had to join the racing teams and the cash offers that had been made to reveal his secrets.

Her mother reminded her regularly that she could have been Mrs. Ted Wallace if she hadn't had higher aspirations than living in Galilee, Georgia. Even Skip chose the Navy knowing the only water Galilee was near was the Savannah River. When JoEllen told her mother about Teresa she was told that it would be better for her not to bring the child home for a visit. People would talk.

That conversation only locked the door that had been closed years ago. Mrs. Dixon had raised her children and that was all she needed to do.

For JoEllen there was only her work and Teresa. Relationships were for people without involvement, and JoEllen Dixon was involved in the lives of others. Glory had called her a lily—proud, pristine, and alone.

Glory had been right.

But Glory was dead, and JoEllen was determined that nothing like that would ever happen again—not if she could help it.

By the early seventies, cases involving a woman's right to choose were being heard across the country, the most famous being *Roe v. Wade* which made abortion legal and changed JoEllen's life in a way she never expected.

Thirty-Five

In the midseventies, *A Chat With Margie Raines* was syndicated and aired on seventy-two local television stations throughout the Southeast and Southwest. Denny disappeared when ABC dropped the children's program *The Mother Goose Hour*. From time to time, Margie thought about him, but not often. There were many men from whom she could choose now. A television personality had to be discreet, but she had choices.

One choice she never thought she'd have to consider as a subject for an interview was Steven Winslow. When he turned up at a Chamber of Commerce luncheon as the representative for Greenway Investments and Securities, she immediately thought of Sam, for there was a family resemblance between the Winslow cousins.

Margie didn't often cross paths with anyone from her past. When she did, she had to work at maintaining her self-confidence. But Steven was a very handsome, polished man, a man she might find a use for. She introduced herself. She didn't have to. Steven remembered Margie, though he remembered her as being a bit overblown and awkward. The woman whose firm handshake he was measuring was tall, sophisticated, and direct.

"Steven, how nice to have you in Atlanta." He'd grown a mustache, full and dark across his upper lip.

The uncertain teenager he remembered was gone. The woman who'd replaced her was stunning. "Margie? It's been a long time."

"Yes."

Neither added what they both were thinking: A long time since Glory's funeral.

"How are you?" Margie was struck again by the similarity between Steven, Sam, and Glory. All three were tall and lean; cousins who shared such a strong family characteristic were rare. And even with the difference in coloring, Margie could have been looking at Glory. She wondered if Steven thought the same when he looked into the mirror.

Steven could have told her he did. From the first time he'd seen Glory in her crib, there had been some instant, unalterable connection. That feeling intensified when Glory's father died and she'd become his shadow. Glory had been a part of Steven's life, both the best and worst of what he'd become. Death hadn't changed the connection, but time and age had made it easier to deal with.

His ex-wife had been right. When she'd left, Elizabeth had accused him of living with a ghost instead of with her. He'd tried to separate himself from Glory and the hold she had on him, but he had never been able to make the break complete. And his wife had known—not the truth, but that she was a substitute for something, or someone, else. Elizabeth had remarried a year ago, and Steven was glad that she'd found someone to love her.

For Steven, life without Elizabeth was little different than it had been before. He was lonely then and was lonely now.

"Have dinner with me, Margie?"

"No, I—"

Steven was still holding her hand. There was a certain awareness between them, and Margie was intrigued. They shared a past. They shared memories of a place that Margie had never quite been able to put behind her. She was surprised as she recognized the same feeling of breathless anticipation that had always come from Glory when she'd come up with some outlandish escapade. Margie told herself that it was natural. Steven made her think of Glory, and she always got a little flutter in the bottom of her stomach when she met a new man.

Margie pulled her hand away and answered softly, "All right. I think I'd like that."

She suggested Anthony's, an antebellum mansion relocated from its original site east of Atlanta in Washington,

306

Georgia. General Sherman had spared the structure because at the time he rode through, a baby had just been born. In the ten years since the house had been moved to Atlanta and opened to the public, it had become a favorite restaurant with an impeccable reputation for both food and romantic atmosphere.

Afraid that she'd allowed her interest to show, Margie followed up by saying, "Let me put it on my expense account. I'm interviewing you."

"No," he argued with a wicked grin. "Let me put it on *my* expense account. You're a potential client."

Steven's eyes didn't agree with his words. Margie Raines might be a lot of things in his future, but a client would be the least important of them. The last thing he'd ever anticipated was that he'd find a new woman to interest him, particularly one from his past, one with the same kind of southern wiles and sexual power that Glory had. He wasn't certain that he wanted to admit it, but Margie's pull was undeniable, and his body began to sing.

She met him at the restaurant. Steven wasn't surprised when she'd said that she'd drive herself. Margie had come a long way from the days when she played follow the leader. Now she was the leader and she made it obvious that she would control the evening. Fine. He'd let her—for now.

Margie was basking in afternoon-production-meeting praise from her producer. Because her interviews were more like fireside conversations, she'd managed to corral Spiro Agnew for a rare interview after he was forced to resign as Gerald Ford's Vice President. The piece had caught the attention of the networks. Now she was having dinner with a handsome man. Life was good.

It was April, a rare warm evening. Her dress was a white lightweight wool, with long sleeves and a gold belt. She wore tan lizard skin shoes and carried a small gold bag. Her hair had been cut and styled in a soft pageboy that fell just below her earlobes. With creamy makeup and a hint of peach color she looked warm but elusive, a style that was becoming her trademark.

Steven was waiting in one of the rocking chairs on the

307

porch when she drove up the promenade lined with hundred-year-old oaks. He stood. As she handed the attendant the keys to her white Buick and walked toward him, Margie was conscious of the picture they'd present once they went inside. They made a stunning couple, light and dark, sunshine and shadows.

They were seated in a corner of one of the new additions to the restaurant. Steven ordered appetizers, little dumplings filled with pork, an herb soup, and fruit salad. He passed on the goat cheese and buffalo meat which was a specialty of the house, choosing instead the rack of lamb with special mint sauce.

"Cocktails first?" the waiter inquired.

"Not me," Margie demurred. "I have to watch my weight. The camera magnifies every ounce."

"And every ounce is lovely," Steven said, ordering iced tea for Margie and white wine for himself.

"So tell me, how did you get to be a television personality, Margie Raines?"

"By accident. I delivered a shoe and became a leprechaun."

"That sounds like you have your fairy tales confused."

"Exactly. That's exactly how it all happened." And she explained how she'd fallen into the starring role on the *Mother Goose Hour*. By the time the lamb was served they'd covered her "trek to catch her comet." She put her fork down. "What about you?"

"Oh, nothing terribly exciting. College, and an internship with Weaver Investments that landed me a job when I graduated. Five years ago, I was named vice president of Greenway and Associates."

"Married?"

Steven gave Margie a puzzled look. She really didn't know anything about him. He'd graduated and left Winslow before the county consolidated the schools, so their paths had never really crossed, except at the funeral. But he'd always assumed that Glory talked about him. Apparently she hadn't.

"Not anymore. I'm divorced now. Three years."

"Children?"

"Two. Steven, Junior, nineteen, and a girl, Melissa,

fourteen. They live in New York with their mother."

"You must miss them."

"Not particularly," he admitted. "I was never a very good husband and father. I've been so busy for the last few years that I haven't had time to see much of them. Their stepfather is a good man. I have them for holidays and summer vacations. They don't seem to mind. Apparently I have only one talent and that's for investments."

"Oh, and what do you recommend?"

"Like you, I'm into television, communications. The Turner Satellite Network, cable television, pay-per-view television is the wave of the future."

"Oh? Then I'll have to let you help me get rich."

"I'd like nothing better."

"At least by moving here you're closer to your mother. How is Evelyn?"

"Not very well, I'm afraid. You know Adele died, too, shortly after Glory . . ." His voice trailed off. "After that, mother seemed to lose her zest for life. Even though I was her only child, we were never really close. She was always sending me away—prep school, college, and, finally, work. I've been gone so long that it hardly seems like home anymore. But she seems to enjoy dragging the grand-children, nieces, and nephews down there."

"Does anybody ever hear from Roger, or—his son?"

"No, except for Mother. Damon spends time with her every summer. He looks on her as a . . . surrogate grand-mother, I suppose."

"And you . . . do you go home often?"

"I've tried, but I just can't seem to. Too many sad memories. What about you?"

"No, I haven't been back since . . ." She took a deep breath. They weren't going to be able to dance around it all night. It might as well be out in the open. "Not since Glory's funeral. After I left Galilee I've been back five times and, except for Sam and Susan's wedding, all the trips were for funerals. You didn't make the wedding, did you?"

"No."

"Neither did Glory."

Margie checked the table for an ashtray, pulled out a cigarette, and reached for her lighter. Steven took it from her and snapped it open, holding the flame to the cigarette.

This was the first time he'd discussed Glory or her son without being overwhelmed with guilt. He didn't know why it was so easy to talk to Margie. It wasn't just the talent she had as an interviewer, and the ease surprised him.

"You know these aren't good for you," he said.

"I know. But little of what I've done in my life has been good for me. Still, in all, I don't guess I have any regrets."

"There are few of us who can say that. No bad decisions?"

"Oh, yes, but bad decisions seem to have propelled me along to whatever success I've had as much as the good ones. I gave up trying to control fate long ago."

"My, so cynical."

"That I am, Steven."

Steven leaned back so that the wine steward could refill his glass. He glanced at her hand. "No ring. Anybody special?"

"No, that I can say with certainty. Nobody special, except Charlie."

"Charlie?"

"My cat, and the only ring he's interested in is one made out of feathers and catnip."

Steven smiled. "Good."

For a moment Margie saw something in his smile that she hadn't seen before. Then the flash was gone, and his expression turned bland. With his sardonic good looks, Margie had the thought that Steven would be a cruel lover. She shivered, and suddenly they'd lost the ease with which they'd talked.

They settled for cappuccino instead of dessert. Afterward, they left in separate cars, each agreeing that they'd have dinner again, each knowing that they'd come close to spending the night together, only to back off at the last minute.

As it turned out, they were both right about the dinner. Margie's subsequent interview with Steven was one of her better serious pieces. His discussion about the market was prophetic as the Dow took an unexpected dramatic rise. And the funds he invested for Margie doubled, then within a year tripled to an astonishing amount of money.

"You were right, Steve. You do seem to have the magic touch." Margie took the news of her latest financial coup with easy acceptance, just as she had Steven's place in her life.

"That I do—for making money. But that isn't my only talent. I wish you'd let me show you how magical my personal touch really can be."

They'd played a word-game courtship for several months. An occasional dinner—very public—and lunch now and then. Margie drove herself to the restaurant and home again. Steven kept suggesting a more personal relationship and Margie kept delaying.

When she'd called Steven this morning she hadn't been certain that she wanted to cross that line she'd drawn between them. Now she decided that she no longer wanted to wait for what would come. She liked Steven and she wanted to see him. She'd held off long enough. "About your personal touch, that's what I called about, Steven, to invite you to be my escort for the local Emmy Awards ceremony."

"Not exactly what I had in mind, but it has possibilities. Are you up for an award?"

"I'm afraid so."

"Which award are you going to win?"

"Probably none. Outstanding Television Personality is the category I've been nominated in. But the competition is pretty stiff."

"You'll win. When is the big night?"

"The ceremony is Saturday. We'll meet at the Hilton. Champagne cocktails begin at seven-thirty, dinner at eight o'clock. I plan to skip the cocktail party, so I'll meet you there about eight?"

"I'll be your escort, Margie. I'll fend off the goblins, charm the ladies, or protect you from the bad guys, but this time, I'll pick you up and take you home. It's time, Margie."

Steven was laying it out. Tonight they'd make love. She could accept, or refuse. It was her play and she knew it. There was a long silence.

"I'm in King's Towers, apartment 1202."

"I know."

Steven left the restaurant with a new spring in his step. For the first time in his life he was interested in a woman, interested in the whole woman, not just her body or what she could do for him. She wasn't necessary to his success and her part in his life was neither an addiction nor a smokescreen.

Margie was somehow a connection with his past and his future. He didn't have to be something he wasn't and he didn't have to hide his true feelings. And best of all she didn't depend on him for her happiness. He'd never realized that kind of dependency sucked a man dry. A strong woman, Margie Raines stood alone, an equal, offering as much as she would take. He began to whistle.

The ballroom glowed with lights. Sequins, beaded gowns, the glittery elegance of the occasion was caught by mirrors and refracted a thousand times. And suddenly Margie knew that tonight was her night. From the moment Steven stepped into her apartment foyer and took a long appreciative look at her, her pulse began to throb.

He was wearing the required dinner jacket, black with a plaid cummerbund and black tie. She'd vacillated between wearing black or white and finally settled on emerald green, a cool hands-off look that would help her keep her poise in the event she was defeated. From the front the dress was simple with a high neckline and long sleeves. But there was no back, at least *almost* none. When she turned around, Steven let out a long vocal breath.

"Wow! I don't want to think about what isn't under that dress or we'll never get out the door. You, as you already know, are playing with fire."

"Is it too risqué?"

"On camera, my darling Margie, you'll stand there and win Atlanta's professional heart as you accept your award. When you turn to leave, you'll grab all their other parts."

"Exactly what I had in mind. And just to make sure you know what I expect, you're along to protect me from the women who'll try to put my eyes out."

"Am I hearing a sexist remark from the highest-ranking female personality in local television?"

"You're damn right, Stevie boy. Tonight I'm pulling out all the stops. Why else do you think I asked you to be my date?"

312

Steven slid his arm around her and pulled her close. "I hope I know."

They were swept into the room by a moving tide of guests. For a moment Margie was blinded by the lights of the television cameras. She caught Steven's arm. Just for a second she felt her glow of confidence falter.

For a moment she wished Leonard were here. But he'd be watching on the public broadcasting channel. Leonard would always know what she was doing and she felt his pride in her accomplishments, even when he never mentioned them.

"Smile, darling," Steven whispered. "These are your people."

"*Beautiful.*"

"*Really talented.*"

"*A real bitch. She used to be a fairy, for God's sake.*"

The fragments of conversation followed their entrance.

"A fairy?" Steven leaned close. "Now that sounds interesting."

"On my children's program . . . Hello, Fred." She nodded at one of the local engineers. "Nice to see you, Governor."

The evening was perfect. Steven wasn't a mystery to the power structure of Atlanta, but he was to their wives. And they were green with envy just as Margie had planned. She and Steven circulated through the throng. Margie was sipping champagne, Steven heavily watered Scotch.

At dinner they were seated with Mayor and Mrs. Jackson, Art London, the president of Channel 8, and his wife, and David Malone and Melanie Starrett, the co-anchors of News at six and eleven.

"Margie," David gave Margie the obligatory kiss, "you look ravishing."

"You're wearing green?" Melanie observed. "Is that symbolic?"

Margie allowed Steven to pull out her chair. "Symbolic? In what way?"

"As I remember, you were wearing green when you got your start on *Mother Goose*. Green is your color."

Art London leaned forward, ready to defuse the ensuing catfight before it started. "What I remember is red. The switchboard, the red switchboard, when every incoming line

313

stayed lit up for days. The whole town must have been watching. And they still are." He held out his hand to Steven. "I'm Art London. I don't think we've been introduced."

"Steven Winslow. Good to be here." Steven shook Art's hand, then David's and Mayor Jackson's before he sat down. They'd drawn the mayor, that sounded promising for Margie, providing Melanie didn't attack her before the ceremony. Steven remembered Margie's plan that he was here to charm the women.

Casually, he allowed his gaze to slide around the table until he found Melanie Starrett. He paused for just a second, long enough for her to see and accept his unspoken signal. She did and began to relax, secure in her belief that she'd found a weapon with which to wound Margie if it became necessary.

Margie picked up her glass and took a sip. "Careful, Steven, you're drooling. Melanie is a witch."

Steven unfolded the napkin and leaned closer. "But darling, isn't that what you hired me for: chief witch hunter?"

She had, and it surprised her that Steven's contact with Melanie bothered her. He was a strong, successful man, and she occupied a similar position of success. They were equals, and neither was a threat to the other. That made the possibility of a relationship acceptable.

"Witch hunter? I don't know. I failed to ask how much you charge?"

"Don't worry, Margie, my services are free."

Margie had never had a relationship with a man like Steven. Every other man in her life was as smooth as she was vulnerable. They were all a part of what had brought Margie this far. Her fate—her karma. What would Steven give her?

Maybe she ought to be asking what Steven would *take*.

"Margie, do you intend to stay with local television, or do you expect to go to New York?" Melanie asked.

Margie smiled. No point in sharing her future plans with her competition. But Margie had her eye on New York and the networks—in time.

"Perhaps," she answered vaguely.

"Oh? Have you had offers?"

Carefully, as if she were interviewing a reluctant guest, Margie phrased her words. "I've never consciously en-

314

visioned my future, Melanie. I've just known that it was there. Once, a long time ago somebody told me to catch my comet and I would soar. I suppose that I'll go wherever it takes me."

Glory. Steven recognized the statement. He'd heard her say it a thousand times. He felt a tightening of his stomach muscles. There'd been a time when he'd thought about Glory constantly, but slowly, the preoccupation had begun to lessen. Instead of bringing Glory to mind, he was surprised when his relationship with Margie had filled his mind with light and laughter—until this moment.

He certainly hadn't expected to think of Glory now. She was part of the past, part of a time when he hadn't known how to define or control his needs. Every move calculated to take him away from temptation seemed to take him back where he started, wanting something he could never have.

Glory's suicide had taken the choice from him, and he'd been ashamed to admit his relief at being set free. The surprise had been that instead of saving his marriage, Glory's death had finally destroyed it. The relief was replaced with even deeper guilt. He'd failed two women: the one he loved and the one he'd married. Elizabeth, who deserved more, finally realized that he had nothing more to give.

The marriage ended and Steven transferred to Atlanta. He could go back home, start over, he thought, at last. But it hadn't worked out like that. He'd come this far, but Winslow and his mother were still troubled waters.

He glanced at Margie. He was glad that she hadn't known about his obsession with Glory. Maybe someday he'd tell her. Steven had changed. He was no longer addicted to a forbidden love. Margie had changed a great deal, too, becoming successful and very beautiful. They were much alike, both reborn, both lonely, both connected to a past that they'd overcome and a future that knew no bounds.

"How long before we can blow this joint?" he whispered, putting his hand on her thigh.

"Soon," she whispered, and covered it with her own. Either she'd win the award or she wouldn't. There was no point worrying about it. For the rest of the meal she allowed her full attention to be captured by the man she'd meant to be a balm for the resident bitches. So? She was a star. A star

315

could change her mind. A star could be honest enough with herself to admit the truth. She wanted Steven for herself.

Outstanding Television Personality was the last award to be given. When they called her name she was stunned. No matter what she'd hoped for, she'd prepared herself to be disappointed. Winning was harder than losing. She had so little experience with it.

"Thanks to all the people in my life who pushed me where I am, and special thanks to Leonard who made me decide where I wanted to go." The remainder of her speech must have been suitable because the audience clapped and stood, giving her an ovation that was caught by the television cameras and beamed across the city. Margie Raines, Outstanding Television Personality, Emmy winner, star. She was giddy with success.

As she sat back down at her table, Steven gave her a proprietary kiss. "So, you've won. Do you feel outstanding?"

"No. But maybe, at last, I've caught the tail of my comet. Now I guess I'll just ride it until it burns itself out. Right now, I think I'm on fire. Let's get out of here." Margie was tipsy from champagne and success. She hugged her Emmy to her, like the teddy bear she'd slept with all these years since she'd left Galilee.

"I'd say you're definitely soaring," Steven agreed a short time later as he helped her into the elevator of her apartment building and punched the twelfth floor.

"Who's Leonard?"

"Leonard? Leonard, my oldest friend, my mentor, my family."

"My competition?"

"No—no, you have none. Here, the key is inside my bag. You'll have to open the door. I don't intend to put this statue down until I'm inside my apartment and the door is locked behind me."

Steven took the silver bag and found the key, propping Margie against the wall while he opened the door. "Why? I don't think anybody can take it away from you now. The whole world watched you accept it."

"Yes, they did, didn't they?" Margie walked over to the fireplace and put the statue in the beam of illumination fed by a series of recessed overhead lights. She stood back and

316

let herself feel the excitement of her success. Finally, Margie Raines, from Galilee, Georgia, was somebody.

"Looks like you already had a place ready, spotlight and all."

"I've had this spot ready for years, Steven Winslow."

Then she slipped her hand to the back of her dress and unzipped the tiny hidden zipper, allowing the dress to puddle in a sea of green around her feet. Still in the spotlight, she turned to face Steven, wearing only a pair of transparent silver pantyhose and strappy high heels.

All the other men in her life had been the aggressors, even Leonard. Tonight, Margie Raines was in charge.

She smiled.

"Make me soar, magic man."

During the next years Steven Winslow and Margie became Atlanta's golden couple, each an important adjunct to the other's career.

For the first time, Margie not only was securely "somebody," but she had a relationship that she felt comfortable with. Only occasionally did she catch a glimpse of something dark beneath Steven's relaxed demeanor. Only occasionally did she wonder if Steven was only another of the men who'd been ready to use her and discard her when her purpose had been served.

They didn't keep tabs on each other. They didn't even live together, though each had a comfortable supply of clothing at the other's apartment. Margie didn't see other men, outside of those at work, and Steven knew it. Margie knew that Steven lived a life of his own, but his life was built on business relationships. That was why when she saw him at lunch with a woman she didn't recognize, she wasn't surprised. She often met attractive men at the Patio Court. Most of Atlanta's elite could be found dining there at one time or another.

The petite woman with Steven this day was dark-haired and vivacious. And it was obvious from the expression on her face that she was totally enamored of Steven.

Margie's first instinct was to turn away, pretend she hadn't seen them. Then she stopped herself. She had no claims on

Steven. This could be one of his clients. There was every likelihood that all his clients were in love with him. He was a compelling man. But if their own relationship was less than she'd believed, she needed to know that, too.

Turning back to the courtyard, she strode toward the table.

"Steven, hello."

Steven looked up. His lips narrowed slightly and he rose. "Margie. I didn't know you'd be free for lunch. Do you know Linda Robbins, the new *Atlanta Journal* entertainment reporter?"

"Of course. At least I know who Linda is. I'm not sure we've actually met."

Margie held out her hand. Linda shook it, drawing back with an uncertain expression on her face. It was that expression that answered Margie's question, the same as the realization that Steven had in fact known that she was to be at the mall this afternoon. She'd had an appointment with the owner of one of the new specialty shops for an interview about her new line of disposable clothing. He'd known that.

What was Steven doing? Had he wanted her to see him with this woman? Margie took a long look at the man who'd shared her life for the last three years. His expression was almost that of a dare. Either accept this for what it is, or let me know you don't, he was saying.

Well, she wouldn't play. He'd made his point. Now it was up to him to play it out. Her knees were shaking and she felt as if she couldn't get her breath. She had to get away.

"Linda, I've been thinking about doing a feature on people behind the entertainment scenes. Do you think the *Journal* would consider allowing a competitor to do a piece on you?"

Linda looked surprised. She glanced from Steven to Margie and back again. "I don't know."

"Talk to them, will you? I'll talk to my people and get back to yours."

Margie gave Linda her best smile, leaned down and planted a teasing kiss on Steven's cheek. "See you tonight, darling."

Margie had made her claim. She turned away. Steven wanted to play. Fine, the next move was his. He made it at midnight. She heard his key in the lock. The door opened and closed. The lamp beside her bed was the only light in the bedroom. She lay in bed, waiting.

"All right, Margie, I'm here. Let's talk." He stood in the shadows. He wasn't smiling. He wasn't going to make their discussion easy.

"Fine. Talk."

"I suppose you guessed that I've been seeing Linda. She wants to get married."

"What do you want?"

"I never thought I'd hear myself say it, but I think I'm ready for more than just a casual relationship with you."

"Marriage?"

"Not necessarily. But a commitment. I want us to live together. I'm tired of going home to a lonely apartment. I'm tired of being the eternal escort."

"I thought things were good the way they are."

"Not anymore."

"Isn't it the woman who's supposed to want commitment?"

"I don't know. I know that when we're in bed together, we're right. We enjoy the same things. We share a common past. Neither of us has to be something different from what we are to please the other. I don't mind being the queen's consort, but I'd like to know that I'm not always on the verge of being displaced if I don't perform up to specification."

Steven didn't mention love. She hadn't expected him to. Margie wasn't certain she knew what love was, but she knew what it meant to lose and she didn't intend to lose Steven. Very calmly she answered his question, in the only way she knew.

"You've always exceeded my expectations, Steven. You may be the only man who ever has. If you think I intend to let that little tart take you away from me, you're mistaken." She sat up, allowing the sheet to slip away revealing her firm body, her peaches-and-cream body. She began to caress her breasts.

Steven stood in the doorway as if he were glued in that spot. Damn it, that wasn't what he wanted her to say. He'd intended to be firm with Margie, to force her into compromising her need to be totally in charge. For once he'd wanted her to worry that he might leave her. Her hand

319

curved under her breast and played across her abdomen.

"Make love to me, Steven."

Not *I love you, Steven.* Not *I want you to marry you, Steven.* Margie had come a long way, but she still didn't understand that it was the woman, not the body that he needed.

Steven groaned. Margie knew that he couldn't resist her. Just as Glory had known. Two women, two totally different women, had managed to take control of his life. It undermined his confidence in his own strength, but the result was inevitable. With everybody else in his life, except Glory, Steven Winslow had been his own master. If he went to Margie it would be because he made a conscious choice, not because he couldn't refuse. Linda Robbins meant nothing to him. He was in love with Margie. His clothes fell to the floor as he walked toward the bed.

"Steven?"

"Don't say anything, Margie. You've proved your point. I want you."

"Good." She took him in her hand and pulled him down to the bed. There was no foreplay, no touching, no kissing. Just Margie beneath him, writhing, spreading her legs so that he could plunge inside her. They were like two animals in heat. He took her roughly, amidst digging fingernails, rough, angry kisses, and grunts of furious desire. The mating was quick and it was intense. Afterward, they both collapsed on the pillows, slick with perspiration and sated with ecstasy.

Steven was gone the next morning when she awoke. There was a note on his pillow, and the male smell of him still lingered in the air.

I don't intend to accept last night as your final answer. I'll be back in about an hour to take you for a drive. I have something I want to show you.

Margie stretched and let herself wonder what he had in mind. She really liked Steven. She might even love him a little. From that first night he'd been ready to do her bidding. Not once had he held back, and in so doing he'd coaxed

Margie into giving as much as she got. They were good together, in bed and in public. It was the ordinary day-to-day living that Margie was uncomfortable with.

She could play a role, almost any role. The interviewer, cool, intimate, sometimes just the girl next door. The rich and powerful television personality. The lover. All roles that, when played out effectively, brought fame, power, and commitment. But deep inside, Margie was still the little girl who slept with her teddy bear when she was alone.

Glory had been right about the comet, but she was wrong in calling Margie a white rose. Margie wasn't a flower at all. She'd always been a scraggly weed, growing between the cracks in the pavement. She kept getting stepped on, crushed. Every day was a struggle to survive. The world might see an American Beauty rose, but she knew that underneath she was still a common weed.

Thirty-Six

With three children to support, Sam found outside work to supplement the farm income. He drove the school bus, worked as janitor for the church, and sold part of the timber his grandfather planted. Susan, trying to fulfill the role for which she'd been trained, kept her own house, grew her own vegetables which she initially took to the cannery but later froze in her own chest freezer. She taught a Sunday school class and worked with the youth groups and filled in occasionally as a substitute teacher at the grammar school.

By the time Marcie graduated from high school and enrolled in Abraham Baldwin College as a forestry major, Jennifer was a college junior and fourteen-year-old Mark had won his first voice competition in a special program set up by the state to recognize excellence in the arts. When he completed high school his grade-point average had won him a national scholarship to the school of his choice, and his voice won him a music scholarship to the University of Alabama.

Sam had switched to soybeans and peanuts. Both crops proved profitable enough to pay for two children in college at the same time, but Mark refused any help. He'd pay his own way. He'd earn his own money.

Jimmy Carter was elected President. Jennifer graduated from college, and so that she could remain close to her future fianceр, took a research job with the agriculture department that dealt with growing new crops. Marcie was accepted into veterinary school. Sam was very proud of his girls.

He tried to be proud of his tall, slim, lookalike son, who sang opera in a language Sam couldn't even identify, but he felt no more comfortable with the seventeen-year-old Mark than he had when Mark was seven. He'd never been able to explain his feelings to Susan. All he knew was that everything about Mark was a reminder of his guilt over Glory.

Mark's gentle disposition and his eagerness to be what his father wanted was embarrassing, for they both knew that he'd always fail. He couldn't bring himself to fire a rifle. Jennifer brought down the deer on his only hunting trip. Fishing he tolerated, but more often than not he'd bring a book and forget his pole. As for driving the tractor, Mark couldn't even start the engine. When Mark left for college, Sam felt a great weight lift from his mind.

"Well, old girl," he joked with Susan that first night, in a rare light-hearted voice, "it looks as if it's just you and me now. At least now we won't run out of milk every other day."

His attempt at humor fell flat. Tears welled up in Susan's eyes and she fled from the room. She wanted to rail out at him. Couldn't he see that she was dying inside? Mark had hardly ever been away from her. Other kids went on scouting trips, but after one disastrous try, Mark never attempted camping again. He often spent the night away during voice competitions, but she always knew that he'd be home the next day. Now he was gone forever, and he'd taken a part of her with him.

"Susan?" Sam knocked softly on the bedroom door before he opened it and came in. "I'm sorry. I guess that didn't come out right, did it?"

"I guess it didn't."

"I know how hard this will be for you."

"No you don't. You never spent any time with Mark. You woulnd't have any reason to be sorry he's gone. His leaving won't affect you."

Susan resented Sam's lack of understanding. He was gone all day, he and the girls. Mark had been the one to share her small conversations, make suggestions, and appreciate the little things she did that nobody else noticed.

There was a long silence.

"Maybe I won't miss Mark like you do, but you'll never know how much I've missed the girls."

Susan heard the pain in his voice, and she was ashamed. Of course he did. The three of them had been inseparable.

She'd understood that and she hadn't minded, for she'd had Mark. Now all three of them were gone. Sam was right, they had each other.

"I'm sorry, Sam. That was cruel of me. You're right. There's still you and me."

But it was as if they'd already used up the love, and there was none left to share with each other. The first Christmas that Mark went skiing with his roommate in Wyoming, Jennifer brought her boyfriend home. He fit right in with Sam and, as if by design, the hole left by Mark was filled. Except for Susan, nobody missed Mark.

Mark gave up opera and joined a rock and roll band. He made only token visits home the next summer. Each time Mark came, his hair was longer and he was more restless. Sam's attempts to show his displeasure with his son's appearance met with Susan's solid resistance and a bristling attempt to defend her son. Sam finally gave up entirely. Susan told herself that time would take care of their differences. Boys were always closer to their mothers until they were older. There was nothing unusual about it.

Jennifer's wedding took place in the spring of Mark's sophomore year. When he canceled out as one of the ushers at the last minute because he was sick, Sam finally exploded.

"It's not that I don't want to come, Mother," Mark had said. "I'm really sick. My group was supposed to open for the BeeGees when they played Montgomery, but I couldn't do that, either."

"What's wrong, Mark?"

"Nothing serious. The doctor thinks it might be the flu. I have a high fever. My lymph nodes are swollen and I just feel like hell."

"I'll come and get you," Susan offered quickly.

"No, Mother. I don't think you need to do that. Just tell Jen I'm sorry."

"You're not going anywhere, Susan," Sam said, loud enough for Mark to hear. "He isn't going to ruin Jennifer's day. If he doesn't come home for the wedding he might as well not come home at all!"

Mark agreed. Susan's next letter was returned, address unknown. Susan couldn't believe that her son would disappear, but he had.

Marcie had completed her second year at the University of

Georgia School of Veterinary Medicine. Jennifer's husband graduated with a degree in agriculture and they came home. They bought a mobile home and set it on the same corner of the Winslow farm where Susan and Sam had planned to put their own little house so many years ago.

In the fall of 1980, a former movie actor from California defeated a Georgia farmer for President and Sam and Susan drifted further and further apart. They both wondered what they had talked about twenty-five years ago. Whatever it was had been said and was gone. Now they just lived together. Susan wrote to Mark every week. She never mailed the letters because she didn't know where to send them and her heart hardened a bit with every letter she wrote.

Life in Winslow went on, the population shrinking a little more each day. The only newcomers were a family of Cuban refugees who'd fled the Castro regime along with a hundred thousand others. They'd work in the fields, for there were no other jobs. The tiny little town had no industry. The last grocery store closed and they'd already lost their post office. In Galilee one doctor died and the other retired. Two drugstores became one. There was no reason for anybody to stay, and few did.

Susan went back to work in the bank. "It'll still be part-time," she explained to Sam. "I'll be working in the bank over at Lynville three days a week."

"Why?" Sam was genuinely puzzled. "With only Marcie in college we don't need the money, not anymore."

"It isn't that, Sam. I just need something to do."

But filling her time wasn't the only thing her job provided. Suddenly Susan became Susan again. She'd been Sam's wife, Marcie and Jennifer and Mark's mother. Now she was enjoying brushing up on her typing. Trying on business clothes that she hadn't worn in years. She put a rinse on her hair, erasing the gray, and filed and polished her nails red for the first time in years. But more than that she looked forward to her day.

At the end of the first two weeks on the job, she actually enjoyed Sam's lovemaking when he reached out for her. Her unexpected response touched something in Sam and with a red face Susan consulted her doctor for birth-control pills, something she'd had little cause to worry about in the last years.

During the next years everything slowly fell into place. Margie's television show continued to do well. JoEllen moved to Atlanta and became clinic manager for a women's medical center, and Glory's son, Damon, had grown up and become an actor, living the life that Glory had always coveted. Life had come full circle. Susan was once more working in the bank. Sam was farming. The dreams from long ago were being replenished by the second generation.

Susan watched the first space pictures sent back by the Voyager I satellite and thought about Glory's prediction. Margie had finally caught the comet's tail. Glory's comet had burned out and disappeared. She didn't know what to think about JoEllen. Mrs. Dixon had said she'd adopted a baby, but she never brought her to Galilee. Then Mrs. Dixon had moved and they'd all lost contact with JoEllen. Susan wondered if Teddy ever heard from her. He never mentioned JoEllen, but he'd never married.

As for Susan, she never looked beyond the life she had. She was a Winslow. Sam's children were the last Winslows to live in the town named for them. But there were no Winslow men to carry on, unless Mark provided an heir and that didn't seem likely. Jennifer should have been a boy. She had followed in her father's footsteps and could have carried on the Winslow name and position. But she was a woman with another name. Susan wasn't certain that Marcie would ever marry. She liked her independence, her uniqueness, and sooner or later she'd win the farmers' acceptance as a veterinarian. Unless Steven's son came home, Sam would be the last Winslow to farm the land.

Susan sighed. Maybe that was best.

Then, in March of 1981 two things happened: President Reagan was shot by John Hinckley and a stranger called Susan from a medical center in California. Mrs. Winslow must come to Los Angeles as soon as possible.

Mark was very ill.

Thirty-Seven

"Mother, where is my daddy?"

JoEllen snapped off the television news program announcing the appointment of Sandra Day O'Connor to the Supreme Court and studied her nine-year-old daughter.

Teresa Dixon was a serious child, never noisy or out of control, a rare occurrence when the mother was a drug user. It was as if she'd come into the world in turmoil and decided that if she were still, people wouldn't notice her.

JoEllen looked into her adopted daughter's eyes and felt her heart expand. She'd never dreamed she had so much capacity for love. For so long she'd carried around such guilt over what she'd done to her own baby. Making amends by raising this child had long ago become her salvation. But more and more frequently Teresa had begun to ask questions about her past. It all started last summer with a Girl Scouts father-daughter campout that Teresa refused to attend when she learned that the other girls' fathers would be coming. Then last week she'd asked why she had no brothers or sisters. Now this.

It was time for JoEllen to be honest. She couldn't keep feeding Teresa half-truths. Teresa was too smart for that. JoEllen pulled out a chair and sat down at the kitchen table beside her daughter and took her hand.

"Teresa darling, the truth is, I don't know where your father is. He disappeared several years ago. Your mother and father weren't married. They lived a different kind of life from ours. There were several men and women who lived together in a kind of family. They all loved each other very

327

much and all the children born belonged to all of them."

"Then why didn't one of them want me?"

"It isn't that simple. I'm sure they all wanted you. But they weren't able to care for you, offer you a nice home, clothes, an education, and your mother knew that I could."

"And she gave me to you? Why would a mother do that?"

"Because she knew that I needed you. That we needed to love each other. I'm very grateful that she loved you enough to share you with an old lady like me."

"Mother, you aren't old!"

Teresa's hug and tentative smile reassured JoEllen for the moment. She dropped Teresa at school and headed to work, glancing in the rearview mirror. Her once light-brown hair was threaded with silver, especially if the sun hit it just right. She'd kept her figure. She'd worked hard to stay in shape. No, she wasn't old, but at forty-one, there were days when she felt as old as some of the Tenth Street buildings she was driving past.

Ironically, Tom Brooks had recently refurbished the old building on the strip between Tenth and Fourteenth streets—the very one that had housed the coffeehouse where declarations of free love were espoused in the era of the flower children.

Free love. There was nothing free about love, JoEllen decided. There was a price for everything, except everybody didn't pay the same amount. She'd been sure that it was wrong to force women to have unwanted children. Glory's death had reinforced that for a time. Then later, when new doubts arose, JoEllen's decision to help other women who found themselves in desperate situations had been put aside by her own ambition.

Until Teresa. She'd found such joy in the child that, under other circumstances, she might have helped abort. Once Teresa came into her life JoEllen had poured all her love into raising the thin, sickly child whose mother had given her away. JoEllen's days were full, too full, but her nights were so very empty.

But the question never stayed answered. Drugs and alcohol, all the addictions that overrode restraint, brought new choices. Rape and poverty couldn't be ignored. when a teenager came in to get a third or fourth abortion, something had to be wrong. She'd thought that the satisfaction she gained from her nursing would sustain her, but it hadn't. She was lonely.

As always, she thought of Teddy. Life had been so simple for him. Everything was either black or white. There were no gray areas, no debates on the issue. He'd thought she was the strong one. But he was wrong. Strength was knowing yourself and holding true to your convictions.

Now she was beginning to rehash the old questions: Was her job making the best use of her talents? Or was she kidding herself? God, she'd turned into some kind of sanctimonious do-gooder in the last ten years.

JoEllen pulled into the parking area and started toward the back of the building, breathing a sigh of resentment. They were out there again, the self-appointed protesters carrying terrible signs about killing babies and murder. It was going to be another one of those days. Half of her patients would see the crowd and run away. The other half would be so unnerved by the time they did get inside that they'd be too upset to go through with the procedure.

"This is the eighties," the card carriers chanted, "when women don't kill their babies. Stop the murder now."

JoEllen wanted to take each one of the protesters and say to them, "Don't tell them what to do if you haven't been there." But more and more often, as she glanced out her window, she realized that the protesters didn't look any different from all the other people she knew. There were the Loretta Greens who told the young women that they were going to hell, that Jesus would save them provided they joined the Baptist Church and ask forgiveness. There were the older men, gaunt-eyed and bitter-looking, the men like Mr. Sims who waxed philosophical about saving lives instead of taking them. But for the most part the sign-carriers were the Susans and the Margies of the world.

The office staff would get through the day, they always did. When she opened the clinic door this morning she saw something was drastically wrong. The receptionist standing in the open doorway to one of the treatment rooms was staring wide-eyed at the frantic activity beyond.

"It's Deborah Brannon," she explained to JoEllen. "You know, the last patient we saw yesterday, the kid who thinks

329

we run a yearly special here. She's hemorrhaging."

JoEllen reached for her surgical gown and rushed inside in time to see Tom Brooks at the end of the table frantically packing the woman's uterus.

"Set up an IV, JoEllen," he said tersely. "You know the procecure."

She knew. She'd lived through it. Quickly she complied, administering the necessary fluids and medications to keep the blood pressure up and stop the bleeding. At the same time she was frantically checking the chart for blood type and ordering plasma.

But they couldn't stop the bleeding. One second Deborah was holding on and the next minute she was gone. And even with the latest equipment, they couldn't bring her back. They hadn't even had time to call an ambulance. A shocked JoEllen removed her gown and collapsed into the chair beside Tom's desk. "I don't think I can do this anymore, Tom," she said quietly.

"Sure you can. This was rough, I know. But you're a great nurse, JoEllen. And you have to look at the lives we save."

"Yes, and the one we just lost."

Tom Brooks arched his neck as he studied his assistant. JoEllen had been his right arm. She'd become, through the years, his friend and his equal. They'd danced around being lovers, enemies, and gradually worked their way to a relationship that he valued greatly. He would have taken it further, but he'd known from the beginning that there was a force burning inside JoEllen that so filled her emotionally that he couldn't get past her shields. He'd settled instead for friendship and, eventually, mutual respect.

Now he was worried. "What's wrong, Jo? We both know that in medicine we can't save everybody. We didn't do anything wrong. It was just an unfortunate situation. You've lost patients before."

"Yes, I have. You always thought that I came to Atlanta to join you because of my own abortion, but you were only partially right. Do you remember Glory, my friend from home?"

"The girl who disappeared from the hotel before we got there?"

"Yes. We helped her abort one baby. Then, years later

330

when she came a second time for help, I tried to talk her out of it. I was having trouble dealing with what I'd done and I made her change her mind and she went home. Did I ever tell you that she killed herself?"

"No. I didn't know."

"She did. And I always felt that if I hadn't been so moralistic she wouldn't have done it. I lost my own baby because I made a wrong choice, and Glory died for the same reason. When Teresa came to me I thought it was a sign that I could start over. But it's happening again. I'm not sure that I'm helping people who really need help."

"Of course you are. You don't have to worry, Jo. Deborah was alone in the world. We aren't going to be sued."

"Sued? Is that what you think? I'm not worried about being sued. I'm worried about Deborah, about not giving her the right kind of help. I always wanted to be needed, to help people. I thought that what we've been doing was the right thing. I still believe in a woman's right to choose, but I don't like what I see happening. You treat a variety of patients in your practice. Every problem isn't an unwanted child. But that's all I deal with. And I'm seeing more and more repeat situations. I always felt that a person was entitled to one mistake and that mistake shouldn't ruin their lives. But so many of our patients have lost any semblance of control. They don't make choices. They just go with the flow. I don't like that, Tom, and I don't like being a part of it."

"You're just emotionally drained, Jo. Go home. I'll handle this."

But Tom was wrong about handling the situation, for Deborah wasn't alone in the world. Her father was one of the most powerful men in the state, a man determined to shut down the Women's Center, and a man who had the political connections to do so.

A barrage of publicity brought about a board of inquiry, but the clinic was found not guilty of neglect. Still, the publicity was so intense that Tom and JoEllen were dogged by reporters and crackpots. The tabloids hinted at an affair, that they were both drug addicts, that the fetuses were carelessly thrown into the dumpster behind the building. Because of the publicity JoEllen decided the only way to shield Teresa was to ask her unwilling grandmother to come

331

for her and take her to Galilee, since JoEllen had to remain in Atlanta until the issue was settled.

Stepped-up protests forced the center to close temporarily, though Tom offered to keep JoEllen on salary. She refused, electing instead to volunteer her services to the women's prisons. For the first time in years she was actually practicing nursing as she'd been trained to do and her patients were always grateful. Three months later a civil suit for malpractice was filed against both Dr. Brooks and JoEllen, charging negligence.

JoEllen felt as if the entire world was judging her and finding her guilty. Of all the people she'd helped through the years, only a handful came to the courtroom in her defense. Most of the spectators were against abortion and had to be admonished repeatedly by the judge. After a week of testimony, the Brannon attorneys rested their case.

The lawyer who represented the Brooks Medical Center made his final statement, reiterating the legality of abortion, the clinic's heretofore unblemished record, and the dedication of both Dr. Brooks and JoEllen. The jury deliberated for a day and a half before returning their verdict.

Not guilty of malpractice.

The courtroom turned into bedlam as opponents began to chant the kinds of accusations JoEllen had heard for years as she went to work. She looked at Tom. "You mean we're free to go?"

"If we can get through that mob without being scalped."

JoEllen had thought she was a strong person. She'd thought she could face almost anything, but suddenly she was tired. She just wanted to go home and get her life in order, except she wasn't certain that she had anyplace to go. She had no job, and her savings had been severely eaten into during the last three months. Tom turned to thank the attorney, leaving JoEllen alone to face the crowd. She knew the moment she stepped outside the courtroom that the reporters would fall on her like buzzards attacking a newly killed animal.

But it wasn't a reporter who made his way down the aisle through the protesters, holding out a welcoming hand. It was a familiar face, a dear face.

"Teddy? What are you doing here?"

332

"I thought you might need an old friend."

It didn't matter that there was grease under his fingernails or that he wasn't wearing a suit. JoEllen stepped into the shelter of his arms and allowed him to sweep her through the crowd and down the steps to his truck. "Oh, yes," she whispered. "I need a friend. I very much need an old friend."

Thirty-Eight

When Susan left Augusta, a cold March wind was blowing. She stepped off the plane in Los Angeles that night and drew in a deep, warm breath. She was here, where Mark was, and he needed her. It had been almost three years since she'd seen him. Now he was sick. She glanced around the busy terminal. She hadn't expected him to be there but she'd allowed herself to hope—hope that the telephone call was all a lie, hope that Mark would dash through the crowd and sweep her into his arms with a smile on his face as he'd done so many times before.

Checking the signs, she found her way to the baggage area and claimed her suitcase, then to the taxi stand outside the door. She directed the driver to take her straight to the hospital.

"This can't be the place," she said when he pulled up in front of a sad, dingy stucco building that looked more like a run-down apartment house than a hospital.

"Read the sign, lady."

The sign said St. Augustus's Center. And underneath in small letters, "All are welcome, in the name of our Father."

That's what the caller had said, St. Augustus's Medical Center. She'd thought it was a hospital, but this was obviously something different. Susan got out, paid the driver, and lugged her suitcase inside the sparse building which smelled strongly of disinfectant.

Behind what passed for a reception desk, a woman looked up. "I'm Sister Sarah. May I assist you?"

"Yes, I'm Mrs. Winslow. I received a call that my son Mark is here."

334

"You're Mark's mother?" There was an element of surprise in her voice.

"Yes, can you tell me what's wrong?"

"You didn't know that Mark was ill?"

"No. I came as soon as I learned." Susan was beginning to be very scared. There was an onimous presence about the woman, the building, even the air she was breathing. Something was very wrong. "Please! Can you take me to him."

"Certainly. Follow me. How long has it been since you've seen your son?"

They were walking down a long corridor, past open doors where men were lying quietly in small rooms. Occasionally a moan would break the silence.

"Almost three years," Susan answered stoically. "I—we didn't know where he was."

"I see. At least he called you. So many times they never do. And you'd be surprised how many of the parents don't come."

"Where are the nurses?" Susan asked.

"We only have one full-time registered nurse. The rest of the staff is volunteer. They're in and out." Sister Sarah stopped at the next door and waited for Susan. "This is Mark's room. I'll be around when you're finished to help answer any questions, if you want to talk."

She turned and made her way quickly and silently back down the corridor. For Susan, the doorway loomed as large as a cavern. She felt the fear growing, and for a long moment she couldn't move. *This is Mark, your son. Whatever is wrong you can handle it now that you've found him again.* She stepped inside.

The boy lying on the bed inside was sleeping. She made herself walk up to him and look. "No," she whispered, not aware that she'd spoken aloud. This couldn't be Mark, not her beautiful son. Mark's skin was fair, but this face was deathly pale. His eyes seemed sunken, his skin pulled too tightly across the bones of his face, and his still-long hair was no longer golden.

"No!" she whispered again, and the boy opened his eyes and blinked in confusion.

"Mother?"

Susan felt her heart crack as she recognized the voice of

335

her son. *Oh, Mark, why didn't you call me earlier?* She gathered him in her arms, pulled his thin body close to her and rocked him as she had so often in the past. "What's wrong?"

"I'm sorry, Mom. Just a little bout of pneumonia that I can't seem to get over. How'd you get here?"

"I flew."

"No, I mean, who told you?"

"I don't know. Someone just called and told me you were ill. I came immediately."

"Are you by yourself?"

Susan felt the old tension in his voice. "Yes, your father would have come, but he couldn't leave the planting."

"Yes, of course." His voice grew stronger as he threw off the remains of sleep and pulled himself out of her arms. "Let me look at you."

"I'm afraid I look a fright. I came straight from the airport and I didn't even take time to do my fingernails before I left."

Mark took her small hand and examined it. "Those long red fingernails," he said. "Such a contradiction for my dutiful mother, the farmer's wife. I've thought about those fingernails so many times."

"Why did you disappear, Mark? I've been so worried about you?"

"It was better, Mother. I didn't fit in in Winslow. I'm not a Winslow, except by name. I thought it was simpler this way."

"I don't care about the Winslows, Mark. You're my son and it's time you came home."

"I wish I could, Mother, but I'm afraid it's too late."

"When can I talk to the doctor about getting you out of here?"

"Not until tomorrow. And he'll let me go, that's not the problem."

"Then what is?"

Mark closed his eyes and let out a sigh. "It's a long story, Mother, and I'm tired. You shouldn't have come. I can't go home with you. God, I wish I could, but it's too late. Go back to Winslow, Mother."

"You keep saying it's too late? You don't mean—"

"That I'm dying? No, not yet, but soon."

"Then you're coming home, as quickly as you're able to travel. I won't have it any other way."

Another woman who appeared to be a nurse came in and Susan was asked to wait outside. She leaned against the wall, trying to understand. They didn't have a hospital in Winslow, or in Galilee. Even JoEllen, who'd come back home, bemoaned the fact that the only doctor for either community was a general practitioner whose office was in Augusta and who only came to Galilee once a week.

What would she do with Mark? She didn't want to think about Sam's reaction to the cost of long-term medical care at Lawson General, and her salary at the bank wouldn't go very far. But Mark was her heart and she'd do whatever was necessary to make him well again.

Unable to stand still, she walked farther down the hall where she found a chapel. She still played the piano for church, but her faith had faltered through the years. What had happened to the Christian life she and Sam had pledged so many years ago?

Jennifer and her husband were carbon copies of Sam, hardworking, dedicated to the farm and the life it offered. With their help, Sam had leased more acreage and expanded his planting schedule. Marcie was in her last year of vet school and was already committed to working with the only other animal doctor in the county.

Susan sighed. They'd have two veterinarians, but they couldn't attract one doctor to treat the people. Too bad people didn't have four feet. There seemed to be more sympathy for God's creatures than man.

Were her children happy? Or had life simply settled down to a routine that had become safe and acceptable?

Susan searched her conscience. What could she have done differently with Mark? From the beginning he'd been different from her other children, from any of the other children in Winslow. Neither Sam nor the girls had ever understood or had much in common with Mark. That lack of understanding had translated to censure.

She'd sensed his uncertainty, his lack of direction, his *difference,* but she hadn't known how to deal with it. When he'd learned about his musical talent, she'd rejoiced, but even that had taken him down a road that exposed his differences. Winslow and all that the name represented were not meant for Mark; rather the name was a restraint that bound him to a life he couldn't tolerate. And he'd gone away.

Now they had a second chance.

Susan stood up and backed away. Her knees were cramped. She didn't know how long she'd been kneeling there. It was only when she turned to leave that she saw him, the man in the back row. He rose, and walked toward her.

"Susan?"

The man was black. There was a half-smile on his face as he waited, as if he were uncertain of her reaction.

Finally he took another step forward. "I guess you don't recognize me."

"Jody? Is it you?"

This time Susan's mind seemed to seal itself in a vacuum. She'd known that he was in California, but there had been no letters in such a long time. Jody was here, with Mark. She couldn't make sense out of that. She could see him, hear herself speak to him, but it was as if she were encased in some kind of bubble that insulated her from what was happening.

"Yes, it's me."

His voice had deepened, lost its southern nuances. "It was you who called?"

"Yes. I hope it was the right thing to do. I wasn't sure.

"How do you know Mark?"

"He auditioned for a part in the television series I write for. I recognized the name and knew there couldn't be two Winslow, Georgias. I've kept in touch."

"Mark auditioned for a part in a television series? I never knew."

"Unfortunately he didn't get the role. He should have, but he didn't. Would you like to go somewhere and have a cup of coffee after you're finished here?" He held out his hand. "To talk about Mark."

"What I'd like to do first is talk to the doctor. But Mark says that isn't possible until tomorrow."

"Yes. I'm afraid that unless they're called, the medical staff is all volunteer. They don't have a set schedule. Perhaps I can explain, if you'll let me."

Susan nodded. "I'd appreciate that. Right now I feel a little overwhelmed. I'd like to stay with Mark. Will you come back for me later?"

For most of the afternoon Susan sat by Mark's bed. He

338

seemed to drift in and out of sleep. When he was awake he talked about going home, about the lake, his music, his room. It wasn't until they brought his dinner that he finally looked at Susan and voiced the question.

"Daddy? What did he say?"

"He said, Go get my son and bring him home."

Susan said a silent prayer that God would forgive her lie. Sam had said nothing. He'd merely left the house and returned late, stumbling, sleeping on the couch.

"I always loved him, you know," he whispered. "I didn't know how to be what he wanted."

"And he didn't know how to love you for what you could be, Mark. It isn't his fault. You never knew your grandfather. If you had, you'd understand better."

She fed Mark the few mouthfuls of soup he'd take, then watched him fall asleep for the night. Tomorrow she intended to see the doctor. If he didn't come to the hospital, she'd go to his office. She was determined to find the answers.

When Jody touched her shoulder she stood, more tired than she'd ever been. Taking his hand, she allowed him to lead her out of the hospital. They began to walk.

"You look good, Susan."

"I've gained weight."

"Yes, but it's flattering. And you still have the long fingernails. I've thought about them so many times, and that big class ring you wore, the one with all the tape around the back so you wouldn't lose it."

"Sam's ring. My husband."

"He didn't come?"

"No." *He has the planting to do.* "You've done well," she said, changing the subject.

"Yes, thanks to you."

"Me? What did I do?"

"You gave me confidence at a time when I needed to believe. But I think you know that."

"And Mark? You've been his friend?"

"I've tried. But now he needs you, Susan. He needs to go back home and face his father, before it's too late."

"Before it's too late? That's what Mark said. What's wrong, Jody. Please tell me."

"I really think it ought to come from Mark, or his doctor."

339

"No, I need to know, to figure out how to deal with the problem before I face Sam. You're wrong about me, Jody. I'm not strong. And I think that Mark needs me to be. Please?"

"Do you know where you are?"

"No. Should I?"

"This is called Sinyan's Point. It's a place where homosexuals gather."

Susan stared at him, then looked around, not yet comprehending what he was trying to say. They'd reached an area made up of little shops and restaurants. There were men on the sidewalks, lounging, talking in little groups, holding hands.

"You don't know anything about that, do you?" Jody's voice was sad. He didn't know if he could tell her. He wanted to fold her in his arms and hold her, to keep her from this kind of truth. But he couldn't. She was willing to be his friend, but anything more would be as impossible now as it had been that summer when he was in the wrong place, a kid, wearing a soldier's uniform and searching for his future.

"No. I mean, I know about things like that, but I never knew anybody involved in—that."

"Yes, you do, Susan. You have to be very strong now. As a mother you have to know and not judge."

"You mean Mark? No. I don't believe it."

But even as she protested, the imaginary bubble burst and she knew. She moaned and reached out, clasping Jody's arms in an attempt to remain standing. She shook her head, trying to speak, but unable to get past the horror of what she was hearing.

"Come, sit down." Jody led her to a table at a sidewalk restaurant and ordered coffee for them both. "Sit there for a minute and breathe easy. Don't try to talk, just listen.

"Mark was—*is* an intense young man who seems to feel lost. As I said, I first saw him at an audition. The fact sheet gave his name and listed Winslow as his place of birth. I don't know why I spoke to him, but I did. I asked him about his family, and he told me about his mother—Susan. I knew it had to be you."

"Does—do—are you . . . ?"

"You mean are Mark and I involved?" Jody laughed. "No, not like that. I felt a kind of responsibility for him. I've arranged a few jobs for him now and then, but he doesn't know. He doesn't know that I know you, either. I wasn't sure how you'd feel."

"Oh, Jody. What can I do? What can I do?"

"There's nothing you can do now, Susan, except be very brave and strong—for Mark."

"You aren't telling me everything, are you? He is going to die, isn't he?"

There was a long silence while the music from a nearby bar spilled into the warm late-afternoon air and murmurs of conversation and laughter echoed in the space beyond the shield that Susan was drawing around her once more. Jody didn't answer. He didn't have to. The expression on his face said it all.

"How long?"

"It's hard to tell. He has some sort of an immune deficiency. His body can't fight off illness. He may get better—for a time, until the disease attacks another part of his body. Or he may go downhill from here. Doctors are only just now beginning to recognize the symptoms of the disease. Apparently the timespan can be different for every patient."

"What? What does he have?" But she didn't need to hear it. She'd heard a few news stories about the unnamed, new killing disease that was sweeping the gay communities in California. She'd paid little attention to the stories because California seemed like another world.

Her child. Her beautiful Mark was dying. Where was Sam? She needed Sam here, with her, to hold her hand and tell her that everything would be all right. But it wasn't Sam's hand that reached out to hold hers, it was Jody's. And she felt her fingers curl around his in supplication.

"Is there anybody? Any doctor, hospital, where they can help him?"

"Not really. The hospice where he's staying cares only for these kinds of patients. They don't have any answers, either. For now all that can be done is treat the infections the body can no longer throw off. Any doctor can do that, if he will."

"Oh, God, Jody, there isn't even a full-time doctor in Galilee anymore, only a doctor who comes one day a week. I'll have to take him to Augusta to— Wait! JoEllen! JoEllen's in Galilee. She'll help."

341

"Sam, Mark's very ill, with a—a virus. I'm bringing him home. I hope you aren't going to fight me on this." Susan clutched the phone with white fingers as she waited for Sam's reply. If he wouldn't let Mark come home she didn't know what she'd do.

"No, I won't refuse my own son" was Sam's terse reply. "When will you arrive?"

"I don't know. He isn't strong enough to leave the hospice just yet. In a few days, I hope. I'll let you know."

"Where are you staying?"

"With a friend of Mark's. That's saving me money on the hotel bill. The number is. . . ." And she gave him Jody's number with the hope that she was doing the right thing. "But you'd better let me call you because I don't know when I'll be here."

"Fine," Sam said, and the silence stretched between them. He wanted to say something to comfort Susan, but he couldn't get beyond the horror of his own reaction. His son, very ill, coming home. He didn't want to think about it. For the last few years he'd tried very hard to close Mark out of his mind entirely. He'd failed. His grandfather had expected Sam to pass on the Winslow name and the farm to the next son. That was not to be.

Mark's illness was an omen, a symbol of Sam's failure.

"Do what you have to," he finally said, adding, "And hurry home."

There was a click and a hum on the empty line. Susan replaced the receiver on its base and let out a deep sigh. "I would have told him who you are, Jody, but he wouldn't have understood."

"I know. Your bedroom is the first one on the left. I've put your suitcase there. Why don't you try and get some sleep. You've had a rough day."

"Yes, thank you." Woodenly she walked down the corridor and let herself in the bedroom. *Rough?* That didn't describe the pain, the horror, the moment when she wanted to run back to that airport and pretend that she'd never learned the truth. But the boy in that bed was Mark, her beautiful son, and she couldn't leave him to die alone.

An unspeakable illness, brought on by unspeakable acts

342

between two men. It didn't even have a name yet. What would the community say when they found out the truth? What would Sam say? Questions swirled round and round her mind until her head was pounding unbearably. But the biggest question she hadn't yet voiced, the question that underlined all the others, that question finally had to be faced. *Why?*

She didn't know how long she'd been standing just inside the bedroom door without moving when she heard the insistent knock behind her. Finally, just as she turned, the door opened and Jody stepped inside, a tray in his hands.

"I thought you might like a cup of hot tea."

"Hot tea?" She began to laugh hysterically. "Tea? You think a farmer's wife from Winslow, Georgia, drinks hot tea?"

As Susan's laughter turned into sobs, Jody put the tray on the table and gathered Susan in his arms. "Sorry, but I don't have any RC Colas or moonshine. But I could manage a little bourbon."

Susan was shaking so that she could barely speak, but the laughter continued until she finally ran out of breath. "Got any Four Roses?" she asked.

"No, I don't think so, but I could get some."

"Not necessary," she whispered. "I just remembered the first time I had whiskey. Glory gave it to me. Glory gave me Mark, too. But Sam doesn't know that I know that. He got drunk one night and told me that he'd had sex with his own cousin, then came home and practically raped me. The next day he didn't remember, or if he did, he never admitted it. Mark was the result of Sam's mistake. Is that why this happened? Are we being punished?"

"Susan, you had nothing to do with this. You're just tired and having a normal reaction to trauma, like shock after an accident. What you need is a hot shower and sleep. Tomorrow you'll think more clearly."

"Yes, a hot bath," she said.

"Sit here and I'll turn on the shower."

"No, don't let me go. I feel as if I'll fly off into a million pieces if you let me go. Hold me, Jody. Hold me."

Jody stood, trying not to feel his response to the woman in his arms. She was already overwrought. She was vulnerable now and he'd be an unspeakable cad to take advantage of

343

her. Drawing on all his control, he walked her into the bathroom, reached past her, and turned on the water.

"I'm going to take off your clothes, Susan. Do you understand?"

She didn't answer, but she didn't flinch when he began to unbutton her blouse. He slid it from her shoulders and unzipped the skirt, holding her up with one arm while the other struggled to remove her clothing. The bra he managed, and her panties and pantyhose. Her strength was completely gone, and if he hadn't been holding her she would have slipped to the bathroom floor.

He lifted her into the shower but releasing her would be akin to drowning her, for she couldn't stand alone. Finally Jody used his free hand to remove his own clothes and stepped into the hot, stinging water with her. He soaped her, using the suds as lotion to massage her body.

"Relax, Susan. Let yourself go. Don't feel anything. You're going to sleep and let your mind accept what you want to avoid."

Susan seemed to hear his words and she draped herself over him, allowing his ministrations to heal, to erase worry and care. But Jody was having less success with his own physical response. He tried to push her away, force her to stand upright, away from his erection. She didn't need this kind of guilt to deal with. If she followed the normal pattern, she'd have enough pangs of conscience over Mark's being gay.

But Susan wasn't cooperating. She reached up and put her arms around his neck, pulling his face down to meet hers. "Thank you, Jody, for being here. For caring about me and my son. I—I—"

As she kissed him, Jody thought he heard her words—"I need you"—but he couldn't be sure. It had finally happened. The woman he'd carried around in his mind for most of his adult years was in his arms, pressing herself against him, kissing him. He lifted her, turned off the water, and walked into the bedroom without breaking the kiss.

As he laid her on the bed he pulled away. "Susan, are you sure? I know you're confused."

"I'm very sure, Jody. Please. Hold me."

He knew it was wrong. He knew he was being weak. But he'd waited so long. Susan had been his inspiration, his

344

dream, and it was time he learned whether or not dreams could be real. Making love to Susan could never be as phenomenal as he'd imagined it to be.

But it was.

And when he left her, sleeping in the moonlight, he knew that this was that rare, wonderful moment that came to a man once and never again. In the morning she'd be embarrassed; she'd regret what had happened. For that he was sorry, but it had happened and nothing could take that away from either of them.

Jody was wrong.

The next morning Susan came into the breakfast room and smiled winsomely. She kissed him lightly and said, "Thank you, Jody. You were there when I needed someone, but I think you know that it can't happen again, even if we'd like it to."

Susan never discussed Mark's illness with him. When he tried to talk to her she refused to listen. He was her child. He was sick and they were going home. That was all that was important.

The next week Susan took Mark home.

Home to face Sam.

Home to die.

Thirty-Nine

Like the peanut farmer from Georgia who'd become President and then been sent home in defeat four years later, Mark Winslow was also coming home. Unlike Jimmy Carter, Mark Winslow had never come close to the fame he'd sought. Now his shame would make him famous and his father would suffer the ultimate disappointment. Mark sighed and glanced out the plane window as it touched the ground. Nothing had changed.

Sam met their plane in Augusta. He took one look at Mark and blanched. Even stoic Sam Winslow couldn't keep himself from reacting.

"Damn, boy, what'd they do to you in California, feed you to those Mediterranean fruit flies they had last summer? You'd better not have brought any of them here with you."

Mark's attempt at laughter was wry. "Fruit flies? You don't know how close to being right you are, Dad."

"Dad? I was Daddy for eighteen years, Mark. I guess I still am."

Sam didn't say anything else. He didn't ask what was wrong, or whether Mark was comfortable. Instead, he kept his eyes on the road and the speedometer on seventy, which was at least ten miles an hour faster than he normally drove.

Susan sat quietly, after having positioned Mark on the backseat to be as comfortable as possible. She grew more anxious by the mile. All she'd thought about was getting Mark home. She hadn't thought further than that. What would she tell the girls, the neighbors, Sam? How would they pay his medical expenses? She reverted to an emotionless dialogue.

"Did you call JoEllen?"

"Yes, she'll come, if you're sure that's what you want. She didn't mention the money for her services and neither did I."

"Money isn't important, Sam." Her voice was too sharp and she knew from past experience that would only make Sam more suspicious. *Keep it calm, like you do when you're having sex.* Not, she told herself, like it had been with Jody. There was a lurch, a twist in her chest, at the flash of memory that came with that thought. Just as quickly she forced the thought away.

Mark was the important one now. Mark was the only one who needed her, the only one who'd ever needed her. She'd make him well. Somehow, they'd find a way to go back and start again. And Sam? Well, Sam would do what was best for Mark now, even if he didn't understand what was happening. Sam was a Winslow and Mark was his son. Susan had no intention of telling Sam that his son was dying of an illness that had no name.

Only JoEllen could know. Only JoEllen and Susan would treat Mark. Nobody else would be at risk of catching what the doctors in California believed to be a virus. He simply had a kind of skin cancer and some kind of mysterious disease that affected his immune system.

Cancer, that's what Mark had.

"JoEllen, I appreciate your coming. Let's walk down to the lake and talk for a minute before we go inside."

Susan ran her fingers through her short, curly hair. She felt the coarseness of the gray hairs. In the last few weeks she'd left off her rinse. Her hair was turning a fashionable salt-and-pepper color, with the emphasis on the salt. Dominicker, Sam called it affectionately, like one of his gray-and-black-speckled laying hens.

She gave a quick glance to her old friend, still thin and neat as always. JoEllen's brown hair had been scissored into a blunt cut that fell in a jaunty wave just below her ears. She wore little makeup, just a touch of blush and lip gloss. There was a quiet confidence about her that calmed and reassured Susan. Nursing had been a choice that Susan hadn't understood, but it fit this JoEllen. The serious, determined friend of her childhood had been magnified and enhanced.

"It's about Mark," Susan began, desperately trying to be strong in spite of the tight knot forming in her throat. She swallowed hard and cleared her throat. "I haven't told the others, but if you're going to be his nurse, you have to know."

"Know what, Susan?"

"The doctors say he's—he's dying. There is some kind of virus that seems to be killing young men in California. The doctors haven't diagnosed it yet. All they know is that it may be contagious and that it attacks the body's ability to fight off disease. So Mark's treatment won't be for the virus, only the symptoms, the part of his body the disease attacks."

"Oh, Susan. I'm so sorry. But we know so much more now about treating illness. I'm sure they'll find an answer."

"No, JoEllen. I can look at him and see it. Mark is going to die. I just don't want him to suffer, and I don't want the world to know."

JoEllen looked at the calm strength in Susan's eyes and knew that of them all, Susan had always been the strong one. Now she was asking for help, and JoEllen knew that she would do anything she could. She'd come full circle, leaving Galilee to contribute, to set an example for her brother, to find her place in life. And life had sent her back here, to Susan, to Galilee, where she'd started.

"Don't worry, Susan. We'll make sure that Mark doesn't suffer. And nobody will ever know. I'll be here for you. I promise."

They sat, looking out across the black-green water at the pine thicket on the other side. A kind of peace fell over them. JoEllen reached out and took Susan's hand. "This reminds me of the lake where we had the picnic," JoEllen said.

"The picnic?"

"The summer the soldiers came to Galilee. Remember? It seems such a long time ago. We were so young, so trusting."

"So naive. So foolish."

"For a long time I thought that, but now I look around me at those who have no dreams, no plans. They seem to drift eternally without much purpose. At least all of us reached the goals we set, didn't we?"

"Yes, I guess we did. Maybe we just didn't dream big enough."

"Does Sam know about Mark?"

"No, and I don't want him to. This will be hard enough on Mark without having people know the truth."

JoEllen studied Susan. *Hard enough.* There was a strength of purpose about her, a determination. It was as if she and Sam had reversed roles. Susan was the caretaker and Sam was following quietly. Good. Susan was going to need that strength. JoEllen hadn't been involved in regular hospital work since this strange virus had made its presence known, but she had friends who had.

Tom Brooks had kept up with the findings, for his surgical duties included men who might be infected. Though the public wasn't alarmed yet, the medical journals were beginning to report the problem which seemed to be confining itself to the homosexual community.

"I thought that between you, Marcie, and myself we would be able to manage. Will you help us, JoEllen? I'll pay you whatever you'd normally get for private-duty nursing."

"Of course I'll help, Susan. But Marcie is a veterinarian and Mark will have to be under the care of a doctor or you won't be able to get the medication he needs. Mother says that Dr. Wade only comes to Galilee one day a week."

"I know. I've brought all Mark's records, along with all the information I've been able to find on the disease. I have an appointment with Dr. Wade on Thursday. I'd like you to come with me."

"I'd like to speak with Mark first," JoEllen said.

"Of course. Please, come to the house."

Mark was lying on his bed, staring at the momentoes of his past: framed awards, pictures of him on stage, a newspaper clipping of him with the Headliners, the rock group he'd sung with briefly. He wondered where his mother had found that.

The world had learned who shot J. R. Ewing of Southfork and Ronald Reagan, into his second year as President, was predicting that the recession would be short. *Cats* had come to Broadway and Mark Winslow, at twenty-two, had hidden his stash of marijuana in his suitcase and come home to die.

Mark thought it was Thoreau who'd once said something about people living lives of quiet desperation. Ever since his mother got on the plane, he'd had the feeling that's what she was doing. He wanted to tell her it was all right to cry, or scream, or ask questions, but he didn't, and she never broke down. It was his father who paused in the doorway of Mark's room without saying anything when he thought Mark was sleeping.

Little about Winslow had changed. His room was just as he'd left it, half-failed farmer and half-struggling musician. The bookcase was filled with model cars in various stages of completion, and well-worn books about the theater and music.

There was a knock at Mark's door.

"Mark? JoEllen is here. She'd like to talk to you. Can she come in?"

It was beginning, the facing of the reality, the withdrawing from a past that seemed less real than the future. "Yes."

"Hello, Mark. How do you feel?"

"Wasted, but that's about par for the course."

JoEllen took in the telltale sores on his face, his thin body, and shallow breathing. "Is it bad?"

Mark glanced behind JoEllen, at the open doorway.

"She's gone to the kitchen. I told her that I wanted to see you alone." JoEllen closed the door and sat down on the chair beside his desk.

"It's bad. I've been fighting it for over a year, and it isn't going to get any better. You don't have to do this. They know it's spread sexually, but they aren't certain if there are other means of becoming infected."

"I've been told that the illness is a bitch, but then, so's life and most of the folks running things. Look, Mark, if what I've heard is anywhere near the truth, this isn't going to be pretty. I can deal with it, but I'm not sure about your mother. As for Sam, I don't have a clue how he'll react. I need to know how you plan to handle that."

"Mother always saw rainbows in the storm. She was my champion."

"She still is."

"I'd rather she not see me die, but that decision was taken out of my hands. Now I'll do whatever is necessary to spare her. As for my father, I doubt he'll see me at all. He never did."

Mark was more right than he knew. Where Sam had worked hard before, now he never stopped. Susan might

350

have noticed his frame growing more and more gaunt, but her entire focus was on Mark. She continued to work part-time, at Mark's insistence. They needed the money to pay JoEllen. But days passed when Sam left before Susan got up and climbed into bed long after she'd gone to sleep.

But late one night she heard Mark cry out and she stumbled out of bed and down the corridor toward his room.

Sam was coming toward her. "What's wrong?"

"It's Mark. He made a noise."

"I didn't hear anything."

"You never do."

"And you hear every breath *he* takes." Sam's gaze swept down her body, taking in the nightgown she wore without a robe. Susan's body was still young and firm, in spite of the years of hard work and the three children she'd borne and nursed. He could see her nipples and the dark thatch of hair between her legs. For a moment he saw her as she was when they'd first married and he felt a stirring of desire.

"Of course. He's my child. And I hear your breathing, too."

"No, it's been a long time since you've even looked at me, Susan." He reached out and touched her breast, tentatively, then more urgently.

Susan gasped and made a move to step around Sam.

"No, not this time, my wife. I've stayed out of your way. I've tried to answer questions about my son's strange medical condition when our friends ask. I've waited for you to tell me what's wrong and when he's going to get better. I've paid the bills without complaining. But tonight, tonight I want my wife to be my wife."

Susan felt stricken. Mark needed her. "Not now Sam, Mark—"

"Yes, now, Susan. Now."

"Not so loud, Sam. Mark will hear you."

"Why shouldn't he know that I want my wife. That I need my wife. That you were my wife before you were his mother, and you still are."

Susan felt all the blood drain from her face. Sam had never been so cold. She was torn between checking on Mark and concealing the lack of concern on his father's part.

"Please, Sam," she whispered. "You don't understand."

"But I do. I waited for you to tell me the truth, but you

never intended to, so I took myself over to Augusta to talk to Dr. Wade. Were you going to let him die without my knowing that my son was a queer, that he was dying of that sex disease? My only son."

Only then did Sam's voice break. Only then did Susan know the pain he was determined to conceal. Only then could she reach out and take his hand. "Oh, Sam. I'm so sorry. I didn't want you—either of you—to hurt. I'd hoped that you'd let Mark know how you feel."

"No, Susan, you don't want me to do that. No more lies. Mark's very conception was tainted. You think I don't know that, that I don't live every day with the knowledge that in some way he came here flawed. The Winslow curse. Granddaddy said I'd escaped it. When Jennifer and Marcie seemed fine, I thought they had, too. But Granddaddy was wrong. Mark is a Winslow all right. His flaw just took a different path."

And then she knew that Sam wouldn't reach out to his son, no matter what. There was a desperate look in his eyes that she'd never seen before. "Your granddaddy was the only cursed one in your family, Sam. He filled your head with a bunch of foolishness and you let him. Now you're doing the same thing all over again."

"Then you explain it to me, Susan. What happened to my son?"

"He's sick, Sam. That's all. They don't know what's wrong with him. All they know is that he has some kind of fatal disease. But it isn't your fault."

"You're wrong about that, Susan. I've known it for a long time. Even Granddaddy couldn't beat it out of me. I knew it. And when Mark was born I saw right away that he was weak. It wasn't his fault. It wasn't Granddaddy's fault. I'm responsible because I knew my weakness and I couldn't fight it. All because of Glory."

Sam pushed past Susan, went into the bedroom, and closed the door. The echo sounded so final. Susan was torn between following Sam and going in to check on Mark. In the end, she walked down the corridor into the kitchen and out to the porch. The wind was cold. The old wellhouse, cast in the yellow light funneling from the pole at the end of the drive, seemed unreal.

She didn't hear Mark until he spoke.

"He's right, Mother, the Winslows are flawed."

"That's foolish, Mark. Everybody is responsible for his own success or failure. If your father didn't become the man his granddaddy wanted, it's his own fault and not because of some curse."

"Mother, how much do you know about Granddaddy?"

"You mean your daddy's father?"

"No, not him. I mean the old man."

"Not much. I saw him occasionally when your father and I were dating. He seemed to be a rather proud man."

"Did you know that he beat Daddy?"

"No. What makes you think a dreadful thing like that?"

"Oh but he did. With a belt. He'd tell him that it was for his own good, so he'd be man enough to take over when his time came."

"How do you know?"

"My granddaddy told me. That's why he never stayed around much, why he left as soon as the old man died. I talked to him once when he came home for a visit. He warned me that the Winslows were decayed and that if I wanted to save myself, I ought to get away before it rubbed off on me."

"Oh, Mark, is that why you ran away?"

"No, Mother. He scared the hell out of me then, but by the time I went to California I already knew he was right. Do you remember when I didn't come home for Jennifer's wedding?"

"Yes, you had the flu."

"No, it wasn't the flu. That's when it began, this thing I have. I started to die then."

"I don't want to hear that. You're not going to die," Susan protested, feeling the crack in her heart widen. She put her arms around her son and pressed her face against him. She could hear the fluid rattling in his chest. The pneumonia was still there. He wasn't getting any better.

"Don't you want to hear about it, Mother? About what I am and why I really left?"

"I don't think that we need to talk about it, Mark. You're home now, and that's all that matters."

He gave a long sigh and rested his chin on her head. She didn't want to know the truth. She didn't want to know about the men he'd known, or why he'd sought them out, long before he left Galilee. That was fine. He'd heard her exchange with his father, felt his father's pain, and for the first time garnered a glimmer of the confusion Sam must have felt. Sam was a simple man. He didn't question whether a thing was right or wrong; he acted instinctively. With Sam there was never a doubt.

And Mark was all doubt. To his father he was either the kind of son he could be proud of, or he simply wasn't there at all. He'd been ignored by Sam for most of his life, and no matter how much he'd like to change that, it wasn't going to happen. Mark stood there in the darkness, holding the only woman he'd ever loved—his mother. His cheeks grew wet with tears.

Forty

Margie turned into the driveway and carelessly parked her Buick at the back of the building, half on the broken concrete and half on the scraggly patch of weeds Leonard called his lawn.

He was in the workroom, slapping purple-blue paint on a large canvas which appeared to be either a strange-colored sky or wallpaper for a stage set. "Leonard," she said softly, "I—do you need some help?"

Leonard planted his gaze on her. "What's wrong?"

"Does it show?"

"Only to me."

"Oh, Leonard, you know me so well. You're the only one, the only one who ever cared enough to understand."

"Yes." He didn't bother to make silly conversation, he simply put the brush in the bucket of water and moved toward her. "Tell me."

Margie let out a long, ragged breath. "I don't know if I can. It's rather personal and I don't want to hurt you."

"Do you love him?"

She couldn't conceal the shock on her face anymore than she could give him foolish answers. "I don't know. I don't know whether or not I know what love is, Leonard. I'm comfortable with him. I depend on him. He makes me feel safe."

"He makes love to you?"

"Yes."

"And that is good?"

"Yes."

"He understands how frightened you are, your need for recognition?"

355

"Frightened? You think I'm frightened?"

"Aren't you? Isn't that why you're here?"

"Yes, I suppose you're right."

"Does he know?"

"No. I don't think so. Nobody ever understood that, except you."

"You never let anybody, did you?"

"No. There have been so many men. Some of them used me. Some of them I used. None of them ever asked me to make a permanent commitment. Damn! I wish I had a cigarette."

"In the desk." He moved past her, opening the drawer and offering the pack to her.

"What, no caution that they aren't good for me?"

"Margie, very little in this world that gives us real pleasure is good for us. That's why the pleasure we are given is so intense. It might never come again."

"It was good between us, Leonard."

"Yes."

She took the cigarette and examined it intently, her mind running toward other things. "Why did you do it? I've always wanted to know. You must have known that by otherwise engaging *Mother Goose* that morning you were running the risk of losing me."

Leonard struck a match and held it out, waited for Margie to take the cigarette between her lips, then held it until it came close to burning his fingertips as he waited for her to take a draw.

"Of course I knew."

"You arranged it. Why? We could still be together."

"No, sooner or later, you'd have gone anyway. The hurt would have been greater then. Besides, it was time that you reached for your comet instead of letting it come to you."

"My comet." She blew out the smoke and gave a thin laugh. "Glory's influence. You know, the man I'm involved with is Glory's cousin? Curious, isn't it? Glory said once that she'd catch the tail of her comet and soar through the air and I'd still be waiting for mine to come along."

"And did she?"

"Not by killing herself."

"What does the cousin say?"

"I don't know. It's strange, but we've never talked about

356

Glory. It's as if when she died, she ceased to exist."

"It's true. That's why we reach for the stars, hoping to capture a little of the magic before it's gone. You've come a long way without reaching, Margie. Sooner or later you're going to have to make a choice that hurts."

Margie dropped the cigarette to the dusty floor and stubbed it out. She took a step forward and slid her arms around Leonard. "Hold me, please," she whispered. "I need you to hold me."

"No," he said simply, "not this time. I can't be your refuge, Margie. It's too hard on me. This time you've got to make your choice and we both know it isn't me."

"Don't you care anymore?" Her anguish made her voice hoarse and loud.

"Of course I care, Margie. I love you. I've loved you since Victoria brought you here when you were eighteen. You went around announcing that one day you were going to be *somebody*. Now you are, Margie, and you don't need me anymore."

"But Leonard, I don't want to give you up."

"You won't. I'm a part of you. All the men in your past are a part of you. They've shaped your dreams, your insecurities, your failures, and your success. Don't you see, my darling Margie, you don't need *them* anymore—unless you choose to."

Leonard watched Margie walk away. He could have told her that Mallory Madorn was his sister, that she'd been an alcoholic even back then, but he kept Mallory's condition private. What had it mattered that she had given up her role under duress? She was on the verge of going under anyway. By bowing out when she did, it had worked out for the best. Except for losing Margie. But he never fooled himself about that. She never belonged to him anyway.

All the way back to her apartment, Margie heard Leonard's words ringing discordant bells inside her mind. He was right. She was a product of all the men she'd known, beginning with the father who'd left her.

She'd had sex, in abundance, but *love?* That was hard. Except for Leonard, she didn't know.

For the first time in her life her relationship with a man

357

was up to her. She and Steven had been together for almost five years. She had nothing to gain by making a commitment to him, and nothing to lose if she didn't. Her contract with Channel 8 was secure, as was the syndication of her interviews. There'd even been a hint that one day ABC might give her a shot at more. Everything she'd ever hoped for was within her grasp and she'd done it all herself.

Still, she liked being with Steven. He was the first man she'd ever met as an equal and, because she hadn't needed to be anything for him, she could be herself.

Steven was waiting in her apartment. He never asked annoying questions about where she'd been or what she was doing and he didn't today. He simply smiled and asked, "Are you ready to go?"

She nodded and they left in Steven's Mercedes, taking Roswell Road to the Chattahoochee and turning east until they came to an entranceway whose locked iron gates yielded to the computer code he entered in a machine just inside the drive.

Steven gave the illusion of being relaxed, but Margie could sense the tenseness in his silence. When they drove through the gates and rounded a curve, she saw the gray-green house built into the side of a green hill. A porch wrapped around its outer edge like the mink collar on her mother's old cashmere coat, cushioning the house from the trees. Steven unlocked the door and drew her inside, through a massive room with cathedral ceilings to the balcony beyond.

"Water?" she said, listening to the music as it moved through the trees beyond the rail they were leaning against.

"The river. Do you like it?"

"Who does it belong to?"

"Me. Us, if you say so. Margie, I want to marry you."

Margie was shocked. She'd expected Steven to demand some kind of full-time living arrangement, maybe even a new apartment. But marriage hadn't been a part of her speculation.

"What, no spontaneous answer? No argument, no questions?"

"I'm just surprised, Steven. I didn't expect this."

"Why not? I thought I'd made it pretty clear."

Margie turned and looked at Steven, trying to put her

358

uncertainties into words. "I suppose you did. I just wasn't hearing you. I thought—I mean, you've been married before, Steven. You have two children. I thought you wouldn't be interested in trying that again."

"I married Elizabeth out of desperation, Margie, because I couldn't marry the woman I loved and I couldn't trust myself not to ruin her life by being free to see her."

If Margie were conducting an interview she would have murmured politely, "I see" or some other inane remark that would lull the subject into continuing.

"That sounds very intense for someone twenty years old," she said instead.

"It was. Intense, consuming, forbidden. What I want now is peace and someone to share it with, Margie. I'll ask no more than you are willing to give."

"And in return?"

"I'll be a loving, supportive, and caring husband. I'll rub your back when you're tired. I'll see that you're free to do whatever your career demands, or I'll give you children, if that's what you want."

"Children? My God, Steven, I'm almost forty-four years old. I probably couldn't carry a child if I wanted to, and the last thing I want in this lifetime is a baby."

"Margie, you're built for making love and having babies. I find it hard to believe that you've never considered it."

Margie laughed. "You won't believe how much I considered it, considered how *not* to get pregnant. I had my opportunities, believe me, and it never happened. I guess I was just lucky."

Steven laughed a wry, strange laugh. "For generations the Winslows only had one living child each. Nobody knew why, it just was that way. Then, when there were only three Winslows left, the pattern changed. Sam has three children. Glory was the only one with just one child."

Glory. Margie didn't want to talk about Glory now. "And you have two children. Surely you don't want more."

"No, I have three children. Two I tried to be a father to and failed. But there was another child, one I could only love in secret. The child doesn't know I'm his father. Nobody does. Nobody can ever know—except you, if you ask me."

"I don't think I will, Steven. Just tell me that child's mother won't intrude in our lives now."

359

"She won't intrude, Margie. She's dead."

And then she knew. She understood what Steven hadn't said. The woman he'd loved had been Glory. She'd been the pivotal point in his life, just as she'd been in Margie's life and in Susan and JoEllen's. Glory had tinged all their lives and sent them spiraling off like the blurred colors on a pinwheel caught in the wind.

They looked at each other in silence. For the first time, Steven allowed Margie to see his pain. He let her feel his anguish. "Marry me, Margie. We need each other."

Was it that simple? Could she trust Steven with her insecurities, her demons of despair? Could she allow him to see her fears and vulnerabilities?

Margie knew that people wouldn't have understood if she'd told them that she wasn't as secure as she appeared. Her success didn't mean as much as she'd thought it would because the people from her past weren't there to see her, the people against whom she'd measured herself. Glory didn't know.

But Margie knew. And she had Steven, if she wanted him. And perhaps Steven would be enough. "All right," she finally said. "Maybe we do need each other. I accept."

"When?"

"Soon."

Steven brushed her lips lightly and drew back. He hadn't been sure that she'd agree, but she had, even after she'd heard him confess to a forbidden love. He should have gone all the way, cleansed his soul by admitting the whole truth, by telling her that the woman he'd loved for most of his life was his cousin Glory.

But he couldn't do that. Marrying Margie would erase that guilt. It would be as if he'd gone back and started again. And finally he'd be able to forget.

In the end, all he said was, "I need you, Margie. Promise me that you won't change your mind."

"I won't."

Forty-One

As JoEllen filed Dr. Wade's medical charts she thought nostalgically about the little house she'd had in Atlanta. Her mother's old apartment was cramped. It hadn't seemed too small for three people when she was growing up, but now that she and Teresa were there she felt smothered. The situation was strained because it had been difficult for her mother to explain Teresa to the community.

Single women didn't adopt children in the seventies, not unless they were relatives. Gossip was rampant that Teresa was in fact JoEllen's child and that the adoption was just a ruse. So much for any guilt over not having her own baby. She'd never have been able to count on any help at all if she'd done that, not even from her mother.

JoEllen had thought that bringing Teresa to Galilee would be hard for the child, but Teresa loved the small, decaying town. She never complained. She simply set her mind on being the best student in third grade, and she was.

The phone rang, pulling JoEllen's attention back to the present. It was Teddy, as it often was these days.

"Hi. Busy?"

"No. Dr. Wade just left. I'm trying to put away the files while I'm waiting for Teresa."

"Want some company?"

"Teddy! What would people say if you came in when the doctor was already gone?"

"They'd say that it was about time. Besides, what do I care what people say?"

"Because you're the mayor and the town's leading businessman and you're an example to the youth of Galilee."

361

"All that? And I thought I was just Teddy."

"You're never just Teddy."

"There was one thing I always wished I had when I was in high school."

"What was that?"

"A telephone, so that I could talk to you late at night and do naughty things to myself."

JoEllen gasped. "Theodore Wallace, you're terrible!"

"No. I was terrible back then, JoEllen. I've learned how to do a lot of things since. In fact, there are some things that I believe I can safely say I've learned to excel at. What say I come over and give you a little demonstration?"

JoEllen waited a long minute before answering. She understood what he was saying and she knew that he deserved an answer. Why was it so hard for her to relax and let herself go?

But she knew the answer to that. The baby. There was a barrier between them, and Teddy didn't even know. He'd been patient. He'd even waited for her, not consciously, perhaps, but he'd never married. And he'd come for her when she needed him. She'd have to tell him the truth. And she would, she vowed. But she needed him now, and she was afraid that once he knew the terrible thing she'd done, she'd lose him.

"Not yet, Teddy. Teresa will be here soon."

"All right then, what if I come by tonight and sit in the swing with you on the porch, so the world can see how proper I'm behaving?"

She heard the disappointment in his voice. She wanted to reach out and touch him; she wanted him here, with her. The strength of that need surprised her.

"Sure, I'll even turn out the porch light."

"Wow!"

JoEllen hung up the phone and glanced at the clock. School was out and Teresa would be along soon. Teresa didn't attend the private school that had been built out in the county. JoEllen couldn't afford it and she wouldn't have sent her even if she could. It hadn't been hard for Teresa to attend the city's mostly black public school, for she'd never known segregation, but JoEllen was concerned about her education and spent extra time working with her.

JoEllen quickly put away the patient records and began

362

straightening the examining rooms. The day's schedule had been hectic. She'd spent six hours assisting Dr. Wade during his usual Thursday hours in Galilee, an arrangement that had come about as a result of his supervising the care of Mark Winslow.

The last patient they'd discussed before Dr. Wade had headed back to Augusta was Mark. Since his return to Winslow two months ago he'd continued to deteriorate. While some patients went into remission, enjoying periods of relative good health, the medical world was learning that there were certain men whose bodies offered no resistance to the virus at all. Perhaps if they'd been able to transfer Mark to the hospital he might have made better progress, but he'd refused to go. Jennifer and Marcie did what they could, but Susan and JoEllen handled most of the nursing care.

At four o'clock the office doorbell rang. As JoEllen opened the door to let Teresa in, a car pulled in the drive and one of the local merchants staggered up the steps.

"JoEllen, something's wrong." He reached the office foyer and collapsed.

"Mr. Barlow, Dr. Wade's already gone. There's nobody here but me."

"It's my chest, girl. I'm hurting bad. Can't you do something?"

JoEllen took one look at the clammy state of his skin and knew he was in trouble. She wasn't certain that she had enough time to get him to the hospital in Augusta. Even the small county facility in Lynville might be too far. She dialed Lawson General. With any luck Dr. Wade had stopped by there to check on his patients.

Ten minutes later she was connected to both Dr. Wade and the emergency-room doctor. Quickly and efficiently she followed directions, feeding the EKG readings directly to the hospital as she described Barlow's condition. In a matter of minutes she'd administered the necessary IVs and medication. She called Teddy, sent Teresa home, and drove Barlow to the hospital herself. He made it in time.

Later, as they discussed the problem, the staff doctor made a surprising suggestion. "You know, JoEllen, we could set up a physician's assistant program through Dr. Wade. You could open his office through the week to treat simple

363

illnesses and monitor emergencies until they can be transported."

"Practice real life-saving medicine?" *Alone, without a doctor present?* To JoEllen the thought was incredulous. "Is that legal?"

"Are you still licensed?"

"Yes, of course."

"Would you be interested?"

"Interested? I'd be ecstatic."

The next night Teddy dropped by. JoEllen was full of excitement. "Just think, Teddy, until another full-time doctor comes to Galilee I could make a real difference."

"You always could," he said quietly, giving a push to the swing. "Do you smell the honeysuckle, JoEllen?"

"Yes, that's what I remember best about Galilee, honeysuckle and watermelon. I used to walk through my neighborhood in Atlanta when the grass was being cut and just breathe in the smell. It always made me think of fresh-cut watermelon."

They continued to swing in silence, watching the local residents drive by in their cars, waving occasionally until it got too dark to see. Since she'd come home Teddy had dropped by occasionally, just to say hello in the beginning and invite Teresa to go fishing with him at the lake. Once he'd invited both Teresa and JoEllen to Atlanta to watch the Atlanta International Race from the pits. Teresa loved the noise and the fumes.

If JoEllen had been postponing her future plans, Teresa wasn't. She was settling in like a seedling, sending her roots into the black dirt and growing. Others might decry the loss of the movie theater, but Teresa loved playing outside at night, chasing lightning bugs and enjoying games of hide-and-seek with the neighborhood children.

"Teresa, time to come in and get ready for bed."

"Not yet, Mother, please?"

"She's changed, Teddy. There was a time when she never argued with me about anything. Never yelled, or talked too loud, or cried. Now she's getting downright sassy."

"Just like her mother. At least I guess that's where she gets it. I've never asked anything about Teresa's father."

"Then she isn't biologically yours?" Teddy asked when JoEllen finished her explanation.

"No, does that matter?"

"Not to me. If she's yours I love her, no matter how she got here. Just like I loved her mother."

Loved. Always in the past tense. That was the way he said it and JoEllen had made no effort to change the status quo. Tonight, along with a mountain of guilt, she allowed herself to express a bit of nostalgia. "Teddy. I'm sorry. I'm so sorry that I hurt you."

"No, *I* hurt *you* and I never knew it. It took me a long time to know that making love to a woman was more than just sex."

"Teddy, it's been twenty-eight years, why haven't you married?"

"Never met anybody else I wanted to marry."

"But you've lived through the sexual revolution, free love, and a time when divorces outnumber marriages. How have you escaped?"

"Don't know. Came close a few times, but at the last minute I just couldn't get past that seedy little motel room in Augusta. It was like that night was a blot on my conscience that I couldn't erase. I can't say I've been a monk, but I never could seem to commit myself for more than fun and games. The women knew. I never lied to any of them. Course I don't know that they believed me, but I was honest with 'em. What about the good doctor? You never married?"

"Tom? No. It wasn't that kind of relationship. There was a blot on that, too, a blot that I couldn't get past. We eventually became friends, but nothing more."

"And there hasn't been anybody else?"

"No. Marriage just didn't seem to be in the cards for me. I don't think it's as easy in a city to meet the right person."

"Well, I don't know about the city, but it gets pretty lonely in the country. Course we've got indoor plumbing now, and heat pumps, but that bed is still icy when I slip into it at night."

"You should try a cat. That's what I had before Teresa came along," she said with a catch in her voice. The conversation was heading back in the direction she'd avoided. Teddy, marriage, beds? She wouldn't allow herself to think about that. She couldn't. Maybe she just wouldn't think at all. For now she'd close out all the negative thoughts she'd carried around for so long.

365

"Cats have claws," he said, and slid his arm around her, letting his hand rest on her shoulder. "Damn! I feel like a fool, trying to figure a way to kiss you without sending you off in a blue funk."

"Maybe you need to stop figuring and just do it, Teddy. Better still, maybe I'll kiss you."

And she did. And just like that, the years melted away and she felt herself relaxing beneath the gentle pressure of his lips. Gone was Teddy's frantic need, the quick, furtive moves meant to bring JoEllen to instant passion and acceptance, the roughness. He simply kissed her for a long moment, then stopped and pulled her into his embrace, resting her head against his chest.

"I think I like this new way of doing things. Women's liberation can be a wonderful thing. Too bad women and men don't have the same rate of liberation development. There'd be fewer folks fooling around with other people when they have what they need at home."

"I don't know, Teddy. Seems to me that the grass is always greener in the other pasture. Nobody seems to pay much attention to the rules. If they interfere with what you want to do, you just change them."

"Maybe, but a man doesn't have to be a billy goat sampling all the vegetation before he picks a place to feed. A man has a brain and all he has to do is use it."

"Aw, shucks, I thought you were about to play traveling salesman with me. Instead, your turning into a professor."

School got out for the summer. The town no longer celebrated the Fourth of July. Instead, people went to the lake, or to Florida, or stayed home and barbecued on their new gas charcoal grills. JoEllen enrolled Teresa in vacation bible school where she made Jesus shoes under the direction of the oldest member of the staff, Mrs. Loretta Green, and memorized more Bible verses than anyone else.

Brooks Medical Center reopened in Atlanta, but for JoEllen the move back had lost its appeal. She didn't know what she'd do, but for now, setting up and operating the physician's assistant program in the county was rewarding. If her life seemed to be in some kind of holding pattern, that was fine. She liked running Dr. Wade's office under his direction and ministering to simple illnesses.

Mark Winslow grew weaker. Susan grew more and more morose. And Teddy continued to make himself a place in JoEllen's life.

Mark lived another year. He finally stopped struggling in September of 1982. He was buried the same day as the lone Marine who was killed when the United States landed in Beirut to keep the peace between the Lebanese and the Palestinians.

The Marine had a hero's funeral. Mark had a quick, quiet service with only the family and a few close friends present. Susan wept openly. His sisters grieved quietly. Sam grimaced, and JoEllen said a silent thank-you that nobody in Galilee or Winslow had learned the truth about Mark's illness. His parents didn't need any more heartache.

As if the residents connected JoEllen's stay with Mark's care, they formally petitioned her to stay in Galilee. They needed her. Even her mother, in a rare moment, admitted that she would miss the grandchild she'd at first been ashamed to claim.

Teddy didn't ask her to stay, but she knew that he wanted it to happen. Teresa openly stated that she wanted to live in Galilee forever.

JoEllen Dixon had been in Galilee almost two years. She hadn't planned to stay and she hadn't planned to leave. But it was time to make a conscious decision, for she and Teresa had lived in the small apartment with her mother long enough, and her mother had received a letter from Skip. He had leave from the Navy and he was coming home. It was time to find her own place. She put it before Teresa. In the end there was no vote.

JoEllen stayed.

Forty-Two

Mark's death wasn't the release Sam had hoped for. First his life, then his death had been imprinted on the walls of the house. If Sam woke at night, he heard his son's labored breathing—or he heard the silence, which was worse.

Susan had buried a part of herself in that grave—her laughter, her quiet joy, the strength she'd drawn on to get through the trauma of watching her son die.

Sam had lost his mother when he was a baby, and his grandmother when he was ten. His grandfather had died suddenly, without warning, without lingering. His father was still alive. Mark's passing was Sam's first close experience with death and he hadn't handled it well. He couldn't talk to Susan about what was happening; he simply closed it up inside him, where it lay like a hard, hot ball of fear.

"Morning, Daddy." Jennifer walked into the barn, pulling on her work gloves.

"What are you doing out here so early?" Sam glanced at his daughter with pride. She was a no-nonsense, dependable girl, ready to work alongside the men like any other hand. Her husband Jack had already loaded hay on the truck and left to feed the cows. The fields were ready for planting as soon as the weather warmed, and the new seed was already ordered.

"Thought I'd give you a hand with that piece of fence that got knocked down by the tree."

"Not today, Jen. It's pretty cold. I think I'll wait for some sunshine."

"What are you doing out here in the barn before breakfast?"

368

"Just looking around . . . What would you think about selling the farm, Jennifer?" he asked abruptly.

Jennifer stopped her motion and stared at her father in shock. "Sell the farm? Why would you want to do that?"

"Your mother wanted to once. She thought I should get a job over in Augusta so that Marcie could be born in a hospital."

"Why didn't you?"

"Sell Winslow land? I couldn't have. She never understood about the land. It's been in the Winslow family for two hundred years. Each generation selects a new caretaker. I was chosen by my grandfather. I could never let it go."

"I know," she said quietly, and put her arms around her father's waist, leaning her head against his chest.

"I thought when Mark was born that he'd be the one to follow me."

Jennifer didn't speak. During all the long days of her brother's illness, her father had never talked about Mark. He'd grown more and more morose, but no matter what Jennifer had said, he'd turned it away. Finally Marcie had been the one to explain the truth. Mark had been a homosexual. He'd been involved with a man, an airline employee who was responsible for infecting Mark with the fatal virus.

"But Mark came here tainted, Jennifer," Sam said. "We can't change that. When it happens, you have to work around it. You must be very careful with your children. It's always out there, waiting for a Winslow. And you never know who it will strike."

Jennifer felt her father shudder. He was talking crazy. Nobody knew what caused men to be homosexuals, but she was reasonably certain that it wasn't a Winslow characteristic. The Winslow men had always been virile, lusty specimens. And the women? There she was less certain. Other than her aunt Glory, and Uncle Steven's daughter, Melissa, whom she knew only slightly, she and Marcie were the only Winslow women.

Granted, Marcie didn't seem to be much interested in men, but she didn't like women that way, either. Marcie simply had her mind set on her work and nothing else touched her. She seemed to be the only one in the family who could deal with Mark's illness. She'd march into Mark's

369

room, ask him, "How's it hanging, buddy?" and tell him a dirty joke. To Marcie, Mark's terrible medical problems were just that, medical problems, and she could divorce herself from any personal feelings.

For Jennifer, being around Mark was harder. She didn't understand him. She never had. And talking to him was uncomfortable, even when he was having a good day. On the bad days, conversation was impossible. Both Jennifer and Sam found an outlet for their unspoken fears in physical labor in some distant corner of the farm. But since the funeral her father had seemed unable to get back into a routine.

"You aren't seriously considering selling the farm, are you, Daddy?"

"No, of course not. But I am thinking of building your mother another house. Mark is so much a part of this one that I—she—might be more comfortable in a new place. I thought I might let you and Jack have the house, if it's not too old- and out-of-date for you."

"Jack and I have the house?"

"Then Marcie could have your trailer. It will all be yours some day, Jennifer. You'll be the caretaker for the land. What do you think?"

Jennifer felt a swell of emotion. She'd loved this farm from the time she learned to walk. Her father had been the biggest, strongest, smartest man she'd ever known and she'd wanted to be just like him. She'd directed all her efforts to that end. When she'd become engaged to Jack it was because she'd carefully chosen a man who'd fit. Jack was a good man, but he was weak. He'd work hard and he'd give her children. And if she was left unsatisfied she'd find her own solutions when she was ready.

She moved her arms beneath Sam's jacket and squeezed him. "I won't disappoint you, Daddy. My son will love the land, too."

Sam tightened his arms about his daughter. Jennifer and Marcie were his strength. He'd shaped their lives, taught them to be strong. His grandfather would have approved. "Don't insist on sons, Jennifer. You may have daughters, too."

"No, Daddy." Jennifer took her father's hand and placed it on her stomach. "I'm carrying a child, Daddy, a son. I'm

370

going to call him Winslow. And one day he'll be the care-taker, too. I'll see to that."

Long after Jennifer went to find Jack, Sam stood in the cold barn, remembering the times his grandfather had sent him there, punished him for showing some weakness, and left him alone in the dark. Tears ran down his face.

He couldn't grieve for Mark when he was dying. He couldn't cry at the funeral. Now, alone in the dark, Sam Winslow wept.

All the years Mark was growing up, Sam had thought he failed. His son was a Winslow, but he'd never been Sam's son: he was Susan's. Sam had tried, but the boy simply hadn't been able to do any of the things Sam had expected of him. And early on Sam had understood that he was being punished, punished because of his own weakness, his sinful obsession for Glory, the woman he could never have.

Forty-Three

Margie and Steven were married in October of 1982, the week after Mark's funeral. The wedding was simple and elegant. No family, only a few business associates and Leonard, attended.

Neither had any desire to invite anyone from their past and neither had, they acknowledged, any close friends.

Their lives changed very little. They got along well. Life was pleasant. The house was lovely, and little by little, it began to take on their personalities. They planned a summer cruise with Steven's son Steve and his daughter, Melissa, who was still in college. At the last minute Margie had to cancel when she got a chance to interview Alexander Haig, who'd resigned as secretary of state after a series of disagreements with President Reagan and some of his advisers. It took the cruise without her for Steven to understand how much he missed her.

Acquaintances gradually became friends. Steven's investment business continued to grow. Margie added more stations to her syndication and plowed vigorously into public service work. Now and then Margie thought about interviewing Victoria. Her group had been remarkably successful in bringing about the desegration of restaurants and public facilities, but her black friend left Victoria behind, garnering headlines by being one of the first students to attend the state university. Gradually Victoria was swallowed up by stronger, younger personalities and now she seemed to be merely tolerated.

Margie thought about Susan and the death of her son. She wondered vaguely if she ought to find a free weekend and drive down for a visit.

But she never did.

The past was finally past and Margie tucked the battered teddy bear into the bottom drawer of her bureau. She didn't need him anymore.

Two years later she received an invitation to the thirtieth reunion of the Galilee High School graduating class of 1954. It would be a combined event of the classes of '53, '54, and '55. She might not have gone had it not been for Steven.

"My children will be there, with Mother," he said. "Even Glory's son, Damon, is visiting."

Margie took a quick look at Steven, wondering if there was more to his statement then he let on. But he went on drinking his morning coffee as usual. Still, an alarm went off in her mind.

"They're all practically grown, Steven. What on earth are they all doing in Winslow at the same time?"

"Mother has finally decided to move into that retirement home. She's dividing up the family treasures. We were all summoned for the ritual. Apparently Damon visits her often. She seems to have taken Adele's place as a grand-mother."

"Sounds odd to me."

It was odd to Steven, too. Damned odd. He was certain that Damon had never been told the truth about who his father was. Yet he'd spent time every summer in Winslow with Adele until she died, and then with Evelyn.

"I see my children so seldom, I really ought to go. And it might be fun for you to see some of your old friends."

Margie didn't know why she held back. Returning to Galilee as a successful television personality should have been the ultimate high, but somehow it wasn't. Even the thought brought back the old uncertainty. For several days she considered dropping the committee a note saying that she was too busy. In the end, she didn't make up her mind until she answered the phone the week before the reunion.

"Margie, this is Susan. Susan Winslow. I thought that since we're cousins-in-law now I ought to call and— No, that's not it. I just wondered if you received your invitation to the reunion."

"Susan? How nice to hear from you. Yes, I got it."

"You are coming, aren't you?"

373

"Well, I don't know. I'm usually so busy in the fall. It's the beginning of a new television season. I'm not sure."

"Please, Margie, come. JoEllen will be here. We thought we'd get rooms at the hotel."

"Hotel? There's a hotel in Galilee?"

"Well, not in town, but on the interstate. It has three stories and calls itself a hotel. I guess by Atlanta standards it's a small motel. Anyway, we can get the connecting rooms on the third floor, overlooking the pool. That's their VIP suite. If you could come down the night before, we can just sit around and talk. It will be like old times, a spend-the-night party for the f—the three of us."

The unspoken "four" hovered there. But there weren't four of them anymore. There hadn't been for a long time. Glory had been dead for seventeen years.

There was an underlying tension in Susan's voice, a plea that Margie couldn't ignore. "It's a bad time, but I'll see what I can do. Steven's children will be with his mother. He already suggested that he should join them."

"Steven? Good, I'd hoped he'd come."

"He'll be with me, yes, but he can stay with his mother. I'll stay at the hotel with you."

"Then you'll come?"

"Yes."

Forty-Four

From the time she and Steven left Lynville heading toward Galilee, sensations billowed over Margie like a dust storm. So many years had passed since she'd been home.

Home. She wondered why a person calls the place where they spent their first years home. Why isn't home the place you are living at that moment? And she lived with Steven in her beautiful house overlooking the river. She'd never expected it to happen, but she liked their house.

Margie had known nothing about decorating, but she'd made many friends through the years and she'd discovered that people were valuable for what they brought to a friendship. Early on she absorbed and cultivated those she needed to know or could use. When she needed a new dress, she'd have lunch with someone who knew fashion. When she needed the house decorated, she asked a friend what she should do.

Until she'd married Steven. Without knowing that her methods were changing, they had. Now it was Steven who was her confidant, who shared the decision-making. Outside of her job, she rarely consulted outsiders anymore.

Still, in her most private moments, Margie felt that if all her layers were removed, there'd be nothing inside but a little girl who'd been left behind by her parents.

They passed the private school, now boarded up and abandoned. After making a firm stand against desegregation so many years ago, all the students in the county now attended the public consolidated Jimmy Carter High School. A new county grammar school was being built.

"The area is really going downhill," Steven said. "It makes

me sad. Do you want to drive around before you go to the hotel? It's not in town you know."

"Yes, I'd like to drive around a bit first."

Steven was right. Many of the houses were empty, their front doors swinging from broken hinges. At the caution light Steven turned left, driving slowly down the street Margie had walked so many times. She felt a knot swell in her throat and she held her breath until her grandmother's house came into view.

"It's still here," she said in a whisper. "They've painted it pink. For God's sake, Steven, they've turned it into a bordello."

"I don't think so, Margie. I understand a nice elderly couple live there. He's a retired railroad man."

"Take me to the hotel, Steven. I don't want to see any more."

Steven saw that she was registered, smiling to himself as the staff members all recognized Margie Raines. He'd expected Margie to bask in her success, but she didn't seem to notice.

"I'll be at Mother's, Margie. I'll bring the children and meet you at the lake tomorrow for the family picnic."

Margie simply nodded. Too many memories were assaulting her. She could still see herself walking from the downtown movie theater up Winslow Road, and, if she were lucky, sitting on the front steps with a boy until her grandfather slammed a door in the back of the house calling her inside. How on earth would she manage to get through the picnic at the lake tomorrow if simply being on Winslow Road had jolted her so?

Why was she subjecting herself to this painful experience? She was the most Outstanding Television Personality in Atlanta, winning the award again this year, not some insecure, ignorant high school girl. She didn't have to come back home for people to know she was a success. Everyone had television sets now, color ones, not like the early black-and-white sets on which they'd watched Ed Sullivan on Sunday nights so long ago.

The lone hotel bellman who hastened to offer his services knocked, inserted her key in the lock, and opened the door.

"Margie!" Susan swept across the room and hugged her, leaned back to look at her old friend, and hugged her again.

376

"You look wonderful."

"Where shall I put your luggage?"

"Oh, just leave it there. Thanks." Carelessly she took the key and handed the boy a folded bill. Once he was gone she took Susan's hands and studied her. "You look good, too, Susan. I was afraid that what you'd been through might have been too much."

"It nearly was, Margie. Nobody will ever know how close I came to total collapse."

"I'm sorry I didn't come for the funeral, but I didn't know until it was over."

"I know. Mark didn't want a fuss and neither did Sam. Sam probably would have buried Mark himself if he hadn't been afraid his body would contaminate the cows."

Margie's eyes flicked in surprise. She hadn't expected Susan's bitterness. "Whooa, girl," she whispered. "Let's go back a few years and pretend it's Christmas."

"Christmas?"

"Yep, it's my turn to bring you gifts." She picked up one of the shopping bags she'd brought and placed it on the table.

Before Susan could look, the door opened again, and JoEllen walked in. Another round of hugs and minute examinations followed. If anything, they decided, they looked better than they had thirty years ago.

JoEllen looked around the room. "Wow! What is this, Galilee's idea of the penthouse suite?"

"Absolutely," Susan explained. "This is the parlor, and we have a bedroom on each side. Actually, there are three connecting bedrooms overlooking the pool. When you order a suite they haul out the bed and bring in a couch and table. I figured we'd flip for the couch. The other two can have their own private bedrooms."

"Great. What's in the bag, Susan?"

"I don't know. Margie brought it for us. Come and look."

JoEllen peered into the bag, raised her gaze to Margie, and shook her head. "Is that what I think it is?"

"Absolutely. Four Roses whiskey. I thought it would be fun to do something wicked again, like we did in high school."

"I never drank whiskey in high school," JoEllen protested.

"That's right, Margie. JoEllen was gone that summer after graduation."

377

"No matter," Margie declared. "She can make up for what she missed. Let's get into something comfortable and open one of the bottles."

"How many bottles *are* there?" Susan asked.

JoEllen glanced at Margie's suitcases and down at the single bag she'd brought. "Enough. I'll take the couch. Give our star one bedroom and our reunion planner the other."

The luggage was transferred in moments and regular clothing had been swapped for big T-shirts and bare feet. JoEllen filled their ice bucket and unwrapped the plastic glasses. "Do we have Cokes? If we're going to do this right, we need Cokes."

"Absolutely." Margie emptied another bag and brought out soft drinks, mineral water, and snacks.

In no time they were sitting on the carpet, leaning against the couch, each woman holding a drink.

"You know I don't really drink," Susan finally said. "Sam never liked me drinking."

"Well, we won't tell. We promise, don't we, JoEllen?"

"I'm very good at keeping secrets. A nurse has to be."

"That's good, because I intend to get smashed." Susan took a big swallow, choked, and took another one.

They took turns bringing each other up to date on their lives. JoEllen glossed over her hospital career, explaining in greater detail her decision to adopt Teresa and work in a women's abortion clinic.

"I heard about what happened when the girl died, Jo. The station wanted me to call you for an interview."

"Why didn't you?"

"I don't know. I thought it would be hard for you, I guess."

"It would have been. Thanks, Margie. I find that I'm not really very brave."

"Of course you are," Margie said sharply. "The difference between you and me is that you really did something to help women. I only talk about it, and sometimes I don't even do that. I just let my guest do something controversial. Let's have more drinks. We're old enough now, guys, aren't we? Hey, we're getting too serious."

"Everything is serious," Susan said. "When we were in high school, we were taught that everything was going to be so wonderful. JoEllen was going to become a nurse and marry Teddy. Margie was going to the city and 'be

378

somebody.' I was going to marry Sam and become a farmer's wife. It's spooky how much of it came true, isn't it?"

JoEllen uncrossed her legs and spread them out in front of her. "Except for me marrying Teddy and—Glory."

"Yes, Glory." Margie rested her head on the seat of the couch and closed her eyes. "I stood there, wearing my best coat so everybody would think I was successful, and I was freezing to death. If I hadn't been so mad I'd have spit on her grave. When they were throwing that dirt on her coffin I actually wanted to kill her. Kill a dead woman."

"And I had to keep telling you to be quiet," JoEllen added. She didn't want to talk about Glory, and she wasn't certain the others did, either. There was a long pause before she changed the subject. "Tell us about you, Margie. You were already a star when I moved to Atlanta. How'd you do it?"

"Initially someone helped me, then it was just a lucky break. I was in the right place at the right time. I guess you could say that when my comet appeared, I grabbed it by the tail."

Susan got to her feet and added more whiskey. She'd emptied her glass without realizing she'd done so. "And you married Glory's cousin?"

"Yes, Steven and I got married. Funny, I never thought of him as Glory's cousin. Since I never knew him back then, I never connected him to Winslow. Of course, his mother still lives there. Steven's children are visiting her now."

Susan laughed. "Do you realize that we're both Winslows, Margie? I never thought about that happening in a million years."

"Neither did I. I used to wish I *was* Glory," Margie admitted, letting out a deep breath, "but I never expected to have her name." *Or that I'd marry the man she wanted.*

"But you don't," JoEllen said. "At least not publicly. The world knows you as Margie Raines. Mr. Jim would be so proud of you."

"I hope so. But he never knew. Susan, I guess we might as well get all the morbid talk behind us, so tell me about Mark."

"Mark died of AIDS." Susan surprised even herself. She hadn't spoken those words aloud once since bringing him back home, until now. "He was a homosexual."

Margie put her hand on Susan's arm. "I'm so sorry, Suse. I

379

didn't mean to make you sad."

"I'm not. At least I'm not sad he chose that lifestyle. And I guess I'm not sad that he's dead. Living with such pain isn't fair. But when he died he took my heart with him."

"Poor Sam," Margie said softly. "How hard it must have been on poor moral, righteous Sam."

Poor Sam? Susan wanted to scream out. *Why, poor Sam? Why not, poor Susan?*

"It was Glory's fault," Susan finally said.

"Glory's fault?" Margie echoed. "Excuse me, but I don't get the connection."

JoEllen felt the tension that suddenly swept through the room. It was as if Glory had walked in and sat beside them. She could almost see her flashing eyes and fiery hair. After all these years she was still enforcing her will over them.

Susan stood and walked toward the table. "She always pulled all our strings. They were invisible, but they were there. We all had them, including Sam. Sam believes all the Winslows are flawed. Mark was flawed. Glory was flawed. Now they're both dead."

Margie and JoEllen looked at each other, each thinking they were the only one to know this truth. The woman adding fresh ice to her glass wasn't the same Susan who'd tried to refuse her drink that afternoon years ago in Glory's bedroom.

"She's had a rough time," JoEllen whispered under her breath. "Mark's death has torn Sam and Susan apart."

"In the end it doesn't matter," Susan said with a dry laugh. "They were Winslows and they couldn't escape the Winslow curse. Be careful, Margie, you're married to a Winslow. It might rub off on you . . . Does anyone want another drink?"

"Sure," Margie said. "I'm game. Let's get drunk and bury Glory once and for all. We'll order from room service for dinner and tell every bit of gossip we know about everybody we ever knew. And what we don't know, we'll make up. Did I tell you that I had a note from Mr. Sims?"

"Our old English teacher?"

"Yep, he saw me on television and recognized me. Said he got married again, and that didn't work out, either. He was working at a school in Kentucky. He never sold his great American novel, and he was living with a mountain woman who had healing powers and visions."

380

"Visions?" JoEllen questioned. "Wonder if she could tell me what's going to happen between Teddy and me."

"You and Teddy?" Margie said. "That's wonderful. At least I guess it is, if you think so."

"It isn't anything yet. When he brought me back to Galilee after the Brannon girl died, I didn't stop to think what that would mean. I was so sure I had my life in control until I collapsed. The trial scared me to death. I love my work and my daughter, but I'd lost all my confidence. My personal life is as barren as Loretta Green's."

"Dear Loretta, such a hypocrite. She told me once that the town didn't approve of me," Susan said with a faraway look in her eyes.

"Not approve of sinless Susan? What would she possibly know about you?"

"It was because I sat beside Jody that Sunday morning at church. She warned me that some of our fine townsfolk would put on white sheets and have a little talk with him. Did you know about that?"

"That black boy?" JoEllen was learning something new. "Did they?"

"No, they never threatened Jody," Susan said. "But they did a lot worse later to some of our local nigras."

Margie tried to digest that bit of information. "You saw Jody after he left Augusta?"

"No, but we corresponded for a while."

"Well, what do you know about that? I went off to Atlanta and got my picture taken over the desegregation of Atlanta restaurants and our good girl was back home writing letters to a black man. Just proves how little we ever really knew about each other, doesn't it?"

Margie emptied her glass and absorbed what she'd learned. JoEllen, who'd left Galilee and Teddy behind, had come back to almost the same spot where she started. And Susan was getting quietly drunk and blaming the failed parts of her life on Glory.

Susan finally broke the silence. "That's pretty funny. Loretta Green tried to tell us how we should live and she couldn't even convert her own husband."

Margie sat up and crossed her legs. "What kind of sin was Mr. Green guilty of?"

"Well, Mrs. Green didn't have any children, but, according to Sam, her husband had a yardful. You know he kept a black woman down in Tinsel Town?"

JoEllen gasped. "And to think she taught us all how to make Jesus shoes." She started to laugh. In a moment they were all laughing. Susan spilled half of her newly filled drink on her T-shirt, soaking the fabric which plastered itself to her breasts.

And suddenly Margie and Susan were seventeen and back in Glory's room. "She was right, you know," Susan said, looking down at her breasts, "that last summer, about what we were."

JoEllen and Margie exchanged questioning glances. "Mrs. Green?" JoEllen asked.

"No, Glory was right about us. You weren't there, JoEllen, but she made us take off our shirts and examine ourselves. We were drinking Four Roses and Coke back then, too."

"Now I'm beginning to understand your strange choice of drinks. I wondered what this was all about."

"She touched herself. I didn't know anything about sex then. I wish I had. I wish I hadn't been so virginal. If I'd known, things might have been different. Do you know that when I went to the bathroom, just before we left, I actually had an orgasm and didn't know it?"

"An orgasm? You're kidding." Margie gave out a disbelieving laugh. "I didn't even know what that meant until I was thirty years old. Can you believe it?"

"None of us knew anything," JoEllen said. "We weren't supposed to. We were warned about catching those unspeakable diseases, but nobody ever mentioned orgasms."

"But Glory knew," Susan said. "And Sam knew. And I suspect Steven knew, too. The rest of us just went blithely along, believing all the lies we were being fed. We'd get married and live happily ever after."

Oh, yes, Steven knew. Margie wanted to say it out loud, but she didn't. Talking about the four of them was one thing, but Steven didn't belong here. Margie was beginning to feel uncomfortable. Maybe she didn't want to know what had happened to her friends. Gossip was one thing, but honesty was something else. She'd lived through the times that women demanded their freedom, but she still wasn't comfortable with this kind of open talk. Honesty was easy for the young. Maybe her generation was still caught up in the lie.

"Ah, I don't know," Margie argued. "What makes you think Glory knew anything more than the rest of us? She just liked being dramatic."

"Sam told me. To Sam, I was the light. Glory was the dark. But Sam was wrong. There's darkness in all of us."

"Not in Teddy," JoEllen said. "He is the kindest, gentlest, most caring person I've ever known."

"And one of the richest, too," Susan observed. "Margie, did you know that Teddy owns land and race cars and he even bought Ed Jordan's construction company?"

"No. Teddy's a success, and he's the guy who just wanted to stay home and work in his brother's gas station."

"Stay home," Susan repeated. "Just like Sam. Are you sleeping with Teddy, JoEllen?"

The question might have come from Glory. Nobody would ever have expected it from Susan. But then nobody would ever have expected Susan to correspond with a black man, either. Margie was beginning to understand that there might be parts of all of them that nobody had ever seen.

"No."

"Do you want to?" Susan persisted.

"I don't know. Yes, I think I do."

"Then why don't you?" Margie asked curiously.

"I've only slept with two men in my life and I paid dearly for both of them. Sex is my hangup."

"But you did sleep with Teddy back then."

"Only once, twenty-five years ago, and it was a disaster. I've been afraid to take a chance on caring about a man again."

"Why is it," Susan asked, "that we allow men to dictate our sex lives? We're as horny as the men. Why can't we let loose and enjoy a good fuck?"

"She's drunk," Margie said. "There's no doubt that our Miss Goody Two Shoes is drunk. I think we'd better order some food before she takes off her clothes and starts dancing on the table."

"Good idea!" Susan said and ripped off her T-shirt. "Let's see you, JoEllen. Glory made us all look at each other. Margie had the biggest boobs, with little pink nipples and blond pussy hair. Glory had dark-purple nipples with big rose-colored circles around them. And that red hair. It looked as if her private parts were on fire. Appropriate, don't you think? For a woman who fucked every man who moved?"

Margie went to the phone, placed an order with room service, and began to recap the liquor bottles on the table.

Susan was cupping her breasts and staring at herself in the mirror. "She said I had the most hair. I probably still do. Do you know what she called us, JoEllen?"

"No, what?"

"Margie was a rose, I was a gardenia. You were a lily and she was a red dahlia. We were all colorless. She was the fire."

"But the fire went out, didn't it?" Margie said.

"Doesn't matter," Susan whispered. "We didn't know it then, that's what our lives have been all about, isn't it. We were all singed by Glory's flame."

"Why are we so obsessed with Glory?" Margie asked the next morning as she and JoEllen waited for Susan to join them in the parlor. They were driving to the family picnic together. Sam and Susan's family, Steven and his children, and Teddy and Teresa would meet them at the picnic.

"God, I feel just like I did that morning when the soldiers came. I don't think this is a good idea, JoEllen. Thomas Wolfe knew what he was talking about."

"I've often wondered, Margie, did you ever hear from Nick-the-Magnificent again?"

"You mean after he deflowered me?"

"No, that isn't what I meant, I just know that he was transferred and he'd planned to stop by that place you were living at in Atlanta and see you."

"I guess he must have changed his mind, or maybe I'd already left by that time . . . Do you think we ought to check on Susan?"

"No, she was in the shower when I went in a few minutes ago. She sounded like one of the three little kittens promising never to lose her mittens again." JoEllen leaned her ear against the door. "She's moving around. Let's just wait. So we're late, it doesn't matter."

"I'm glad they made this a three-class reunion."

"Members of the classes from 1953 through 1955. That

covers all of us—Teddy, Susan and me, and you. And we'll still do good to have a hundred people, I'll bet.

"I hate to admit it, but I wish Glory were here. None of this seems right without her."

"Well, at least her son is coming." Susan appeared in the doorway, dressed in a skirt and blouse much like the one she'd worn that fateful summer.

"I know. Steven says that Damon visits Evelyn every summer. When Adele died he adopted Evelyn as his Winslow grandmother."

Susan gave Margie an odd smile. "Have you seen Damon recently?"

"Not since Glory's funeral, and he was just a kid then."

"Well, I think you're going to be very surprised," Susan said. "We're going in my car. Sam finally bought me my own vehicle, a used station wagon, but it's mine."

JoEllen and Margie gathered up their swimsuits and beach bags and waited by the door. Susan moved slowly toward them, willing the pounding in her head to stop. Sam wouldn't like it if he knew that she'd gotten drunk. But then, Sam liked very little of what she did. To hell with Sam, she decided, and stopped by the table where the liquor bottles were. She further shocked her friends by pouring a small amount of whiskey straight into one of the cups and swallowing it in one gulp, following it with a breath mint she fished from her purse.

"Are you ready?" She moved past them into the corridor and hit the elevator button.

Moments later JoEllen and Margie were following Susan to her station wagon.

"Do you want me to drive, Susan?" JoEllen asked cautiously. This was a side of Susan she'd never seen and her years of nursing told her that Susan was dangerously close to a mental breakdown.

"Of course not. Get in."

The drive to the lake was little different from the one thirty years earlier. All three women were tense and uncertain, each imagining the scenario they expected to be played out. None of them was expecting the welcome they received. Nor were they prepared for their first look at Glory's grown-up son, Damon.

Gathered around the picnic table Teddy had staked out

were Sam, his two daughters Jennifer and Marcie, Steven, Steven's daughter, Melissa, his son, Steve, and Glory's son, Damon. And they all could have been cut from the same mold. All tall, thin, and dark-eyed. Not a red hair in Damon's head. All four men were Winslows through and through.

"Now you see what I mean," Susan said in a low voice. "Glory isn't here, but her men are."

"Why didn't you tell me that Damon looked more like you than your own son?" Margie asked a subdued Steven.

"I guess I didn't know."

"It's uncanny how much all of you look alike."

"Yes, we're all Winslows, all right. If you had my grandfather, Glory's father, and Sam's father here, you'd see that they all have the same characteristics."

"What about your father?"

"No, he had sandy-colored hair and he was much more muscular. I just happened to inherit the Winslow features. He took after his mother, I suppose. I never saw her."

"He was killed in the war?"

"Yes, he and Glory's father both died in the War in the Pacific."

"Glory barely remembered her father. Right?"

"Yes, she was only six when he died. I was ten."

Steven was answering her, but Margie could tell that his attention was elsewhere. She was more convinced than ever that coming back was a mistake. Susan was getting drunk again. JoEllen was sitting away from the group, using her little girl as some kind of shield between her and Teddy, and Steven was behaving as if he were hypnotized.

"Your daughter has blue eyes. She must have gotten them from her mother." Margie felt compelled to keep talking.

"What? Oh, yes. Elizabeth had blue eyes."

"Isn't it odd that Jennifer is the only one of the children who has married. If Steve doesn't marry, there won't be any more Winslows."

"Sam thinks that's a good thing," Susan said, sitting on the bench beside Margie. "He thinks the Winslows are cursed. He thought the line might end with Mark. But Jennifer's pregnant. She's sure it will be a boy and she's going

386

to name him Winslow. Aren't you two going swimming?"

"No, I think we'll just watch the rest of you," Margie answered for both of them.

"Well, I intend to. I was the only one who didn't that summer, and I always wondered what would have happened if I had."

"What summer?" Steven asked curiously.

"The summer after we graduated from high school. The town threw a Fourth of July celebration and brought in three busses of soldiers from Camp Gordon. JoEllen was already in nursing school, but she came down to help look after those who'd come from the hospital. Susan, Glory, and I were hostesses. You probably don't remember."

Don't remember? Oh, yes, he remembered that morning as vividly as if it had just happened. That was the morning he awoke to find Glory in his bed, in his arms. The morning that changed his life forever. The morning Damon had been conceived. He couldn't keep his eyes from his dark, brooding son. As a child Damon had come often to Adele's house, but Steven had always managed to avoid seeing him.

He'd known that Damon would be here. He'd expected him, but he hadn't known what a shock seeing him would be. When he'd walked into his mother's house and found his son standing there, he'd been struck emotionally dumb. As if Damon knew how he felt, he'd returned Steven's handshake, then drawn away and faced him with the challenge of the knowledge on his face.

Loving Glory had been the obsession of Steven's life. Now the living proof of that obsession was there, watching him through Glory's eyes.

"Let it be, Steven," his mother had said. "No good ever came from Glory. This child is her son."

"He's mine, too, Mother."

"No, he only belongs to himself. His name is Sasser. Leave it that way."

And he might have if he hadn't watched his son Damon sitting on a picnic table talking to Melissa, who was staring up at her older cousin with complete adoration. As he watched, Damon stood, held out his hand to Melissa, and started down to the lake.

"No!" Steven said, coming to his feet. "No, not my daughter!"

387

Susan followed the line of his vision and let out a dry laugh. "You can't stop it, Steven. No more than you could ever stop Glory. Not you, not Sam. He's corrupt. He's Glory's son."

Steven groaned.

"I must," he murmured under his breath as he started after them. "He's my son, too."

He caught them at the water's edge. "Melissa, go back to the table, I want to have a talk with Damon."

"But, Dad—"

"Now!"

Melissa gave her father a look of disbelief and Damon a shrug of her shoulders that plainly said he was a parent and should be forgiven for his idiocy.

"Something wrong?" Damon asked, lifting an insolent eyebrow.

"I think you see that Melissa is becoming infatuated with you, Damon. And that won't do at all."

"Oh? And why would you say that, sir?"

"Because, damn it, you're cousins and cousins don't get—involved. See that you stop it—now."

"I see. Perhaps, sir, it would be well to speak to your daughter, too. Sometimes it's hard to handle a Winslow woman who's made up her mind."

Damon turned and walked down the shoreline, following the path that led around the lake to the secluded spit of water beyond the blackberry bushes.

Steven watched in silence, Damon's words digging into his mind. *Sometimes it's hard to handle a Winslow woman who's made up her mind.*

And Melissa was a Winslow woman.

Forty-Five

Steven, Margie, JoEllen, Teddy, Sam and Susan shared a table at the reunion dinner dance. There was little attempt at conversation. Sam was his usual taciturn self. Steven was remote and preoccupied. Only Teddy breached the cold cavern of silence into which they'd descended.

Margie looked around, more convinced than ever that she shouldn't have come. There was an ominous presence, as if they were being watched. Old friends were mere acquaintances now and she wondered if she'd ever liked any of them. She wondered if she'd ever *known* them. All she could see were sad faces with painted smiles and frenzied laughter.

"You know JoEllen is running a physician's assistant medical practice here in Galilee," Teddy was saying. He explained that meant she could treat simple illnesses without the doctor's presence. "Galilee is showing some new signs of life. There's even a Japanese firm looking into locating an automobile plant in the county.

"Teddy is working with the site-selection committee," Susan offered. "If it comes in, he'll be the local member of the management team."

JoEllen looked up in surprise. "You didn't tell me that you'd decided to take their offer."

"Of course he will," Sam growled. "He's the logical one. Ted's always been the one to look after things at home."

JoEllen allowed Sam's words to sink in. *Teddy's always been the one to look after things.* He was right. He'd sowed his wild oats as a teenager, but since then he'd been the most solid one of the group. You might not know what any of

389

them would do next, but Teddy had always been there.

Now, as dinner ended and the band struck up a song, Teddy held out his hand to JoEllen. Teddy, the one who'd gone away that dreadful summer. Teddy, the one who'd come back. There was a sense of déjà vu. Suddenly she felt as if she were in high school again.

"May I have this dance?"

"Of course," she said, and stopped into his arms. "You always were the best dancer in Galilee."

"The girls always said so. Dancing and sports, that was good old Teddy. Good moves and the glory."

"Glory? Not you, too."

"Oh, no. She scared me to death. I always thought there was something a little wrong with her."

"There was, but it took the three of us a long time to figure it out. Who knows how our lives might have gone if it weren't for Glory and that summer."

"That summer. I always regretted that, JoEllen. It took me a long time to understand what I'd lost. I'm sorry."

"Oh, Teddy. It wasn't just you. We all went a little crazy that summer. We discarded our old set of rules and we hadn't established new ones. It was crazy."

"Nobody knows that better than me. Nothing was the same during my senior year. Oh, I was still the big athlete, but without any of you there to appreciate my moves, they didn't seem as important. I wish we could go back and do it all over."

JoEllen missed a step. "I'm not sure I would want to do that," she said. "Too much has happened."

"Well, maybe not all of it. But I do think that there are some things I've learned to improve on. And I think, one day soon, we ought to talk about that."

It had come: Judgment Day. The final ending, or a new beginning? JoEllen wasn't certain, but she knew with sudden clarity that Teddy had carried around the burden of his guilt just as she had. It was time they absolved each other.

"One day?" she said. "How about one night?"

"How about tonight?"

"No motel," she said.

And she leaned against him, certain now that she'd come full circle. Teddy had changed her life; now he was changing it again. This was a weekend for truth. And she'd have to tell

Teddy everything. His reaction would determine the course of their lives.

JoEllen took a deep breath. "Agreed."

"Would you like to dance, Susan?" Steven needed to get up, move around, find something on which to focus his attention. The impact of seeing Damon was unsettling. And Susan looked as if she were about to run.

"I'd love to."

As Susan moved into Steven's arms she saw that Margie had coaxed Sam onto the floor. Ignoring the hellos from old friends, Susan and Steven danced to a song she remembered well, Eddie Fisher's "I'm Walking Behind You on Your Wedding Day." Steven was going through the motions, but he was a million miles away.

The ease with which Steven fitted into the circle of friends surprised her. Though he was Sam's cousin, she'd never spent enough time with him to feel that she knew him at all, until tonight. But as they danced, she could feel his tension. She recognized it, for she'd spent a lot of time covering up her own fear.

"Don't let her keep doing it to you, Steven."

"What?" Steven pulled away and looked down at Susan.

"Glory. She always did cause strife. I never understood that until now. She's already spoiled her life and destroyed mine. You've escaped. Don't let her ruin what you have with Margie."

"What do you mean?"

"I mean, look at Sam and Sam's father, both victims of your grandfather. Granddaddy Winslow was the evil one. There was something very wrong with him. There was something wrong with Glory, too."

"Grandfather Winslow? I don't know what you mean." But he did. He'd known about his grandfather's peculiar opinion of women, of Winslow duty and obedience. Steven had seen how badly his grandmother had been treated. And he'd known about the beatings. He'd seen Sam once, after he'd been beaten. And he'd sworn then that he'd never let that happen to him.

Only once had his grandfather tried it with him, once

391

when he'd chided Steven for his lack of interest in the farm, in his heritage. "I wouldn't be a farmer if you paid me," Steven had said. "I'm going to study business and get as far away from this broken-down one-horse town as I can."

"You'd pass up your inheritance?"

"Absolutely! Give it to Sam. He wants it."

Steven hadn't fully understood what that meant. And he had spent little time in Winslow afterward to find out. But it hadn't been his grandfather who kept him away, it had been Glory. All during his childhood it had been him and Sam and Glory. As a teenager she'd tormented both of them unmercifully. That last summer before Sam had met Susan, he and Sam spent hours discussing Glory, her body and what she made them want to do, but it never occurred to Steven that Sam had taken his desire any further.

Steven had held himself in check. They touched and kissed, and explored, but until that summer thirty years ago, he'd never allowed them to consummate their love. And like Pandora's box, once it had been opened there was no closing it again.

Steven's thoughts returned to the present. "What do you mean, Susan?"

"I mean that Glory was infatuated with all the Winslow men. She wasn't satisfied with just you, she contaminated Sam, too. Even now, after all this time, she's reaching out with her red lips to wipe her sins on you. Don't let her, Steven."

"Sam, too?"

"That's why I wanted Margie to come. I thought you'd come, too. Sam is about to crack, Steven. I can't reach him because he won't let himself admit his fascination with Glory. But you can. Talk to him, Steven. Stop this madness before it goes any further."

Across the room, Margie was trying in vain to follow Sam's lead. Her sense of disaster was making her desperate because she couldn't find its source. "You know, Sam, you're the only one I could never dance with. You always made me feel like I had two left feet."

"You had two all right, but it wasn't feet that messed up my rhythm."

"Messed up your rhythm?"

"Sure. I was committed to Susan. You were a nice girl and

392

nice boys didn't let nice girls know how their bodies reacted to them."

"Says who?"

"Granddaddy."

"Sure, and according to our mothers, nice girls didn't let boys know that they were hot for their bodies, either, but that didn't make it true."

"You mean you . . ."

"Sure. I wanted you. You were the best-looking boy in school. I just didn't know how to do anything about it. You were Susan's boyfriend and Susan was my friend. Hell, that's not the real reason. We were all scared to death of getting pregnant. If we'd had the Pill in '54, none of you guys would ever have gone steady."

"Susan did."

"Did what?"

"Let me know she wanted me. She would have gone all the way, if I'd let her."

"*Gone all the way.* God, those words still sound ominous. I can't for the life imagine why you didn't let her. Was there something wrong with you, Sam?"

Sam came to a stop. "Why would you ask that?"

"Well, for one thing you always knew you were going to marry Susan, and if your hormones were raging as wild as mine, I can't imagine you turning down anybody. You weren't going to get pregnant. Why didn't you?"

"It would have been wrong. Granddaddy took me to a place where the women didn't matter. And they were— willing."

"Sam, this is very interesting, but don't you think we look a little odd just standing here on the dance floor."

"Oh, yes. I'm sorry." He took her in his arms again.

"And, just once I'd like to be able to follow you. I think it would help if you weren't two feet away."

Sam's eyes narrowed for a moment, then he pulled Margie against him, exposing his erection to her without apology. "There, now you know the truth. I stayed like that most of the time. I still do, and since Susan and I don't—"

"Why the hell not? Susan's your wife and I know she isn't frigid. Anybody can look at Susan and see she worships the ground you walk on. She always has. What's your problem, Sam?"

393

Margie couldn't believe she was having this conversation with Sam. Never had he done more than pass the time of day with her. Now she was telling him to take his wife home and make love to her. She kept expecting the evening to end like they used to when she had to find her own way home, alone. This was turning into a very strange affair.

"I can't."

"Why not?"

"Susan's not a whore like Glory. Susan is my wife."

Steven couldn't believe she was buying this story. Of the four, only Steven had become aroused that day, that night, and then. While she was telling him to relax with Delores and like it because Sam was watching, Steven smiled at her. She remembered that no matter how much her touch and Delores' aroused Sam, it was her touch that...

Forty-Six

Later, when Steven finally asked her to dance, Margie was still caught up in Sam's words. *Not a whore like Glory.*

"Steven, how close are you to Sam?"

"Now? Not at all. Though there was a time when we were."

"A time before Glory."

"I'm not sure what you mean. There was always Glory, Sam, and me. Why are you asking?"

"I'm beginning to figure it out, my husband. I've never said this to you, but I think that the woman you loved, the woman who was forbidden to you, who had your child, had to have been Glory."

Steven was so surprised that all he could say was, "Yes."

"What you may not know was that Sam had the same kind of hangup about her. He still does. Sam isn't sleeping with his own wife because he can't. She's his wife. He can only sleep with women like Glory."

"I know, Susan just told me about Sam's obsession."

"Isn't this the night for confessions! Do you have a suggestion on how the four of us can bury Glory once and for all?"

"If I knew, I would have done it long ago."

Margie hadn't expected Steven to deny her accusation, but she'd hoped. He hadn't. He was as screwed up as Sam, over a dead woman. They all were. She wanted to scream. These were men, strong men, Winslow men, not a bunch of wimps. She could almost see Glory laughing at them.

"Well then," Margie said, hiding her fear in recklessness, "shall we ease each other's burdens?"

"I don't know what you mean."

395

"Simple. I'll take Sam home with me and you can satisfy Susan. That ought to round things off nicely. If the Winslow men can't make love to their wives, the wives ought not to suffer."

"You and Sam?" That thought hit Steven in the stomach like an ice pick. What was wrong with Margie? She'd never made such a crude statement before. "You've had too much to drink."

"I haven't had nearly enough, Steven. Besides, I can't see why the Winslow wives shouldn't swap husbands. The men don't have a corner on the market. Everybody in the Winslow family seems to be sexually deprived, including our Glory, and since we're all so flawed anyhow, we might as well admit it. We could even make it a foursome. You wouldn't mind that, would you? You don't have any of those old hangups that men who love their wives have."

"Don't be foolish, Margie. I'm married to you."

"Another marriage of convenience, isn't it, like your marriage to Elizabeth? I know now you married her to ease your conscience. But neither Susan or I are Glory, are we? No, don't answer. Tell me, why didn't you just take Glory and run away to some foreign country. There are some places where first cousins marry and nobody cares."

"That's what Glory wanted."

"Why didn't you?"

"Because—that wasn't all. There were other risks."

"Do tell. What else could there possibly be to keep two soulmates apart?"

She wasn't to learn Steven's answer, for JoEllen was tapping her on the shoulder. "Margie, Teddy and I are going to call it a night. I hope you don't mind if I skip our spend-the-night party tonight. I'll still pay my share of the bill. See you later."

From the look in JoEllen's eyes Margie understood that what she meant was *much* later, like tomorrow. "No, go on. Susan seems to have disappeared. Maybe she went home with Sam after all. I could end up in the suite all by myself."

"Want some company?" Steven asked quietly as JoEllen and Teddy moved away.

"I don't believe you said that, Steven."

"Why not? You said the Winslow men are depraved, and

396

we're always good together in bed."

"You've let yourself get hot remembering Glory, and you want me to satisfy you?"

Hot? No, it wasn't Glory who had set him on edge, it was something else. Steven didn't like Margie's bitterness. He didn't understand what was happening. What had started out as a simple reunion of old friends had turned into an angry free-for-all. He just wanted to stop her, before they both went too far.

"I like making love to you, Margie. We give each other pleasure. I didn't expect it, but I think we need each other. It's up to you."

"Forget it. As a matter of fact, I think I'll turn in, too. I think I want this day to be over, before something worse happens." She paused and looked up at Steven, finally recognizing the look of fear in his eyes. "Are you all right?"

"Yes. It's Damon, seeing how much like Glory he is. I guess that's what unsettled me."

"Oh, yes, Damon, the new snake in the Garden of Eden. I don't think I like Glory's son. Did you separate him from your daughter?"

"I did. By tomorrow I'll have Melissa shipped back to her mother on Long Island. With Damon on his way to California, they ought to be far enough apart. That just leaves Steve."

"Everyone seems to have a private agenda for coming here. What's Steve's?"

"Steve's asked me for a job. And I'm going to give him one." The song ended and Steven stepped away, continuing to hold Margie's hand. "I'll walk you to your room."

Neither Susan nor Sam were anywhere to be seen when Margie and Steven left the dance floor and stepped into the elevator. Steven stopped at Margie's door. "Are you certain you don't want me to come in?"

"I'm certain. This weekend has been an emotional roller coaster and I don't think I can stand any more physical stimulation."

"All right." Steven looked at Margie for a long moment, then brushed her lips lightly. "You were the loveliest woman here."

"Thank you," she answered honestly. "But I still don't compare with the woman who wasn't."

"Where are we going?"

Teddy was driving out of town. The car windows were open wide and crisp, clean air curled around JoEllen's face, tousling her hair.

"It's a surprise."

"Will I like it?"

"I don't know. I hope so."

As they passed the private school, now used as a grammar school, Teddy slowed the car. "You've never been out here, but this is my shop, where I build the race cars."

She'd expected some junkyard. She was wrong. The building was enormous. It was surrounded by a high fence and lit up like daylight.

"I had no idea it was so—so big."

"There's more to my success than this building, JoEllen. I want you to know it all. When we originally built the school, we had to adjust the location because of a vein of something like kaolin that ran across the corner of the site. I discovered that the substance was laced with what we later decided was a petroleum-like product. I still don't know all the properties of the white mud, only that it's a freak of nature."

"I don't understand."

"I accidentally learned that it could be used to clean and lubricate the inside of the engine. And that's the magic that's accounted for the success of my cars on the track."

"I don't understand. Why doesn't everybody use this stuff?"

"Apparently this is the only spot where it's been found. I do know that this whole area was once under water because I keep dredging up sea shells and black rocks which might mean an ancient volcano."

"And nobody knows about it except you?"

"Not until now. We still don't know exactly what's in the mud, but it's being analyzed."

"Why now?"

"That's how I bribed the Japanese into locating their automobile plant here. It will be the first one in this country. Can you imagine what it will mean to the local economy?"

"You mean you're giving the cleaner to a foreign country?"

"I offered it to the American manufacturers first, but they turned it down. If I wouldn't sell my secret to them outright, they wouldn't play. And I'm not giving it to anybody permanently. The Japanese have the rights to it for five years, then the mud is available to anybody who wants to buy it, from me."

JoEllen was astounded. Teddy, with only a high school education from tiny little Galilee High, had pulled off an industrial miracle. He'd lured a manufacturing plant from a foreign country to Galilee and he'd retained the rights to his dirt.

"How much of this mud is there?"

"I'm not certain, and I could never do much research for fear that the secret would get out. Part of the vein runs under the school and I won't let that be disturbed until is isn't needed anymore for the children. The rest, so far as I can tell, belongs to me."

"Well, I can't say this is what I was expecting when we left the reunion, but it's truly amazing. I'm proud of you, Teddy."

"Oh, this isn't all I had in mind. This is just the beginning. I wanted to be completely honest with you. Teresa said this would work. I hope she's right."

Honest? That thought hit her in the gut. Teddy was being honest and she was still carrying around a secret that could forever ruin what they were rediscovering. "Teresa? Teresa knows about all of this?"

"Not the mud, but about the rest of my surprise. At least part of it. I know I'm over the hill, but don't you think we could pretend we're seventeen again and you could come a little closer?"

He laid his arm across the top of the seat and JoEllen didn't debate for a second. She slid across the seat and laid her head against his shoulder.

"Is this about what you had in mind?"

"Not yet, but we're getting there." And he kissed her. Gently, without pressure, he kissed her, as if they had all the time in the world.

And it felt right.

Then he pulled back, let out a deep breath, and allowed

the car to move on. A few minutes later he was maneuvering the vehicle into a thicket of oak trees and rolling to a stop. "Do you remember this place?"

The moonlight was shining through the moss-hung trees, edging the flat darkness beyond with little scallops of silver.

"The lake? Is this the lake where we always came?"

"Yes it is, but we're on the other side. You can't see it now, but in the daytime, if we were down around that little finger of land, you'd recognize the picnic area on the other side."

"You used to bring me out here, to—"

"Neck," he finished for her. "And if you'll look in the backseat, you'll find a blanket."

"Teddy, you're kidding. You're not seriously suggesting that we—"

"I'm absolutely serious. Come with me."

Teddy opened the door and took her hand, pulling her across the seat and out the driver's side. Moments later he was spreading the blanket on the bank of the lake. He removed his jacket and tie, and pitched them in the car, then rolled up his sleeves.

"Teddy, I don't know how to tell you this, but I'm not really very experienced. If you spend any more time getting ready I'm liable to take off down the road."

"Come and sit down, JoEllen, I want to tell you about the rest of the surprise." He sat down on the blanket and leaned back, resting on his elbows. "Please? If you want, we can just talk, that's all."

Talk, yes. That was what she'd meant to do. She just hadn't expected Teddy to make it so difficult. Still, she couldn't run away. It had to be done. She sank to her knees on the blanket beside him.

"Is it so hard, JoEllen? Sitting here with me? We're not seventeen. That seems like so long ago."

"In some ways. And then it could have been yesterday."

"I always liked this spot, JoEllen. After—after that summer I used to come here and sit and think. I want to be honest with you. I hurt, and I knew I'd hurt you, but I didn't know what to do about it."

There it was again: *honest with you.* "Please, Teddy. Don't. We both hurt each other, in different ways. And there's something you don't know. Until you do, we can't—be together."

"I don't care about the doctor. I don't blame you for turning to someone you had something in common with."

"I turned to him, Teddy, but not for the reason you think."

"You don't have to tell me."

"Yes I do, and when I'm finished talking, if you want to take me straight back to town, I'll understand. I should have done this long ago. Just listen."

"All right."

"You remember that night when you—when you—"

"When I practically raped you?"

"No, you didn't do that, Teddy. You were just young and—and besides, I let you. I never understood why, but I could have stopped you if I'd wanted."

"I'm not so sure about that, but I'm glad you think so."

"Anyway, I—I was pregnant, Teddy. I was pregnant and I had an abortion. It was botched and I had a rough time after. When you came to the hospital to see me, it was because of the abortion. Tom Brooks helped me."

"You were pregnant and you didn't tell me?"

"I couldn't. You'd have insisted that we get married. You had another year of high school and I was starting my second year of nursing school. It would have been a disaster, Teddy. We were too young, and too different."

"JoEllen, I'm so very sorry."

"You don't have anything to be sorry about. I'm the one who should be saying she's sorry."

She got through the confession by tensing every muscle in her body. Now she was ready to shatter into a thousand pieces as she waited for him to think about what she'd said. He'd be hurt—angry. She was prepared for his censure.

Instead he reached out and took her hand.

"Is that why you stayed away?"

"No. I stayed away because I felt as if I didn't belong anywhere anymore. I had to think about Skip, about my mother. All I could do was try to make up for what I'd done by helping other women. I didn't deserve you, Teddy. And now I can never have another child. The abortion took that away from me."

"If you could go back and do it over, would you have had our child?"

"I don't know. I'd like to think I would, but I don't know. The world has changed so much in thirty years. It's hard to

401

believe how small our parameters were then, or how large they've grown now. Sometimes I wonder if we haven't lost the cushion of security that tradition offered us."

"Maybe that's why I've stayed here, JoEllen. By staying I could control change. But that doesn't work, either. There comes a time when we have to open up to life or die in the vacuum we've created. JoEllen, come down here. Near me. Galilee is about to change and I don't think I want to go through what's coming without you. Besides," he paused, giving her a gentle tug, "Teresa's already picked out the spot where she wants our house."

"Our house?"

"I bought this land, JoEllen. I bought us a piece of the past and we're going to build on it for our future. Now are you coming down here or do I have to find a motel?"

"I'm forty-eight, Teddy, don't you think that's a little too old to be making out on the ground?"

"Not at all," he said, and pulled her down. "I think it's just about right. Remember all those times you said no?"

"God, yes."

"Well, so do I, and I think you owe me something."

"Teddy, I know it may come as a surprise," she repeated, "but I'm a very inexperienced woman in these matters."

"As I told you back at the dance, I've been practicing. It's time I taught you what I learned."

"Can we start over, Teddy?"

"I don't know, JoEllen. I only know that I want to try."

Forty-Seven

Margie couldn't sleep. Susan hadn't returned to their room and JoEllen was out somewhere with Teddy. Finally she wandered out on the patio and stood staring down at the pool in the darkness. A figure was swimming back and forth, steadily, exhaustingly.

A nude figure.

A woman.

Steven wished that Margie had invited him to stay, but she hadn't. After he left the elevator he changed course, swerving into the bar where he found Sam hunched over a stool, staring morosely into a half-filled glass of whiskey.

"Care for some company, Sam?"

"It's a free country."

"Not the last time I noticed."

Steven ordered, and for several minutes they drank silently. "You should have heard what Margie suggested for the rest of the evening."

"I'm sure it was something—enlightening."

"I'd say it was more climactic. She thought she ought to take you up to the suite and I should go home with Susan. Sex to exorcise our mutual demon."

Sam turned a burning glare to his cousin. "It doesn't work."

"I know. I spent a lot of years trying to get rid of mine. Sam, I know about you and Glory. Or at least I know enough to recognize the symptoms."

"Glory's been dead for seventeen years, Steven. We both know that."

403

"Maybe you believe that, but I don't. Each of us still carries her around. I guess you know about Damon?"

"Damon? Glory's son? No, what about him?"

Steven ordered refills for them both. "Let's walk outside, Sam. I think we need some privacy."

They strolled between the trees toward the darkened pool area. Steven considered his words and wondered if what he was about to do was wise, then decided that the situation could hardly deteriorate any further. "You really don't know the truth about Damon?"

"I really don't know what you're talking about."

"Sit down, Sam. This is going to be a long night."

They found a table in the shadows and sat.

"Sam, I don't know how to put this other than directly: Damon is my son."

"Your son? But Glory married that doctor."

"I got Glory pregnant, but I didn't know it. Adele found out and married Glory off to the doctor. I couldn't marry her and I couldn't stay away from her, so I married Elizabeth. I thought that would stop it. It didn't."

"Glory had your child. You bastard! You got Glory pregnant, your own cousin." Sam staggered to his feet, grabbing Steven by his collar and forcing him to stand. "I'll kill you. I'll—"

He swung wildly, allowing Steven to dance away.

"Stop it, Sam. I don't want to fight with you."

"You're a coward. You always were. Even Granddaddy knew what a poor excuse for a Winslow you were. You were weak." He feigned a stumble, and as Steven reached for him, landed a hard blow on Steven's chin, followed by another blow to the stomach.

"Stop it, Sam," Steven wheezed as he spit blood from his mouth. "I'm not going to hit you. Granddaddy was an evil man, Sam. He couldn't conquer me, so he started in on you. Don't you see the truth? He was warped. All the Winslows are warped. It's time you saw our saintly grandfather as the devil he was."

Sam's voice rose steadily. "You're wrong. He was a strong, pious man, determined to make me strong, too."

"He was a devil. Two of his sons were killed and the only one left was your father, who he believed to be as flawed as he. So he started to work on you. And he's done a pretty fair job of turning you into a reflection of himself. Why do you suppose so few Winslow children survived?"

"I—I don't know."

"Because there is a genetic aberration there and, God help us, we're passing it on."

"You're wrong. I had two normal children," Sam argued.

"Yes, and you had one you considered flawed, and so did I. Too bad Glory wasn't a boy. She was probably the only real Winslow in the family."

Sam sat back down in the chair, shaking his head. "No. Granddaddy chose me. I was the true Winslow. You left, and Glory's dead."

"But they're both still reaching out, Sam. I'm no better than you. The only difference is that I know what I did, what I was, and what damage I caused. You're still going around with it screwing up your mind. You married Susan when you wanted Glory. And you've spent twenty-five years punishing her for that."

"Don't you dare compare Susan to Glory. Susan was— Susan is a lady. Glory was evil."

"Yes. She was."

There was a long silence as Sam stared into the darkness. Behind them the filter in the pool bubbled. Sounds of laughter came from the parking lot and cars moved by on the highway beyond.

"But I wanted her," Sam said, finally. "God, how I always wanted her. I'd see her come on to you and it would drive me crazy. I'd go home and—it's a wonder I have a cock left, I worked it so hard. Granddaddy found me once. That's when he took me to a whore. He explained that all the Winslow men were oversexed, that they had to find a release. A lady could never satisfy them. He was right. I'd be with a prostitute and then I'd come home to Susan. I couldn't let her act like they did."

"Why not?"

"Bad things would happen. Bad things did happen."

"What kind of things?"

"I tried not to do it. The last time I was with Glory I went a little crazy. She wanted me. She wouldn't take no. Afterward I came home and I raped Susan. And she liked it, Steven. That was a sin. And I was punished for it."

"Sin? Hell. That's just sex. How were you punished?"

405

"We had Mark. My son was a queer, a flaming queer. He was a Winslow and he was flawed. What would Granddaddy say if he knew that I produced a Winslow who died of AIDS? And that it was my fault."

"Oh, Sam. Even if Mark was a homosexual, you weren't responsible. Blame it on Grandfather. Blame it on the Winslow curse. Blame it on Glory. But don't blame it on Susan."

"But Susan liked what I did to her. If she'd fought me off I could have understood. But how could Susan . . . I mean, Susan was a *wife.*"

"Susan was a *woman.* Women have needs and desires, just like Glory. Glory wanted me and she used you to punish me for not being with her. Susan isn't like Glory. She's in love with her husband, not her brother."

"Brother? Glory never had a brother."

"And that's the final part of the evil, Sam. Glory did have a brother. Me."

"You? I don't understand."

"That's why I couldn't go away with Glory, why I couldn't save either of us from our obsession. When you and Susan got married, Glory and I spent the weekend in a hotel in Augusta. Adele found us. And told me the truth."

The woman who'd been swimming in the pool held her breath from behind the bathhouse. She wanted to close her ears, scream out, run away, but she couldn't. Susan already understood what Sam was refusing to hear.

"What truth?" he asked.

"Blackie Winslow, Glory's father, was my father, too."

"You and Glory had the same father? I don't believe it. I don't believe that you and Glory slept together like that, either."

"Believe it, Sam. And there's more. You have to get over Grandfather's influence and Glory's death. I can never do that because of Damon. But you still have a chance."

"Sure, your son Steve is still alive. And Damon is a Winslow, even without the name. Anybody could look at him and tell. My only son is dead. All I have left are my girls."

"Good. Maybe the evil will stop here."

"You don't know what you're saying, Steven. You don't know what hell is."

406

"Yes I do, Sam. I know what hell is in a way you'll never know. You see, Glory called me, just before she killed herself. She was frantic. She asked me to come to her. I refused. I know about hell, Sam. It's because of me that Glory's dead. Sam. When Glory killed herself she was pregnant again. She was carrying my child."

Forty-Eight

"You're right, Teddy. You have learned." JoEllen was lying content in Teddy's arms. He'd been more than right. Sometime in the years they'd lost, he'd learned how to make love to a woman.

"JoEllen, I'm almost fifty years old. I've lived by myself for a long time, but I don't want to be alone anymore."

Overhead, stars blinked in the darkness like fireflies. The sound of crickets and tree frogs drifted across the lake. There was the smell of fall in the cool air. JoEllen lay, quietly taking in the peace of the night.

"Oh?"

"I'm worried about bringing the plant in," Teddy said. "I'm going to be accused of being un-American. But the plant means jobs, people, doctors, maybe even a small hospital for Galilee."

"A hospital?"

"Yes, a place for you to really help our people."

"Strange how things work out. I left to do great things and the most important thing I ever do may be coming back. You're bringing Galilee to life again, Teddy."

"Well, it's not done yet."

"Yes it is. Of all of us, you've accomplished the most."

"There may be some opposition to the Japanese. I'm not sure it's right to ask you to take the heat I'm going to face."

"I've faced the public's wrath before, Teddy, and survived."

"I guess what I really need to hear you say is that you think we've learned enough to have a future here. Together."

"If you're asking me to marry you, Teddy, the answer is

408

yes. I thought at first that the only thing I wanted in life was respect. But the only real respect a person has is his respect for himself."

Across the lake they heard a car start up and drive slowly away. The driver didn't turn on the lights.

"Lovers," Teddy said, planting a kiss on JoEllen's palm. "I didn't know any of them used parked cars anymore."

"Neither did I. I guess everything comes full circle."

"If we're lucky."

Forty-Nine

Sam wavered slightly and stumbled away from the pool into the darkness. He stopped at the back of the refreshment stand and leaned his head against the wall, gasping for breath. Vaguely he heard splashing, as if someone were in the pool. He couldn't face anybody, not now. Rounding the building he slumped to the ground with a cry of pain.

Steven let him go, turned, and, oblivious to the blood dripping from his split lip, walked toward his car. He suddenly felt very old. Pausing to glance up at the penthouse, he thought for a moment he saw a figure watching from the balcony. Then he blinked and it was gone. It couldn't have been Margie. Margie would be watching some late-night talk show, unaware of anything that didn't concern her career. She'd always been able to submerge herself in her private world and close out anything that threatened her success, including, he was beginning to understand, him.

The reunion was over. The first fifty-two years of Steven's life were over. Tomorrow he'd take Elizabeth's children and drive back to Atlanta. Elizabeth's children. He'd never thought of them as his, not until he saw Steve standing beside the other Winslow men. Steve was a Winslow, and if Steven never accomplished anything else in his life, he intended to make certain that the Winslow curse never touched his son.

Belatedly he intended to be a father. Belatedly he'd exorcise the demon that had hovered over most of his life. Belatedly he felt a strong need to involve himself in the lives of his daughter and his son.

His son? No, he had two sons. Steve and Damon. He wondered if his mother knew? Of course she did. That's why Damon had been a visitor so often, why he was here now as she divided up her portion of the Winslow treasures. Evelyn knew that Damon was her grandson.

But Damon had another name and another father. Roger Sasser was responsible for Damon and that's the way Steven would leave it. Neither Damon nor Roger knew the truth and perhaps that would make Damon safe.

He was less sure about Margie. The raging passion he'd carried around for Glory had made all the other women in his life pale in comparison. But Margie had never competed for the part of him that Glory had claimed. Margie was more like a friend. They shared the same taste in food, entertainment, and friends. She was easy to be with, never demanding, never making him feel as if he'd failed her.

But more than anything, he'd been able to give to Margie and she'd made him feel good about himself. Love and passion were both the same, yet two different things. Passion allowed to run free overwhelmed. Love? Perhaps the most real love offered when it was shared, was the absence of destruction and the freedom to make choices.

Satisfied that he'd reached some kind of bizarre understanding about the future, Steven got into his car and started the engine. With the windows down he took the Winslow Road. He wouldn't come here again until he came to bury his mother. It was time he put the past to rest.

When Susan saw Sam fall, she didn't stop to think about what she was doing. She hadn't stopped to think when she stripped off her dress and dove into the pool, either. She'd had too much to drink and she'd been hurting. Swimming had always been her salvation from pain and she'd never worn a suit when she swam alone.

But Sam was injured. He'd been beaten, by his own cousin, all because of Glory who'd been dead for seventeen years. Susan knelt beside him.

"Susan? You heard?"

"Yes. I heard it all. Do you want me to leave?"

He didn't answer for a long time. Then his voice came low and strangled. "No. Stay with me."

411

She lay down beside him and began to rub his back. When the children were small she'd done that. It seemed to comfort them. "Cry, Sam. It's time."

"I'm not crying."

"I think you are, deep inside. We're both crying, Sam. For all the hurts we've caused each other and our children, for all our misplaced guilt."

"You have nothing to feel guilty about, Susan."

"Yes I do. I think it's time we talk, really talk, about us, who we really are, about how we feel about each other."

"Us? You can still say us, after what I said back there. You're not going to leave me?"

"I don't know, Sam. All I know is we still have a connection. We've had three children and we've lost one. I don't want to lose the others. Besides, where would I go?" *My father doesn't want me, and my mother's gone. I thought Galilee was my sanctuary. There is none.*

Sam turned over and laid his head on Susan's bare breast.

"You're wet, and you're not wearing any clothes."

"I was swimming. I always swim nude when I'm upset. Of course you never knew."

"I think there are a lot of things I don't know about you."

"Yes, there are."

"I'm sorry. I guess it's too late for me to learn."

"I don't know. But the one thing I do know, Sam, is that we thought we loved each other once. I don't know whether it's enough, but it's a start. I like making love with you, Sam. There's never been anything like us together."

"No, there hasn't. And I never understood that."

"I know."

"Please don't leave me, Susan."

"I don't know if I can stay, Sam, unless you find a way to get your grandfather out of our bedroom. If you can do that, we'll talk about 'us.' It's up to you."

"Susan, about Mark—"

"Not yet. Let's not talk about Mark now. It's too soon. Just let me tell you that you aren't to blame, not any more than I am. Your grandfather was wrong about so many things. I'm only just now learning that we're all responsible for our own lives. And so was Mark."

"But you loved him best."

"Only because you didn't. And I felt responsible, too.

412

Someday I'll tell you about my guilt and ask your forgiveness, but not yet. We've both heard enough truth tonight. Can you get up?"

"I think so. Here, take my jacket."

Susan came to her knees. She slipped her arms into Sam's coat and held out her hand. He clasped it and allowed her to help him back to his truck.

"What about your friends? Won't they be expecting you?"

"They'll always be my friends, but they have their own lives. Tonight I'm going home."

Margie closed the doors on the balcony and stepped back into the room. Steven's and Sam's voices had carried across the pool and she'd heard enough of what they'd said to learn the whole truth.

She hadn't realized that the swimmer was Susan until she and Sam walked from behind the refreshment stand and crossed the concrete toward the parking lot. It looked as if she'd be alone in the reunion suite tonight. That was all right, she'd always been alone. Margie slid the dead bolt closed and turned out the bathroom light, allowing only the glow from outside to fall across the floor.

The last bottle of Four Roses stood on the table. Margie filled a glass with the whiskey, walked back into her bedroom, and switched on the TV. There was a late-night interview show on ABC and she wanted to watch. She hadn't mentioned it to Steven, but the new inquiry she'd had from the network was more than just a nibble. The current host was being replaced and she was in line for the spot.

Accepting the job would mean leaving Atlanta for New York. It could mean leaving Steven, too, for he was too firmly ensconced in his job to move. And that was the decision she had to make. Did she want to leave Steven? Did she want to live without him?

But the job was in New York. She'd finally make it to the place where she'd started out to go.

Margie had considered herself brave. She'd gotten on a train and come to Atlanta alone, found a job and a place to stay, and started on the long road leading to her success. But in truth, most of her decisions hadn't been carefully-thought-out choices. She'd gone wherever the path led,

413

always depending on someone else to direct her. There'd been Glory at first, then some man.

Nick-the-Magnificent had sent her fleeing from Galilee. In some peculiar way Arthur Noland took her off the stage. Richard started her toward her first real thirst for knowledge and made her take an analytical look at the world. Leonard, dear Leonard had given her Mother Goose and Denny had lost it for her. The only direct move she'd ever made was to ask Arthur for the interview that started *A Chat with Margie Raines*.

Even her marriage to Steven had been a matter of expedience. She'd told Leonard that she didn't know what love was. She still wasn't certain she did. But she felt comfortable with Steven. She could be herself without apology, for he didn't judge her. He had a way of giving her confidence, making her feel good about herself, and him. She didn't know if it was from respect for her or because nobody could ever be Glory and his expectations were never very high.

Allowing her attention to wander from the program, she made a mental list of what she'd be giving up if Steven didn't choose to come along with her. He was a handsome man and he made her look good. She was able to bounce ideas off him, often taking his suggestions. Her life was better organized because of Steven; he dealt with the maid, the gardener, and any caterers or decorators that were necessary. He was her bookkeeper, her fashion consultant, her chauffeur, and her cheerleader.

And he warmed her feet at night.

And he made her laugh at herself without feeling insecure.

Divorcing Steven would be a wrench, an inconvenience, a deep black hole in her life, for she liked living with Steven Winslow.

But deep down, maybe the biggest thing of all was being a Winslow. That gave her a certain kind of perverse pleasure. The world didn't know, but wearing this name from her past still provided a certain amount of emotional insurance. And *After Hours with Margie Raines* offered the fame she'd always craved.

Nobody, even Steven, knew about that deep pain she carried in her soul. She'd loved her grandparents, but she'd never understood why her mother and father had left her to

414

live with them. What was wrong with them that they always had to move on to some new place?

Just as she had done.

Margie had known all her life that there was something wrong with her or she wouldn't have been abandoned. If there *hadn't* been something wrong with her she wouldn't have been the only one of the four friends who never had a steady boyfriend. She had been afraid to try to use her good looks.

Margie knew that she was smart, but that wasn't enough. She'd carried her bad feelings around inside. She was terrible at spelling and math. She was creative, but she managed to put off the very people she could have worked with.

Margie Raines didn't have to use her body anymore, and she had a secretary to do her spelling and Steven to see to everything else. But it was Steven who made it work. Could she do it without him?

Margie poured herself another drink and faced that big black demon of fear and uncertainty. She might have to choose between Steven and her career. She could turn down the network offer and stay in Atlanta where she was the queen and keep Steven.

With a network show Margie would know that she was finally somebody. Too bad the one person she wanted to see her, the specter who'd found that black hiding place inside her and fulminated there, couldn't see her now.

Glory.

Glory, who had left her mark on everyone she came in contact with, still reached out and toyed with the emotions and dreams of her friends. Even Glory's death had somehow been designed to punish. And seventeen years later she was still wielding her power.

Glory had been wrong that summer of the soldiers. She'd called Susan a gardenia who would be easy to bruise. Susan had been the strong one, facing the worst life had to offer, and surviving.

JoEllen had been the lily, white and pure. But JoEllen had been accused of medical wrongdoing. She'd come back home in disgrace, bringing a child, a child who had no father.

And Margie was the rosebud that would open, have its moment, and fade away. Glory had been wrong about Margie most of all. And about herself.

The fiery dahlia was the flower Glory had envisioned for herself, vivid against the paleness of the other three. Vivid had been right, but the dahlia had burned up and three colorless flowers had survived.

And Margie would continue to survive. And she'd make her own choices. She'd choose Steven *and* New York. But if Steven stayed behind she'd survive. Margie Raines could make it in New York without Steven.

She hoped she wouldn't have to.

And she didn't need to be better than Glory. "Not anymore, Glory Winslow," Margie said recklessly. "Because I'm alive, and, what's more, I'm the one who got what you wanted most: Steven.

"So here's to you, Glory Winslow," she said, and lifted her drink in mock salute. "Go fuck yourself!"

The car from the lake reached the Winslow house just minutes before Steven's did. The couple inside got out, pausing for one last kiss at the front door.

"You start filming that black man's movie next month?"

"Yes. Joseph Cheatham is the hottest film director in Hollywood."

"But you'll call me, won't you, Damon?"

"Of course."

"No," Melissa observed wisely, "you won't. You never do. But that's all right. I'll call you."